The men they love are heroes,
so it is only a matter of time
before three very special
women become

SOLDIERS'
Brides

by

Debbie Macomber

Lois Faye Dyer

Katherine Stone

"Warm and wise, these novellas…
are certain to resonate with
readers everywhere."
—*Romantic Times*

SOLDIERS'
Brides

DEBBIE MACOMBER
LOIS FAYE DYER
KATHERINE STONE

*M&B™ and M&B™ with the Rose Device
are trademarks of the publisher.*

*First published in Great Britain 2007
by Harlequin Mills & Boon Limited, Eton House,
18-24 Paradise Road, Richmond, Surrey TW9 1SR*

SOLDIERS' BRIDES © by Harlequin Books S.A. 2007
(Originally published as *Hearts Divided* in USA)

The publisher acknowledges the copyright holders
of the individual works as follows:

5-B Poppy Lane © Debbie Macomber 2006
Liberty Hall © Lois Faye Dyer 2006
The Apple Orchard © Katherine Stone 2006

ISBN: 978 0 263 85004 8

024-0407

*Printed and bound in Spain
by Litografia Rosés S.A., Barcelona*

TABLE OF CONTENTS

5-B POPPY LANE
Debbie Macomber

My dearest readers,

All I was planning to do was meet my dear friends Katherine Stone and Lois Faye Dyer for lunch. Before I knew it, the three of us were plotting some loosely connected stories about three war brides – and their granddaughters. Katherine had been discussing the idea with her editor (who is also mine) and she asked if Lois and I wanted to be part of it.

My mother was a war bride. Not in the traditional sense, however, as my mother and father married at home during the war. Shortly after their marriage, Dad shipped out to Europe and they didn't see each other again for three very long years.

The concept for this anthology appealed to me for another reason, too. My father fought in France and was captured by the Germans during the Battle of the Bulge in 1944, near Bastogne. He never spoke of his imprisonment until the end of his life. With his World War II experiences on my mind, I sat in the doctor's waiting room one day – and stumbled upon a magazine article about the work of the French Resistance. It fascinated me, and my story was born.

I decided to give my fictional war bride a home in Cedar Cove, Washington, the setting of my ongoing series of books, which started with *16 Lighthouse Road*. I thought that Cedar Cove was the right sort of town for Helen, and I hope you'll agree.

I also hope you enjoy *5-B Poppy Lane*. This story is special to me because I wrote it in memory of my parents and the love they shared for over sixty years.

Debbie Macomber

PS I love to hear from readers. You can reach me at www.debbiemacomber.com or at PO Box 1458, Port Orchard, WA 98366, USA.

To my parents
Ted and Connie Adler
who married July 25, 1942
before my father
headed off to war

Prologue

Helen Shelton
5-B Poppy Lane
Cedar Cove, Washington
April 1

My dear Winifred,
You've been on my mind all week, and I decided the best thing to do was simply write. I'm much more comfortable with a pen in my hand than sitting at a computer, not that I have one. I do envy you and Clara communicating via the Internet, though. I got a kick out of Clara's e-mail address—if that's the correct term. Clara@AppleButter Ladies.com. Yours is obviously because of the secret codes you learned during the war. Unfortunately, those computer machines intimidate me. My granddaughter, Ruth, keeps saying they're not as difficult as they seem, but I don't know....

You remember my friend Charlotte Jefferson-Rhodes. She, too, has encouraged me to learn. She tried to persuade me to sign up for a computer class at the Senior Center, and I considered it for a time—a *brief* time. But somewhat to Charlotte's chagrin, I decided I'm just too old and set in my ways. I find holding a fountain pen intensely satisfying, old-fashioned or not. I realize my reluctance is a disappointment to you and Clara, and I apologize. I agree it would be a wonderful way for us to keep in touch. The two of you are as dear to me as family. In my heart, you *are* family. After the war, it was you, and Sam, of course, who showed me that life was still worth living. I'm deeply indebted to you both.

Speaking of the war, I find myself thinking more and more about those years in France. I woke in a cold sweat last night, dreaming of Jean-Claude. I've never spoken to my children about my experiences during the Second World War because I didn't know how to tell them I'd been married before and that I'd loved a man other than their father. As you know so well, Sam was my hero, my second chance at love and life. He saved me, and gave me a reason to live. I'll always be grateful that he brought me to you and Clara. You are the sisters of my heart.

All these years, I've pushed the war memories into the depths of my mind, but now they're here again, unwanted and unyielding, refusing to leave. I'm thinking that perhaps I should write them down for the family to read after I'm gone. As you've so often said, they have a right to know. I'm beginning to agree with you.

Now enough about that! Let me go on to more pleasant subjects. The main one is your birthday.

Your 80th! For years you bemoaned the fact that you were younger than Clara and me. I haven't heard you mention *that* lately. At any rate, your birthday's coming soon and it's the perfect opportunity for the three of us to get together. Winifred, just imagine—eighty years. Who would ever have believed we'd live this long? I know I didn't. But then, I always assumed I'd die before Sam. That wasn't to be; God had other plans.

In any event, this is a special birthday and we should celebrate. Traveling isn't as easy for me as it once was, and I suspect it isn't for you, either, so that trip we always talked about—the three of us going to Hawaii and Hong Kong—is out. But we're not dead yet! I've still got some spring to my step and so do you! However, I doubt either of us could keep up with Clara.

What would you think if I booked us on the passenger ferry up to Victoria, British Columbia? It's spectacular there this time of year. We could stay at the Empress Hotel and tour Butchart Gardens. The hotel is lovely, and their high tea is not to be missed. I've already written Clara and suggested the three of us go there together. How does that sound? I'll wait to hear back from you before I make the hotel reservations.

I wanted to ask your impression of how Clara's doing. Losing one's life mate is devastating. It hurts so terribly, as you and I both know. Although it's been nearly twenty years since Sam died, he's still with me...still a part of me. I know you understand what I'm trying to say. Those first few weeks I was numb, and I know Clara probably is, too. I'm thankful her family's close by.

You asked about Ruth. Yes, my granddaughter's still living in Seattle, attending the University of Washington and working toward her master's in education. I was thrilled when I learned that she'd chosen to finish her schooling in Washington State in order to be closer to me. She's very good about staying in touch but can't visit as frequently as we'd both hoped. I'll give her a call next week and see if she can come to Cedar Cove for lunch. Ruth is a delightful child. Grandchildren are indeed a blessing. How fortunate you are to have three granddaughters. Three! Ruth is my only one and I feel especially close to her—and she to me.

Do get in touch soon, and let me know if you can manage a trip to Victoria in June. The three of us will have a grand time! And since you're the youngest, Clara and I will expect you to carry the luggage.

Much love,

Helen

One

Ruth Shelton hurried out of her classroom-management lecture at the University of Washington, where she was completing her master's of education degree. Clutching her books, she dashed across campus, in a rush to get home. By now the mail would have been delivered to her small rental house three blocks from the school.

"Ruth," Lori Dupont called, stopping her in the hallway just outside the door. "There's another antiwar rally this afternoon at—"

"Sorry, I've got to run," Ruth said, flying past her friend and feeling more than a little guilty. Other students cleared a path for her; wherever she was headed must have seemed urgent—and it was, but only to her. Since Christmas, four months ago, she'd been corresponding with Sergeant Paul Gordon, USMC, who was stationed in Afghanistan. There'd been recent reports of fighting, and she hadn't received a letter or an e-mail from Paul in three days. Three interminable days. Not since they'd initially begun their correspondence had there been such a lapse. Paul usually wrote every day and she did, too. They e-mailed as often as possible. Ruth had strong feelings about the war in Iraq, although her opinions didn't match those of her parents, who endorsed this undeclared war.

Earlier in the school year, Ruth had been part of a protest rally on campus. But no matter what her political views on the subject, she felt it was important to support American troops wherever they might be serving. In an effort to do that, Ruth had voluntarily mailed a Christmas card and letter to a nameless soldier.

Paul Gordon was the young man who'd received that Christmas card, and to Ruth's surprise he'd written her back and enclosed his photograph. Paul was from Seattle and he'd chosen her card because of the Seattle postmark. He'd asked her lots of questions—about her history, her family, her interests—and closed with a postscript that said he hoped to hear from her again.

When she first got his letter, Ruth had hesitated. She felt she'd done her duty, supported the armed services in a way she was comfortable doing. This man she'd never met was asking her to continue writing him. She wasn't sure she wanted to become that involved. Feeling uncertain, she'd waited a few days before deciding.

During that time, Ruth had read and reread his letter and studied the head shot of the clean-cut handsome marine sergeant in dress uniform. His dark brown eyes had seemed to stare straight through her—and directly into her heart. After two days, she answered his letter with a short one of her own and added her e-mail address at the bottom of the page. Ruth had a few concerns she wanted him to address before she could commit herself to beginning this correspondence. Being as straightforward and honest as possible, she explained her strong feelings against the war in Iraq. She felt there was a more legitimate reason for troops to be in Afghanistan and wanted to know his stand. A few days later he e-mailed her. Paul didn't mince words. He told her he believed the United States had done the right thing in entering Iraq and gave his reasons. He left it up to her to decide if she wanted to continue their correspondence. Ruth e-mailed him back and once again listed her objections to the American presence in the Middle East. His response came a day later, suggesting they "agree to disagree." He ended the e-mail with the same question he'd asked her earlier. Would she write him?

At first, Ruth had decided not to. They were diametrically opposed in their political views. But in the end, even recognizing the conflict between their opinions, she did write. Their correspondence started slowly. She enjoyed his wry wit and his unflinching determination to make a difference in the world. His father had fought in Vietnam, he said, and in some ways this war seemed similar—the hostile terrain, the unpredictability of the enemy, the unpleasant conditions. For her part, she mentioned that at twenty-five she'd returned to school to obtain her master's of education degree. Then, gradually, without being fully aware of how it had happened, Ruth found herself spending part of every day writing or e-mailing Paul.

After they'd been corresponding regularly for a couple of months, Paul asked for her picture. Eventually she'd mailed him her photograph, but only after she'd had her hair and makeup done at one of those "glamour" studios. Although she wasn't fashion-model beautiful, she considered herself fairly attractive and wanted to look her absolute best for Paul. Already he was becoming important to her. For years, she'd been resigned to the fact that she wasn't much good at relationships. In high school she'd been shy, and while she was an undergraduate, she'd dated a little but tended to be reserved and studious. Her quiet manner didn't seem to appeal to the guys she met. It was only when she stepped in front of a classroom that she truly came out of her shell. She loved teaching, every single aspect of it. In the process, Ruth lost her hesitation and her restraint, and to her astonishment discovered that this enthusiasm had begun to spill over into the rest of her life. Suddenly men started to notice her. She enjoyed the attention—who wouldn't?—and had dated more in the past few months than in the preceding four years.

For the picture, her short brown hair had been styled in loose curls. Her dark-brown eyes were smiling and friendly, which was exactly the impression she hoped to convey. She was a little shocked by the importance of Paul's reaction—by her need that he find her attractive.

She waited impatiently for his response. A week later she received an e-mail. Paul seemed to like what he saw in her photograph and they were soon writing and e-mailing back and forth at a feverish pace. A day without some form of communication from Paul felt empty now.

Ruth had never had a long-distance relationship before, and the intensity of her feelings for this man she'd never met took her by surprise. She wasn't a teenager with a schoolgirl crush. Ruth was a mature, responsible adult. Or at least she had been until she slipped a simple Christmas card into the mailbox—and got a reply from a handsome marine sergeant named Paul Gordon.

Ruth walked quickly to the tiny rental house she shared with Lynn Blumenthal, then ran up the front steps to the porch. Lynn was eighteen and away from home and family for the first time. The arrangement suited them both, and despite the disparity in their ages and interests, they'd gotten along fairly well. With her heart pounding hard, Ruth forced herself to draw in a deep breath as she started toward the mailbox.

The screen door flew open and Lynn came out. "What are you doing home?" she asked, then shook her head. "Never mind, I already know. You're looking for a letter from soldier boy."

Ruth wasn't going to deny the obvious. "I haven't heard from him in three days."

Lynn rolled her eyes. "I don't understand you."

"I know." Ruth didn't want to get into another detailed discussion with her roommate. Lynn had made her feelings known about this relationship from the first, although as Ruth had gently tried to tell her, it was none of her business. That didn't prevent the younger woman from expressing her views. Lynn said that Ruth was only setting herself up for heartache. A part of Ruth actually agreed, but by the time she realized what was happening, she was emotionally involved with Paul.

"You hardly ever see Clay anymore," Lynn chastised, hands on her hips. "He called and asked about you the other night."

Ruth stared at the small black mailbox. Depending on his assignment duty, Paul didn't always have computer access and sometimes wrote letters instead. "Clay and I are just friends."

"Not according to him."

It was true that they'd been seeing each other a lot following a Halloween party last October. Like her, Clay Matthews was obtaining his master's of education, and they seemed to have a lot in common. But her interest in him had already started to wane before she'd mailed that Christmas card to Paul. The problem was, Clay hadn't noticed.

"I'm sorry he's disappointed."

"Clay is decent and hardworking and I think the way you've treated him the last few months is...is terrible." Lynn, who at five foot ten stood a good seven inches taller than Ruth, could be intimidating, especially with her mouth twisted in that grimace of disapproval.

Ruth had tried to let Clay down easily, but it hadn't worked. They'd gone to the library together last Thursday. Unfortunately, that had been a mistake. She'd known it almost right away when Clay pressured her to have coffee with him afterward. It would've been better to end the relationship entirely and forget about staying friends. He was younger, for one thing, and while that hadn't seemed important earlier, it did now. Perhaps it was wrong to compare him to Paul, but Ruth couldn't help it. Measured against Paul, Clay seemed immature, demanding and insecure.

"You said he phoned?" Frowning, she glanced at Lynn.

Lynn nodded. "He wants to know what's going on."

Oh, brother! Ruth couldn't have made it plainer had she handed him divorce papers. Unwilling to be cruel, she'd tried to bolster his ego by referring to all the positive aspects of his personality—but apparently, that had only led him to think the opposite of what she was trying to tell him. He'd refused to take her very obvious hints, and in her frustration, she'd bluntly announced that she wasn't interested in seeing him anymore. That seemed pretty clear-cut to her; how he could be confused about it left Ruth shaking her head.

The fact that he'd phoned and cried on her roommate's shoulder was a good example of what she found adolescent about his behavior. She was absolutely certain Paul would never do that. If he had a problem, he'd take it directly to the source.

"I think you're being foolish," Lynn said, and added, "Not that you asked my opinion."

"No, I didn't," Ruth reminded her, eyeing the mailbox again. There was an ornamental latticework design along the bottom, and looking through it, she could tell that the day's mail had been delivered. The envelope inside was white, and her spirits sank. There just *had* to be something from Paul. If not a real letter, then an e-mail.

"He asked me to talk to you," Lynn was saying.

"Who did?" Ruth asked distractedly. She was dying to open the mailbox, but she wanted to do it in privacy.

"Clay," Lynn cried, sounding completely exasperated. "Who else are we talking about?"

Suddenly Ruth understood. She looked away from the mailbox and focused her attention on Lynn. "You're attracted to him, aren't you?"

Lynn gasped indignantly. "Don't be ridiculous."

"Sit down," Ruth said, gesturing toward the front steps where they'd often sat before. It was a lovely spring afternoon, the first week of April, and she needed to clear the air with her roommate before this got further out of hand.

"What?" Lynn said with a defensive edge. "You've got the wrong idea here. I was just trying to help a friend."

"Sit," Ruth ordered.

"I have class in twenty minutes and I—" Lynn paused, frowning at her watch.

"Sit down."

The eighteen-year-old capitulated with ill grace. "All right, but I already know what you're going to say." She folded her arms and stared straight ahead.

"I'm fine with it," Ruth said softly. "Go out with him if you want. Like I said earlier, I'm not interested in Clay."

"You would be if it wasn't for soldier boy."

Ruth considered that and in all honesty felt she could say, "Not so."

"I don't understand you," Lynn lamented a second time. "You marched in the rally against the war in Iraq. Afghanistan isn't all that different, and now you're involved with Paul what's-his-face and it's like I don't even know you anymore."

"Paul doesn't have anything to do with this."

"Yes, he does," Lynn insisted.

"I'm not going to have this conversation with you. We agree on some points and disagree on others. That's fine. We live in a free society and we don't have to have the same opinion on these issues or anything else."

Lynn sighed and said nothing.

"I have the feeling none of this is really about Paul," Ruth said with deliberate patience. She hadn't known Lynn long; they lived separate lives and so far they'd never had a problem. As far as roommates went, Ruth felt she was fortunate to have found someone as amicable as Lynn. She didn't want this difference of opinion about Clay—and Paul—to ruin that.

The other girl once again looked pointedly at her watch, as if to suggest Ruth say what she intended to say and be done with it.

"I don't want to see Clay." She couldn't make it any more explicit than that.

"You might have told him that."

"I tried."

Lynn glared at her. "You should've tried harder."

Ruth laughed, but not because she was amused. For whatever reason, Clay had set his sights on her and wasn't about to be dissuaded. Complicating matters, Lynn was obviously interested in him and feeling guilty and unsure of how to respond to her attraction.

"Listen," Ruth said. "I didn't mean to hurt Clay. He's a great guy and—"

"You shouldn't have lied to him."

Ruth raised her eyebrows. "When did I lie to him?"

"Last week you said you were going to visit your grandmother in Cedar Cove and that was why you couldn't go out with him this weekend. I overheard you," she added.

Oh, that. "It was a white lie," Ruth confessed. She definitely planned to visit her grandmother, though. Helen Shelton lived across Puget Sound in a small community on the Kitsap Peninsula. Ruth had spent Thanksgiving with her grandmother and visited for a weekend before Christmas and then again close to Valentine's Day. Her last visit had been early in March. She always enjoyed her time with Helen, but somehow the weeks had slipped away and here it was April already.

"A lie is a lie," Lynn said adamantly.

"Okay, you're right," Ruth agreed. "I should've been honest with Clay." Delaying had been a mistake, as she was now learning.

That seemed to satisfy her roommate, who started to get to her feet. Ruth placed her hand on Lynn's forearm, stopping her. "I want to know why you're so upset about this situation with Clay."

"I already told you…. I just don't think this is how people should treat each other."

"I don't like the way Clay's put you in the middle. This is between him and me. He had no right to drag you into it."

"Yes, but—"

"You're defending him?"

Lynn shrugged. "I guess."

"Don't. Clay's a big boy. If he has something to say, then he can come to me all on his own. When and if he does, I'm going to tell him *again* that I'm no longer interested in dating him. I'm—"

"Stuck on some gun-wielding—"

A look from Ruth cut her off.

"Okay, whatever," Lynn muttered.

"What I want you to do is comfort him," Ruth said, patting Lynn's forearm.

"I could, I suppose."

"Good," Ruth said, hoping to encourage her. "He might need someone to talk to, and since you're sensitive to his feelings, you'd be an excellent choice."

"You think so?"

Ruth nodded and then Lynn stood up. She went inside to get her books and left with a cheerful goodbye as if they'd never had an argument. With her roommate gone, Ruth leaped off the step and across the porch to the mailbox. Lifting the top, she reached inside, holding her breath as she pulled out the electric bill in its white envelope, a sales flyer—and a hand-addressed air mail letter from Sergeant Paul Gordon.

Two

April 6

My Dear Ruth,

We've been out on a recon mission for the last four days and there wasn't any way I could let you know. They seemed like the longest four days of this tour, and not for the reasons you might think. Those days meant I couldn't write you or receive your letters. I've been in the marines for eight years now and I've never felt like this about mail before. Never felt this strongly about a woman I've yet to meet, either. Once we were back in camp, I sat down with your letters and read through each one. As I explained before, there are times we can't get on-line and this happened to be one of those times. I realize you've probably been wondering why I wasn't in touch. I hope you weren't too concerned. I would've written if I could.

I have good news. I'm coming home on leave....

Ruth read Paul's letter twice. Yes, he'd definitely said he was headed home, to Seattle, for two weeks before flying to Camp Pendleton in California for additional training. He was looking forward to spending most of his leave with her. His one request was that Ruth make as much time for him as her studies would allow and, if possible, keep her weekends free.

If Ruth thought her heart had been beating hard a few minutes earlier, it didn't compare to the way it pounded now. She could barely breathe. Never had she looked forward to meeting anyone more.

Sitting on the edge of her bed in her tiny room, Ruth picked up the small framed photograph she kept on her nightstand. Paul's image was the first thing she saw when she woke and the last before she turned off her light. In four months, he'd become an important part of her life. Now, with his return to Seattle, their feelings for each other would stand the real test. Writing letters and e-mail messages was very different from carrying on a face-to-face conversation. At the same time, Ruth was afraid. She feared their differing views on the war in Iraq would come between them. She feared, too, that if he was being sent for additional training, he might soon be stationed there.

At the end of his letter, Paul suggested they meet at 6:00 p.m. on Saturday, April 17, at Ivar's restaurant on the Seattle waterfront. She didn't care what else was on her schedule; any conflicting arrangement would immediately be canceled.

Rather than begin her homework, Ruth sat down and wrote Paul back, her fingers flying over the computer keys as she composed her response. Yes, she would meet him. Nothing would keep her away. While she was nervous at the prospect of meeting Paul, she was excited, too.

Her letter was coming out of the printer when the phone rang. Absently Ruth grabbed the receiver, holding it against her shoulder as she opened the desk drawer and searched for an envelope.

"Hello?"

"Ruth, it's your grandmother."

"Grandma," Ruth said, genuinely pleased to hear from Helen. "I've been meaning to call you and I haven't. I'm sorry."

Her grandmother chuckled. "I didn't call to make you feel guilty. I'm inviting you to lunch."

"When?"

"In a couple of weeks—on Sunday the seventeenth if that works for you. I figured I'd give you plenty of time to fit me into your schedule. I thought we'd sit out on the patio, weather permitting, and enjoy the view of the cove."

Her grandmother's duplex was on a hill overlooking the water with the lighthouse in the distance. Her grandparents had lived in Cedar Cove for as long as Ruth could remember. Because she'd been born and raised in Oregon, Ruth had visited the small Washington town often through the years. "I've wanted to get over to see you."

"I know, I know, but unless we both plan ahead, it won't happen. In no time you'll have your master's degree and then you'll move on and we'll both regret the missed opportunities. I don't want that."

"I don't, either." Her Grandma Shelton was Ruth's favorite relative. She was well educated, which wasn't particularly common for a woman her age, and spoke French and German fluently. Her father hadn't said much about his mother's life prior to her marriage, and one of the reasons Ruth had chosen to attend the University of Washington was so she could get to know her grandmother better.

"I can put you down for lunch, then?"

"Yes, that would be perfect." Her gaze fell on Paul's letter and Ruth realized that the date her grandmother had suggested was the first weekend Paul would be in town. He'd specifically asked her to keep as much of that two-week period free as she could. She wanted to spend time with him and yet she couldn't refuse her grandmother. "Grandma, I'm looking at my calendar and—"

"Is there a conflict?"

"Not…exactly. I've sort of got a date," she said, assuming she and Paul would be seeing each other. It would be ideal if he could join her. "It isn't anything official, so I—"

"Then you do have something scheduled."

"No…" This was getting complicated.

"I wasn't aware that you were dating anyone special. Who is he?"

The question hung there for a moment before Ruth answered. "His name is Paul Gordon and we aren't really dating." She would've explained, except that her grandmother broke in again.

"Your parents didn't say anything about this." The words were spoken as if there must be something untoward about Paul that Ruth didn't want to divulge.

"No, Mom and Dad wouldn't," Ruth muttered, not adding that she hadn't actually mentioned Paul to her parents. She'd decided it wasn't necessary to enlighten them about this correspondence yet. Explaining her feelings about Paul to her family would be difficult when everyone knew her stand on the war. More importantly, she wasn't sure how she felt about him and wouldn't be until they'd met.

So far, they were only pen pals, but this was the man she dreamed about every night, the man who dominated her thoughts each and every day.

"Grandma, I haven't said anything to Mom and Dad because I haven't officially met Paul yet."

"Is this…" Her grandmother hesitated. "Is this one of those…those *Internet* relationships?" She spit out the word as though meeting a man via the Internet was either illegal or unseemly—and probably both.

"No, Grandma, it's nothing like that."

"Then why don't your parents know about him?"

"Well, because…because he's a soldier in Afghanistan." There—it was out.

Her announcement was met with silence. "There's something wrong with that?" Helen eventually asked.

"No…"

"You say it like you're ashamed."

"I'm *not* ashamed," Ruth insisted. "I like Paul a great deal and I'm proud of his service to our country." She downplayed her political beliefs as she expanded on her feelings. "I enjoy his letters and like him more than I probably should, but I don't like the fact that he's a soldier."

"You sound confused."

Ruth sighed. That was certainly an accurate description of how she felt.

"So this Paul will be in Seattle on leave?"

"Yes. For two weeks."

"He's coming here to meet you?"

"His family also lives in the area."

"Invite him along for lunch," her grandmother said. "I want to meet him, too."

"You do?" Ruth's enthusiasm swelled. "That's great. I wanted to, but I wasn't sure how you'd feel about having him join us."

"I meant what I said. I want to meet him."

"We've only been writing for a few months. I don't know him well, and..." She let the rest fade.

"It'll be fine, Ruth," her grandmother assured her. Helen always seemed to know what Ruth was feeling and thinking. She'd found ways to encourage the special bond between them.

"Grandpa was a soldier when you first met him, wasn't he?" Ruth remembered her father telling her this years ago, although he'd also said his mother didn't like to talk about those years. Ruth assumed that was because of Grandpa Sam's bad memories of the war, the awful things he'd seen and experienced in Europe. She knew her grandparents had met during the Second World War, fallen in love and married soon afterward. Ruth's father had been born in the baby boom years that followed World War II, and her uncle Jake had arrived two years later. Ruth was Helen's only granddaughter, but she had three grandsons.

"Oh, yes." She sighed wistfully. "My Sam was so handsome, especially in his uniform." Her voice softened perceptibly.

"How long did you know him before you were married?"

Her grandmother laughed. "Less than a year. In wartime everything's very intense. People married quickly because you never knew if you'd still be alive tomorrow. It was as if those of us who were young had to cram as much life into as short a time as possible."

"The war was terrible, wasn't it?"

Her grandmother hesitated before whispering, "All war is terrible."

"I agree," Ruth said promptly.

"So you and this soldier you've never met are discussing marriage?"

"No!" Ruth nearly choked getting out her denial. "Paul and me? No, of course not. I promise you the subject has never even come up." They hadn't written about kissing or touching or exchanged the conventional romantic endearments. That didn't mean she hadn't *dreamed* about what it would be like to be held by Paul Gordon. To kiss him and be caressed by him. She'd let her imagination roam free....

"So you say," her grandmother said with amusement in her voice. "By all means, bring your friend. I'll look forward to meeting him."

That was no doubt true, Ruth thought, but no one looked forward to meeting Paul Gordon more than she did.

Three

"How do I look?" Ruth asked her roommate. She hated to sound so insecure, but this was perhaps the most important meeting of her life and Ruth was determined to make a perfect impression.

"Fabulous," Lynn muttered, her face hidden behind the latest issue of *People* magazine.

"I might believe you if you actually looked at me," Ruth said, holding on to her patience with limited success. The relationship with her roommate had gone steadily downhill since the confrontation on the porch steps two weeks earlier. Apparently Clay wasn't interested in dating Lynn. What Ruth did know was that Clay hadn't contacted her since, and her roommate had been increasingly cold and standoffish. Ruth had tried to talk to her but that hadn't done any good. She suspected that Lynn *wanted* to be upset, so Ruth had decided to go about her own business and ignore her roommate's disgruntled mood. This might not be the best strategy, but it was the only way she could deal with Lynn's attitude.

Her roommate heaved a sigh; apparently lifting her head a couple of inches required immense effort. Her eyes were devoid of emotion as she gave Ruth a token appraisal. "You look all right, I guess."

That was high praise coming from Lynn. Ruth had spent an hour doing her hair, with the help of a curling iron and two brushes. And now it was raining like crazy. This wasn't the drizzle traditionally associated with the Pacific Northwest, either. This was *rain*. Real rain. Which spelled disaster for her hair, since her umbrella wouldn't afford much protection.

If her hair had taken a long time, choosing what to wear had demanded equal consideration. She had a lovely teal-and-white summer dress from last year that made her eyes look dark and dreamy, but the rain had altered *that* plan. Now she was wearing black pants and a white cashmere sweater with a beige overcoat.

"You're meeting at Ivar's, right?"

"Right." Ruth didn't remember telling her roommate. They were barely on speaking terms.

"Too bad."

"Too bad what?" Ruth demanded.

Lynn sighed once more and set aside the magazine. "If you must know, soldier boy phoned and said you should meet him outside the restaurant." She grinned nastily. "And in case you haven't noticed, it's pouring out."

"I'm supposed to meet him outside?"

"That's what he said."

Ruth made an effort not to snap at her. "You didn't think to mention this before now?"

Lynn shrugged. "It slipped my mind."

Ruth just bet it did. Rather than start an argument,

she collected her raincoat, umbrella and purse. Surely she would receive a heavenly reward for controlling her temper. Lynn would love an argument but Ruth wasn't going to give her one; she wasn't going to play those kinds of childish games with her roommate. The difference in their ages had never seemed more pronounced than it had in the past two weeks.

Because of the rain, Ruth couldn't find convenient street parking and was forced to pay an outrageous amount at a lot near the restaurant. She rushed toward Ivar's, making sure she arrived in plenty of time to meet Paul by six. Lynn's sour disposition might have upset Ruth if not for the fact that she was finally going to meet the soldier who'd come to mean so much to her.

Focusing on her hair, dress and makeup meant she'd paid almost no attention to something that was far more important—what she'd actually say when she saw Paul for the first time. Ideas skittered through her mind as she crossed the street.

Ruth hoped to sound witty, articulate and well informed. She so badly wanted to impress Paul and was afraid she'd stumble over her words or find herself speechless. Her other fear was that she'd take one look at him and humiliate herself by bursting into tears. It could happen; she felt very emotional about meeting this man she'd known only through letters and e-mails.

Thankfully, by the time she reached Ivar's, the rain had slowed to a drizzle. But it was still wet out and miserably gray. Her curls, which had been perfectly styled, had turned into tight wads of frizz in the humid air. She was sure she resembled a cartoon character more than the fashion model she'd strived for earlier that afternoon.

After the longest ten-minute wait of her life, Ruth checked her watch and saw that it was now one minute past six. Paul was late. She pulled her cell phone from her bag; unfortunately Paul didn't have a cell, so she punched out her home number. Perhaps he'd been de-layed in traffic and called the house, hoping to connect with her.

No answer. Either Lynn had left or purposely chose not to pick up the receiver. Great, just great.

To her dismay, as she went to toss her cell phone back inside her purse, she realized the battery was low. Why hadn't she charged it? Oh, no, that would've been *much* too smart.

All at once Ruth figured it out. Paul wasn't late at all. Somehow she'd missed him, which wouldn't be that difficult with all the tourist traffic on the waterfront. Even in the rain, people milled around the area as if they were on the sunny beaches of Hawaii. Someone needed to explain to these tourists that the water dripping down from the sky was cold rain. Just because they'd dressed for the sunshine didn't mean the weather would coop-erate.

By now her hair hung in tight ringlets all around her head. Either of two things had happened, she speculated. First, her appearance was so drastically changed from that glamour photo she'd sent him that Paul hadn't recognized her and assumed she'd stood him up. The other possibil-ity was even less appealing. Paul had gotten a glimpse of her and decided to escape without saying a word.

For a moment Ruth felt like crying. Rather than waste the last of her cell phone battery phoning her roommate again, she stepped inside the restaurant to see if Paul had left a message for her.

She opened the door and lowered her umbrella. As she did, she saw a tall, lean and very handsome Paul Gordon get up from a chair in the restaurant foyer.

"Ruth?"

"Paul?" Without a thought, she dropped the umbrella and moved directly into his embrace.

Then they were in each other's arms, hugging fiercely.

When it became obvious that everyone in the crowded foyer was staring at them, Paul reluctantly let her go.

"I was outside—didn't you tell Lynn that's where we were meeting?"

"No." He brushed the wet curls from her forehead and smiled down at her. "I said inside because I heard on the weather forecast that it was going to rain."

"Of course, of course." Ruth wanted to kick herself for being so dense. She should've guessed what Lynn was up to; instead, she'd fallen right into her roommate's petty hands. "I'm so sorry to keep you waiting."

A number of people were still watching them but Ruth didn't care. She couldn't stop looking at Paul. He seemed unable to break eye contact with her, too.

The hostess came forward. "Since your party's arrived," she said with a smile, "I can seat you now."

"Yes, please." Paul helped Ruth off with her coat and set the umbrella aside so it could dry. Then, as if they'd known and loved each other all their lives, he reached for her hand and linked her fingers with his as they walked through the restaurant.

The hostess seated them by the window, which overlooked the dark, murky waters of Puget Sound. Rain ran in rivulets down the tempered glass, but it could have been the brightest, sunniest day in Seattle's history for all the notice Ruth paid.

Paul continued to hold her hand on top of the table.

"I was worried about what I'd say once we met," she said. "Then when we did, I was just so glad, the words didn't seem important."

"I'd almost convinced myself you'd stood me up." He yawned, covering his mouth with the other hand, and she realized he was probably functioning on next to no sleep.

"Stood you up? I would've found a way to get here no matter what." She let the truth of that show in her eyes. She had the strongest feeling of *certainty,* and an involuntary sense that he was everything she'd dreamed.

He briefly looked away. "I would've found a way to get to you, too." His fingers tightened around hers.

"When did you last sleep?" she asked.

His mouth curved upward in a half smile. "I forget. A long time ago. I probably should've suggested we meet tomorrow, but I didn't want to wait a minute longer than I had to."

"Me, neither," she confessed.

He smiled again, that wonderful, intoxicating smile.

"When did you land?" she asked, because if she didn't stop staring at him she was going to embarrass herself.

"Late this morning," he told her. "My family—well, you know what families are like. Mom's been cooking for days and there was a big family get-together this afternoon. I wanted to invite you but—"

"No, I understand. You couldn't because—well, how could you?" That didn't come out right, but Paul seemed to know what she was trying to say.

"You're exactly like I pictured you," he said, and his eyes softened as he touched her cheek.

"You imagined me drenched?"

He chuckled. "I imagined you beautiful, and you are."

His words made her blush. "I'm having a hard time believing you're actually here," she said.

"I am, too."

The waitress came for their drink order. Ruth hadn't even looked at her menu or thought about what she'd like to drink. Because she was wet and chilled, she ordered hot tea and Paul asked for a bottle of champagne.

"We have reason to celebrate," he announced. Then, as if it had suddenly occurred to him, he said, "You do drink alcohol, don't you?"

She nodded quickly. "Normally I would've asked for wine, but I wanted the tea so I could warm up. I haven't decided what to order yet." She picked up the menu and scanned the entrées.

The waitress brought the champagne and standing ice bucket to the table. "Is there something special you're celebrating?" she asked in a friendly voice.

Paul nodded and his eyes met Ruth's. "We're celebrating the fact that we found each other."

"Excellent." She removed the foil top and wire around the cork and opened the bottle with a slight popping sound. After filling the two champagne flutes, she left.

Ruth took her glass. "Once again, I'm so sorry about what happened. Let me pay for the champagne, please. You wouldn't have had a problem finding me if I'd—"

"I wasn't talking about this evening," he broke in. "I was talking about your Christmas card."

"Oh."

Paul raised his glass; she raised hers, too, and they clicked the rims gently together. "Do you believe in fate?" he asked.

Ruth smiled. "I didn't, but I've had a change of heart since Christmas."

His smile widened. "Me, too."

Dinner was marvelous. Ruth didn't remember what she'd ordered or anything else about the actual meal. For all she knew, she could've been dining on raw seaweed. It hardly mattered.

They talked and talked, and she felt as if she'd known Paul her entire life. He asked detailed questions about her family, her studies, her plans after graduation, and seemed genuinely interested in everything she said. He talked about the marines and Afghanistan with a sense of pride at the positive differences he'd seen in the country. After dinner and dessert, they lingered over coffee and at nine-thirty Paul paid the tab and suggested they walk along the waterfront.

The clouds had drifted away and the moon was glowing, its light splashing against the pier as they strolled hand in hand. Although she knew Paul had to be exhausted from his long flight and the family gathering, she couldn't deny herself these last few minutes.

"You asked me to keep the weekends free," Ruth murmured, resting her head against his shoulder.

"Did you?"

She sighed. "Not tomorrow."

"Do you have a date with some other guy?"

She leaned back in order to study his face, trying to discern whether he was serious. "You're joking, right?" she murmured hesitantly.

He shrugged. "Yes and no. You have no obligation to me and vice versa."

"Are *you* seeing someone else?"

"No." His response was immediate.

"I'm not, either," she told him. She wanted to ask how he could even *think* that she would be. "I promised my grandmother I'd visit tomorrow."

"Your grandmother?" he repeated.

"She invited you, too."

He arched his brows.

"In fact, she insisted I bring you."

"So you've mentioned me to your family."

She'd told him in her letters that she hadn't. "Just her—she's special. I'm sure you'll enjoy meeting her."

"I'm sure I will, too."

"You'll come, won't you?"

Paul turned Ruth into his arms and stared down at her. "I don't think I could stay away."

And then he kissed her. Ruth had fantasized about this moment for months. She'd wondered what it would be like when Paul kissed her, but nothing she'd conjured up equaled this reality. Never in all her twenty-five years had she experienced anything close to the sensation she felt when Paul's mouth descended on hers. Stars fell from the sky. She saw it happen even with her eyes tightly closed. She heard triumphant music nearby; it seemed to surround her. But once she opened her eyes, all the stars seemed to be exactly where they'd been before. And the music came from somebody's car radio.

Paul wore a stunned look.

"That was...very nice," Ruth managed after a moment.

Paul nodded in agreement, then cleared his throat. "Very."

"Should I admit I was afraid of what would happen when we met?" she asked.

"Afraid why? Of what?"

"I didn't know what to expect."

"Me, neither." He slid his hand down her spine and moved a step away from her. "I'd built up this meeting in my mind."

"I did, too," she whispered.

"I was so afraid you could never live up to my image of you," Paul told her. "I figured we could meet and I'd get you out of my system. I'd buy you dinner, thank you for your letters and e-mails—and that would be the end of it. No woman could possibly be everything I'd envisioned you to be. But you are, Ruth, you are."

Although the wind and rain were chilly, his words were enough to warm her from head to foot.

"I didn't believe you could be what I'd imagined, either, and I was right," Ruth said.

"You were?" He seemed crestfallen.

She nodded. "Paul, you're even more wonderful than I'd realized." At his relieved expression, she said, "I underestimated how strong my feelings for you are. Look at me, I'm shaking." She held out her hand as evidence of how badly she was trembling after his kiss.

He shook his head. "I've been in life-and-death situations and I didn't flinch. Now, one evening with you and my stomach's full of butterflies."

"That's lack of sleep."

"No," he said, and took her by the shoulders. "That was what your kiss did to me." His eyes glittered as he stared down at her.

"What should we do?" she asked uncertainly.

"You're the one with reservations about falling for a guy in the service."

Her early letters had often referred to her feelings about exactly that. Ruth lowered her gaze. "The fundamental problem hasn't changed," she said. "But you'll eventually get out, won't you?"

He hesitated, and his dark eyes—which had been so warm seconds before—seemed to be closing her out. "Eventually I'll leave the marines, but you should know it won't be anytime in the near future. I'm in for the long haul, and if you want to continue this relationship, the sooner you accept that, the better."

Ruth didn't want their evening to end on a negative note. When she'd answered his letter that first time, she'd known he was a military man and it hadn't stopped her. She'd gone into this with her eyes wide open. "I don't have to decide right away, do I?"

"No," he admitted. "But—"

"Good," she said, cutting him off. She couldn't allow their differences to come between them so quickly. She sensed that Paul, too, wanted to push all that aside. When she slid her arms around his waist and hugged him, he hugged her back. "You're exhausted. Let's meet in the morning. I'll take you over to visit my grandmother and we can talk some more then."

Ruth rested her head against his shoulder again and Paul kissed her hair. "You're making this difficult," he said.

"I know. I'm sorry."

"Me, too," he whispered.

Ruth realized they'd need to confront the issue soon. She could also see that settling it wasn't going to be as easy as she'd hoped.

Four

Paul met Ruth at the Seattle terminal at ten the following morning and they walked up the ramp to board the Bremerton ferry. The hard rain of the night before had yielded to glorious sunshine.

Unlike the previous evening, when Paul and Ruth had talked nonstop through a three-hour dinner, it seemed that now they had little to say. The one big obstacle in their relationship hung between them. They sat side by side on the wooden bench and sipped hot coffee as the ferry eased away from the Seattle dock.

"You're still thinking about last night, aren't you?" Ruth said, carefully broaching the subject after a lengthy silence. "About you being in the military, I mean, and my objections to the war in Iraq?"

He nodded. "Yeah, there's the political aspect and also the fact that you don't seem comfortable with the concept of military life," he said.

"I'm not, really, but we'll work it out," she assured him, and reached for his free hand, entwining their fingers. "We'll find a way."

Paul didn't look as if he believed her. But after a couple of moments, he seemed to come to some sort of decision. He brought her hand to his lips. "Let's enjoy the time we have today, all right?"

Ruth smiled in agreement.

"Tell me about your grandmother."

Ruth was more than willing to change the subject. "This is my paternal grandmother, and she's lived in Cedar Cove for the past thirty years. She and my grandfather moved there from Seattle after he retired because they wanted a slower pace of life. I barely remember my grandfather Sam. He died when I was two, before I had any real memories of him."

"He died young," Paul commented sympathetically.

"Yes… My grandmother's been alone for a long time."

"She probably has good friends in a town like Cedar Cove."

"Yes," Ruth said. "And she's still got friends she's had since the war. It's something I admire about my grandmother," she continued. "Not only because she speaks three languages fluently and is one of the most intelligent women I know. She's my inspiration. Ever since I can remember, she's been helping others. Even though she's in her eighties, Grandma's involved with all kinds of charities and social groups. When I enrolled at the University of Washington, I intended for the two of us to get together often, but I swear her schedule's even busier than mine."

Paul grinned at her. "I know what you mean. It's the same in my family."

By the time they stepped off the Bremerton ferry and took the foot ferry across to Cedar Cove, it was after eleven. They stopped at a deli, where Paul bought a loaf of fresh bread and a bottle of Washington State gewürztraminer to take with them. At quarter to twelve, they trudged up the hill toward her grandmother's duplex on Poppy Lane.

When they arrived, Helen greeted them at the front door and eagerly ushered Paul and Ruth into the house. Ruth hugged her grandmother, whose white hair was cut stylishly short. Now in her early eighties, Helen was thinner than the last time Ruth had visited and somehow seemed more fragile. Her grandmother hugged her back, then paused to give Paul an embarrassingly frank look. Ruth felt her face heat as her grandmother spoke.

"So, you're the young man who's captured my granddaughter's heart."

"Grandma, this is Paul Gordon," Ruth said hurriedly, gesturing toward Paul.

"This is the soldier you've been writing to, who's fighting in Afghanistan?"

"I am." Paul's response sounded a bit defensive, Ruth thought. He obviously preferred not to discuss it.

In an effort to ward off any misunderstanding, Ruth added, "My grandfather was a soldier when Grandma met him."

Helen nodded, and a faraway look stole over her. It took her a moment to refocus her attention on Ruth. "Come, both of you," she said, stepping between them. She wrapped her arm around Ruth's waist. "I set the table outside. It's such a beautiful afternoon, I thought we'd eat on the patio."

"We brought some bread and a bottle of wine," Ruth said. "Paul got them."

"Perfect. Thank you, Paul."

While Ruth sliced the fresh-baked bread, he opened the wine, then helped her grandmother carry the salad plates outside. An apple pie cooled on the kitchen counter and the scent of cinnamon permeated the sun-lit kitchen.

They chatted throughout the meal; the conversation was light and friendly as they lingered over their wine. Every now and then Ruth caught her grandmother staring at Paul with the strangest expression on her face. Ruth didn't know what to make of this. It almost seemed as if her grandmother was trying to place him, to recall where she'd seen him before.

Helen seemed to read Ruth's mind. "Am I embarrassing your beau, sweetheart?" she asked with a half smile.

Ruth resisted informing her grandmother that Paul wasn't her anything, especially not her beau. They'd had one lovely dinner together, but now their political differences seemed to have overtaken them.

"I apologize, Paul." Helen briefly touched his hand, which rested on the table. "When I first saw you—" She stopped abruptly. "You resemble someone I knew many years ago."

"Where, Grandma?" Ruth asked.

"In France, during the war."

"You were in France during World War II?" Ruth couldn't quite hide her shock.

Helen turned to her. "I haven't spoken much about those days, but now, at the end of my life, I think about them more and more." She pushed back her chair and stood.

Ruth stood, too, thinking her grandmother was about to carry in their empty plates and serve the pie.

Helen motioned her to sit. "Stay here. There's something I want you to see. I think perhaps it's time."

When her grandmother had left them, Ruth looked at Paul and shrugged. "I have no idea what's going on."

Paul had been wonderful with her grandmother, thoughtful and attentive. He'd asked a number of questions during the meal—about Cedar Cove, about her life with Sam—and listened intently when she responded. Ruth knew his interest was genuine. Together they cleared the table and returned the dishes to the kitchen, then waited for Helen at the patio table.

It was at least five minutes before she came back. She held a rolled-up paper that appeared to be some kind of poster, old enough to have turned yellow with age. Carefully she opened it and laid it flat on the cleared table. Ruth saw that the writing was French. In the center of the poster, which measured about eighteen inches by twenty-four, was a pencil sketch of two faces: a man and a woman, whose names she didn't recognize.

"Who's that?" Ruth asked, pointing to the female.

Her grandmother smiled calmly. "I am that woman."

Ruth frowned. Although she'd seen photographs of her grandmother as a young woman, this sketch barely resembled the woman she knew. The man in the drawing, however, seemed familiar. Gazing at the sketch for a minute, she realized the face was vaguely like Paul's. Not so much in any similarity of features as in a quality of…character, she supposed.

"And the man?"

"That was Jean-Claude," Helen whispered, her voice full of pain.

Paul turned to Ruth, but she was at a complete loss and didn't know what to tell him. Her grandfather's name was Sam and she'd never heard of this Jean-Claude. Certainly her father had never mentioned another man in his mother's life.

"This is a wanted poster," Paul remarked. "I speak some French—studied it in school."

"Yes. The Germans offered a reward of one million francs to anyone who turned us in."

"You were in France during the war and you were *wanted?*" This was more than Ruth could assimilate. She sat back down; so did her grandmother. Paul remained standing for a moment longer as he studied the poster.

"You and Jean-Claude were part of the French Resistance?" Paul asked, but it was more statement than question.

"We were." For a moment her grandmother seemed to have a hard time speaking. "Jean-Claude was my husband. We married during the war. He was my everything, strong and brave and handsome. His laughter filled a room. Sometimes, still, I think I can hear him." Her eyes grew teary and she dabbed at them with her linen handkerchief. "That was many years ago now and, as I said, I think perhaps it's time I spoke of it."

Ruth was grateful. She couldn't let her grandmother leave the story untold. She suspected her father hadn't heard any of this, and she wanted to learn everything she could about this unknown episode in their family history before it was forever lost.

"What were you doing in France?" Ruth asked. She couldn't comprehend that the woman she'd always known as a warm and loving grandmother, who baked cookies and knit socks for Christmas, had been a freedom fighter in a foreign country.

"I was attending the Sorbonne when the Germans invaded. My mother had been born in France, but her own parents were long dead. I was studying French literature. My parents were frantic for me to book my passage home, but like so many others in France, I didn't believe the country would fall. I assured my mother I'd leave when I felt it was no longer safe. Being young and foolish, I thought she was overreacting. Besides, I was in love. Jean-Claude had asked me to marry him, and what woman in love wishes to leave her lover over rumors of war?" She laughed lightly, shaking her head. "France seemed invincible. We were convinced the Germans wouldn't invade, convinced they'd suffer a humiliating defeat if they tried."

"So when it happened you were trapped," Paul said.

Her grandmother drew in a deep breath. "There was the Blitzkrieg.... People were demoralized and defeated when France surrendered after only a few days of fighting. We were aghast that such a thing could happen. Jean-Claude and a few of his friends decided to resist the occupation. I decided I would, too, so we were married right away. My parents knew nothing of this."

"How did you join the Resistance?" Paul asked as Ruth studied her grandmother with fresh eyes.

"Join," she repeated scornfully. "There was no place to sign up and be handed a weapon and an instruction manual. A group of us students, naive and foolish, offered resistance to the German occupation. Later we learned there were other groups, eventually united under the leadership of General de Gaulle. We soon found one another. Jean-Claude and I—we were young and too stupid to understand the price we would pay, but by then we'd already lost some of our dearest friends. Jean-Claude and I refused to let them die in vain."

"What did you do?" Ruth breathed. She leaned closer to her grandmother.

"Whatever we could, which in the beginning was pitifully little. The Germans suffered more casualties in traffic accidents. At first our resistance was mostly symbolic." A slow smile spread across her weathered face. "But we learned, oh yes, we learned."

Ruth was still having difficulty taking it all in. She pressed her hand to her forehead. She found it hard enough to believe that the sketch of the female in this worn poster was her own grandmother. Then to discover that the fragile, petite woman at her side had been part of the French Resistance...

"Does my dad know any of this?" Ruth asked.

Helen sighed heavily. "I'm not sure, but I doubt it. Sam might have mentioned it to him. I've told only my friends Clara and Winifred. No one else." She shook her head. "I didn't feel I could talk to my sons about it. There was too much that's disturbing. Too many painful memories."

"Did you...did you ever have to kill anyone?" Ruth had trouble even getting the question out.

"Many times," Helen answered bluntly. "Does that surprise you?"

It shocked Ruth to the point that she couldn't ask anything else.

"The first time was the most difficult," her grandmother said. "I was held by a French policeman." She added something derogatory in French, and although Ruth couldn't understand the language, some things didn't need translation. "The police worked hard to prove to the Germans what good little boys they were," she muttered, this time in English. "I'd been stopped and questioned, detained by this pig of a man. He said he was taking me to the police station. I had a small gun with me that I'd hidden, a seven millimeter."

Ruth's heart pounded as she listened to Helen recount this adventure.

"The pig didn't drive me to the police station. Instead he headed for open country and I knew that once he was outside town and away from the eyes of any witnesses, he would rape and murder me."

Ruth pressed her hand to her mouth, holding back a gasp of horror.

"You'd trained for self-defense?" Paul asked.

Her grandmother laughed. "No. How could we? There was no time for such lessons. But I realized that I didn't need technique. What I needed was nerve. This beast of a man pulled his gun on me but I was quicker. I shot him in the head." She paused, as if the memory of that terrifying moment was as clear as if it had happened only hours before. "I buried him myself in a field and, as far as I know, he was never found." She wore a small satisfied look. "His mistake," she murmured, "was that he tightened his jaw when he reached for his gun— and I saw. I'd been watching him closely. He was thinking of what might happen, of what could go wrong. He was a professional, and I was only nineteen, and yet I knew that if I didn't act then, it would've been too late."

"Didn't you worry about what could happen, too?" Ruth asked, not understanding how her grandmother could ever shoot another human being.

"No," Helen answered flatly. "I *knew* what would happen. We all did. We didn't have a chance of surviving, none of us. My parents would never have discovered my fate—I would simply have disappeared. They didn't even know I'd married Jean-Claude or changed my name." She stared out at the water. "I don't understand why I lived. It makes no sense that God would spare me when all my friends, all those I loved, were killed."

"Jean-Claude, too?"

Her eyes filled and she slowly nodded.

"Where was he when you were taken by the policeman?" Paul asked.

Her grandmother's mouth trembled. "By then, Jean-Claude had been captured."

"The French police?"

"No," she said in the thinnest of whispers. "Jean-Claude was being held by the Gestapo. That was the first time they got him—but not the last."

Ruth had heard horror stories of the notorious German soldiers and their cruelty.

Helen straightened, and her back went rigid. "I could only imagine how those monsters were torturing my husband." Contempt hardened her voice.

"What did you do?" Ruth glanced at Paul, whose gaze remained riveted on her grandmother.

At first Helen didn't answer. "What else could I do? I had to rescue him."

"You?" Paul asked this with the same shock Ruth felt.

"Yes, me and…" Helen's smile was fleeting. "I was very clever about it, too." The sadness returned with such intensity that it brought tears to Ruth's eyes.

"They eventually killed him, didn't they?" she asked, hardly able to listen to her grandmother's response.

"No," Helen said as she turned to face Ruth. "I did."

Five

"You killed Jean-Claude?" Ruth repeated incredulously, her heart hammering wildly.

Tears rolling down her cheeks, Helen nodded. "God forgive me, but I had no choice. I couldn't allow him to be tortured any longer. He begged me to do it, begged me to end his suffering. That was the second time he was captured, and they were more determined than ever to break him. He knew far too much."

"You'd better start at the beginning. You went into Gestapo headquarters?" Paul asked, moving closer as if he didn't want to risk missing even one word. "Was that the first time or the second?"

"Both. The first time, in April 1943, I rescued him. I pretended I was pregnant and brought a priest to the house the Gestapo had taken over. I insisted with great bravado that they force Jean-Claude to marry me and give my baby a name. I didn't care if they killed him, I said, but before he died I wanted him to give my baby his name." She paused. "I was very convincing."

"You weren't pregnant, were you?"

"No, of course not," her grandmother snapped. "It was a ploy to get into the house."

"Was the priest a real priest?"

"Yes. He didn't know I was using him, but I had no alternative. I was desperate to get Jean-Claude out alive."

"The priest knew nothing," Ruth repeated, meeting Paul's eyes, astounded by her grandmother's nerve and cunning.

"The Father knew nothing," the older woman concurred, smiling grimly. "But I needed him, and so I used him. Thankfully the Gestapo believed me, and because they wanted to keep relations with the Church as smooth as possible, they brought Jean-Claude into the room."

Ruth could picture the scene, but she didn't know if she'd ever possess that kind of bravery.

"Jean-Claude was in terrible pain, but he nearly laughed out loud when the priest asked him if he was the father of my child. Fortunately he didn't have to answer because our friends had arranged a distraction outside the house. A firebomb was tossed into a parked vehicle, which exploded. All but two Gestapo left the room. I shot them both right in front of the priest, and then Jean-Claude and I escaped through a back window."

"Where did you find the courage?" Ruth asked breathlessly.

"Courage?" her grandmother echoed. "That wasn't courage. That was fear. I would do anything to save my husband's life—and I did. Then, only a few weeks later, I was the one who killed him. What took courage was finding the will to live after Jean-Claude died. *That* was courage, and I would never have managed if it hadn't been for the American soldier who saved my life. If it hadn't been for Sam."

"He was my grandfather," Ruth explained to Paul.

"I want to know more about Jean-Claude," Paul said, placing his arm around Ruth's shoulders. It felt good to be held by him and she leaned into his strength, his solid warmth.

Her grandmother's eyes grew weary and she shook her head. "Perhaps another day. I'm tired now, too tired to speak anymore."

"We should go," Paul whispered.

"I'll do the dishes," Ruth insisted.

"Nonsense. You should leave now," Helen said. "You have better things to do than talk to an old lady."

"But we *want* to talk to you," Ruth told her.

"You will." Helen looked even more drawn. "Soon, but not right now."

"You'll finish the story?"

"Yes," the old woman said hoarsely. "I promise I'll tell you everything."

While her grandmother went to her room to rest, Ruth and Paul cleaned up the kitchen. At first they worked in silence, as if they didn't know quite what to say to each other. Ruth put the food away while Paul rinsed the dishes and set them inside the dishwasher.

"You didn't know any of this before today?" he asked, propping himself against the counter.

"Not a single detail."

"Your father never mentioned it?"

"Never." Ruth wondered again how much her father actually knew about his mother's war adventures. "I'm sure you were the one who prompted her."

"Me?" Paul asked with a frown. "How?"

"More than anything, I think you reminded her of Jean-Claude." Ruth tilted her head to one side. "It's as if this woman I've known all my life has suddenly become a stranger." Ruth finished by wiping down the counters. She knew they'd need to leave soon if they were going to catch the ferry.

"Maybe you'd better check on her before we go," Paul suggested.

She agreed and hurried out of the kitchen. Her grandmother's eyes opened briefly when Ruth entered the cool, silent room. Reaching for an afghan at the foot of the bed, Ruth covered her grandmother with it and kissed the papery skin of her cheek. She'd always loved Helen, but she had an entirely new respect for her now.

"I'll be back soon," Ruth whispered.

"Bring your young man."

"I will."

Helen's response was low, and at first Ruth didn't understand her and strained to hear. Gradually her voice drifted off. Ruth waited until Helen was asleep before she slipped out of the room.

"She's sleeping?" Paul asked, setting aside the magazine he was reading when Ruth returned to the kitchen.

Ruth nodded. "She started speaking to me in French. I so badly wish I knew what she said."

They left a few minutes later. Caught up in her own thoughts, Ruth walked down the hill beside Paul, neither of them speaking as they approached the foot ferry that would take them from Cedar Cove across to Bremerton.

Once they were aboard the ferry, Paul went to get them coffee from the concession stand. While he was gone, Ruth decided she had to find out how much her family knew about her grandmother's war exploits. She opened her purse and rummaged for her cell phone.

Paul brought the coffee and set her plastic cup on the table.

Ruth glanced up long enough to thank him with a smile. "I'm calling my parents."

Paul nodded, tentatively sipping hot coffee. Then, in an obvious effort to give her some privacy, he moved to stand by the rail, gazing out at the water.

Her father answered on the third ring. "Dad, it's Ruth," she said in a rush.

"Well, Ruthie, this is a pleasant surprise. I'll get your mother."

Her father had never enjoyed telephone conversations and generally handed the phone off to Ruth's mother.

"Wait—I need to talk to you," Ruth said.

"What's up?"

That was her dad, too. He didn't like chitchat and wanted to get to the point as quickly as possible.

"I went over to see Grandma this afternoon."

"How is she? We've been meaning to get up there and see her *and* you. I don't know where the time goes. Thanksgiving was our last visit."

How is she? Ruth wasn't sure what to say. Her grandmother seemed fragile and old, and Ruth had never thought of her as either. "I don't know, Dad. She's the same, except—well, except she might have lost a few pounds." Ruth looked over at Paul and bit her lip. "I…brought a friend along with me."

"Your roommate? What's her name again?"

"Lynn Blumenthal. No, this is a male friend."

That caught her father's attention. "Someone from school?"

"No, we met sort of…by accident. His name is Paul Gordon and he's a sergeant in the marines. We've been corresponding for the past four months. But Paul isn't the reason I'm phoning."

"All right, then. What is?"

Ruth dragged in a deep breath. "Like I said before, I was visiting Grandma."

"With this marine you're seeing," he reiterated.

"Yes." Ruth didn't dare look at Paul a second time. Nervously, she tucked a strand of hair behind her ear and leaned forward, lowering her voice. "Grandma was in France during World War II. Did you know that?"

Her father paused. "Yes, I did."

"Were you aware that she was a member of the French Resistance?"

Again he paused. "My father mentioned something shortly before he died, but I never got any more information."

"Didn't you ask your mother?"

"I tried, but she refused to talk about it. She said some things were better left buried and deflected all my questions. Do you mean to say she told you about this?"

"Yes, and, Dad, the stories were incredible! Did you know Grandma was married before she met Grandpa Sam?"

This statement was greeted by a shocked silence.

"Her husband's name was Jean-Claude," she added.

"A Frenchman?"

"Yes." She frowned as she tried to recall his surname from the poster. "He was part of the movement, too, and Grandma, your *mother,* went into a Gestapo headquarters and managed to get him out."

"My mother?" The question was obviously loud

enough for Paul to hear from several feet away, because his eyebrows shot up as their eyes met.

"Yes, Dad, *your* mother. I was desperate to learn more, but she got tired all of a sudden, and neither Paul nor I wanted to overtax her. She's taking a nap now, and Paul and I are on the ferry back to Seattle."

Ruth thought she heard her father mutter something like "Holy Mother of God," then take a long, ragged breath.

"All these years and she's never said a word to me. Dad did, as I told you, but he didn't give me any details, and I never believed Mom's involvement amounted to much—it was more along the lines of moral support, I always figured. My dad was over there and we knew that's where he met Mom."

"Did they ever go back to France?" Ruth asked.

"No. They did some traveling, but mostly in North America—Florida, Mexico, Quebec…"

"I guess she really was keeping the past buried," Ruth said.

"She must realize she's getting near the end of her life," her father went on, apparently thinking out loud. "And she wants us to know. I'm grateful she was willing to share this with you. Still, it's pretty hard to take in. My mother…part of the French Resistance. She told me she was in school over there."

"She was." Ruth didn't want her father to think Helen had lied to him.

"Then how in heaven's name did she get involved in that?"

"It's a long story."

"What made her start talking about it now?" her father asked.

"I think it's because she knows she's getting old, as you suggested," Ruth said. "And because of Paul."

"Ah, yes, this young man you're with."

"Yeah."

Her father hesitated. "I know you can't discuss this now with Paul there, so give us a call later, will you? Your mother's going to want to hear about this young man."

"Yes, Daddy," she said, thinking with some amusement that she sounded like an obedient child.

"I'll give Mom a call later," her father said. "We need to set up a visit ourselves, possibly for the Memorial Day weekend."

After a quick farewell, she clicked off the phone and put it back inside her purse.

Paul, still sipping his coffee, approached her. She picked up her own cup as he sat down beside her.

"I haven't enjoyed an afternoon more in years," Paul said. "Not in years," he added emphatically.

Ruth grinned, then drank some of her cooling coffee. "I'd like to believe it was my company that was so engaging, but I know you're enthralled with my grandmother."

"And her granddaughter," Paul murmured, but he said it as if he felt wary of the fact that he found her appealing.

Ruth took his hand. "We haven't settled anything," he reminded her, tightening his hold on her fingers.

"Do we have to right this minute?"

He didn't answer.

"I want to see you again," she told him, moving closer.

"That's the problem. I want to see you again, too."

"I'm glad." Ruth didn't hide her relief.

Paul's responding smile was brief. "All right, we'll do this your way—one day at a time. But remember, I only have two weeks' leave."

She knew instinctively that these would be the shortest two weeks of her life.

"By the time I ship out, we should know how we feel. Agreed?"

"Agreed," she said without hesitation.

He nodded solemnly. "Do you own a pair of in-line skates?" he asked unexpectedly.

"Sure, but I don't have them in Seattle. I can easily rent a pair, though."

"Want to go skating?"

"When?"

"Now?"

Ruth laughed. "I'd love to, with one stipulation."

"What's that?"

Ruth hated to admit how clumsy she was on the skates. "If I fall down, promise you'll help me up."

"I can do that."

"If I get hurt…"

"If you get hurt," Paul said, "I promise to kiss you and make it better."

Ruth had the distinct feeling that she wasn't going to mind falling, not one little bit.

Six

Helen Shelton
5-B Poppy Lane
Cedar Cove, Washington
April 23

Dearest Clara,

Of course I understand why you won't be able to take the Victoria cruise with Winifred and me. Don't give it another thought. You'll be with us in spirit. We'll miss you, but believe me, we both understand.

It's important that you be kind to yourself and not overdo things. You've suffered a major loss; you and Charles were married for sixty-four years. After Sam died, and that's been over twenty years ago now, I felt as if I'd lost my right arm. But I can promise you that this terrible sense of loss does grow easier to bear with time. The first year was the most difficult—the first summer without him, the first birthdays, the first Christmas.

On a happier note, has your granddaughter set her wedding date yet? I know you've been anxious to see Elizabeth settled. I have news on the romance front myself. Ruth was over last week with a soldier she's been writing to who's on leave from Afghanistan. He's a delightful young man and it was easy to see that her feelings for him are quite intense. His name is Paul Gordon. When Ruth first introduced us, I'm afraid I embarrassed us both by staring at him. Paul could've been Jean-Claude's grandson, the resemblance is that striking.

For the past few weeks, I've been dreaming and thinking about my war experiences. You've been encouraging me for years to write them down. I've tried, but couldn't make myself do it. However…I don't know if this was wise but I told Ruth and her young man some of what happened to me in France. I know I shocked them both.

My son phoned later the same day, and John was quite upset with me, especially since I'd told Ruth and not him. I tried to explain that these were memories I've spent most of my life trying to forget. I do hope he understands. But Pandora's box is open now, and my family wants to learn everything they can. I've agreed to allow Ruth to tape our conversations, which satisfies everyone. I'm afraid you're right, my dear friend—I should've told my children long ago.

Do take care of yourself, and write soon. Once

Winifred and I are back from our Victoria adventure, we'll make plans to see each other this summer.

Bless you, dear Clara,

Your friend always,

Helen

"I want you to meet my family," Paul announced a little more than a week after their first date. They'd spent every available moment together; they'd been to the Seattle Center and the Space Needle, rowing on Lake Washington, out to dinner and had seen a couple of movies. Sitting on the campus lawn, he waited for Ruth after her last class of the day. He stood when she reached him, and Ruth noticed he wasn't smiling as he issued the invitation.

"When?"

"Mom and Dad are at the house."

"You mean you want me to meet them *now?*" Ruth asked as they strolled across the lush green grass toward the visitors' parking lot. If she'd known she was meeting Paul's parents she would've been better prepared. She would've done something about her hair and worn a different outfit and…

"Yeah," Paul muttered.

Ruth stopped and he walked forward two or three steps before he noticed. Frowning, he glanced back.

"What's going on here?" she asked, clutching her books to her chest.

Paul looked everywhere but at her. "My parents feel they should meet you, since I'm spending most of my time in your company. The way they figure it, you must be someone important in my life."

Ruth's heart did a happy little jig. "Am I?" she asked flirtatiously.

A rigid expression came over him, betraying none of his feelings. "I don't know the answer to that yet."

"Really?" she teased.

"Listen, Ruth, I'm not handing you my heart so you can break it. You don't want to be involved with a soldier. Well, I'm a soldier, and either you accept that or at the end of these two weeks, it's over."

He sounded so…so military. As if he thought a relationship could be that simple, that straightforward. Life didn't divide evenly into black and white. There were plenty of gray areas, too. All right, so Paul had a point. In the back of her mind, Ruth hoped that, given time, Paul would decide to get out of the war business. She wasn't the kind of woman who'd be content to sit at home while the man she loved was off in some faraway country risking his life. Experiencing dreadful things. Suffering. Maybe dying.

"You'd rather I didn't meet your family?" she asked.

"Right."

That hurt. "I see."

Some of her pain must have been evident in her voice, because Paul came toward her and tucked his finger beneath her chin. Their eyes met for the longest moment. "If my family meets you, they'll know how much I care you," he said quietly.

Ruth managed to smile. "I'm glad you care, because I care about you, too," she admitted. "A *lot*."

"That doesn't solve anything."

"No, it doesn't," she agreed, leaning forward so their lips could meet. She half expected Paul to pull away, but he didn't.

Instead, he groaned and forcefully brought his mouth to hers. Their kiss was passionate, deep—honest. She felt the sharp edges of her textbooks digging painfully into her breasts, and still Ruth melted in his arms.

"You're making things impossible," he mumbled when he lifted his head from hers.

"I've been known to do that."

Paul reached for her hand and led her into the parking lot. "I mentioned your grandmother to my parents," he said casually as he unlocked the car doors.

"Ah," Ruth said, slipping into the passenger seat. "That explains it."

"Explains what?"

"Why your family wants to meet me. I've brought you to my family. They feel cheated."

Paul shook his head solemnly.

"I really don't think that's it. But…speaking of your grandmother, when can we see her again?"

"Tomorrow afternoon, if you like. I talked to her this morning before my classes and she asked when we could make a return visit."

"You're curious about what happened, aren't you?" Paul asked as he inserted the key into the ignition.

"Very much so," Ruth admitted. Since their visit to Cedar Cove, she'd thought about her grandmother's adventures again and again. She'd done some research, too, using the Internet and a number of library books on the war. In fact, Ruth was so absorbed by the history of the Resistance movement, she'd found it difficult to concentrate on the psychology essay she was trying to write.

She'd had several days to become accustomed to Helen's exploits during the Second World War. And yet she still had trouble imagining the woman she knew as a fighter for the French Resistance.

"She loved Jean-Claude," Paul commented.

Ruth nodded. Her grandmother had loved her husband enough to kill him—a shocking reality that would not have made sense at any other time in Helen's life. And then, at some point after that, Helen had met her Sam. How? Ruth wondered. When did they fall in love? Family history told her that Sam Shelton had fought in the European campaign during the Second World War. He'd been in France toward the end of the war, she recalled. She wondered how much he'd known about Helen's past.

Ruth could only hope her grandmother would provide some answers tomorrow.

The meeting with Paul's family was going well, Ruth decided. His parents were delightful—immediately welcoming. Barbara, his mother, had an easy laugh and a big heart. She brought Ruth into the kitchen and settled her on a stool at the counter while she fussed with the dinner salad.

Paul and his father, Greg, were on the patio, firing up the grill and chatting. Every now and then, Ruth caught Paul stealing a glance in her direction.

"I want to help," Ruth told his mother.

"Nonsense," Barbara Gordon insisted as she tore lettuce leaves into a large wooden bowl. "I'm just so pleased to finally meet you. It was as if Paul had some secret he was keeping from us."

Ruth smiled and sipped her glass of iced tea.

"My father was career military—in the marines," Barbara said, chopping tomatoes for the salad. "I don't know if that was what induced Paul to join the military or not, but I suspect it had an influence."

"How do you feel about him being stationed so far from home?" Ruth asked, curious to hear his mother's perspective. She couldn't imagine any mother would want to see her son or daughter at that kind of risk.

Barbara sighed. "I don't like it, if that's what you're asking. Every sane person hates war. My father didn't want to fight in World War II, and I cried my eyes out the day Greg left for Vietnam. Now here's my oldest son in Afghanistan."

"It seems most generations are called upon to serve their country, doesn't it?" Ruth said.

Barbara agreed with a short nod. "Freedom isn't free—for us or for the countries we support. Granted, some conflicts we've been involved in seem misguided, but unfortunately war appears to be part of the human condition."

"Why?" Ruth asked, although she didn't really expect a response.

"I think every generation has asked that same question," Barbara said thoughtfully, putting the salad bowl aside. She began to prepare a dressing, pouring olive oil and balsamic vinegar into a small bowl. "Paul told me you have a problem with his unwillingness to leave the marines at the end of his commitment. Is that right?"

A little embarrassed by the question, Ruth nodded. "I do."

"The truth is, as his mother, I want Paul out of the marines, too, but that isn't a decision you or I can make for him. My son has always been his own person. That's how his father and I raised him."

Ruth's gaze followed Paul as he stood with his father by the barbecue. He looked up and saw her, frowning as if he knew exactly what she and his mother were talking about. Ruth gave him a reassuring wave.

"You're in love with him, aren't you?" his mother asked, watching her closely.

The question took Ruth by surprise. "I'm afraid I am." Ruth didn't *want* to be—something she hadn't acknowledged openly until this moment. He'd described his reluctance to hand her his heart to break. She felt the same way and feared he'd end up breaking hers.

There seemed to be a tacit agreement not to broach these difficult subjects during dinner.

The four of them sat on the patio around a big table, shaded by an overlarge umbrella. His mother had made corn bread as well as the salad, and the steaks were grilled to perfection. After dinner, Ruth helped with the cleanup and then Paul made their excuses.

"We're going to a movie?" she whispered on their way out the door, figuring he'd used that as a convenient pretext for leaving.

"I had to get you out of there before my mother started showing you my baby pictures."

"I'll bet you were a real cutie."

"You should see my brother and sister, especially the nude photos."

Ruth giggled.

Instead of the theater, they headed for Lake Washington and walked through the park, licking ice-cream cones, talking and laughing. Ruth couldn't remember laughing with anyone as much as she did with Paul.

He dropped her off after ten, walked her up to the front porch and kissed her good-night.

"I'll pick you up at noon," he said. "After your morning class."

"Noon," she repeated, her arms linked around his neck. That seemed too long. Despite her fears, despite the looming doubts, she *was* in love with him.

"You're sure your grandmother's up to having company so soon?" he asked.

"Yes." Ruth pressed her forehead against his shoulder. "I think the real question's whether we're ready for the next installment. I don't know if I can bear to hear what happened to Jean-Claude."

"Perhaps not, but she needs to tell us."

"Yes," Ruth said. "She couldn't talk about it before."

"I know." Paul kissed her again.

Ruth felt at peace in his arms. Only when she stopped to think about the future, *their* future, did she become uncertain and confused.

Seven

Ruth and Paul sat with her grandmother at the kitchen table in her Cedar Cove house as rain dripped rhythmically against the windowpane. The day was overcast and dreary, often the case with spring in the Pacific Northwest.

Helen reached for the teapot in the middle of the table and filled each of their cups, then offered them freshly baked peanut-butter cookies arranged on a small dessert plate. Ruth recognized the plate from her childhood. She and her grandmother had often had tea together when she was a youngster. Her visits to Cedar Cove were special; her grandmother had listened while Ruth chatted away endlessly, sharing girlish confidences. It was during those private little tea parties that they'd bonded, grandmother and granddaughter.

Today the slow ritual of pouring tea and passing around cookies demanded patience. Ruth badly wanted to throw questions at Helen, but she could see that her grandmother would begin her story again only when she was ready. Helen seemed to be bracing herself for this next installment.

"I've been thinking about the things I mentioned on your last visit," Helen finally said, sipping her tea. Steam rose from the delicate bone-china cup. "It was a lot for you to take in at one time."

"I didn't know *anything* about your adventures, Grandma." And they truly were adventures, of a kind few people experienced these days. *Real* adventures, with real and often involuntary risks.

Helen nodded. "My children didn't, either. But as I said before, it's time." Helen set the fragile cup back in its saucer. "Your father phoned and asked me about all this." She paused, a look of distress on her face. "I hope he'll forgive me for keeping it from him all these years."

"I'm sure he will," Ruth assured her.

Helen obviously wanted to believe that. "He asked me to tell him more, but I couldn't," she said sadly.

"I'm sure Dad understood."

"I couldn't relive those memories again so soon."

Ruth laid a comforting hand on her grandmother's arm. This information of Helen's was an important part of her family history. Today, with Helen's agreement, she'd come prepared with a small tape recorder. Now nothing would be lost.

"Jean-Claude had a wonderful gift," her grandmother said, breaking into the story without preamble. "He was a big man who made friends easily—a natural leader. Our small group trusted him with our lives."

Paul nodded encouragingly.

"Within a few minutes of meeting someone, he could determine if he should trust that person," Helen continued. "More and more people wanted to join us. We started with a few students like ourselves, who were determined to resist the Nazis. Soon, others found us and we connected with groups across France. We all worked together as we lit fires of hope."

"Tell me about the wanted poster with your picture and Jean-Claude's," Ruth said.

Her grandmother smiled ruefully, as if that small piece of notoriety embarrassed her. "I'm afraid Jean-Claude and I acquired a somewhat exaggerated reputation. Soon almost everything that happened in Paris as part of the Resistance movement was falsely attributed to us, whether we were involved or not."

"Such as?"

"There was a fire in a supply depot. Jean-Claude and I wished we'd been responsible, but we weren't. Yet that was what prompted the Germans to post our pictures." A smile brightened her eyes. "It was a rather unflattering sketch of Jean-Claude, he told me, although I disagreed."

"Can you tell me some of the anti-Nazi activities you were able to undertake?" Ruth asked, knowing her father would want to hear as much of this as his mother could recall.

Helen considered the question. "Perhaps the most daring adventure was one of Jean-Claude's. There was an SS officer, a horrible man, a pig." This word was spit out, as if even the memory of him disgusted her. "Jean-Claude discovered that this officer had obtained information through torturing a fellow Resistance member, information that put us all at risk. Jean-Claude decided the man had to die and that he would be the one to do it."

Paul glanced at Ruth, and he seemed to tell her that killing an SS officer would be no easy task.

Helen sipped her tea once more. "I feared for Jean-Claude."

"Is this when he…died?" Ruth asked.

"No." For emphasis, her grandmother shook her head. "That came later."

"Go on," Paul urged.

"One night Jean-Claude left me and another woman in a garden in the suburbs, at the home of a sympathetic schoolteacher who'd made contact with our group. He and his wife went out for the evening. Jean-Claude instructed us to dig a grave and fill it with quicklime. We were to wait there for his return. He left with two other men and I was convinced I'd never see him again."

"But you did," Ruth said.

The old woman nodded. "According to Jean-Claude, it was either kill the SS officer or he would take us all down. He simply knew too much."

"What did Jean-Claude do?"

"That is a story unto itself." Helen sat even straighter in her chair. "This happened close to the final time he was captured. He knew, I believe, that he would die soon, and it made him fearless. He took more and more risks. And he valued his own life less and less." Her eyes shone with tears as she gazed out the rain-blurred window, lost in a world long since past.

"The SS officer had taken a room in a luxury hotel on the outskirts of Paris," Helen went on a minute later. "He was in the habit of sipping a cognac before retiring for the evening. When he called for his drink, it was Jean-Claude who brought it to him wearing a waiter's jacket. I don't know how he killed the SS man, but he did it without alerting anyone. He made sure there was no blood. The problem was getting the body out of the hotel without anyone seeing."

"Why? Couldn't he just leave it there?"

"Why?" Helen repeated, shaking her head. "Had the man's body been discovered, the entire staff would have been tortured as punishment. Eventually someone would have broken. In any event, Jean-Claude managed to smuggle the body out."

"But how?"

Again her grandmother smiled. "Jean-Claude was clever. His friends hauled him and the body of the SS officer up the chimney. First the dead man and then the live one. That was necessary, you see, because there was a guard at the end of the hallway."

"But once they got to the rooftop, how did he manage?"

"It was an effort," Helen said. "Jean-Claude told me they tossed the body from that rooftop to the roof of another building and then another—an office building. They lowered him down in the elevator. When the men arrived with the body, we all worked together and buried him quickly."

"The SS officer's disappearance must have caused trouble for the Resistance," Paul said.

Helen nodded ardently. "Oh, yes."

"When was Jean-Claude captured the second time?" Ruth asked. She was intensely curious and yet she dreaded hearing about the death of this brave man her grandmother had loved.

Helen's eyes glistened and she lifted her teacup with an unsteady hand. "It isn't what you think," she prefaced, and the cup made a slight clinking sound as it rattled against the saucer. Helen placed both hands in her lap and took a moment to compose herself. "We were headed for the Metro—the subway. By then I'd bleached my hair and we'd both changed our appearances as much as possible. I don't think my own mother would have recognized me. Jean-Claude's, either," she added softly, her voice a mere whisper.

Paul reached for Ruth's hand, as if sensing that she needed his support.

When her grandmother resumed speaking, it was in French. She switched languages naturally, apparently without realizing she'd done so. All at once, she covered her face and broke into sobs.

Although Ruth hadn't understood a word, she started crying, too, and gently wrapped her arms around her grandmother's thin shoulders. Hugging her was the only thing she could do to ease this remembered pain.

"It's all right, it's all right," Ruth cooed over and over. "You don't need to tell us any more."

Paul agreed. "This is too hard on her—and you," he said.

They stayed for another hour, but it was clear that reliving the past had exhausted her grandmother. She seemed so frail now, even more so than during the previous visit.

While her grandmother rested in her room, Ruth cleared the table. As she took care of the few dirty dishes, her eyes filled with tears again. It was hard to think about the horrors her grandmother had endured.

"When she was speaking French, she must've been reliving the day Jean-Claude died," Ruth said, turning so her back was pressed against the kitchen counter.

Paul nodded. "She was," he answered somberly.

Ruth studied him as she returned to the kitchen table, where he sat. "You said you speak French. Could you understand what she was saying?"

He nodded again. "At the Metro that day, Jean-Claude was picked up in a routine identity check by the

French police. Through pure luck, Helen was able to get on the train without being stopped. She had to stand helplessly inside the subway car and watch as the police hauled him to Gestapo headquarters." Paul paused long enough to give her an odd smile. "The next part was a tirade against the police, whom she hated. Remember last week when she explained that some of the French police were trying to prove their worth to the Germans? Well, apparently Jean-Claude was one of their most wanted criminals."

"They tortured him, didn't they?" she asked, although she already knew the answer.

"Yes." Paul met her eyes. "Unmercifully."

Ruth swallowed hard.

"Helen tried to save him. Disregarding her own safety, she went in after him, only this time she went alone. No sympathetic priest." Paul's face hardened. "They dragged her into the basement, where Jean-Claude was being tortured. They had him strung up by his arms. He was bloody and his face was unrecognizable."

"No!" Ruth covered her eyes with both hands.

"They taunted him. Said they had his accomplice and now he would see her die."

Ruth could barely talk. "They…were going to…kill Helen—in front of Jean-Claude?"

"From what she said, it wouldn't have been an easy death. The point was for Jean-Claude to watch her suffer—to watch her die a slow, agonizing death."

"Dear God."

"She didn't actually say it," Paul continued. "She didn't have to spell it out, but Jean-Claude obviously hadn't been broken. Seeing her suffer would have done it, though, and your grandmother knew that. She also knew that if he talked, it would mean the torture and death of others in the Resistance." Paul looked away for a moment. "Apparently he and his friends had helped a number of British pilots escape German detection. At risk was the entire underground effort. Jean-Claude knew more than anyone suspected."

"Helen couldn't let that happen," Ruth said.

"No, and Jean-Claude understood that, too."

"Remember how she said she was the one who killed him? She didn't mean that literally, did she?"

"She did."

This was beginning not to make sense. "But…how?"

Paul leaned forward and braced his elbows on the table. "Her voice had started to break at this point and I didn't catch everything. She talked about a cyanide tablet. I'm not sure how she got hold of it. But I know she kissed him…. A final kiss goodbye. By this stage she was too emotional to understand clearly."

The pieces started to fall together for Ruth. "She gave him the pill—you mean instead of taking it herself?"

"That's what it sounded like to me," he said hoarsely.

"Was this when he'd asked her to kill him? And then she kissed him and transferred the pill?"

"I think so." Paul cleared his throat, but his voice was still rough. "She said Jean-Claude had begged her to kill him. He spoke to her in English, which the Germans weren't able to understand."

Ruth pictured the terrible scene. Helen and Jean-Claude arguing. If Helen swallowed the pill, she'd be dead and the Gestapo would lose their bargaining chip. Even knowing that, Jean-Claude couldn't bear to see his wife die. It truly would have broken him.

"Speaking in another language added enough confusion that she had the opportunity to do what he asked," Ruth speculated.

"Last time she told us about being driven by fear instead of courage," Paul reminded her. "I'm sure she didn't stop to think about what she was doing—she couldn't. Nor could she refuse Jean-Claude."

Ruth wanted to bury her face in her hands and weep.

"Jean-Claude thanked her," Paul added.

"She would have refused." Ruth could see it all in her mind, the argument between them.

"I'm convinced she did refuse at first. She loved Jean-Claude—he was her husband."

Ruth couldn't imagine a worse scenario.

Paul's voice dropped slightly. "She said Jean-Claude had never begged for mercy, never pleaded for anything, but he told her he couldn't bear any more pain. Above all, he couldn't bear it if they killed her. He begged her to let him die."

"He loved her that much," Ruth said in a hushed whisper.

"And she loved him that much, enough to spare him any more torture, even at the risk of her own death."

"They didn't kill her, though," Ruth said, stating the obvious. "Even though they must have figured out that she was responsible for his death?"

Paul's eyes widened as if he couldn't explain that any more than she could. "She didn't say what happened next."

Ruth stood, anxious now to see her grandmother before they left. "I'd better check on her."

Ruth went to her grandmother's room to find her resting fitfully. Helen's eyes fluttered open when Ruth stepped quietly past the threshold.

"Have I shocked you?" Helen asked, holding out her hand to Ruth.

"No," Ruth told her grandmother, who had to be the bravest woman she would ever know. She sat on the edge of the bed and whispered, "Thank you, Grandma—for everything you did. And for doing Paul and me the honor of sharing it with us."

Helen smiled and touched her cheek. "You've been crying."

Taking her grandmother's hand between her own, she kissed the old woman's knuckles. A lump filled her throat and she couldn't find the words to express her love.

"When did you meet Grandpa?" she finally asked.

Helen smiled again and her eyes drifted shut. "Two years later. He was one of the American soldiers who came with Patton's army to free us from the concentration camp."

This was an entirely different aspect of the story.

"When it was learned that I was an American citizen, I was immediately questioned and given priority treatment to be sent home."

"Two years," Ruth said in a choked voice. "You were in a camp for two years?" Just when she was convinced there was nothing more to horrify her, Helen revealed something else.

"Buchenwald... I don't want to talk about it any longer," Helen muttered.

It was little wonder her grandmother had never spoken of those years. The memories were far worse than the worst Ruth had been able to imagine.

Her grandmother brushed the hair from Ruth's brow. "I want you to know I like your young man."

"He reminded you of Jean-Claude, didn't he?"

Her smile was weak, which told Ruth how drained this afternoon's conversation had left Helen. "Not at first, but then he smiled and I saw Jean-Claude in Paul's eyes." She swallowed a couple of times and added, "I wanted to die after Jean-Claude did. I would've done anything if only the Germans had put me out of my living hell. They knew that and decided it was better to let me live and remember, each and every day, that I'd killed my own husband." A tear slid down her face. "I can't speak of it anymore."

Ruth understood. "I'll leave you to rest. Try to sleep."

Her grandmother's answering sigh told Ruth how badly she needed that just then.

"Come back and see me soon," she called as Ruth stood.

"I will, I promise." She bent down to kiss the soft cheek.

Paul was waiting for her in the living room, flipping through the *Cedar Cove Chronicle,* but he got up when Ruth returned. "Is she all right?"

Ruth shrugged. "She's tired." Her eyes were watering again, despite her best efforts not to cry. She couldn't stop thinking about the pain her grandmother had endured and kept hidden all these years.

Paul held open his arms and she walked into his embrace as naturally as she slipped on a favorite coat. Once there, she began to cry—harsh, broken sobs she thought would never end.

Eight

Once again Ruth and Paul spoke little on the ferry ride
back to Seattle.

Ruth's entire perspective on her grandmother had
changed. Until now, she'd always viewed the petite,
gentle woman as…well, her grandmother. All of a sudden Ruth was forced to realize that Helen had been
young once, and deeply involved in events that had
changed or destroyed many lives. She'd been an ordinary young woman from a fairly privileged background.
She'd been a student, fallen in love, enjoyed a carefree
existence. Then this ordinary young woman had been
caught up in extraordinary circumstances—and risen to
their demands.

Ruth was curious about the connection between her
grandmother's life during the war and her life afterward.
Clearly the link was her grandfather, whom she'd never
had a chance to know.

Paul stood with Ruth at the railing as the ferry glided
through the relatively smooth waters of Puget Sound.
The rain had stopped, and although the sky remained

cloudy and gray, the air was fresh with only the slightest hint of brine.

"Every story I hear leaves me amazed that this incredible woman is my grandmother," Ruth said fervently, grateful that Paul was beside her.

"I know. I'm overwhelmed, and I just met her."

They exchanged tentative smiles, and then they both sighed in appreciation, Ruth thought, of everything Helen Shelton had been and done.

"I wish I'd known my grandfather," she said. "He seems to have been the one who gave my grandmother a reason to live. He loved her and she loved him." Ruth knew that from every word her grandmother and her dad had said about Sam Shelton.

"How old were you when he died?" Paul asked.

"Two or so." She turned so she could look directly at Paul. "When I saw my grandmother in her bedroom, she said he was with a group of soldiers who freed the inmates in the concentration camp."

"She was in a concentration camp?"

Ruth nodded. "She was there at least a couple of years."

Paul frowned, obviously upset.

"I can't *bear* to think what her life was like in one of those obscene places," Ruth said.

"It would've been grim. You're right—they were obscene. Places of death."

Ruth didn't welcome the reminder. "I'm so glad you've been with me on these visits," she told him. Paul's presence helped her assimilate the details her grandmother had shared. He'd given her a feeling of comfort and companionship as they'd listened to these painful wartime experiences. Ruth genuinely believed there was something about Paul that had led Helen to divulge her secrets.

After the ferry docked, Paul and Ruth walked along the Seattle waterfront, where they ate clam chowder, followed by fish and chips, for dinner. Their mood was somber, and yet, strangely, Ruth felt a sense of peace.

The next day, after her classes, she hurried back to her rental house and ran into Lynn. As much as possible, Ruth had avoided her roommate. Her relationship with Lynn had been awkward ever since the argument over Clay. Lynn's lie, which she'd told in an effort to keep Ruth from meeting Paul, hadn't helped.

Lynn was coming out just as Ruth leaped up the porch steps. Her roommate hesitated.

Ruth did, too. She'd never said anything to Lynn about her intentional mix-up that first night she was meeting Paul. Her classes would be over at the end of May and she was more than ready to move out.

"Hi," Lynn offered uncertainly.

Ruth's pace slowed as she waited, half expecting Lynn to make some derogatory remark about Paul. Because Ruth had been with him so often lately, she'd had very little contact with her roommate.

"Are you seeing Paul again?"

The question lacked the scornful tone she'd used when referring to him previously. She seemed more prompted by simple curiosity than anything else.

"We're meeting some friends of his later. Why?" Ruth couldn't help being suspicious. If he'd phoned with a change of plan, she needed to know about it. She knew from experience that Lynn couldn't be trusted to relay the message.

Lynn shrugged. "No reason."

"Is there something you aren't telling me?" Ruth's voice was calm.

Her roommate had the grace to blush. "He didn't call, if that's what you're asking."

"Like I could believe you."

"You can—okay, maybe what I did that night was pretty stupid."

"Maybe?" Ruth echoed.

"All right, it was. I was upset because of Clay." She didn't meet Ruth's eyes. "I thought Clay was really hot and you dumped him for soldier boy, and I thought that was just wrong."

"I don't need you to decide who I'm allowed to date." Ruth couldn't keep the anger out of her voice. What Lynn had tried to do still rankled. If her cell phone battery hadn't been low, she and Paul might have missed each other completely. That thought sent chills down her spine.

Lynn released a long sigh. "I'll admit it—you were right about Clay."

"How so?"

"He's…he's stuck on himself."

Ruth suspected that meant he wasn't interested in Lynn.

"I…I like Paul," her roommate confessed.

Ruth wasn't even aware that Lynn had met him and said so.

"He stopped by one afternoon when he thought you were back from classes, only you weren't and I was here. We talked for a bit. Then he left to look for you at the library."

Funny that neither had mentioned the incident earlier. "I had the impression you were dead set against him."

"Not him," Lynn said. "I'm against the war in Iraq…. I thought you were, too."

"I don't like war of any kind. This war or any war. Still, the United States is involved in the Middle East, and no matter what, it's our young men and women who are fighting there. Politics aside, I want to support our troops."

"I know." Lynn suddenly seemed to find something absolutely mesmerizing about her shoes.

Ruth moved past her on the porch. "I'd better go in and change."

"Ruth," Lynn said sharply. Ruth turned to face her. "I'm sorry about the other night. That really was an awful thing to do. I was upset and I took it out on you."

Ruth had pretty much figured that out on her own. "Paul and I connected, so no harm done."

"I know, and I'm glad you did because I think Paul is great. I know he's a soldier and all, but he's a nice guy. I only met him that one time, but I could see he's ten times the man Clay will ever be. He's the kind of guy I hope to meet."

Paul had obviously impressed her during their brief exchange. She wondered what they'd talked about.

"All's well that ends well," Ruth said.

"Shakespeare, right?" Lynn asked. "In other words, all is forgiven?"

Ruth laughed and nodded, then started into the house.

Paul picked her up at five-thirty and they drove to a Mexican restaurant in downtown Kent. Paul had arranged for her to meet his best friend.

Carley and Brian Hart were high school sweethearts and Brian had known Paul for most of his life.

"We go way back," Brian said when they were introduced. He slid out of the booth and they exchanged handshakes, with Paul standing just behind Ruth, his hand on her shoulder.

"I'm pleased to meet you both." They were a handsome couple. Carley was a delicate blonde with soulful blue eyes, and her husband was tall and muscular, as if he routinely worked out.

"We're pleased to meet you, too," Carley said when Ruth slipped into the booth across from her.

Paul got in beside Ruth.

"I insisted Paul introduce us," Carley said as she reached for a chip and dipped it in the salsa. "Every time we tried to get together during his leave, he already had plans with you."

Ruth hadn't thought of it that way, but realized she'd monopolized his time. "I guess I should apologize for that."

"We only have the two weeks," Paul explained.

"You'll be back in Seattle after the training, won't you?" Brian asked.

"Maybe, but…" Paul hesitated and glanced at Ruth.

"We only just met and…" Ruth let the rest fade away. He would be back and they'd see each other again, but only if she could accept his career in the military.

This fourteen-day period was a testing time for them both, and at the end they had a decision to make.

"I'm giving Ruth two weeks to fall head over heels in love with me." Paul said it as if it were a joke.

"If she doesn't, there's definitely something wrong with her," Carley joked back.

Ruth smiled, but she felt her heart sinking. She

hadn't made her decision yet; the truth was, she'd been putting it off until the last possible minute.

Time was dwindling and soon, in a matter of days, Paul would be leaving again. She wasn't ready—wasn't ready to decide and wasn't ready for him to go.

Brian and Carley had to be home before eight because of their babysitter, so they left the restaurant first.

Ruth had enjoyed the spicy enchiladas, the margarita and especially the teasing between Paul and Brian. Carley had told story after story of the two boys and their high-school exploits, and they'd all laughed and joked together.

Paul and Ruth lingered in the booth over cups of dark coffee, gazing into each other's eyes. He'd switched places so he could sit across from her. If she'd met him under any other circumstance, there'd be no question about her feelings. None! It was so easy to fall in love with this man. In fact, it was already too late; even Paul's mother had seen that. Ruth *knew* him. After all the letters and e-mails, all the conversations, she felt as if he'd become part of her life.

"I know what you're thinking," Paul said unexpectedly.

"What am I thinking?" she asked with amusement.

"You're wondering why I find life in the military so attractive."

She shrugged. "Close."

"Do you want to know my answer?"

Ruth was already aware of his reasons, but decided to hear him out, anyway. "Sure, go ahead."

"I like the structure, the discipline, the knowledge

that I'm doing something positive to bring about freedom and democracy in the world."

This was where it got troubling for Ruth.

Before she could state her own feelings, Paul stopped her. "I know you don't agree with me, and I accept that, but I am who I am."

"I didn't challenge that—I wouldn't."

He stiffened, then reached for his coffee and held it at arm's length, cupping his hands around the mug. "True enough, but the minute I started talking, you looked like you wanted to challenge my answer."

She hadn't known her feelings were that transparent.

"I guess now is as good a time as any to ask where I stand with you."

"What do you mean?" An uneasy feeling began to creep up her spine. They had only a couple of days before he was scheduled to leave, and she was going to need every minute of that time to concentrate on this relationship.

"You know what I'm asking, Ruth."

She did. She met his eyes. "I'm in love with you, Paul."

"I'm in love with you, too." He stretched his hand across the table and intertwined their fingers.

Her heart nearly sprang out of her chest with happiness and yet tears filled her eyes.

To her astonishment, Paul laughed. "This is supposed to be a happy moment," he told her.

"I *am* happy, but I'm afraid, too."

"Of what?"

"Of you leaving again. Of your involvement in the military. Of you fighting in a war, any war."

"It's what I do."

"I know." Still, she had a hard time reconciling her emotions and beliefs with the way Paul chose to make his living.

"But you don't like it," he said, his voice hard.

"No."

He sighed harshly. "Then tell me where we go from here."

Ruth wished she knew. "I can't answer that."

His eyes pleaded with her. "I can't answer it for you, Ruth. You're going to have to make up your mind about us."

She'd known it would come down to this. "I'm not sure I can. Not yet."

He considered her words. "When do you think you'll be able to decide?"

"Let's wait until you've finished your training and we see each other again.... We'll both have a better idea then, don't you think?"

"No. I might not be coming back to Seattle. I have to know soon. Now. Tonight." He paused. "I sound unfair and pushy, and I apologize."

"Apologize for what?" she asked. Her hand tightened around his fingers. Already she could feel him pulling away from her, if not physically, then emotionally.

"I've been trained to be decisive. Putting things off only leads to confusion. We've been writing for months."

"Yes, I know, but—"

"We've spent every possible minute of my leave to-gether."

"Yes…"

"I love you, Ruth, but I won't lie to you. I'm not leav-ing the marines. I've chosen the military as my career and that means I could be involved in conflicts all over the world. I have to know if you can accept that."

"I…"

"If you can't, we need to walk away from each other right now. I don't want to drag this out. You decide."

Ruth didn't want a part-time husband. "I want a man who'll be a husband to me and a father to my children. A man of peace, not war." She didn't mean to sound so adamant.

Paul didn't respond for a long moment. "I think we have our answer." He slid out of the booth and waited for her. They'd paid their tab earlier, so there was nothing to do but walk out the door to the parking lot.

Ruth wasn't finished with the conversation, even if Paul was. "I need time," she told him.

"The decision's made."

"You're pressuring me," she protested. "I've still got two days, remember?"

"It doesn't work that way," he said.

"But this isn't fair!"

"I already admitted it wasn't." He opened the passenger door, and a moment later, he joined her in the car. "I wish now I'd waited and we still had those two days," he said bleakly. "But we don't."

He started the car and Ruth noticed that his fingers had tensed on the steering wheel.

Ruth bit her lip. "Sure we do. Let's just pretend we didn't have this conversation and enjoy the time we have left. You can do that, can't you?" Her voice took on a pleading quality.

"I wish I could, but…I can't." He inhaled deeply. "The decision is made."

They didn't have much to say during the rest of the

ride to the university district. When Paul pulled up in front of the rental house, Ruth noticed the lights were on, which meant Lynn was home.

They sat side by side in the car without speaking until Paul roused himself to open the car door. He walked around to escort her from the passenger side. Silently he walked her to the porch.

Ruth half expected him to kiss her. He didn't.

"Will I see you again?" she asked as he began to walk away.

He turned back and stood there, stiff and formal. "Probably not."

"You mean this is it? This is goodbye…as if I meant nothing…as if we were strangers?" She felt outraged that he could just leave her like this, without a word. It was unkind and unfair…and life wasn't that simple.

"Is there anything left to say?" he asked.

"Of course there is," she cried. She didn't know what, but surely there was *something*. Hurting and angry, Ruth gestured wildly with her arms. "You can't be serious! Are you really going to walk away? Just like that?"

"Yes." The word was devoid of emotion.

"You aren't going to write me again?"

"No."

This was unbelievable.

"Call me?"

"No."

She glared at him. "In other words, you're going to act as if you'd never even met me, as if I'd never mailed that Christmas card."

A hint of a smile flickered over his tightly controlled features. "I'm certainly going to give it my best shot."

"Fine, then," she muttered. If he thought so little of her, then he could do as he wished. She didn't want to be with a man who didn't care about her feelings, just his own.

Nine

True to Paul's word, Ruth didn't hear from him after their Tuesday-night dinner with Carley and Brian. The first day, her anger carried her. Then she convinced herself that Paul would contact her before he left for Camp Pendleton. Not so. Paul Gordon—correction, *Sergeant* Paul Gordon, USMC, was out of her life and that was perfectly fine with her. Only it wasn't.

A week later, as she sat in her "Theories of Learning" class, taking notes, her determination faltered. She wanted to push all thoughts of Paul out of her mind forever; instead, he was constantly there.

What upset her most was the cold-blooded way in which he'd dismissed her from his life. It seemed so easy for him, so…simple. She was gone for him, as if she meant nothing. That hurt, and it didn't stop hurting.

Ruth blinked, forcing herself to listen to the lecture. If she flunked this class, Paul Gordon would be to blame.

After class she walked across campus, her steps slow and deliberate. She felt no urge to hurry. But when her cell phone rang, she nearly dropped her purse in her eagerness. Could it be Paul? Had he changed his mind? Had he found it impossible to forget her, the same way she had him? A dozen more questions flew through her mind before she managed to answer.

"Hello?" She realized she sounded excited and breathless at the same time.

"Ruth." The familiar voice of a longtime friend, Lori Dupont, greeted her. They talked for a few minutes, and arranged to meet at the library at the end of the week. Four minutes after she'd answered her cell, it was back in her purse.

She was too restless to sit at home and study, which was how she'd spent every night since her last date with Paul, so she decided to go out. That was what she needed, she told herself with strained enthusiasm. Find people, friends, a party. Something to do, somewhere to be.

Although it was midafternoon, she took the bus down to the waterfront, where she'd met Paul the first night. That wasn't a smart idea. She wasn't up to dealing with memories. Before she could talk herself out of it, Ruth hopped on the Bremerton ferry. A visit with her grandmother would lift her spirits in a way nothing else could. Besides, if Helen felt strong enough, she wanted to hear the rest of the story, especially the role her grandfather had played.

As she stepped off the foot ferry from Bremerton to Cedar Cove, it occurred to Ruth that she should've phoned first. But it was unlikely her grandmother would be away. Even if she was, Ruth figured she could wander around Cedar Cove for a while. That would help fill the void threatening to swallow her whole.

The trudge up the hill that led to her grandmother's house seemed twice as steep and three times as long. Funny, when she'd been with Paul, the climb hadn't even winded her. That was because she'd been laughing and joking with him, she remembered—and wished she hadn't. Alone, hands shoved in her pockets, she felt drained of energy.

Reaching 5-B Poppy Lane, she saw that the front door to her grandmother's duplex stood open, although the old-fashioned wooden screen was shut. The last remaining tulips bloomed in primary colors as vivid as the rainbow. Walking up the steps, Ruth rang the doorbell. "Grandma! Are you home?"

No one answered. "Grandma?"

Alarm jolted through her. Had something happened to her grandmother? She pounded on the door and was even more alarmed when a white-haired woman close to her grandmother's age came toward her.

"Hello," the older lady said pleasantly. "Can I help you?"

"I'm looking for my grandmother."

The woman unlatched the screen door and swung it open. "You must be Ruth. I don't think Helen was expecting you. I'm Charlotte Rhodes."

"Charlotte," Ruth repeated. "Helen's spoken of you so often. It's wonderful to meet you."

"You, too," Charlotte said, taking Ruth's hand. "I'm happy to make your acquaintance."

Ruth nodded, but she couldn't help blurting out, "Is anything wrong with my grandmother?"

"Oh, no, not at all. We're sitting on the patio, talking and knitting. Helen's counting stitches and asked me to get the door. She assumed it was a salesman and my

job was to get rid of him…or her." Charlotte laughed.
"Not that *I'm* much good at that. Just the other day, a
Girl Scout came to my door selling cookies. When I
bought four boxes, she announced that every kid comes
to my house first, because I'll buy anything. Especially
for charity."

Ruth grinned. "I think my grandmother must be like
that, too."

"Why do you think she sent *me* to the door?" Charlotte joked. "Your grandmother's decided to knit a Fair
Isle sweater. It's her first one and she asked me over to
get her started."

"Perhaps I should come back at a more convenient
time?" Ruth didn't want to interrupt the two women.

"Nonsense! She'd never forgive me if you left. Be-
sides, I was just gathering my things to head on home.
My husband will be wondering what's kept me so long."
Charlotte led the way through the house to the patio.

As soon as Ruth stepped onto the brick patio, her
grandmother's eyes lit up with pleasure. "Ruth! What
a welcome surprise."

Ruth bent forward and kissed Helen's cheek.

Charlotte Rhodes collected her knitting, saying
she'd talk to Helen at the Senior Center on Monday,
and left.

"Sit down, sit down," Helen urged, motioning at the
chair next to her. "Help yourself to iced tea if you'd
like." Strands of yarn were wrapped around both index
fingers as she held the needles. One was red, the other
white. "You can find a glass, can't you?"

"Yes, of course, but I'm fine," Ruth assured her, enjoying the sunshine and the sights and sounds of Cedar
Cove. The earth in her grandmother's garden smelled

warm and clean—the way it only smelled in spring. Inhaling deeply, Ruth sat down, staring at the cove with its sparkling blue water.

"Where's Paul?" her grandmother asked, as if noticing for the first time that he wasn't with her.

Ruth's serenity was instantly destroyed and she struggled to disguise her misery. "He went to the marines camp in California."

"Oh." Her grandmother seemed disappointed. "I imagine you miss him."

Ruth decided to let the comment slide.

"I liked him a great deal," her grandmother said, rubbing salt into Ruth's already wounded heart. Helen's focus was on her knitting, but when Ruth didn't immediately respond, she looked up.

Ruth met her eyes and exhaled forcefully. "Would you mind if we didn't discuss Paul?"

Her request was met with a puzzled glance. "Why?"

Ruth figured she might as well tell her. "We won't be seeing each other again."

"Really?" Her grandmother's expression was downcast. "I thought highly of that young man. Any particular reason?"

"Actually," Ruth muttered, "there are several. He's in the military, which you already know."

Her grandmother carefully set her knitting aside and reached for her glass of iced tea, giving Ruth her full attention. "You knew that when you first met, I believe."

"Yes, I did, but I assumed that in time he'd be released from his commitment and return to civilian life. He told me that won't be the case, that the military's his career." *In for the long haul,* as he'd put it. Granted, she'd known about his dedication to the marines from the beginning, but he'd known about her feelings, too. Did her preferences matter less than his?

"I see." Her grandmother studied her.

Ruth wondered if she truly did. "What really upsets me is the heartless way he left. I told him I wasn't sure I could live with the fact that he'd chosen the military." The memory angered her, and she raised her voice. "Then Paul had the audacity to say that I wouldn't be hearing from him again and he...he just walked away." Ruth hadn't planned to spill out the whole story minutes after she arrived, but she couldn't hold it inside a second longer.

Her grandmother's response shocked her into silence. Helen *smiled*.

"Forgive me," her grandmother said gently, leaning forward to give Ruth's hand a small squeeze. "Sam did something similar, you see."

The irritation died instantly. "I wanted to ask you about my grandfather."

A peaceful look came over Helen. "He was a wonderful man. And he saved me."

"From the Germans, you mean?"

Helen shook her head. "Technically, it was General Patton and the Third Army who saved us. Patton knew what Buchenwald was. He knew that a three-hour wait meant twenty-thousand lives because the Germans had been given orders to kill all prisoners before surrendering. Against every rule of caution, Patton mounted an attack, cutting off the SS troops from the camp. Because of his decisive move, the Germans were forced to flee or surrender. By that time, the German soldiers knew they were defeated. They threw down their guns and surrendered. Sam was with Patton on the march, so, yes, he contributed to my rescue and that of countless others. But when I say your grandfather saved me, I mean he saved me from myself."

"I want to hear about him, if you're willing to tell me." Ruth straightened, perching on the edge of her seat.

Her grandmother closed her eyes. "I cannot speak about the years in Buchenwald, not even to you."

Ruth reached for Helen's hand, stroking the soft skin over the gnarled and prominent knuckles. "That's fine, Grandma."

"I wanted to die, wished it with all my heart. Without Jean-Claude, it was harder to live than to die. Living was the cruelest form of punishment." Tears pooled in her eyes and she blinked them away.

"When the Americans arrived," Helen continued, "the gates were opened and we were free. It was a delicious feeling—freedom always is—but one never appreciates it until it's taken away. The soldiers spoke English, and I went to them and explained that I was an American. I had no identification or anything to prove my claim, so I kept repeating the address where my parents lived in New York. I was desperate to get word to them that I was alive. They hadn't heard from me in almost five years.

"One of the soldiers brought me to their headquarters. I was completely emaciated, and I'm sure the stench of me was enough to nauseate anyone standing within twenty feet. The young man then took me to his lieutenant, whose name was Sam Shelton. From that moment forward, Sam took care of me. He saw that I had food and water, clothes and access to showers and anything else I needed."

Ruth shuddered at the thought of her grandmother's physical and mental condition following her release.

Her grandmother paused to take a deep breath, and when she spoke again, it was in another language, what Ruth assumed was German. Pressing her hand on Helen's, she stopped her. "Grandma, English, please."

Her grandmother frowned. "Sorry."

"Was that German?"

She shrugged, eyes wild and confused. "I don't know."

After all those years inside a German camp, it made sense that she'd revert to the language. In her mind she'd gone back to that time, was reliving each incident.

"Go on. Please," Ruth urged.

Helen sighed. "I don't remember much about those first days of freedom."

Ruth could understand that easily enough.

"Still, every memory I have is of the lieutenant at my side, watching over me. I was hospitalized, and I think I slept almost around the clock for three days straight, waking only long enough to eat and drink. Yet every time I opened my eyes, Sam was there. I'm sure that's not possible, but that's how I remember it."

She picked up her tea with a trembling hand and sipped the cool liquid. "After a week—maybe more, I don't know, time meant nothing to me—I was transported out of Germany and placed on a ship going to America. Sam wrote out his name and home address in Washington State and gave it to me. I didn't know why he'd do that."

"Did you keep it?" Ruth asked.

"I did," Helen confessed, "although I didn't think I'd ever need it. By the time I got back to New York, I was still skin and bone. My own parents didn't even recognize me. My mother looked at me, covered her face and burst into tears. I was twenty-four years old, and I felt sixty."

Ruth was in her twenties and couldn't imagine living through any of what her grandmother had described.

"Five months after I arrived, Sam Shelton knocked on my parents' brownstone. I'd gained weight and my hair had grown back, and when I saw him I barely remembered who he was. He visited for two days and we talked. He'd come to see how I was adjusting to life back in America."

Ruth had wondered about that, too. It couldn't have been easy.

"I hadn't done very well. My parents owned a small bakery and I worked at the counter, but I had no life in me, no joy. Now that I was free, I felt I had nothing to live for. My husband was dead, and I was the one who'd killed him. I told this American soldier, whom I barely knew, all of this. I told him I preferred to die. I told him everything—not one thing did I hold back. He listened and didn't interrupt me with questions, and when I was finished he took my hand and kissed it." The tears came again, spilling down her cheeks. "He said I was the bravest woman he'd ever known."

"I think you are, too," Ruth said, her voice shaky.

"When I'd finished, Sam told me he was part of D day," Helen said. "His company was one of the first to land on Omaha Beach. He spoke of the fighting there and the bravery of his men. He'd seen death the same way I had. Later, in the midst of the fighting, he'd stumbled across the body of his own brother. He had no time to mourn him. He didn't understand why God had seen fit to spare him and not his brother.

"This lieutenant asked the very questions I'd been asking myself. I didn't know why I should live when I'd rather have died with Jean-Claude—or instead of him." She paused again, as if to regain her composure.

"After that, Sam said he'd needed to do a lot of thinking and praying, and it came to him that his brother, his men had sacrificed their lives so that others could live in freedom. God had spared him, and me, too, and it wasn't up to either of us to question why. As for Jean-Claude and Tim, Sam's brother, they had died in this terrible but necessary *war*. For either of us to throw away our lives now would be to dishonor them—my husband and Sam's brother."

"He was right, you know."

Her grandmother nodded. "Sam left after that one visit. He wished me well and said he hoped I'd keep in touch. I waited a week before I wrote the first letter. Sam hadn't given me many details of his war experiences, but deep down I knew they'd been as horrific as my own. In that, we had a bond."

"So you and Grandpa Sam wrote letters to each other."

Helen nodded again. "For six months we wrote, and every day I found more questions for him to answer. His letters were messages of encouragement and hope for us both. Oh, Ruth, how I wish you'd had the opportunity to know your grandfather. He was wise and kind and loving. He gave me a reason to live, a reason to go on. He taught me I could love again—and then he asked me to marry him." Helen drew in a deep breath. "Sam wrote and asked me to be his wife, and I said no."

"You refused?" Ruth asked, hardly able to believe it.

"I couldn't leave my parents a second time…. Oh, I had a dozen excuses, all of them valid."

"How did he convince you?"

Her smile was back. "He didn't. In those days, one didn't hop on a plane or even use the phone unless it was a dire emergency. For two weeks he was silent. No letters and no contact. Nothing. When I didn't hear from him, I knew I never would again."

This was the reason her grandmother had smiled when Ruth told her she hadn't heard from Paul.

"I couldn't bear it," Helen admitted. "This soldier had become vitally important to me. For the first time since Jean-Claude died, I could *feel*. I could laugh and cry. I knew Sam was the one who'd lifted this heavy burden of pain from my shoulders. Not only that, he loved me. Loved me," she repeated, "and I'd turned him down when he asked me to share his life."

"What did you do next?"

Helen smiled at the memory. "I sent a telegram that said three words. *Yes. Yes. Yes.* Then I boarded a train and five days later, I arrived in Washington State. When I stepped off the platform, my suitcase in hand, Sam was there with his entire family. We were married two weeks later. I knew no one, so he introduced me to his best friends and the women they loved. Winifred and Clara became my dearest friends. They were the people who helped me adjust to normal life. They helped me find my new identity." She shook her head slowly. "Not once in all the years your grandfather and I were together did I have a single regret."

Ruth's eyes remained teary. "That's a beautiful love story."

"Now you're living one of your own."

Ruth didn't see it like that. "I don't want to be a military wife," she said adamantly. "I can't do it."

"You love Paul."

Ruth noted that her grandmother hadn't made it a question. She knew that Ruth's heart was linked with Paul's. He was an honorable man, and he loved her. They didn't have to share the same political beliefs as long as they respected each other's views.

"Yes, Grandma, I love him."

"And you miss him the same way I missed Sam."

"I do." It was freeing to Ruth to admit it. The depression that had hung over her for the past week lifted.

All at once Ruth knew exactly what she was going to do. Her decision was made.

Ten

Barbara Gordon answered the doorbell, and the moment she saw Ruth, her eyes lit with delight. "Ruth, it's so good to see you!"

Ruth was instantly ushered into the house. She hadn't been sure what kind of reception to expect. After all, she'd disappointed and possibly hurt the Gordons' son.

"I was so hoping you'd stop by," Barbara continued as she led the way into the kitchen.

Obediently Ruth followed. "I came because I don't have a current address for Paul."

"You plan on writing him?" Barbara seemed about to leap up and down and clap her hands.

"Actually, no."

The happiness drained from the other woman's eyes.

"I know it's a bit old-fashioned, but I thought I'd send him a telegram."

The delight was back in place. "Greg," she shouted over her shoulder. "Ruth is here."

Almost immediately Paul's father joined them in the

kitchen. His grin was as wide as his wife's had been. "Good to see you, good to see you," he said expansively.

"What did I tell you?" Barbara insisted.

The two of them continued to stand there and stare at her.

"About Paul's address?" Ruth prodded.

"Oh, yes." As if she'd woken from a trance, Barbara Gordon hurried into the other room, leaving Ruth alone with Paul's father.

It was awkward at first, and Ruth felt the least she could do was explain the reason for her visit. "I miss Paul so much," she told him. "I need his address."

Greg Gordon nodded. "He's missing you, too. Big-time."

Ruth's heart filled with hope. "He said that?"

"Not in those exact words," Greg stated matter-of-factly. "But rest assured, my son is pretty miserable."

"That's *wonderful*." Now it was Ruth who wanted to leap up and down and clap her hands.

"My son is miserable and you're happy?" Greg asked, but a teasing light glinted in his eyes.

"Yes…no… Yes," she quickly amended. "I just hope he's been as miserable as I have."

Greg's smile faded. "No question there."

The phone rang once; Barbara must have answered it right away, and within a few minutes she returned to the kitchen, carrying a portable phone. "It's for you."

Greg started toward her.

"Not you, honey," she said, nodding at Ruth. "The call is for Ruth."

"Me?" She was startled. No one knew she'd come here. Anyone wanting to reach her would automatically use her cell-phone number. Her frown quickly disappeared as she realized who it must be.

"Is it Paul?" she asked, her voice low and hopeful.

"It is. He thinks Greg's about to get on the line." She clasped her husband's elbow. "Come on, honey, let's give Ruth and Paul some privacy." She was halfway out of the room when she turned back, caught Ruth's eye and winked.

That was just the encouragement Ruth needed. Still, she felt decidedly nervous she picked up the portable phone resting on the kitchen counter. After the way they'd parted, she didn't know what to expect or how to react.

"Hello, Paul," she said, hoping to sound calm and confident, neither of which she was.

Her greeting was followed by a slight hesitation. "Ruth?"

"Yes, it's me." Her voice sounded downright cheerful—and more than a little forced.

"What are you doing at my parents' place?" he asked gruffly.

"Visiting."

Again he paused, as if he wasn't sure what to make of this. "I'd like to speak to my father."

"I'm sorry, he and your mother stepped out of the room so you and I could talk."

"About what?" He hadn't warmed to her yet.

"Your calling ruins everything," she told him. "I was going to send you a telegram. My grandmother sent one to my grandfather sixty years ago."

"A telegram?"

"I know it's outdated. It's also rather romantic, I thought."

"What did you intend to say in this telegram?"

"I hadn't decided. My first idea was to say the same thing Helen said to my grandfather. It was a short message—just three little words."

"I love you?" He was warming up now.

"No."

"No?" He seemed skeptical. "What else could it be? Helen loved him, didn't she?"

"Oh, yes, but that was already understood. Oh, Paul, I heard the rest of the story and it's so beautiful, so compelling, you'll see why she loved him as much as she did. Sam helped her look to the future and step out of the past."

"You're avoiding the question," he said.

That confused her for a moment. "What's the question?"

"Do you love me enough to accept me as a marine?"

"I wasn't sending *that* answer by way of Western Union." The answer that was going to change her life…

"You can tell me now," he offered casually.

"Before I do, you have to promise, on your word of honor as a United States marine, that you'll never walk away from me like that again."

"You think it was easy?" he demanded.

"I don't care if it was easy or not, you can't ever do it again." His abandonment had hurt too much.

"All right," he muttered. "I promise I'll never walk away from you again."

"Word of honor?"

"Word of honor," he agreed.

He'd earned it now. "I'm crazy about you, Paul Gordon. *Crazy.* Crazy in love with you. If having the marines as your career means that much to you, then I'll adjust. I'll find a way to make it work. But you need to compromise, too, when it comes to my career. I can't just leave a teaching job in order to follow you some-where."

The last thing Ruth expected after her admission was a long stretch of silence.

Then, "Are you serious? You'll accept my being in the military?"

"Yes. Do you think I'd do this otherwise?"

"No," he admitted. "But what you don't know is that I've been thinking about giving up the marines."

"Because of me?"

"Yes."

"You were?" Never once had it occurred to Ruth that he'd consider such a thing.

"My dad and I have had a couple of long talks about it," he went on to say.

"Tell me more."

"You already know this part—I'm crazy about you, too. I wasn't convinced I could find a way to live the rest of my life without you. One option I've looked into is training. I've already talked to my commander about it, and he thinks it's a good possibility I'd be able to stay in the marines, but I'd be stationed in one place for a while."

Ruth slumped onto a kitchen stool, feeling deli-ciously weak, too weak to stay upright. "Oh, Paul, that's wonderful!"

"I felt like a fool," he said. "I made my big stand, and I honestly felt I was right, but I didn't have to force you to decide that very minute. My pride wouldn't allow me to back off, though."

"Pride carried me the first week," she said. "Then I went to see my grandmother, and she told me how she met my grandfather at the end of the war. Their romance was as much of an adventure as everything else she told us."

"She's a very special woman," Paul said. "Just like her granddaughter."

"I'll tell you everything later."

"I can't wait to hear it. I'm just wondering if history might repeat itself," Paul murmured.

"How?"

"I'm wondering if someday you'll be my bride."

"That's the perfect question," Ruth said, and it *was* perfect for what she had in mind.

She closed her eyes and sighed deeply. "I do believe I'll send you that telegram after all."

Yes. Yes. Yes.

Helen Shelton
5-B Poppy Lane
Cedar Cove, Washington
May 9

Dear Winifred,

It's time to celebrate—your birthday and my granddaughter's engagement. Yes, Ruth has agreed to marry Paul Gordon, the young man she introduced me to in April. They've decided to have a December wedding in Oregon, where her family lives. Paul is a fine young man and I feel she's chosen well.

Yes, my dear friend, I'll meet you in Seattle and we'll board the ferry for Victoria together. It's been far too long since we've had an extended visit. I'm looking forward to hearing about your granddaughters.

I'm feeling good. Ruth and my sons know all about my war adventures. It was time, as you've been telling me all these years. Ruth has the tapes

and is making copies for everyone in the family.
She claims this is more than family history, this
is *history*. Maybe she's right....

  I'll see you next week.

The warmest of wishes,

Helen

LIBERTY HALL
Lois Faye Dyer

Acknowledgements

My thanks to explosives expert Skeeter Burnett for
sharing his knowledge; to Paula Eykelhof, Meg Ruley
and Christina Hogrebe for their compassion and
understanding; and to my critique group, my
children, sisters, brother and friends for support
above and beyond the call of duty.

Dear Reader,

I grew up listening to my grandparents relaying stories about "the war years." The courage and dedication of ordinary citizens who donned uniforms and left their homes to defend their country never failed to leave me awed and amazed. It was difficult to imagine my charming Uncle Bill as a sailor in the Pacific, or Uncles Karl and Knute as soldiers in North Africa. They were funny and lovable and kind – how could they be warriors?

As an adult, it is just as awe-inspiring to me to hear reports of military men and women. Thus, the opportunity to explore whether a cautious English professor like Chloe Abbott and a battle-hardened soldier like Jake Morrissey could find a future together was irresistible.

I'm delighted to be sharing this collection with two of my favourite authors and dear friends, Debbie Macomber and Katherine Stone. I hope you enjoy reading them as much as we enjoyed the planning of this anthology over lunches filled with laughter.

Warmest regards,

Lois Faye Dyer

c/o Paperbacks Plus
1618 Bay Street
Port Orchard, WA 98366, USA
www.specialauthors.com/who/bio_dyer.html

In memory of my husband, Bud.
Psalm 23: 1–6

Prologue

From: Winifred@Codebreakers.org
To: Clara@AppleButterLadies.com
Sent: Wednesday, May 16
Subject: Good morning—

Dear Clara,
Thank you so much for forwarding your apple crisp recipe. My bridge club loved it and I feel quite proud to have an "apple expert" as my dear friend. : -)

The postman brought a letter from Helen yesterday. (We must find a way to convince her to try the World Wide Web so she can share morning e-mail with us!) I was so pleased to learn she's talked to her granddaughter about her wartime experiences. I confess I was a bit surprised that she chose her granddaughter, Ruth, as her confidante—I thought she might have told her son first. But I don't think it matters *who* she told, as long as she told someone in her family. As far as I know, Ruth is the first person

Helen has talked to about her involvement in the French Underground—except for her husband, me and you, Clara.

I've never forgotten her torment and the pain in her eyes when she told us. I think that was the moment when the three of us bonded, crying together in her hotel room while our husbands waited downstairs in the lobby with Sam. She seemed so fragile, clutching her wedding bouquet. Remember how she wept when she told us about losing her husband in France? And how worried she was about whether she was being fair to Sam by marrying him when she was still devastated by what happened in France? I'm so glad we were there to support her that morning and convince her to go through with her wedding, especially since her marriage to Sam turned out so well. Now that she's shared her secrets with Ruth, too, I'm hopeful she'll find a measure of peace.

Helen's note said her granddaughter's in love! There must be something in the air this spring—first we learn your granddaughter, Elizabeth, is engaged and now Helen's Ruth finds love with Paul. I'm so delighted for both of you. What happy times are in store for you and Helen with engagements, weddings and great-grandchildren on the horizon.

I confess I'm envious, Clara, since my own three granddaughters show no signs of hurrying toward marriage. Chloe, Alexie and Lily are busy with their careers, and when I ask them about marriage, their response inevitably is "no time, Gran." Sigh. Perhaps I should try a bit of matchmaking, since I'm apparently the only one with free time to search for husbands for them. : -)

I do wish we lived closer so I could pop in and visit you daily for coffee and a nice long chat. I vividly remember how difficult it was for me the first year after I lost my Richard. He's been gone for six years now, and although I still miss him every day, the awful sadness and sense of being lost and adrift gradually eased. I know the grief will grow less for you, too, Clara, but until it does, please remember you can call me anytime, day or night, if you need to talk. I'm sure Helen would say the same.

I must stop chattering and get busy—I have a Women's Club meeting today. We're working with the Rehabilitation Department at the University of Washington Medical Center on a project that's dear to my heart. I've even convinced Chloe to get involved—such fun to work with my granddaughter! Have a wonderful day, Clara. Talk to you soon...

All my love,

Winifred

One

Jake Morrissey strode down the hall at the University of Washington Medical Center, scanning the signs above the doors until he found one that read Rehabilitation Medicine. He pushed open the big double doors and looked for his friend, Dan.

The room was surprisingly uncrowded. Across from him, two women talked with a doctor wearing a lab coat. The white-haired older woman and the doctor faced him, the other woman had her back to him.

And a very nice back it was. Tall and slender, she wore a simple, curve-hugging white dress, and her black hair was a sleek fall that brushed her shoulders.

Classy, he thought. *Wonder what the front view is like.*

A nurse in operating-room scrubs joined the group, and the brunette turned to greet her. She smiled, her eyes glowing emerald-green against fair skin, her face lit with amusement as she spoke to the nurse.

Jake went from idle appreciation of a beautiful female to serious lust. The unusual reaction stunned him.

"Hey, Sarge." Dan's voice broke the spell that held Jake motionless, staring at the brunette. He turned to his right and saw Dan, seated in a wheelchair farther down the room. A male nurse walked behind him, but the young soldier himself propelled the chair.

"Dan." Jake moved toward him and the two met halfway.

A broad grin split the young marine's face as they shook hands. "Man, it's good to see you! What are you doing here?"

"I've been out of town. I didn't know you were in Seattle until I flew back last night. I found out the VA Hospital sent you here for experimental therapy when I talked to Tomaselli around midnight."

"No kiddin'—you talked to Tomaselli? I heard he was back in the States and that he was shot. Didn't hear where he was or what happened, though."

"His unit was cleaning out a nest of insurgents in the hills near the Khyber Pass in Afghanistan, and he took a bullet in his leg." Jake glanced downward. "That's where they got you, too, he told me. Right leg or left?"

"Left." Dan shifted the lap robe to reveal a prosthetic attached just below his knee.

"Damn. I'm sorry," Jake said with feeling. "Tomaselli didn't tell me you lost the leg."

"Hell, Jake. I didn't lose it. I know exactly where it went." Dan grinned and Jake laughed, shaking his head. But before he could say anything, Dan looked past him and grimaced. "Hang around, will you?" he whispered. "I've gotta do some PR stuff. I promised the doc—and I could use some backup."

Jake glanced over his shoulder, following Dan's gaze. The pretty brunette and the small group she'd been talking with were walking in their direction. They'd been joined by a midthirties woman in jeans and sweater and a tall lanky guy with cameras slung around his neck.

"PR?" He looked back at Dan.

"Yeah. A newspaper reporter is doing a story on the equipment in here."

That takes care of the guy with the cameras and the woman in jeans, Jake thought. "Who are the two women with the doctor?"

"They must be from the Seattle Women's Club—the group that donated the equipment I've been using."

"Sure, I'll stay."

"Thanks," Dan murmured.

Jake stepped aside, silently observing as Dan said hello to his doctor and was introduced to the older woman, Winifred Abbott, and her granddaughter, Chloe Abbott.

"Hey, Sarge," a male voice called.

Chloe looked over her shoulder. A pajama-clad patient sat in a wheelchair across the room, grinning broadly at the tall, burly man walking toward him. Dressed casually in a light-blue cotton shirt tucked into belted jeans, black boots on his feet, the visitor seemed to dominate the room.

"Our patient has arrived," Dr. Jacobson said. "Are you ready to talk to Dan?" he asked the reporter.

"In a moment." She gestured at the male nurse and the other man standing next to the patient in the wheelchair. "Tony, can you get a few candid shots first?" The photographer nodded, lifting his camera to focus on the trio.

Dr. Jacobson waited until the photographer lowered his camera. "I think we're ready. Ladies, shall we…?" He waved the reporter ahead of him, following with Winifred and Chloe.

The man talking to the patient turned and stared straight at Chloe, his eyes narrowed. She'd only seen his profile earlier; now she realized that her earlier impression of "good-looking" hadn't done him justice. His eyes were a bright blue in a ruggedly handsome face. Short black hair, dark eyebrows and lashes, high cheekbones and a strong jaw combined to create a sense of strength and purpose.

His eyes didn't waver from her as she crossed the room with Dr. Jacobson, and the group was introduced to Dan West, the wheelchair-bound Marine.

"I'd like you all to meet Jake Morrissey," Dan said after shaking their hands. "Two years ago, he was our master sergeant during my first tour of duty in the Middle East."

Jake shook hands with the reporter and photographer, Dr. Jacobson and the nurse, then Winifred, before he reached Chloe.

"Chloe." His fingers and palm were slightly rough with calluses, engulfing her much smaller hand. "It's a pleasure to meet you."

"Mr. Morrissey," Chloe said politely. He held her hand a few seconds too long until she tugged discreetly. He immediately released her, a slight smile of apology curving his mouth. Amused, she smiled back at him and his gaze sharpened, holding a glint of admiration.

"Mr. Morrissey." The reporter claimed his attention. "Since you worked with Dan, I'd like to include you in the article. Do you mind?"

"Not at all." He gave the reporter a half smile before looking at Chloe and Winifred. "As long as it's all right with the ladies?"

"Whatever makes the article more effective is fine with me," Winifred said. "Our goal is to generate more donations to the medical center's equipment fund."

Chloe murmured her agreement.

"Excellent. I'd like to get some shots of you using the equipment first, Dan, then we'll take group photos."

The reporter bustled off with the photographer, Dr. Jacobson and Dan in tow.

"It's a terrible thing to lose a limb, especially at his age," Winifred said. "He's such a nice young man."

"He's a good soldier, too," Jake replied.

"I believe Dan said you served together before you left the military. Are you retired, maybe playing golf full-time?" Chloe asked, curious.

Jake laughed, his teeth a flash of white in his tanned face. "Not hardly. I started my own company when I left the Marine Corps more than five years ago—Morrissey Demolition. We're headquartered just south of Pioneer Square. And two years ago, my reserve unit was called up and I was on active duty for twelve months. I've been back in Seattle running the company again for the past year."

"How interesting. What exactly do you demolish?"

"Large buildings, mostly. We also have a contract with the Colville Tribe's construction company. We remove boulders and rock from logging roads on their reservation in eastern Washington."

"Isn't that dangerous?" Chloe tried to envision working with explosives on a daily basis.

"Not if you know what you're doing." Jake shrugged. "I specialized in explosives in the military, and my crew has years of experience in this kind of work."

"Chloe," the reporter called, "will you join us, please?"

"Excuse me." Chloe walked over to the small group surrounding Dan.

"You have a very attractive granddaughter, Mrs. Abbott," Jake said, watching Chloe as she bent to talk to Dan.

"Yes, I know."

Jake turned his head and his gaze met Winifred's, her green eyes shrewd as she studied him.

"You aren't the first man to admire Chloe," she said. She tilted her head, and a small smile raised the corners of her mouth. "But I must say you're the first one I've thought had serious potential."

"Potential?" Jake repeated warily.

"Chloe is a strong-willed woman," Winifred continued as if Jake hadn't spoken. "And very bright. Just like my son and me, she stayed on to become a professor at the University of Washington after graduating magna cum laude."

"Is that right?" Jake said evenly. "I have an engineering degree but I earned it in bits and pieces. The Marines moved me around fairly often."

Winifred waved her hand dismissively. "It's not about *where* a person is educated, it's about how intelligent that person is in all aspects of his or her life." She leaned closer. "My husband never went to college, but he was one of the most intelligent men I've ever known. Well rounded, that's the important thing."

Jake nodded without commenting, his eyes returning to Chloe.

"She teaches English at the University of Washington," Winifred said. "Her office is in Liberty Hall, although I believe I'll let you find out her phone number yourself. And Chloe recently bought a nice little house in the Queen Anne District. Where do you live, Mr. Morrissey?"

"I have an apartment on the top floor of the building I own, near Pioneer Square." Jake grinned, amused by Winifred's no-nonsense approach. "I'm also healthy, my bank account isn't overdrawn, I've never been married and I don't have any children. What do you think, Mrs. Abbott? Do I pass inspection?"

She laughed, her eyes gleaming with approval. "Yes, son, you pass. Now all you need to do is convince Chloe."

"That might take a while. I'm heading back to Vegas tonight to finish a job. It'll be four or five days before I'm back in Seattle."

Winifred nodded. "Then I'll expect you to attend my monthly brunch two weeks from this Sunday, promptly at 1:00 p.m. I assume you'll be bringing Chloe?"

"Yes, ma'am, I'll certainly try." Jake chuckled. The old lady was a force to be reckoned with. If Chloe was anything like her grandmother, he was in for a hell of a trip.

The Seattle Tribune lay open on the table. The article and photos taken at the UW Medical Center took up half of page six.

Rage hissed and uncoiled in his belly, spreading its heat through his veins. His fingers curled into fists, creasing the edges of the newspaper.

He reread the paragraphs, his morning routine disrupted as he ignored his customary breakfast of half a grapefruit and a single slice of rye toast, cut in a precise line from corner to corner. The mug of Starbucks coffee grew cold while he stared at the picture.

Three civilians stood next to a wounded solder in a wheelchair. The caption identified the patient as a marine private. The white-haired older woman was Winifred Abbott, a founding member of the Seattle Women's Club. The club's fund-raising had purchased the rehab equipment being used by the recovering marine. On Winifred's left was a late-twenties brunette identified as her granddaughter, Chloe Abbott.

He didn't have to read the name of the man standing to the right of Chloe Abbott. Jake Morrissey was all too familiar. He'd meticulously researched Morrissey for the past year and tracked his schedule and whereabouts for the past two months. Morrissey currently had a contract to implode a casino in Las Vegas; the demolition crew had been there for two weeks and weren't due to return for another two days.

He'd been unaware of Morrissey's return to Seattle this week. He was sure it wasn't in the original plans for the Las Vegas job. He didn't like it when schedules changed.

The *Tribune* article said Master Sergeant Morrissey had once served overseas with the wounded marine.

This marine was alive.

Other young men serving with Morrissey hadn't been so lucky.

The fresh-faced marine, the older woman, the granddaughter and Morrissey smiled directly at the camera in the group photo. In a second photo, Morrissey's head was bent toward the younger woman, his lips brushing her ear as he whispered to her, and her hand rested on his forearm with intimate ease. The look on the ex-master sergeant's face said Chloe Abbott meant something to him. Their body language hinted that they knew each other well.

Despite intense covert observation of Morrissey's life over the past six weeks, he'd uncovered no evidence of close family members and only casual ties to women friends. Morrissey's personal life appeared to lack anyone whose death would cause him the devastation and grief he deserved.

That situation had apparently changed.

At last. At long last.

Time for the revenge his soul craved. He had the woman's name, and he'd check her out. This might be his chance to destroy Jake Morrissey's life just as his had been destroyed.

All things come to those who wait.

"Perfect. It's absolutely perfect." Chloe Abbott cradled the rosewood mantel clock in her hands, turning it to inspect each side. Sunlight poured through the windows of the antique shop on Fourth Avenue in Seattle, gleaming off chests of silver, displays of china and crystal, and finding deep red highlights in the clock's wooden box.

She couldn't detect a single fault with it. The wood had the fine patina of age, and when the clock struck the hour, the carved doors on the front opened. The delicate figures of two dancers in Louis IV court dress popped out to twirl to the strains of a Strauss waltz.

"Gran's going to love this." Delighted, Chloe set the clock carefully on the glass counter. "Thank you so much for finding it for me."

"I'm glad you like it." The shop owner, a thin, elegant man in an impeccable gray suit and tie, abandoned his normal reserve and fairly beamed at her. "I knew the moment it came into the shop that it was meant for Winifred. There's only one tiny detail that detracts from its value. Someone modified the clockworks to add a modern battery-operated alarm inside."

"I don't care, David, and I doubt Gran will, either." Chloe's eyes half closed as she swayed to the lilting music. "'The Blue Danube' was my grandfather's favorite waltz. Gran told me they danced to it the night they became engaged."

"I seem to recall Winifred telling me that story."

Chloe opened her eyes and chuckled at his expression of fond indulgence. David McPherson had grown up with Chloe's grandmother Winifred and grandfather Richard in the community of Ballard, only a few miles from the heart of downtown Seattle. In 1943 Winifred had signed on as an assistant to her father, a cryptographer employed in the Seattle section of the Office of Strategic Services, precursor to the CIA. That same year, Richard Abbott and Winifred were married four days before he and David donned army uniforms and marched off to war. They'd returned to Seattle to take up their lives after peace was won. Winifred had resumed her university studies, earning her doctorate and stayed on to become a professor of literature. Richard inherited Abbott Construction from his father, while David had opened an antique shop in downtown Seattle. Both men had been stunningly successful, and although David was widowed at forty-two and never had children, he'd been adopted into Richard and Winifred's family. Chloe thought of him as a much-loved great-uncle.

Which was why, when she'd wanted a special gift to mark her grandmother's eightieth birthday, she'd called on David.

"Of course you remember. You were probably at the same dance."

His blue eyes twinkled. "I'm sure I was. In fact, I distinctly remember slipping money to the bandleader so he'd play the waltz at just the right moment."

Chloe laughed and hugged him. "Clever, David, very clever."

"Sometimes true love needs a helping hand," he said sagely, patting her back.

"Hmm." Chloe herself had never experienced true love, so she'd have to take his word for it. She stepped back and looked once more at the clock, gleaming in splendor on the glass counter. "I'll buy it, of course. It's wonderful."

"Give me a few minutes to pack it properly." David walked behind the counter and disappeared through a curtained doorway.

The antique bell mounted above the outer door chimed. Chloe smiled politely at the three older woman who entered the shop before her gaze moved on to the big display window. Outside, the sidewalks were busy, thronged with pedestrians walking briskly past. A solitary man stood motionless, looking through the glass into the interior of the shop. He was of average height and weight, dressed in khaki pants with a neatly pressed plaid shirt. Mirrored sunglasses concealed his eyes below the bill of a Mariners baseball cap that covered all but a glimpse of short-cropped black hair.

Chloe's skin prickled and she shivered. She couldn't see the man's eyes behind the dark glasses, but she had the uneasy conviction that he was staring at her. Something about his absolute stillness was unnerving. How long had he been watching her?

"Here we are." David returned with a cardboard box, tissue paper and an elegant plastic bag.

Chloe turned to look at David, and when she glanced back at the window, the man was gone. Shrugging off the unsettling moment, she leaned against the counter. "Where did you find the clock?"

He carefully wrapped the tissue paper around the mantel clock before slipping it into the white box with his shop logo, Elegance, in tasteful script across the top.

"At an estate sale in the Capitol Hill District. Fortunately," David told her, taping the lid of the box closed, "I had the opportunity for a private viewing before the house was open to the public and I picked up several nice pieces, including this clock."

"What else did you find?"

Chloe listened with interest as David pointed out the various newly acquired items in his chic, cluttered shop. Finally she said goodbye and left, the clock held safely in her arms within its multiple layers of packing.

She checked her watch. She had to lecture college freshmen on the basics of English composition at two o'clock. If she was lucky and there were no traffic snarls, she could make it back to the campus with ten minutes to spare. She quickened her steps as she headed toward her car and was soon driving north on Dexter Avenue before crossing the Fremont Bridge to hook up with Pacific Avenue on her way to Lake Union and the University District. The University spires were already in sight when her cell phone rang. She flipped open the phone, read the caller ID information and held the slim silver phone to her ear.

"Hi, Alexie, what's up?"

"Did you get Gran's present?" Chloe's sister didn't bother with a greeting.

"Yes, and it's gorgeous. You're going to love it."

"Good. Which one of us is picking up the cake?"

"I will."

"Excellent." Alexie sounded relieved. "With Mom and Lily still in England, and you and me responsible for Gran's birthday, I'm a little worried that we'll forget something. Speaking of forgetting, why didn't you tell me about the guy you met at the UW Medical Center?"

"What guy?"

"The guy kissing you in the *Tribune* photo."

"Jake Morrissey? He wasn't kissing me."

"Ohh, yes, he was," Alexie drawled. "And I cut out the photo to prove it. Oops, gotta run, I'm due in court in thirty minutes. We'll discuss this later. Call me after work."

Chloe turned off the phone and reached across the console to tuck it back into her purse.

She'd thought Jake was interested, maybe a lot interested.

But he hadn't called. She frowned. The article and photos weren't published in the *Tribune* until this morning's edition, but the photos had been taken three days earlier. She'd been sure Jake would call and was surprised at how disappointed she felt that he hadn't.

She nosed the Volvo into the stream of cars crossing the University Bridge and checked her watch again. By the time she turned onto Pacific Avenue and arrived at the north-central side of the university campus, she had just enough time to slip into a faculty parking space, grab her purse, briefcase and an armful of books, and dash across campus.

Halfway to Liberty Hall, she had the feeling that someone was following her. She looked over her shoulder, but although students crowded the sidewalk, none of their faces were familiar and none appeared to be paying particular attention to her. Frowning, she dismissed the oddly disturbing sensation and picked up her pace once again.

Chloe's freshman English classes were held in one of the original brick university buildings. The small single-story hall was used as the first campus church but during the mid-1950s, had been converted into a classroom. Now it contained only one lecture theater, accessed by students via a steep flight of concrete stairs leading to the double oak doors at the front. Professors entered at the lectern level through a side door that opened directly onto a sidewalk and the campus lawns beyond.

When Chloe walked inside, the three hundred tiered theater seats were half-filled with students. She dropped her briefcase and books on the table.

"Professor Abbott?"

Chloe glanced up from organizing her lecture notes and reference books and smiled at the first-year student seated in the front row.

"Yes?"

"I read the article in the *Tribune* this morning—the one about the solider in rehab? The article said your grandmother was a codebreaker."

"Yes, she worked for the Office of Strategic Services at a satellite office here in Seattle. Her father was a cryptographer working for the OSS and he hired her as his assistant when she was only eighteen years old. She loved the work."

An hour later, Chloe assigned a three-page essay as homework. Class time had been used for a lively and passionate discussion fueled by the *Seattle Tribune* article with the photos of Dan West, and Chloe had encouraged students to voice their views. The papers were to explore the impact made on each student's life by the wounding or death of American military personnel stationed around the globe.

"The essays are due next Wednesday. If you drop them through the door slot at my office, they have to be there no later than 4:00 p.m. on Wednesday afternoon," she said, raising her voice to be heard over the sound of books slamming shut. "And don't forget to take a copy of the handouts on the table next to the exit. The page-three article on the style of Jane Austen is part of your required reading for next week."

She gathered up her books and slung her purse over her shoulder, making a mental note to confirm with the student editor about using the Opinions section of the university newspaper. She'd promised her class the winning essay would be published in the column, and the editor had agreed.

The lectern-level exit door stood ajar, letting fresh air and the scent of flowers into the hall. With her arms full, Chloe bumped the door with her shoulder to open it and the heavy metal panel crashed into something solid just outside.

"Hey!"

Chloe peered around the edge of the door. The janitor perched on the ladder grabbed the wall next to the empty light socket above the doorjamb.

"Are you all right, Fred?"

"Yeah." The dour, midfifties man frowned, his carrot-colored brows pulling down into a V over his beaky nose. "The light bulb isn't, though."

Chloe followed his gaze. Pieces of shattered glass lay on the concrete sidewalk. "I didn't see you there behind the door. I'm so sorry."

Fred grunted an acknowledgment and descended to the walkway. "I'll have to go to the maintenance shop and get another bulb. I'm leaving the ladder here."

He paused, looking at her pointedly, and Chloe waved at the lawn and busy campus beyond. "It's safe from me. I'm going to my office."

"Uh-huh."

He eyed her suspiciously before Chloe walked briskly away. The taciturn man had worked at Liberty Hall, her campus office building, for the past year and he had yet to warm up to any casual conversation beyond "hello." She glanced over her shoulder. He was moving the ladder, carefully arranging it against the side wall. Then he took a small hand broom and dustpan from his toolbox, knelt down and began to sweep up the broken glass.

He takes his job so personally, she thought. *As though the university is his own private place. But then, that's probably a good trait in a janitor.*

Jake Morrissey shaded his eyes with one hand. Despite his sunglasses, the Las Vegas sun was blinding, and he narrowed his eyes against the glare. The searing heat of the desert city was light years away from the cooler Puget Sound region he'd left yesterday.

He'd flown out of SeaTac airport on a red-eye express

to Las Vegas barely twelve hours after he'd met Chloe
Abbott at the UW Medical Center. There hadn't been
time to talk to her again, although he could've called her
today, either on his cell or the hotel room phone. But
like most of the jobs he took on, imploding the multi-
story casino-hotel was complicated and required all his
attention. He wanted the work completed and out of the
way so he could focus on Chloe. He'd grabbed three
hours of sleep at the hotel before heading for the job site
with his crew, already looking forward to finishing and
flying home.

He hadn't met a woman who intrigued him this much
in years. Maybe never. The half hour he'd spent talking
with Chloe and her grandmother had only increased his
interest.

Chloe Abbott was beautiful, sexy, smart and had a
quick, wry sense of humor. He was positive the attraction was mutual, but he was too far away to act on it.

He wanted her within reach when he talked to her,
not a thousand miles away. Her grandmother had mentioned that Chloe lived in Queen Anne, a Seattle district
only a ten- or fifteen-minute drive from the industrial
end of First Avenue where his building was located.

Setting the explosives to implode the old casino
would take roughly five more days. He'd be on a flight
back to Seattle by the time the dust settled.

Two

"So tell me about the guy in the *Tribune* photo with you and Gran," Alexie demanded as she closed the freezer door in Winifred's kitchen. Ice-cream container in hand, she pulled open a drawer.

Chloe groaned silently. That photo. How on earth had the photographer managed to make it look as if Jake was nibbling her ear? She lifted the cake out of its box. "I'm guessing you're referring to the photos taken at the medical center?" Her older sister wasn't likely to be distracted enough to drop the subject of Jake Morrissey, but Chloe tried.

"Drank it in with my morning latte. Nice article, by the way," Alexie said.

"I think so, too. The reporter did a great job and I loved that she included Gran's background as a code-breaker during World War II." Chloe slipped the three-tiered chocolate cake onto a heavy crystal cake stand.

"Yes, nice touch. Are you about ready with that?"

"I just need to put the candles on top." Chloe quickly poked ten short pink candles into the dark chocolate frosting, eyed the arrangement critically, then nodded with approval.

"Let's get back to you explaining the hot guy nibbling on your ear."

"I was hoping you'd forget."

"No chance. Who is he?"

"Didn't you read the caption under the picture?"

"Of course—it gave me his name, rank and how long he's been a civilian. What I want to hear from you is how you *feel* about him."

"What do you mean how I feel about him? I just met him! We spent maybe twenty minutes talking, and most of the conversation was about the medical center and Gran. I don't even know him." *Not that I don't want to,* Chloe thought. She pulled open two drawers before she located a book of matches. She tucked them into the pocket of her retro, swingy pink skirt and picked up the cake plate.

Alexie's huff of disbelief spoke volumes. "The expression on Jake Morrissey's face in that photo practically singed the edges of my morning paper and you have nothing to tell me about him? The man was kissing your ear."

"He was *not* kissing my ear. He said something to me and I couldn't hear him. When I asked him to repeat it, he leaned closer to ask me a question about Dan West and the annoying photographer chose that moment to snap the picture. That's all there was to it." Chloe had a swift mental image of Jake Morrissey holding her hand a shade too long when they were introduced, his dark eyes filled with male interest. She'd found it a bit disconcerting to have all that male intensity focused exclusively on her. Jake wasn't her usual, easygoing kind of man, but she was attracted in spite of herself and had thought he was, too. But he hadn't called.

"I might believe you if I hadn't seen the look on his face." Alexie used her elbow to hold open the swinging door between the kitchen and dining room and gestured

Chloe to precede her. As Chloe walked past, she hissed, "This conversation isn't over."

"Maybe we should discuss *your* latest guy," Chloe murmured, laughing when Alexie rolled her eyes. "Here we are," she announced. Winifred, seated at one end of the gleaming mahogany table, looked up.

"Eight candles?" Winifred lifted an inquiring eyebrow, her sharp gaze sweeping Chloe and Alexie. "Why not eighty?"

"We were afraid we'd melt the frosting if we lit that many candles, Gran." Alexie grinned, mischief on her face. "So we settled on one candle for each decade."

Chloe set the cake plate on the table and pulled out the book of matches, lighting the candles with a flourish.

"An excellent solution." Winifred leaned forward, drew in a deep breath and blew out the candles while her granddaughters clapped and cheered.

"I'll cut the cake while Alexie scoops." Chloe slid cake onto a plate before passing it to her sister to add ice cream.

"Thank you, dear." Winifred's white hair was cut short in a natural cap of snowy curls that framed her face. Her tailored long-sleeved silk blouse had mother-of-pearl buttons from waistline to neck, the emerald silk making her eyes glow a deeper green. She wore a treasured heirloom cameo pin at her throat, a gift from her husband when he'd returned from London more than fifty years earlier. At five foot six, her posture was still nearly perfect, her carriage erect, her walk graceful. "I'm so glad you two could be here tonight."

"It's tradition, Gran. What would a birthday be without a gathering of The Abbott Women?" Chloe adored her grandmother. Winifred Abbott was a force to be reckoned with, both inside and outside their tight-knit family circle. "And we'll do this again when Mom and Lily get home in a few weeks."

"Two birthday parties?" Winifred's eyes twinkled. "Hmm, maybe we should do two every year." She ran a loving hand over the glossy surface of the rosewood clock sitting on the table next to her. "Especially if it means I get another present as nice as this one."

"I'll talk to Mom and Lily," Chloe said promptly.

"I was telling Chloe earlier that I read the *Tribune* article about the rehab equipment, Gran," Alexie commented. "The reporter did a good job."

Chloe flicked a threatening glance at her sister. Alexie caught the look and mouthed "What?" Chloe turned to her cake again and kept her head down.

"Thank you, Alexie," Winifred said. "I hope the publicity generates more donations for the medical center."

"I thought the reporter planned to interview only the soldier, you and Chloe?"

"That was her original plan, but Mr. Morrissey happened to be in the ward when we arrived, and since he once served with Dan West, she added him to the mix."

"He owns a company called Morrissey Demolition?" Alexie asked.

"That's right. I believe they do a variety of work," Winifred replied. "But he apparently specializes in imploding large buildings. He's in Las Vegas blowing up a casino-hotel this week, isn't that correct, Chloe?"

"I didn't hear him mention where he's currently working, Gran." *But if he's out of town, maybe that's why he didn't call.* Although there were certainly telephones in Las Vegas.

"He must've told me about Las Vegas while you were getting ice water for young Dan. He said he's been working there for several weeks and flew home to Seattle to attend a meeting but had to return to Nevada that evening. I'm sure he said it was a casino he was blowing up and that he'd be there for at least a few more days."

"Does his wife travel with him?" Alexie asked casually.

"He isn't married. He seemed quite taken with Chloe, however."

Fully aware that two pairs of eyes immediately focused on her, Chloe shook her head. "He wasn't all that interested, Gran. Besides, he's not really my type."

"Not your type?" Alexie pulled the newspaper clipping from her pocket and unfolded it in the center of the table for all to see. "Look at this picture. How could he *not* be your type? What is it about 'tall, dark and handsome' that doesn't appeal to you?"

"Those aren't the only qualities a woman wants," Winifred put in mildly.

"Of course not, Gran," Alexie said. "But it's hard to imagine that any of the khaki-pants-and-glasses, Woody Allen-wannabe men in Chloe's life could compete with Jake Morrissey."

"I don't date men who look like Woody Allen," Chloe protested, affronted.

"The math professor you brought to Lily's New Year's Eve party was a nerd," Alexie said.

"Sam is a very nice man. And I don't date him, we're just friends."

"But he's a nerd." Alexie stared at her until Chloe gave in.

"All right. But he's a *nice* nerd. And we've never been romantically involved."

"It's a sure bet Nice Nerd Sam would never nibble on your ear and look at you like Jake Morrissey did." Alexie seemed to feel she'd had the last word, jabbing her fork at the clipping for emphasis.

"I remember when my Richard looked at me like

that." Winifred sighed, a reminiscent smile curving her lips.

"You're mistaking annoyance for interest," Chloe said. "Just before the reporter snapped that photo, we argued over whether Dan should go to work for him when he's released from the hospital."

"I'm guessing Jake thought he should?" Alexie asked. "And you thought he shouldn't?"

"Of course I thought he shouldn't take a job working with explosives." Chloe frowned. "He's already lost a leg."

"Let's get back to the subject of Jake Morrissey—I can't believe you found him *annoying*." Alexie waved her fork in the general direction of the clipping. "He's way too good-looking."

"I felt he was a very nice young man," Winifred declared. "I didn't find him difficult at all."

"That's because he went out of his way to be charming to you, Gran," Chloe said wryly.

"He did have a certain rough-around-the-edges, Humphrey Bogart appeal," Winifred agreed.

"From Woody Allen to Bogart." Alexie laughed out loud. "That's a quantum leap, Chloe."

"I'm not sure I buy your analysis, Gran," Chloe muttered.

"That's it! That's how he's looking at you in the photo. It's that Bogart and Bacall thing," Alexie declared.

Much to Chloe's relief, the conversation shifted to movie actors and actresses in classic pairings, and away from her and Jake Morrissey. The rest of their visit with Winifred passed with much laughter and friendly arguing over whether Bogart and Bacall led the list of top-ten best couples ever.

Alone in her bedroom later that evening, Winifred sat on the edge of her turned-down bed and picked up Richard's photo from her nightstand.

"Richard, why can't the girls find a man like you? Where are all the good men?" She smoothed her fingertips over the glass separating her from his smile. "Jake Morrissey might be the one for our Chloe. I think she might be more attracted to him than she's willing to admit."

She pressed a kiss to the photo and returned the silver frame to its place on the white crocheted doily decorating the polished mahogany nightstand.

"Good night, Richard."

He parked in the shadow of a large elm, across the street and half a block away from Winifred Abbott's stately Victorian home. Chloe Abbott had been ridiculously easy to follow from her house in Queen Anne to her grandmother's. She'd arrived alone, but while she was still unloading parcels from her car, another vehicle pulled in and parked behind her in the driveway. A second woman got out. He heard them laughing and talking before doors slammed and the two of them entered the house. The neighborhood subsided into relative quiet once more.

He slumped in the driver's seat and waited until he was sure Chloe was staying put. Then he left, parking some distance away from the house in the opposite direction. Seattle residents vigorously supported Neighborhood Watch and they were also dog-lovers. The last six weeks he'd spent following Morrissey had taught him that residents walking their dogs tended to notice and grow suspicious if he was parked too long in one place.

Around ten o'clock, the two women drove away. He followed Chloe's Volvo back to Queen Anne and watched her enter the tidy Craftsman bungalow.

Satisfied, he drove home to neatly enter details of the day's activities and observations in his log book. Reading his afternoon notes, jotted while slumped in the last seat of the top tier in the far-left corner of the lecture hall, brought a resurgence of the outrage he'd felt as he listened to Chloe's class voice their opinions. What did any of these late-teens and early twenties students know about the tearing pain felt by the family after a soldier died in combat? He was convinced he was the only person in the lecture hall who'd actually experienced the loss of an American soldier and the devastation that accompanied it.

Only he could write an essay that told the truth. And he would, he decided.

He printed a note in the margin, the block letters precise, the message brief. *Deliver essay to Liberty Hall, Chloe Abbott's office, one week from today.*

Then he continued transcribing his personal shorthand into sentences on the page.

Chloe Abbott would make an easy target. She seemed to lead an ordinary life, with set work hours and close family connections.

A predictable schedule and rudimentary surveillance requirements. You're easy prey, Miss Abbott.

The spacious parking lot surrounding the casino was empty except for Jake, his crew and the building's owner with his entourage.

Jake stepped away from the small crowd, turning his head to speak into his earpiece.

"You ready over there, Ed?"

"Good to go, Sarge. Ready whenever you are."

Jake nodded, waved a hand at Ed, visible across the expanse of bare pavement, and turned back to the observers.

"We're ready, Kyle." He joined the crowd and lifted

the protective plastic guard from the black box. "It's all yours."

Normally Jake enjoyed this moment when he was able to indulge the ten-year-old child within an adult client and let him or her trigger the control to blow up a huge building. But today, he had difficulty concealing his impatience. He was booked on a 7:00 p.m. flight home to Seattle. With luck, by nine-thirty or ten o'clock he'd be back in his apartment.

Kyle set off the first round of explosives and the building's upper stories imploded. Jake listened, counting the subsequent explosions as each charge detonated in sequence, further weakening the structure and allowing it to fold in on itself, collapsing to the ground with slow grace. Clouds of dust rose. Hiding a grin, Jake watched the well-dressed crowd scatter like chickens in a downpour as the wall of dust moved across the parking lot toward them.

He headed for his rented SUV. All he had left to finish in Vegas was a celebration dinner and drinks with the client and he could go home to Seattle.

The next day, Jake decided not to call Chloe after all. Instead, he phoned the florist and arranged to have flowers delivered with a note asking her to lunch—today, tomorrow or whenever she was free. He drove to the University of Washington just before noon and parked the Porsche, then he took a last look at the map he'd printed off the UW Web site and started across campus.

Liberty Hall was easy to find. Built in 1949 and dedicated to World War II veterans, the four-story brick building had majestic Norman arches and a bell tower. It housed faculty offices for the English Department. Jake paused at an information desk to inquire after Professor Abbott's whereabouts. Then he followed the secretary's directions down a wide hallway.

Halfway down the hall, a white nameplate with black lettering marked Chloe's space. The door, its bottom half glossy dark wood with a wide mail slot and the top section opaque glass, stood slightly ajar. He rapped lightly on the doorjamb.

"Come in."

He pushed the door wide and stepped across the threshold. The small office was neat and tidy, but crowded with a desk, two wooden guest chairs, a bookcase and a corner coatrack. Chloe stood next to the deep window embrasure across the room, where a vase held a lush spring bouquet.

"You got my flowers."

"Yes, I did. Thank you—they're beautiful."

His mouth curved upward in response to the smile that warmed her face and lit her eyes. He'd have to remember she loved flowers, he thought. "Any chance you're free for lunch? Today would be great, but I'll come back tomorrow or the next day, if you're busy."

"Actually, I was planning on eating yogurt and a banana at my desk while I corrected papers. But the world's best pizza is just across campus." She walked to the desk, opened a drawer and took out a straw purse, then looked up at him. "Do you like pizza?"

"Love it."

"Excellent." She moved past him, waiting while he followed her and pulled the door closed. Then she locked the door.

They left the building, dodging students seated on the dozen steps outside the front door. A warm breeze carried the scent of water from Lake Washington, where the University's rowing team practiced on the rippled lake surface, the white racing sculls skimming over the blue. Pink, white and red azaleas and rhododendrons made brilliant splashes of color against the background of green fir trees and the ivy that climbed brick-and-stone buildings.

"Gran said you've been working out of town?"

"Yes, in Vegas." Jake slipped his sunglasses on, shielding his eyes.

"So that's where you got the tan. I knew you couldn't have been sunning yourself in Seattle, because until last week, most of our days have been rainy." Amusement tinged her slightly husky voice. Jake glanced at Chloe to find her smiling.

"The Pacific Northwest's version of liquid sunshine," he commented.

"Exactly. Are you a native Northwesterner?"

"Born and raised on the Kitsap Peninsula. You?"

"I was born in Seattle. I've lived here all my life, except for a few years while my father taught at UC Berkeley."

"Your father's a professor, too?"

"He was—his field of study was mathematics. He passed away when I was six." Chloe gestured across campus at the math and science buildings. "Abbott Library over there is named after him."

"So you're a third-generation UW professor. That makes you a legend here."

Chloe laughed. "That's true." Her smile became a frown and she slowed, looking over her shoulder.

"Something wrong?"

She didn't answer immediately, but he saw her shiver as she scanned the students on the sidewalk behind them.

"What is it?" Jake asked.

"Nothing. At least, nothing I can see."

"What do you mean?"

"I've had this creepy feeling for the past few days—as if someone's watching me. If I didn't know better, I'd swear I'm being followed."

Jake stopped, drawing her with him off the sidewalk and onto the grass. The flow of pedestrian traffic continued past them, the walkway crowded with noisy students on their way to lunch.

"You think you're being stalked?" He searched her face, read the uneasiness on her features and looked back at the busy sidewalk, studying the crowd for any visible threat.

It can't be a coincidence that she feels she's being followed so soon after meeting me, Jake thought grimly.

He'd never forgive himself if he'd made Chloe a target for whoever had been following him for the last six weeks.

Three

Jake shifted her behind him, concealing her from the crowd with his body while he continued to inspect the busy walkway.

"I haven't actually *seen* anyone following me but I have this…this eerie feeling that I'm being watched." Chloe's fingers closed over his forearm and she felt his muscles flex. "I swear the hair rises on the back of my neck."

"When in doubt, trust your gut instinct," he said. "If something doesn't feel right, it probably isn't. Soldiers learn that lesson the first week in a combat zone."

"I've never had anything like this happen to me before," Chloe told him. "I've read about it, and seen it in movies. But in real life and to me personally? No."

"You sound more annoyed than scared." Jake swept one more glance over the surrounding area. "Do you still feel you're being watched?"

Chloe paused, assessing, and was relieved when she realized the eerie feeling had disappeared. "No."

"Good." He checked his watch. "Let's resume this over lunch." He took her arm and they left the grass for the sidewalk. He didn't return to the subject of a possible stalker until they were seated at the restaurant with slices of hot pizza and cold drinks in front of them.

"What about a boyfriend?"

Startled, she looked up, her glass of ice water halfway to her lips. "I beg your pardon?"

"Have you had a fight with a boyfriend lately?"

"I'm not dating anyone at present." Chloe caught a quick flash of satisfaction.

"What about ex-boyfriends? Any relationships that ended badly? Guys who might be looking for revenge?"

"No." She shook her head. "Definitely not a possible scenario."

"That leaves us with professional enemies."

"I work in the English Department at a university," Chloe said. "None of my fellow assistant professors are the James Bond type. In fact…" She smiled. "My sister calls them Woody Allen–wannabes."

"Really?" He raised his eyebrows. "That bad, huh?"

"Not bad," she protested. "They're very nice men."

"Hmm," he murmured, but didn't comment further. "So you have a sister?"

"I have two, actually."

"Either of them have a reason to follow or threaten you?"

"No." A swift mental image of Alexie made Chloe laugh.

"What?"

"I just pictured Alexie trying to stalk me. She has no patience—she'd last maybe two minutes before she confronted me and told me exactly what she wanted."

"I think I like her." Jake's lips curved in a smile. "Apparently both you and Alexie inherited some of your grandmother Winifred's character traits. You said you have two sisters?"

Chloe nodded. "Alexie is my older sister. Lily is younger than me by five years. And before you ask…" She held up her hand to forestall his next question. "Lily's on a buying trip in Europe for her lingerie boutique. And my mother's with her, so neither of them could possibly be connected to this. Not that there's any possibility of that, anyway," she added. "I have a normal family, Jake. And I live a perfectly average life. I have no idea why someone would want to follow me or who this person might be."

"Maybe you have nothing to worry about," he said calmly. "Have you talked to the police?"

"No. What would I tell them—that I *feel* someone watching me?" She frowned. "They'd call in a psychiatrist and have me committed."

"Not necessarily. They get more complaints like yours than you might think."

"I'm guessing they file them in the 'paranoid' folder." Chloe was unconvinced. "I'd rather wait until I have something concrete to tell them before I call."

"What sort of evidence are you waiting for?"

"I don't know." Chloe bit her lip, considering. "Something beyond an uneasy feeling. If I'd actually seen the person who's following me, then I'd have something solid for the police to investigate."

"But you haven't noticed anyone unusual or out of the ordinary? No one who made you feel uncomfortable?"

Chloe instantly thought of the man wearing sunglasses outside David's shop.

"What is it?"

"Probably nothing."

"Tell me."

"The other afternoon I was in downtown Seattle, picking up a gift for my grandmother's birthday. I saw a man outside the shop who seemed to be staring at me through the glass. But I may have been imagining it. I turned to speak to David and when I looked back, the man was gone."

"Could you describe him?"

She called up the image of the man at David's shop and told Jake the few things she remembered.

"Any distinctive features?" Jake asked.

"No."

"Have you seen the man since then?"

"No."

"But you still feel as if someone's following you." Jake's words were more a confirmation than a question.

Chloe stared at him. His face was set in grim lines. Despite the sunshine that poured through the window behind her, Chloe shivered. "You think I'm being stalked. You believe me."

"Yes." Jake's eyes narrowed. "You've gone pale as a ghost."

Chloe crossed her arms. The short-sleeved, light cotton sweater she wore over her sleeveless summer dress suddenly wasn't heavy enough to warm her. "Telling you about it has somehow made it more real."

"I didn't mean to scare you more than you already are, Chloe." Jake stretched across the table and took her hand, folding it between his palms. The heat from his hands warmed her chilled fingers and reached past the fear to stir the sexual awareness that always simmered just below the surface when he was near. "We'll find out who the man is, why he's following you and what he wants."

"But I didn't know the man I saw through the window. I have no idea who he is or why he'd follow me."

"First things first. We should tell the police. Even though you don't have a lot of information, they can at least take a report and establish a file. Who knows?"

Jake shrugged. "Maybe something you tell them will fit into a bigger puzzle, since we have no idea what connection you have with this man."

"I have a one o'clock lecture, but after that I'm free for the rest of the afternoon. I'll drive downtown to the Seattle Police Department when I'm finished."

"I'll make a couple of calls. I'm sure they'll send an officer out here to talk with you."

"I'd rather meet the officer off campus. I'd like to keep this from my colleagues and students, if possible."

"All right." Jake looked at his watch. "We'd better leave if you're going to make your one o'clock class."

"Is it that late already?" Chloe checked her own watch, slid out of the booth and grabbed her purse, waiting while Jake paid their bill.

He took her arm as they left the restaurant, surveying the student and faculty pedestrians as they crossed the campus.

"As first dates go, this has been memorable," he said when they reached her office at Liberty Hall. He leaned against the doorjamb, waiting for her.

Chloe slipped her lecture notes and two volumes of poetry into her briefcase and rejoined him. "Are you telling me most women you take out for pizza don't require bodyguard services?" she asked wryly.

"Not usually, no." He looked sideways at her and grinned. Sunlight shafted through the high windows at the end of the hall and burnished his dark hair. Chloe couldn't help smiling back. She felt safer with him nearby.

She touched his hand. "Thank you," she said softly. "I didn't realize how worried I've been. I feel safer just knowing you're taking me seriously."

His eyes darkened and he covered her hand with his, trapping her fingers against his warm skin. "I'm glad."

A door slammed down the hall, the noise breaking the charged moment between them, and Chloe slipped her hand from his. "I'd better go."

"I'll walk with you."

Jake fell into step beside her as they left Liberty Hall and walked the short distance to her classroom. She said goodbye and entered the lecture hall on the lower level; Jake followed her, stopping on the threshold to peruse the room. Directly in front of him was a speaker's table where Chloe was arranging a couple of books and a sheaf of notes. Beyond the small instructor area, theater seats rose in tiers to a set of upper doors where students were entering. The room was filling quickly. Satisfied that Chloe was safe for the moment, Jake stepped outside, lowered the doorstop to keep the door open and moved to the shade of a walnut tree several yards across the lawn. He dropped onto a bench beneath the big old tree and pulled out his cell phone to call his office.

"Morrissey Demolition."

"Barbara, I need you to cancel my afternoon appointments."

"Sure, boss. Should I reschedule?"

"No. Tell them I'm dealing with an emergency situation and you'll call tomorrow to arrange another time."

"All right. Everything okay?"

"Everything's fine. I should be in the office late this afternoon. Thanks, Barbara." He hung up and dialed the cell-phone number for Gray Stewart, an old friend and a detective with the Seattle Police Department. While he waited for Gray to answer, he watched Chloe through the open hall door. She walked back and forth as she spoke, pausing to ask and answer questions, unmistakably passionate about the subject under discussion, whatever it might be.

"Hello."

"Gray, it's Jake. I've got a problem. I think whoever's been following me has started stalking a woman I'm seeing."

"The brunette in the *Tribune* photo?"

Jake groaned out loud. "Has the entire world seen that picture?"

"Probably all of Seattle, at least," Gray said, clearly amused.

"Well, hell." He paused. "Yeah, it's the same woman. I just had lunch with her and she told me she's felt someone watching her, off and on, since a day or so after the picture was in the paper."

"The timing's pretty suspicious. Anything else happen to her? Any threatening letters or a dead rat left on her doorstep?"

"No. And I don't want her to know about the letter and the blown-apart sewer rat I got. I'd like you to talk to her, though."

"All right. Tell her to come to the station this afternoon."

"I'd rather take her myself and meet you somewhere outside your office. She's teaching a class right now, but we could be there by two-thirty."

"All right. Meet me at Rosa's Downtown at two-thirty. And you're buying my coffee and doughnuts. You still owe me twenty bucks from the last poker game."

"You got it."

For the next hour, Jake returned messages and caught up on business calls, sitting under the walnut tree. He stood up and waited inside the doorway when Chloe dismissed class. As she collected her books and purse, he assessed the students leaving through the exit at the top of the tiered seats. None of them did anything to rouse his suspicions; they all appeared to be typical college freshmen. Students still crowded the aisle leading to the exit above when Chloe joined him.

"I called the Seattle P.D. and made arrangements for you to talk to Gray Stewart."

"Is he the officer handling harassment reports?"

"Not exactly." Jake took her briefcase. "Gray and I went to high school together. After we graduated, I enlisted in the Marine Corps and he joined the Seattle P.D. He's a detective now."

"I see."

"I'm parked this way." He pointed toward the visitors' lot.

"My car's in the faculty lot in the opposite direction." Chloe reached for her briefcase. "Thanks for all your help, Jake."

He shook his head. "I'll drive you downtown. We'll come back and pick up your car when you're finished talking with Gray."

"I can't let you do that," she protested. "I'm sure you must have a dozen ways to spend your afternoon that would be more fun than waiting for me in a police station."

"Nope, not a thing." He took her arm and turned her toward the lot where he'd left his car. "Besides, Gray's meeting us at Rosa's Downtown, a restaurant near his office. I told him I'd come with you."

"I feel guilty for taking up so much of your day," Chloe said as she walked beside him toward his car.

"I'm sure we can think of a way for you to repay me," he drawled.

His voice was blatantly suggestive. Chloe glanced over and caught him watching her.

"Really? And what might that be?" Her voice was cool.

Jake laughed. "Nothing gets past you, does it? All I meant was that you can let me take you to dinner. Preferably soon."

"Hmm." She was very sure that wasn't what he'd meant.

"Not that I won't be happy to cooperate if you have something friendlier in mind," he said.

"I'll let you know when I do," she murmured.

"You do that. Here we are." Jake touched the button on his key chain, and the brake lights flashed on a black Porsche.

He opened the passenger door and Chloe slid into the seat, fastening her seat belt. He rounded the hood of the car and stowed her briefcase before he got in.

Chloe ran her hand over the soft leather upholstery and eyed the panel of gauges on the dashboard. "Nice car."

"Thanks. I like it." The engine turned over with a throaty growl when he twisted the ignition key. He shifted into gear and backed out of the parking space.

"Did I mention I drive a Volvo?" she asked mildly.

"No." He looked at her and smiled. "But if you're wondering how fast I drive, I never race on city streets or the freeway."

"Good to know."

He watched the black Porsche's taillights blink red when the car slowed at the exit before pulling out into traffic.

He no longer wondered whether the connection between Morrissey and the lady professor was important. He wasn't positive just how deep the lady's feelings went, but he'd observed Jake Morrissey with other women. This one was different.

Excellent.

It was time to set in motion the next phase of his plan. Just as Morrissey had been responsible for the death of his son, so would he be responsible for the death of Chloe Abbott. Morrissey Demolition's current job site was located southeast of downtown Seattle in a rural area. The small building holding Jake's powder magazine was padlocked and enclosed inside chain-link fencing, along with the huge earth-moving equipment used by the highway contractor.

He knew exactly how to bypass the alarm, enter the building and get to the powder magazine that held the company's supply of dynamite. All the equipment required was a small bolt cutter and wire cutters. He didn't need to steal more than one stick of dynamite and a detonator cap for the justice and revenge he craved.

He smiled, imagining Chloe Abbott and Liberty Hall's bell tower blowing sky-high.

It was almost too easy.

Four

"There's Gray." Jake pointed at a booth near the back of the restaurant. He dropped his hand to her waist to gently urge Chloe ahead of him and they made their way to the rear of the room.

The man who rose to meet them was as tall as Jake, but his build and coloring were the opposite. With tawny hair and brown eyes, Gray was lean where Jake was burly. Jake introduced Chloe and she slid into the booth, studying the two men while they talked.

"I ordered coffee for us."

"No doughnuts?" Jake said.

"No, but since you're buying, I'm thinking of ordering an eight-course meal for four."

"It's too late for lunch and too early for dinner," Jake pointed out.

"I'll ask for a doggie bag."

"Yeah, right."

The waitress interrupted them, pouring coffee into their cups.

"So, Chloe." Gray shifted his focus when she'd left.

"Jake tells me you're having a problem with someone following you?"

"I haven't exactly had a problem yet. It's more like I'm afraid I *might* have a problem. So far, I've had the uneasy feeling that someone's watching me, sometimes following me, but that's all." She tore open a packet and stirred sugar into her coffee, looking up in time to catch a swift exchange of glances between Gray and Jake.

"If you're being followed, someone has a reason. Have you had any disagreements with students that got out of hand?"

"No." She shook her head. "One of my freshman composition classes had a debate about the military after the *Tribune* story appeared, but that's about it."

"What kind of debate?"

"Some of the students argued that international peacekeeping wasn't worth the loss of American soldiers' legs or lives. Others believed the cost to our country and our soldiers was necessary to help maintain peace around the world."

Gray's eyes narrowed. "Did any of the students argue directly with you?"

"No. I tried to stay neutral. The discussion grew heated, but I don't remember any student who was angry with me specifically."

"Tell him about the man outside the shop window," Jake prompted.

Chloe repeated what she'd told Jake earlier.

"Do you remember what he looked like?" Gray asked, taking a pen and notebook from his pocket and flipping it open.

"Average height, weight, black hair. There really wasn't anything distinctive about him. He wore a baseball hat pulled down over his eyes and dark sunglasses, so I couldn't see much of his face."

"Do you remember how he was dressed—jacket, shirt?"

"Yes." Chloe related the details she could recall.

"When you saw him, did you have the same uneasy feeling that you said you felt today on campus?"

Chloe's eyes widened as she considered the question. "Yes, it was exactly the same."

"Then maybe you *have* seen the man who's stalking you." Gray looked at his notes, then back at Chloe. "Have you received any threatening phone calls or letters?"

"No, of course not."

"You're sure?"

"I'm positive. Trust me, I'd remember if I'd received anything like that."

"I believe you." Gray closed his notebook and sat back, eyeing the two of them across the table. "Unfortunately, until whoever's stalking you actually does something, there's nothing I can do except take your information and file a report."

"I was afraid of that," Chloe said, glancing at Jake. His face was grim and a muscle flexed along his jawline.

"There must be some way we can flush this guy out," Jake muttered.

"The department's budget doesn't provide for enough manpower to have Chloe followed," Gray said. He nodded thoughtfully. "But unofficially, maybe…"

"What?" Jake demanded.

Gray reached into his inner coat pocket and pulled out a narrow envelope, tapping it against the table. "My aunt gave me her two tickets for the Seattle symphony tomorrow night at Benaroya Hall. If Chloe's willing to go with you, I'll follow you. If we're lucky, our stalker will be so busy watching you he won't notice me."

"I don't like it." Jake scowled. "It puts Chloe in a potentially dangerous situation."

"It's not as if this person has actually threatened me, Jake," she said. "In fact, he hasn't really done anything except watch me. It's creepy, granted, but it's possible he's someone from campus with a crush on me, maybe a student from one of my classes. And if we confront him, it's likely he'll stop. Don't you think that makes sense, Gray?"

The two men exchanged an unreadable look.

"Benaroya Hall is a public place, Jake. It's not likely he'll try anything in a crowd that big," Gray said. "The head of security at the hall is an ex-Seattle PD captain. He can move people around and get me a seat above you so I can search the crowd for anyone who might be watching you instead of the stage. And you'll be with Chloe the entire time, which means he won't have a chance to get near her while she's alone."

"Can we guarantee her safety?"

"I don't think anything in life is a hundred-percent certain, but the odds are in our favor. And," Gray added, "it's our best chance to catch him, or at least get a visual and possible ID. As it stands, we don't have anything solid to work with here."

"All right," Jake said reluctantly. "I'm not crazy about the idea but it sounds like all we've got."

"For now." Gray lifted his coffee cup and silently toasted them. "Here's to catching the SOB, whoever he is."

"Have you heard from that nice Mr. Morrissey?"

"Yes, Gran, I did. In fact, I had lunch with Jake yesterday and he's taking me to the symphony tonight."

Winifred restrained a crow of approval. *Good work, Jake.* She spoke calmly despite her excitement. "How nice, dear. The symphony is always a pleasant evening's entertainment. Benaroya Hall is one of my favorite places. The acoustics are wonderful. What composer is scheduled?"

"Believe it or not, Gran, the program tonight is pop music, mostly Broadway show tunes."

"Really?" Winifred's respect for Jake went up a notch. "I must say I'm impressed with your young man's fortitude."

Chloe laughed. "So am I, Gran. Remember how Grandad grumbled when you and Mom made him take you to a pop music concert?"

"Yes, I do. Your grandfather really disliked pop music. He was a staunch Beethoven and Tchaikovsky man, all the way."

"I remember." Chloe's voice was filled with warmth. "I'd better scoot, Gran, I have to get ready for my date."

"Have fun," Winifred said before she hung up the phone. She looked at the photo of her late husband, framed in crystal and sitting on the kitchen windowsill, next to the phone. "Richard," she said softly, smiling with delight. "The situation between Chloe and Jake is proceeding even better than I'd hoped."

Chloe switched off the portable phone and dropped it on the bed. It landed next to the lacy, pale-green underwear laid out on the spread. A backless emerald sheath with matching silk shawl hung on a padded hanger hooked over the open closet door.

She walked into the bathroom, stripped off her clothes and tossed them in the hamper before stepping into the shower. With quick efficiency, she shampooed, soaped and rinsed, then left the glass stall to towel off and smooth body lotion over still-damp skin. Drying her hair took only moments. It occurred to her as she began to apply makeup that she wouldn't be anticipating the evening quite this happily if Jake wasn't her date.

Okay, so it's not just love of music that has me excited, she thought.

She paused, eye shadow brush in hand, and examined her reflection in the mirror. *Excited.* Yes, she was definitely excited. Jake intrigued her. He made her aware of him as no other man ever had. And he made her want him.

Despite the brief time she'd known Jake, there was something about him that made her heart shriek "mine" whenever she saw him. Her rational mind had no control over the gut-level reaction.

Maybe it was because of the unusual circumstances caused by the possibility of danger from an unknown stalker. Perhaps she was instinctively drawn to Jake's protectiveness.

Or not. She could be totally off base. She had a degree in English literature, not psychology.

I hope Gray catches this man tonight, whoever he is. I never thought I'd say this, but a normal, ordinary, sometimes boring life is beginning to sound better and better.

She finished dressing and went downstairs, shawl and small evening purse in hand. Reaching the foot of the stairs and the slate-floored entryway, she glanced into the living room at the mantel clock just as the doorbell rang. She peered through the side window, verified that the man on her porch was Jake and opened the door.

"Hello." *My, oh, my.* From the top of his well-combed hair to the tips of his polished black shoes—and the black Ralph Lauren suit that clothed the toned, muscled body between—Jake was gorgeous. *If Alexie could only see you, she'd never tease me about my male friends again.*

His gaze swept swiftly downward before returning slowly, lingering, making heat bloom under her skin. She shivered as if he'd trailed his fingertips over her.

"Hi," he said softly. "Ready to go?" He held out his hand, took the shawl from her unresisting fingers, and Chloe suddenly realized that she was standing perfectly still, simply staring at him. Jake's expression was blatantly hungry; she wondered if hers held the same open need.

"Yes."

He stepped closer and slipped the shawl around her shoulders, then tugged gently. She obeyed the slight pressure, joining him on the porch. He bent his head until his lips touched her ear. "In case someone's watching…" he murmured.

Chloe's gaze met his for a brief moment before she tilted her head in silent invitation. The bright blue of his eyes darkened to indigo, and he brushed his lips against hers once, twice, before his mouth settled over hers.

The world narrowed to his mouth on hers. Chloe's knees weakened. Her fingers clutched his sleeve and she leaned into him, his chest and the hard muscles of his thighs supporting her.

When he lifted his head, he left her craving more. She opened her eyes and tightened her grip on his jacket sleeve to keep him from leaving her—until she realized they were standing on her front porch, in full view of her neighbors and anyone passing by.

And that's the point, she remembered belatedly. *We're hoping someone is watching.*

"Let's get out of here." His voice was rougher than usual. He took her hand and led her down the steps, tucking her into the passenger seat of the Porsche.

Chloe checked the side mirror several times as they neared downtown Seattle. "I don't see Gray, do you?"

"He picked us up two blocks from your house."

She searched the mirror again but didn't see a car following them. Traffic was moderately heavy, and all around them cars, trucks and SUVs switched lanes, turned off the street or sped up to pass Jake's Porsche. None of the vehicles appeared to remain steadily behind them. "I can't find him."

"Good." Jake flashed a grin. "Then he's doing his job." He flicked a glance in the mirror. "He's about six cars behind us, opposite lane. He's off duty so he's driving his own car, a gray SUV."

Chloe looked over her shoulder, counted back six cars and found Gray. "Clever. He's very good at this, isn't he?"

"That's why he's a detective."

"I hope he knows how much I appreciate that he's giving up his off-duty time to help me."

"Don't worry about it."

Jake slowed, merging with the line of cars waiting to turn into the Second Avenue entrance to the underground parking lot. It was fifteen minutes before they found a space and left the Porsche.

Chloe draped the shawl around her shoulders and took Jake's arm. "Is Gray parked here, too?"

"One aisle over. The only time we'll be out of his sight is when we take the elevator upstairs to the Boeing Company Gallery. But we'll have lots of other people around us." Jake nodded at the well-dressed couples streaming toward the bank of elevators. "Even if our man is here, the crowd will provide a buffer."

"Right." Chloe's fingers tightened unconsciously on his sleeve.

"Nervous?"

"A little." She looked up to find him watching her. Confidence and strength sat easily on his shoulders and the butterflies in her stomach instantly quieted. She drew a long breath. "I'm fine. Lead on, Macduff."

Jake laughed. "Yes, ma'am."

They rode the elevator up to the gallery and joined the chatting, laughing crowd as it moved on to the Grand Lobby. The curved bank of windows that separated the lobby from the city skyline allowed late-evening sunshine to fall across the plush carpet. Sconces were already lit inside the vast, elegant room, their light glittering on ladies' jewels and highlighting the bright colors of their dresses.

Jake pushed back his cuff and looked at his watch. "We have another fifteen minutes. Would you like a glass of wine?"

"I think I'd just as soon find our seats, if you don't mind."

"Not at all." Jake covered her hand with his where it rested on his arm, pressing it closer in reassurance, before he released her to get their tickets from his coat pocket.

The usher led them down a hallway and then through a door and held open a curtain for them.

"Box seats?" Chloe smiled with delight. "You didn't tell me Gray's aunt had season box seats."

"No?" Jake shrugged. "That's why Gray thought this would work. He's two boxes over and one level up. He can see almost the entire auditorium from there and he'll watch the audience with binoculars. Anyone whose eyes are on us instead of the stage will stand out like a sore thumb."

"If the man's actually in the audience," Chloe said.

"Right," Jake agreed. "And if he isn't, maybe he'll follow us home and Gray will spot him then. And if not," he continued, picking up her hand and threading her fingers through his, "we've spent a nice evening at the symphony. No hardship, right?"

"No." She shook her head. "Definitely not a hardship."

Four hours later, Jake pulled the Porsche into Chloe's driveway and turned off the engine. Chloe reached for the door handle.

"Wait."

She froze. "What is it?" she whispered.

"Maybe nothing."

In the street behind them, a plain blue sedan drew near. The car didn't slow down, didn't speed up. It did nothing to arouse suspicion as it drove past them, the sole occupant never even glancing their way. A moment later, Gray's SUV passed by.

"That was Gray. Do you think he's following the other car?"

"Yeah. I do." Jake pushed open the driver's door and got out, coming around to open Chloe's. He bent toward her and murmured, "Don't look down the street after Gray. Pretend we're just a couple returning from an evening out." She nodded and he took her hand, drawing her from the car, and they walked up the sidewalk to the porch, climbing the steps to her front entry.

Chloe unlocked the door and went inside. Jake followed her, closing the door behind him.

"Don't turn on the lights." He moved swiftly to the narrow side window and shifted the curtain a scant inch to look outside.

Chloe stood in the center of the tiled entryway, her shawl clutched to her chest, barely breathing as the minutes ticked by. The sound of her heartbeat thudded in her ears.

Jake's cell phone rang.

"Yeah?" He was silent, glancing at Chloe. "Thanks, Gray." He switched off the phone and slipped it into his jacket pocket. "Gray thinks the man in the blue car was following us, but he lost him. Whoever was driving the car abandoned it three blocks from here and disappeared. He probably had another car parked near the site and was gone before Gray got there. Gray wasn't close enough to get a visual of the driver."

Chloe's heart sank. "So we still don't have any information about him."

"Don't give up hope. Gray ran the plate numbers on the car and they belong to a pickup truck in Bellevue. I'm guessing both the plates and the car were stolen earlier tonight in separate thefts. Our stalker's careful and he's smart. I'm going to help Gray go over the car." Jake wrapped his arms around Chloe. "Are you okay staying here by yourself?"

She nodded. "Of course."

"Good." Jake dropped a hard kiss on her lips and released her, pulling open the door. "Lock this after me."

"I will." Chloe waited until he'd stepped onto the porch and shut the door, then she slid the dead bolt home and twisted the lock. Peering through a gap in the curtains, she watched him back the Porsche out of her drive, taillights winking red as he disappeared down the block.

Unable to settle down, she poured a giant mug of milk, added three tablespoons of chocolate syrup and popped it into the microwave. While she waited for it to heat, Chloe leaned on the counter, gazing out the window over her sink into the backyard. A full moon rode high in the sky, turning the familiar shapes of lilac tree, rhododendrons, wisteria, apple tree and tall blue spruce into shadowy, mysterious forms.

This was her world, and for the first time, she felt a niggle of fear as she contemplated what might be in her moon-dappled garden besides flowers and trees.

Five

Stealing the stick of dynamite and blasting cap from Morrissey Demolition hadn't been difficult at all.

Morrissey's work site in Black Diamond, southeast of Seattle, had an equipment shack in a large area enclosed within chain-link fencing. The locked-off area held parked bulldozers, backhoes, massive concrete-and-metal culverts and other equipment owned by Warren Construction, the Washington State contractor responsible for building a twenty-mile section of road. The contractor had a security service that patrolled the area once every hour to protect the expensive equipment and supplies stored inside the fence.

He had no interest in any of that. He only cared about Morrissey's dynamite.

The small bolt cutters snipped through the chain links of the fence and made short work of the padlock securing the Morrissey storage shed. Once he was inside, it was a matter of minutes to locate the powder magazine, cut the bolts holding the double-hooded locks that secured it, slice through the locks and open the steel box. The magazine's interior was lined with wood to ensure no accidental spark from exposed metal could threaten the stability of the explosives. He found just a handful of dynamite sticks but he didn't care. He needed only one.

He removed the eight-inch-long brown stick and placed it in a narrow wooden box, then stowed the box in his jacket pocket. Carefully closing the powder magazine, he rearranged the locks so a casual observer would see nothing amiss.

The detonator caps were stored in a second locked box. He cut through the locks, removed a cap with its attached wires and tucked it into the small tote he'd carried in with him. When he'd closed the box, he rearranged the locks, then picked up the black tote bag and his bolt cutters, and checked his watch.

He smiled. His timing was perfect. The security guard wasn't due for another twenty minutes. He eased the shed door open and peered out. The bright moonlight was the only flaw in his plan. Fortunately, the huge pieces of earthmoving equipment and stacks of supplies threw giant shadows over the exposed spaces between him and safety.

He crept out of the shack and hung the sliced padlock back on the hasp. Its appearance wouldn't withstand close scrutiny, but in the dark, it would suffice.

He stood very still, scanning the area. Nothing moved. Satisfied, he ran toward the fence, moving quickly from shadow to shadow. He slipped through the fence, taking time to bend the wire into place again.

With a last backward glance, he melted into the brush and trees. Ten minutes later, he was driving northwest. Within the hour, he'd reached his apartment in Seattle's Capitol Hill district and was hidden once more.

He wondered which one of Morrissey's crew had followed him from Chloe Abbott's house earlier. Stealing license plates and pairing them with nondescript stolen cars was a strategy he'd used often while tailing Morrissey over the past six weeks. Tonight his caution had paid off.

He opened his journal and began to write, satisfaction buoying him.

Morrissey didn't have enough hours left to stop the sequence of events that was about to destroy him.

From: Winifred@Codebreakers.org
To: Clara@AppleButterLadies.com
Sent: May 22
Subject: Good morning—

Dear Clara,

I have interesting news to share! I spoke with Chloe last night and learned she'd had lunch with Jake Morrissey yesterday. And he took her to the symphony last night. (Picture me gleefully dancing a jig in my living room. : -)

I really like this young man and it appears Chloe might, too. Wouldn't it be lovely if all three of our granddaughters were planning weddings??!! Stay tuned for further developments.

Helen telephoned yesterday to discuss the final details for our trip to British Columbia to celebrate my birthday. She wants to tour Victoria in a horse-drawn carriage after high tea at the Empress Hotel. I voted "yes" on that suggestion, of course, and we both want to browse the shops for tins of good English tea. I'd like to find a new Scottish wool blanket, also, just a small one to cover my lap while I'm reading on rainy winter days. Is there anything special we can pick up for you, Clara? I wish you were going with us—it just won't be the same without you there. But next year, the three of us will spend my birthday somewhere equally fun.

I'd better get busy. I'll let you know the moment
I hear from Chloe about her date with Jake.
All my love,
Winifred

Chloe carried a large glass of ice water and the stack
of essays onto her back deck and set them on the glass
table in the shade of the patio umbrella. She dropped
into a wrought-iron chair. Stretching out her legs, she
crossed her ankles and sighed with pleasure. The late-
afternoon sun slanted across the gray-painted wood
deck, warming her bare legs. The umbrella's shade
blocked the sunshine from her upper body. Still, the
heat and bright sky were a welcome change from the
showers and gray days of two weeks earlier.

*Only in Seattle do you need a wool sweater under
your raincoat one week, and two weeks later, you can
sit in the sun wearing shorts with a tank top,* she
thought. *Gotta love this city.*

She straightened her arms over her head and arched
her back, stretching luxuriously. Then she pulled the
stack of essays closer, picked up the top one and began
to read. Red pencil in hand, she worked her way through
half the pile before taking a break.

Jake had called earlier to fill her in on developments
since last night. They hadn't found any identifying information or fingerprints in the abandoned sedan. The
truck owner had reported his license plates stolen this
morning and had no idea why they were on a sedan.
Gray was running the VIN number in an attempt to
trace the car, but he expected that the sedan had been
stolen, too.

Jake also mentioned that he'd spent most of the day
at his company's current work site in Black Diamond.
During the night, someone had broken into the Mor-

rissey Demolition storage shed and stolen dynamite. The foreman of the road construction crew swore nothing was missing from his list of equipment and supplies, so it appeared the thief had targeted only the explosives.

Jake sounded frustrated with the dead ends and delays, and she was just as disappointed as he was when he had to cancel their dinner plans. She'd settled for a mixed salad with slices of barbecued chicken, eaten on her patio in the sunshine.

Taking a water bottle with her, Chloe returned to the deck and sank into her chair again. It was now almost eight o'clock. She picked up the next essay, but two paragraphs in, she frowned and sat up straighter. Each paragraph had a group of letters—gibberish—enclosed in parentheses.

She flipped to the cover sheet to check the writer's name, and to her surprise, there wasn't one. The other necessary elements were present—class title and number, professor's name, date, the title of the essay: "The American Military: Friend or Enemy?"

Even more puzzled, she went through the stack of essays on the table, then her list of students enrolled in the class. There were five fewer essays than students, but three of them had already contacted her and been given permission to deliver their work late. One of those students had broken his arm in a pickup game of football; one's National Guard unit had been activated and she was training in Yakima; the third was at a funeral in Tucson. The remaining two students had distinctive writing styles and she felt sure she could rule them out.

If none of the students registered in her class had written this essay, then who had? Chloe knew anyone could have dropped the paper through the mail slot in her door; students delivered work that way all the time. She didn't remember finding this particular document on her office floor and filing it with the other essays, but it was more than likely she'd done so without giving it a thought. Still, why would anyone have gone to such lengths—writing and delivering a paper for a class in which he or she wasn't even registered?

She picked up the mysterious essay to resume reading where she'd left off, and by the time she'd finished, her inner alarms were shrieking. There was something decidedly off-kilter about the essay. Not only were all the paragraphs interspersed with parentheses enclosing collections of letters that she couldn't understand, but the author made angry, disparaging remarks about the military in general and the Marine Corps in particular. Something about the gibberish in the parentheses felt vaguely familiar, but she couldn't seem to grasp why.

The essay ended with a paragraph alleging government collusion to conceal the truth about the death of marines in combat situations abroad. Thee was a specific reference to military personnel dying in Afghanistan.

Chloe stared at the typed pages, trying to see a pattern that might reveal a hidden message or a clue that might tell her the identity of the writer. Unfortunately, she found nothing that made sense.

Gran could probably take one look at this and know if the writer had hidden a message in the words.

She pushed back her chair decisively, gathered up the papers and hurried into the house. She dropped the stack of essays on the table and ran upstairs to collect a light sweater. She grabbed her purse, slipping her feet into leather sandals, and after checking to make sure all the locks in the house were secure, drove to Winifred's.

Chloe mulled over the style and the content of the essay tucked into her purse. However, she was no closer to deciphering the puzzle when she reached her grandmother's home.

Winifred answered her knock almost immediately and smiled with pleasure. "Why, Chloe, come in, dear."

"Hi, Gran." Chloe stepped past Winifred and into the entryway, turning to look at her grandmother. "Sorry to come by so late, but I need your help."

"Of course." Winifred's gaze sharpened and frown lines appeared between her brows. "Join me in the kitchen. I was going to have a glass of iced tea. You can tell me all about it."

Chloe followed Winifred down the hall to the big kitchen, sitting down in a chair at the oak table by the big window. The table already held a crystal pitcher, a Wedgewood plate with several cookies and a tall glass. Winifred took another glass and spoon from the cupboard and sat across from her.

"I'll pour," Winifred said as she picked up the pitcher. "While you tell me what has you so worried."

"It's this essay, Gran." Chloe removed the three-page document from her purse and laid it on the table between them. "Whoever wrote it clearly has issues with the American military, particularly the Marines, but there are also weird words, gibberish really, spaced throughout. I can't make any sense of it."

"Whoever wrote it? What do you mean? Isn't the writer one of your students?" She finished pouring the iced tea, set a glass in front of Chloe and stirred sugar into her own.

"That's another odd thing." Chloe slid the stapled papers closer to her grandmother and pointed at the top sheet. "The writer didn't sign his or her name. It's anonymous."

Winifred raised her eyebrows, bending forward to read the cover page. "Well, that certainly *is* odd. How does he expect to get credit for his work?"

"I don't think he does. I don't think the writer is one of my students."

"Then why would he turn in the essay?" Winifred asked slowly, setting aside glass and spoon to pick up the papers.

"I don't know," Chloe said. "I'm sure this essay was with a group of several others that students dropped through the slot in my office door. There's something about the gibberish that nags at me. I feel as if I should know what it means, but I don't. It's just letters strung together. I'm hoping you can give me some insight."

Winifred began to read. Chloe sipped her tea, nibbled on a Hob Nob cookie and waited impatiently for her to finish.

Finally, Winifred reached the last page and looked up.

"Well? What do you think it means?"

"First, I agree with you. There's something familiar about the letters in parentheses," Winifred said thoughtfully. "I don't think they're merely random." She paused, a faraway look in her eyes, her fingers drumming on the table. "Of course." She pushed back her chair.

"What?"

"I'll be right back." Winifred hurried out of the room. Chloe heard her footsteps as she moved quickly down the hall, and guessed she'd gone to her office off the living room. Moments later Winifred reappeared, carrying a thick hardcover book, a pad of paper and a pen.

She sat down, handed Chloe the pen and notepaper, and opened the book to the index.

Chloe turned her head, twisting to read the title of the book. *Codebreakers Through History*. She straightened in her chair. "Gran, do you see a pattern? Do you think the letters are a code?"

"They might be…."

Chloe pulled the essay closer and looked at the first grouping of letters enclosed in parentheses. "Yildoc," she read out loud. "You think that's a word?"

"It might be. Ah, here it is." Winifred leafed through the book, stopping to scan a page before turning to the next. "Yes," she said with satisfaction. "I need you to spell out the letters for me, then write down what I tell you, Chloe."

"Okay. The first one is Y-I-L-D-O-C."

Winifred ran her fingertip down a list. *"J."*

"The letter *J?*" Chloe asked.

"Yes. What's the next set of letters within parentheses?"

"T-S-E-N-I-L."

"That's an *A.*" She waited for Chloe to jot down the letter and find the next parenthetical set of letters.

"J-A-D-H-O-L-N-I."

"That's a *K.* Next."

"A-H-N-A-H."

"That's an *E.* Next."

Chloe stared at the letters she'd written down. "Gran."

Winifred looked up. "Yes?"

"We just spelled *Jake.*"

Winifred nodded abruptly. "Then I was right. Whoever wrote the essay used the World War II code based on the Navajo language."

"So you're saying a Navajo wrote the essay?"

"Not necessarily. The code was never broken during the war and was kept top secret. It wasn't officially recognized by the Pentagon until 1992. But since then, there have been articles written about the Navajo code-breakers and how the code worked. I believe Hollywood even made a movie called *Windtalkers* about the use of the Navajo code during the war in the Pacific. Public knowledge about the subject has definitely increased over the past several years."

"So anyone who wanted to could look up the code and learn how to use it."

"Technically speaking, yes. I'm sure the details are available on the Internet somewhere, since most things are these days. Using the code orally would be almost impossible for anyone except a Navajo because the language itself is extremely complex. It's almost unintelligible to anyone except a native. But to write it—" Winifred tapped the essay in front of Chloe "—that's quite easy, really. All you'd have to do is look up the English letters of the alphabet and the Navajo words assigned to them."

"But these don't look like words."

"I know. Whoever wrote them neglected to hyphenate them where needed. For instance, 'yildoc' is really Yil-Doc, and 'jadholni' is Jad-Ho-Loni. Nonetheless, it's clear to me that the Navajo code is the basis for the words enclosed in parentheses."

"And the first word is *Jake*. Why would someone encode his name in an essay given to me?"

"That's the real mystery, isn't it?" Winifred's expression was solemn. "Let's finish going through the letters in parentheses and see what words we have when we're done."

Several moments later, Chloe and Winifred stared at the three names.

"Jake Morrissey, Chloe Abbott and Kenny Dodd," Winifred read slowly. "Why is your name here, Chloe? And who is Kenny Dodd?"

"I don't know, Gran, but I'm going to find out." Chloe took her cell phone from her purse and dialed Jake's number.

Six

When Jake received Chloe's call, Gray was at his apartment. They arrived at Winifred's house together, Jake's Porsche closely followed by Gray's SUV as they pulled into the circular driveway.

Chloe met them at the front door.

"What happened?" Jake demanded, his gaze running over her, searching for signs of damage.

"Come into the kitchen. Gran can help me explain." She said hello to Gray, standing behind Jake. "I'm glad you're here, Gray. You need to hear this, too."

She led them down the hall to the kitchen and introduced Gray to Winifred.

"Sit down, gentlemen." Winifred gestured at two empty chairs and looked at Chloe. "Why don't you start, Chloe."

Chloe nodded and, as succinctly as possible, told them about the essay and the encoded words.

Gray turned to Jake. "Who's Kenny Dodd?"

"He's a kid who died in Afghanistan." Jake's face was grim. "He was in the wrong place at the wrong time when I detonated a charge I'd set to take out a bridge."

Chloe's heart cramped at the expression of stark pain that flashed across his features. *He feels responsible for that young soldier's death.*

Gray whistled softly. "So the stalker is connected to the military, not to your demolition work."

"Yeah," Jake said. "I guess so. We've been looking in the wrong place, at the wrong people."

"No wonder we didn't find anything."

"Whoa." Chloe lifted her hand. "What are you saying? You've 'been looking.' Is this my stalker or your stalker?"

Jake's eyes were unreadable, but they met hers without flinching. "It's possible the person following you may really be after me."

Chloe could only stare at him, speechless, as scenes from the last few days ran through her mind—the man outside David's shop window, the eerie feeling that someone was following her on campus, the blue sedan driving by her house after the symphony. The man was stalking her because she'd met Jake?

"Gray and I suspected that might be the case. You told me the feeling that someone was watching you didn't start until after the photos of us appeared in the *Tribune*," Jake continued.

"That's true," she murmured, frowning.

"The photo may have been the catalyst that caused the stalker to link you with me."

Chloe thought about the group of photos that had accompanied the article and cold fear gripped her. "My grandmother was in those pictures, too."

"Have you noticed any strangers watching you, Mrs. Abbott?" Jake asked. "Maybe a car following you when you leave the house?"

"No. Nothing like that," Winifred said firmly. "And

I would have noticed." She turned to Chloe. "Why didn't you tell me what's been going on?"

"I thought it was probably a student with a crush on me, Gran. It made me nervous because it's a little creepy, knowing someone might be stalking me, but I wasn't really afraid for my safety."

"And there's every reason to believe you shouldn't be afraid, even now," Gray put in. "As we've said, the primary target appears to be Jake. Someone's been shadowing him for weeks, and the fact that you're having the same experience so soon after the photos were made public indicates you're a secondary interest."

"You're sure? Because I won't leave town if Chloe's in danger." Concern shaded Winifred's voice.

"Gran's taking the *Queen Victoria* cruise ship to Victoria, B.C., in the morning," Chloe explained, answering Jake's unspoken question. "It's only an overnight trip—a birthday gift from a friend."

"Ah." He nodded. "I don't think Chloe's in real danger, Mrs. Abbott. We believe the man's after me and he's only interested in Chloe because he saw her with me in the photo."

"Okay, then." Chloe drew a deep breath and covered Winifred's hand with hers. "I think you should go to Victoria, Gran, and have a great time. Have high tea at the Empress Hotel, visit Butchart Gardens and shop till you drop. With any luck, by the time you get home, Jake and Gray will have found this person and solved the puzzle. And our lives will go back to being quiet, normal and totally boring."

Winifred's eyes twinkled. "At my age, Chloe, a little excitement makes life interesting. But I'll settle for tea at the Empress."

"Great." Chloe kissed her cheek, relieved that her grandmother would be safely out of town until Jake and Gray had time to apprehend the stalker, whoever he was.

The three took their leave of Winifred. Jake walked Chloe to her car and opened the door.

"I'll be back in a minute. I need to talk to Gray."

"All right." Chloe slid into the driver's seat, watching in her rearview mirror as Jake walked back to Gray's SUV, parked behind his Porsche, which was blocking Chloe.

The two men spoke for a few minutes, then Gray reversed out of the driveway to park on the street while Jake walked back to her car.

He leaned down, resting his forearms on the window. "Come home with me, Chloe."

"What?" Startled, she could only stare at him.

He swore under his breath. "Not to sleep with me. Not unless you want to," he amended, his lips curving in a slight grin that swiftly disappeared. "I'd just feel better if you were close enough for me to keep an eye on tonight."

"I don't want to leave my home."

He sighed. "I didn't think you would. So I've asked Gray to have one of his off-duty cop friends stand guard outside your house tonight. Calling in a favor," he added. "Since we still don't have enough evidence to get the police involved, we'll continue to handle this unofficially."

"You're that worried?"

"No. I'm that careful."

Chloe's eyes darted to her grandmother's house, but before she could speak, Jake reassured her. "Gray's going to stay and watch over Winifred." He looked over his shoulder. "He backed out of the driveway to let us leave. He'll pull back in when we're gone and park in plain sight. If our stalker plans to bother Winifred, Gray will be waiting for him."

"Thank goodness." Relief washed over Chloe. "Will he stay until the limo picks her up in the morning?"

"Yes." Jake leaned into the car and pressed a hard kiss against her mouth. "I'll follow you home. By the time we get there, Gray's friend should have arrived and he'll park outside your house, just like Gray's doing here."

"Where will you be?" She struggled to speak above a whisper. He'd stolen her breath and sidetracked her ability to think with that kiss.

"At my apartment working. I need access to my computer and other files to track down information on Kenny Dodd. Otherwise, I'd be the guard in the car outside your door."

Chloe smiled at him, touched. "You're such a Galahad."

"Not hardly," he growled. "And if I ever get you alone at my place, I'll prove it."

She laughed and he walked back to his car. The engine turned over with a throaty growl and he backed the sports car out of Winifred's driveway, waiting for her to precede him.

Chloe glanced out the living room window the following morning. The silver sedan with Gray's friend behind the steering wheel was still parked in her driveway.

"Bless you, Jake," she said out loud. "What would I do without you and your friends?"

She walked into the kitchen where the automatic timer had switched on the grind-and-brew coffeemaker fifteen minutes earlier. The welcoming aroma of fresh coffee pervaded the air and she poured a cup, taking a sip before setting it on the counter. When she'd replenished the bird feeder outside, she'd get some coffee for the officer, too. She filled a plastic quart pitcher with birdseed from a large bag in the pantry and opened the door to the deck overlooking her backyard. As soon as she stepped outside, her foot connected with something solid.

"What...?"

A large shoe box sat on the gray deck and the contact with her sandal had knocked the lid askew. Chloe couldn't see exactly what was inside, but what she could see chilled her blood.

Feathers spattered with crimson, and thin shattered bones were visible.

Chloe spun on her heel and ran back into the house, locking the door behind her. She grabbed the phone from its base and dialed Jake's number.

"Jake? There's something on my back deck. I—I think it's dead."

Fifteen minutes later, Jake pulled into Chloe's driveway, loped up the sidewalk and knocked loudly on her door. It was opened by the rumpled, young off-duty cop with bleary eyes who'd spent the night outside her house.

"Hey, Jake." He jerked his head toward the kitchen. "She's in there."

"What did she find?"

"A shoe box with pieces of a dead seagull inside. Looks like somebody blew it up, maybe with a big firecracker of some sort, then put it inside the box. Her name was written in big block letters on the lid. She didn't touch it and neither did I. I called the PD. They're sending out someone to collect the evidence and take a report."

"Damn." Jake strode quickly down the hall and into the kitchen. Chloe sat at the table, cradling a mug of coffee in her hands. She glanced over her shoulder, saw him and stood. Her face was pale, her green eyes dark and vulnerable.

He held open his arms and she walked into them, her hands clutching the back of his shirt.

"Hey, babe," he murmured. "You okay?"

"No." Her voice was muffled against his throat. "It was awful, Jake. Why would anyone do that to a bird?"

"I don't know. Some people's actions are beyond understanding."

She nodded, her hair brushing his throat and chin. "Yes." Her voice was steadier, stronger. She leaned back and looked up at him. "How long before you catch this person?"

"Maybe today."

Her eyes widened with interest.

"I was up most of the night tracking down information on Kenny Dodd. He joined the Marines with a friend, Alan Granstrom. Granstrom's currently living in Mason city, Oregon, the same town where he grew up. I'm driving down there this morning."

"You think Alan Granstrom might have information about the person stalking us?"

"I think it could be Granstrom himself who's following us. When Dodd was killed, Alan Granstrom was there and he blamed me for his death. He went crazy, even threw a few punches at me. I chalked it up to shock and grief under battle pressure and forgot about it. I never thought he'd be carrying a grudge after all this time."

"But someone has, and it might be him."

"It might be him," Jake said. "In fact, I hope it is, because then we'll have a name and a face for our stalker. Up until now, we've been looking for a phantom. If we'd been able to get fingerprints from the sedan, we could've included Granstrom or ruled him out because his prints are in the military database. But whoever our man is, he was smart enough to wipe the car clean." Jake paused. "I have to check out Alan Granstrom in person."

"How long will you be gone?"

"Most of the day. It's a three-to-four-hour drive, one way. And I have no idea how long it'll take to find Granstrom and talk to him. I doubt I'll be back in Seattle before tonight."

"I'm going with you," Chloe said decisively. "I'll call my department head and ask if someone else can cover my two classes today."

Jake thought swiftly, weighing the value of having her safely under his watchful eye versus the unknown situation waiting for him in Oregon. Having her near him, where he could make sure she was safe, won out. "All right." He released her and looked at his watch. "It's after nine. Make your call and get whatever you need."

"Why isn't Gray going with you?" Chloe asked, suddenly remembering the detective's interest in their stalker.

"He has to testify in court today on another case."

Within the hour, they were driving south on Interstate 5 toward Portland, Starbucks lattes in the cup holders on the console between them, the Dave Matthews Band growling out "Crash" on the car's CD player.

"There's the exit." Chloe pointed at the highway sign with Mason City spelled out in big white letters against a forest-green background.

The town's cluster of buildings was visible from the highway, and Jake slowed to a crawl as they drove through the business center. Shops and stores lined both sides of the wide street, and although small, the town appeared to be prosperous and well kept.

"Alan Granstrom's address is 238 Tenth Street." Jake noted the cross streets as they approached an intersection.

"We just passed Eighth," Chloe said.

"So, do we turn right or left on Tenth?"

"I vote for left."

Jake waited for an oncoming car to pass before he turned left. The Porsche's engine purred as they moved down the street, which changed from a small-business area to a residential one.

Chloe peered out the open car window to read house numbers. "Six-forty, six-twenty, six hundred," she mumbled to herself. "We're going in the right direction."

The tree-shaded boulevard drowsed in the early afternoon sunshine. Sprinklers arced sprays of water across green lawns and children played at a corner city park.

"There." Chloe pointed to a tidy bungalow, set well back on a neat square of lawn with flower borders edging the walk.

Jake parked the Porsche at the curb and turned to her. "I want you to stay in the car."

"Why?"

"If Granstrom's our stalker, there's no way of knowing how he'll react. I don't want you in the line of fire."

"I'll feel much safer with you than staying out here alone."

Jake was silent for a moment. Then he shrugged, thrust open the driver's side door and got out. By the time he reached the sidewalk, Chloe was waiting for him, impatient to proceed.

"I hope someone's home," she said as they walked to the porch and climbed the steps.

"So do I," Jake agreed. "And I hope Granstrom's our guy." He rapped on the locked screen door and waited, then rapped again, louder this time.

"Coming!" The feminine voice was followed by the hurried sound of footsteps on a wooden floor. A young woman appeared, a toddler perched on her hip. She studied them through the screen. "Yes?"

"We're looking for Alan Granstrom. Is he home?"

"Yes—he's got a day off. Can I tell him who's visiting?"

"A friend—I served in Afghanistan with Alan. We're passing through town and just wanted to say hello."

She smiled, obviously reassured by Jake's words,

and pushed open the screen. "Come on in." She raised her voice and half turned to call over her shoulder. "Alan! You have company."

The door eased shut behind Jake and Chloe just as the toddler began to cry. The woman patted the baby's back and waved them toward the living room. "Go on in. Excuse me—I have to change her diaper." She hurried off, disappearing up the stairs.

Chloe lifted an eyebrow at Jake, who merely shrugged and gestured toward the room. As they stepped through the archway, he moved ahead of her, placing his body between her and the man walking toward them.

The lanky, blond-haired man in his early thirties, wearing jeans and a T-shirt, halted abruptly when he saw Jake. "Morrissey? What are you doing here?"

"Granstrom." Jake nodded hello, his tone neutral. "This is Chloe Abbott."

Chloe and Alan exchanged polite nods before he looked at Jake once again, clearly puzzled.

"We have a few questions to ask you about Kenny Dodd," Jake continued.

"Kenny?" Alan shook his head in confusion. "What about Kenny?"

"Someone threatened Chloe in a document that included Kenny's name."

Alan's eyebrows shot up and he stared at Chloe. "I don't get it. What does that have to do with me?"

"It's pretty simple. Chloe's been threatened and stalked by someone in Seattle. So have I. And both our names have been tied to Kenny by the person who's following us." Jake's expression was lethal. "You went ballistic when Kenny died, and you made it clear that you blamed me for his death. You were the first person I thought of when Kenny's name came up."

Understanding dawned and Alan immediately shook

his head. "Oh, no. You've got the wrong guy. In the first place, I haven't left town. Ask anybody—ask my wife, ask my boss. And even if I had the time, I don't have the need. I put what happened in Afghanistan behind me when I got out of the marines. I've got a life here, a wife, a baby, a decent job…. Nope." He shook his head again, underlining his words. "The only person I know who's still obsessed with Kenny's death is his dad."

"His father? Have you talked to him recently?" Jake asked.

"Sure. He lives two streets over from me. I've known him since I was a kid. Kenny and I grew up together. We were pretty much inseparable, and if he wasn't at my house, I was at his. We even enlisted together."

"When did you last see Kenny's father?"

"About two months ago, I guess, maybe a little longer. He was stirred up over a copy of the incident report he finally got from the military about Kenny's death. Come to think of it…" He paused, eyeing Jake. "He told me he'd figured the Marines would make you pay for killing Kenny. He ranted about the military failing to make sure justice was done."

"What can you tell me about him?"

"Why are you asking all these questions about Kenny's dad?" Granstrom's eyes narrowed with suspicion. "Why should I tell you anything?"

Jake shrugged. "You can tell me or you can tell the police. It's up to you. But if there's a squad car parked outside your door, the neighbors are going to get curious. Your call."

Granstrom's eyes flickered to the stairway. "All right, ask your questions," he said in a low voice. "What do you want to know?"

"For starters, what's his full name?"

"George Dodd."

"How old is he?"

"I'm guessing late fifties, maybe a bit older."

"What does he do? Is he retired or still working?"

"He's a widower. Retired—has been for a few years. He left the union just before my dad did."

"The union?"

"Yeah. My dad and Kenny's dad were electricians. They worked out of the Union Hall over in Greensburg."

Although a foot of space separated them, Chloe felt Jake tense.

"You said Dodd lives near here—do you have his address?"

Alan gave them the information and after a few more questions and answers, Jake and Chloe left. They were in the car, pulling away from the curb, before Chloe spoke.

"This man's an electrician and he's retired, which means he has an independent income and can travel. Plus, he has reason to hate you."

"Yeah, add it all up and George Dodd is looking more and more like our prime suspect."

Seven

They easily located the address Alan had given them. The walkway leading from the street to the front door of the 1940s bungalow was lined with neglected flower beds.

"It doesn't seem like anyone's home," Chloe said, surveying the ragged grass and yellowing newspapers lying on the doorstep.

"Not for some time," Jake agreed. He knocked on the door, then knocked again, harder. There was only silence. "Let's try around the back."

They followed the sidewalk that curved around the house to the rear. Despite the overgrown flower beds, it was apparent that the house itself had been well-cared-for by its owner.

Jake pounded on the back door. No response. He turned in a slow circle, scanning the backyard. A high wooden fence blocked the neighbors' view, while the house concealed them from any passerby on the street or sidewalk.

He bent and slipped a knife from inside his boot.

Chloe almost gasped. The blade was long and wickedly lethal. "What are you going to do with *that?*"

"Unlock the door." He nodded toward the walkway at the side of the house. "Keep watch, will you? Some neighbor might start wondering why a strange car is parked out front."

Chloe left the doorstep and peered around the corner of the house. The lawn, sidewalk and the street beyond were quiet in the warm sunshine.

"Ah, got it."

She looked over her shoulder. Jake pushed open the door, pausing to slip the knife back into the hidden sheath in his boot top. He beckoned and she left her post to rejoin him.

They stepped into the silent kitchen, closing the door. The room was spotlessly clean, the tiled floor gleaming, the counters and white cabinets immaculate.

"I've never been in a man's house this clean," Chloe whispered.

"Yeah, it's practically sterile."

Jake walked out of the kitchen, with Chloe behind him. The small dining area was as pristine and neat as the kitchen. They passed through it, skirting the square maple table with four chairs aligned precisely opposite each other, and entered the living room. The furnishings were neither expensive nor new, and the sofa, with its matching upholstered chair, had wear marks on the arms, but all was tidy and clean.

"I don't see evidence of anything other than that George Dodd is amazingly neat." She moved down the hall and looked into the bathroom, the door open wide. "And even though that's unusual for a man living alone, it doesn't prove he's our crazy stalker."

"No." Jake's voice came from farther down the hall. "It doesn't. But I've got a feeling about Dodd." He opened and closed doors, glancing briefly into rooms, before joining Chloe again. "Let's get out of here. It's clear no one's been here for some time, and if Dodd is our man, then he's somewhere in Seattle."

They retraced their steps through the living room, dining room and into the kitchen.

"Wait." Chloe stopped him just before he opened the door leading to the backyard. A phone was mounted on the wall next to the refrigerator. The top corner of the fridge door held a narrow pad of paper with a magnetized back. A pencil stub was attached to the pad by a neatly knotted length of fishing line.

"What is it?"

"Shouldn't we check the message pad? I've read hundreds of mystery novels, and the amateur detectives always check the blank pad for pencil impressions."

"Couldn't hurt. Go for it." Jake half grinned, waiting patiently while Chloe went to stare at the pad.

She squinted at it, frowning. "I think he might actually have written something on the pad, then torn off the paper. There seem to be words…." She took the dangling pencil stub and carefully rubbed the lead over the paper.

Jake bent closer to read the shaded letters. "Sunshine Real? No, Sunshine Realty. And the rest is a phone number—with Seattle's area code."

Chloe dropped the pencil and ripped off the sheet. "The phone number for a Realtor in Seattle? Maybe he used them to find an apartment or a house to rent?"

"I'm betting you're right." He took the paper, folded it and tucked it into his shirt pocket. "Smart lady."

They left the house, locking the door behind them. Jake called Gray as soon as they were in the car and on their way out of town.

"Gray? It's Jake." He turned onto the highway and headed north. "Granstrom didn't pan out, but he gave us some valuable information. Kenny Dodd's father still lives in Mason City. Granstrom says Dodd blames me for Kenny's death and he left town about eight weeks ago, right after receiving the military incident report."

Chloe listened to Jake's half of the conversation.

"Hold on a sec." He lowered the phone to hold it and the steering wheel in one hand while he fished the slip of paper out of his pocket with the other. "He left the phone number of a Seattle realty office on the pad in his kitchen. Want to check it out?" He read off the number, then glanced at Chloe and the corner of his mouth lifted in a half smile. "No. He tore off the note, but Chloe saw the impression his pencil made on the pad beneath."

His smile disappeared. "Yeah, do that." He looked at his dashboard clock. "We should be back in town by eight or so—too late to do anything tonight. Right, see you tomorrow." Gray apparently had another question. Jake responded. "No, she's staying with me until we figure this out. Right."

He rang off, put down the phone and slipped the folded paper back into his pocket.

"You told Gray I'm staying with you?"

"Yes." He met her gaze briefly, then looked again at the empty highway stretching ahead of them. "Gut instinct tells me there's more to this than we know. And I always listen to my gut."

Chloe was silent for a moment, considering. "I have to admit I'm more than a little leery about Mr. Dodd myself. So I'll accept your offer to be my bodyguard until we find him." His mouth curved in a swift smile, filled with more than a little satisfaction. "But if you're offering to guard me just to get me up to your apartment alone…" She paused.

Jake sent her a questioning glance.

"You didn't need to go to these lengths," she said softly. "All you had to do was ask me up to see your etchings. I would've said yes."

His eyes heated. "I'll remember that."

"Please do."

"I love a woman who knows her own mind." He reached across the console and took her hand from her lap, raised it to his mouth and pressed a hot, open-mouthed kiss into her palm. Then he laid her hand, palm down, on his thigh.

Chloe shivered, fully aware that she'd taken an irrevocable step. Anticipation pulsed through her veins, heated by the flex of powerful muscles beneath her hand as he shifted gears. She settled back and watched the scenery flash by.

It was after 9:00 p.m. when they arrived in Seattle and turned into the alleyway behind Jake's building. He triggered a remote control. Ahead of them, a garage door set into the brick wall of the warehouse began to rise. Once they'd driven inside, the headlights swept over the cavernous interior. The door rumbled smoothly down behind them, shutting out the night.

Chloe had a quick impression of space and high ceilings before Jake switched off the engine and headlights, throwing the area into blackness. The Porsche's dome light came on when Jake pushed open the door; Chloe got out, too, quickly surveying the surrounding space. Then the big room went dark again. The only illumination came from a glowing yellow bulb mounted over a door at their far right.

"Hey, Jake."

"Max." Jake caught Chloe's hand and drew her with him toward the doorway. "Any problems?"

"None. If anything, it's too quiet." A man stepped out of the shadows, an assault weapon cradled in his arms.

"Let's hope it stays like that."

Max nodded and turned away. Chloe noticed light

eyes in a handsome face and dark hair tied back at his nape before he disappeared into the shadows.

"Who was that?" she whispered to Jake as they went through the doorway and climbed a set of stairs.

"Max Luken. He works for me." He unlocked a door at the top of the stairway, pushed it inward and waited for Chloe to enter.

Moonlight poured through skylights, throwing cool light and dark shadows over the apartment.

Jake's hands closed over her shoulders and he brushed his mouth against the side of her throat. Chloe turned in his embrace, sliding her arms around his neck.

He pinned her against the wall with his body and covered her mouth with his.

"Next time, we'll make it to the bedroom," he muttered. "I promise."

Jake drove Chloe to UW the next morning, in time for her ten o'clock class, leaving her at the open lecture-hall door. She walked inside and dropped her books on the table, reassured by his solid presence in the shade of the big old walnut tree.

An hour later, Chloe left the lecture hall by the side door. Despite the unresolved threat posed by George Dodd, anticipation at the prospect of spending the next few hours with Jake made her lighthearted. Her smile faded when she discovered that he wasn't waiting for her. She reached the tree and stopped beneath its leafy shade, but there was no sign of him anywhere.

"Where is he?" she wondered out loud.

After a few minutes, she gave up and set off alone down the walkway toward Liberty Hall.

Keys in one hand and cell phone in the other, she punched in Jake's number as she slipped the office key into the lock. The pile of books in her arms began to slide and she grabbed for the top two but there were too many to catch. Gravity took control and she let the phone slide into her skirt pocket while she struggled to keep from dropping the entire stack.

"Darn it." Annoyed, she pushed open the door, concentrating on juggling the armload of books and still hold on to her purse and briefcase while she hurried into her office. She tumbled the pile onto her desk; two of the books kept sliding and hit the floor behind the desk.

She heard the door click shut.

"Miss Abbott. How nice of you to join us."

Chloe spun to face the closed door. A man stood with his back against it. He wore a gray suit and a cap with Executive Limos embroidered in black above the shiny bill. The small, lethal-looking black gun, pointed directly at her, was rock steady in his hand.

In the corner to his right was Winifred, her hands secured with plastic handcuffs in front of her, silver duct tape over her mouth.

"Gran!" Chloe jerked, taking a quick instinctive step toward her grandmother. The man's voice stopped her.

"No, no. Stay where you are." He smiled gently. "Unless, of course, you want to see your grandmother hurt."

"Who are you?"

"My name is George Dodd. But I'm sure you've guessed that by now."

Jake leaned against the walnut tree's trunk and watched through the open door as Chloe began her class. Ten minutes into her scheduled hour, his phone rang. Gray had the address of George Dodd's Seattle residence. Jake immediately paged Max, stationed in the parking lot to watch the Porsche in case Dodd decided to target it. Max took over guard duty for Chloe, and Jake broke speed limits on his way to Capitol Hill.

Gray was waiting for him on the sidewalk outside a run-down apartment building near downtown Seattle.

"This is the address you have for Dodd?"

"Yup."

Jake ran a quick, assessing glance over the old building's worn facade. "It doesn't look like Dodd. He's obsessively neat and clean."

Gray shrugged. "Maybe he chose this place on purpose because it's the direct opposite of his usual living space."

"Could be." Jake followed Gray into the small foyer. "What floor is he on?"

"Third. Apartment 302." Gray looked at the elevator's grimy buttons and shook his head. "This thing's older than dirt. I say we walk up."

"Good plan."

The third floor of the building had six doors opening off the hallway. The walls were painted institutional green and matched the worn green carpet on the floor. Both men drew weapons, taking opposite sides of the door to Apartment 302.

"You got a concealed-weapon permit for that thing?" Gray asked.

"Yeah."

"Just checkin'. Wouldn't want to have to arrest you."

"Oh, hell. Just open the damn door."

Gray grinned, banging on the door panel. "Open up. Police."

No one answered.

Gray knocked once more, repeated his words, and was again met with silence.

Jake bent, slipped the knife from his boot sheath and lifted an eyebrow in silent inquiry.

Gray rolled his eyes, looked up and down the hall-way and nodded.

It took only seconds for Jake to open the door.

"You know, Morrissey, even cops can get busted for breaking and entering," Gray said as they walked into the small apartment.

"No one will ever know," Jake promised.

"No one except you—and you'll probably blackmail me." Gun drawn, Gray moved swiftly across the unit and cleared the bathroom. "Nothing here. In fact, this place doesn't look like anyone lives here."

"Not in the living room. But the bedroom sure as hell does."

"What's in there?" Gray strode to the doorway of the bedroom and stopped abruptly. All four walls were cov-ered with maps, sheets of closely printed notes and blown-up photographs. Some of the photos were of a young man in a Marine uniform, smiling proudly. One wall held pictures of Jake, both alone and with Chloe. What surprised Gray were several photographs of Chloe's grandmother.

He stepped inside the room, registering the desk pushed against the far wall, and the computer, monitor and printer atop the dust-free surface. No papers were stacked on the desk, no clutter of pens or paper clips were strewn across the polished wood.

Jake's phone rang. Glancing at the caller ID, he flicked it on. "Hi, Chloe. What's up? Chloe?"

Gray turned from his study of one of the maps to look at him.

Jake stopped talking. "What the hell?" He listened for a second, then covered the mouthpiece with his fin-gers and jerked his head toward the door.

"What's going on?" Gray followed him into the hall and closed the door.

"Chloe's phone is on and I can hear her talking to a man. I think it might be Dodd."

"Shit."

They ran down the stairs, through the lobby and outside. Jake fished in his pocket for his keys and tossed them to Gray. "You drive. I'll keep the line open."

"Where is she?" Gray turned on the ignition and shifted the car into gear.

"Liberty Hall."

Please, Jake, answer your phone. If he didn't pick up, the call would be switched to the automated answering service.

"We're going for a walk. You will remove the tape from your grandmother's mouth and place the scarf over her hands." He gestured with his gun at the crumpled gold silk on the floor at Winifred's feet.

Winifred's gaze, steady and strong, held Chloe's as she carefully pried loose the tape. The skin beneath was reddened and she winced as the tape came loose.

"Sorry, Gran," Chloe murmured.

"Not your fault." Winifred shifted her gaze to George Dodd when Chloe bent to pick up the scrap of silk. "Where are you taking us, Mr. Dodd?"

"To the Bell Tower." He smiled and Chloe's skin prickled with warning. There was no humor in his smile. "I've arranged a place for you there."

Chloe glanced at Winifred as she carefully wrapped the gold silk around her wrists, concealing the connected loops made of small ties, the kind that came with garbage bags. They effectively bound her hands together. Her grandmother shook her head, a slight, nearly imperceptible movement. Chloe narrowed her eyes to acknowledge the message that she should bide her time, then stepped to the side, facing their captor.

Dodd noted the scarf. "Very good. Chloe, you will walk ahead of us while your grandmother walks with me. Any attempt on your part to summon help will result in my having to shoot her. We'll take the South Annex stairway up to the Bell Tower." He gestured Chloe forward.

She crossed to the door and opened it.

"Remember, not a word or your grandmother dies."

Chloe nodded. "You want me to walk ahead of you all the way to the Liberty Hall Bell Tower?" she asked, speaking more loudly than usual.

He glared at her. "That's what I said. Outside. Now."

She pulled open the door and stepped into the empty hallway.

Jake, please be listening.

Eight

"He's taking them to the Bell Tower at Liberty Hall."

"Which end of the building is that?"

Jake visualized the map he'd used to find Chloe's office the first day he'd taken her to lunch. "South end. I think there's a ground-floor entrance." He checked his watch. "Damn it. We're still at least fifteen minutes away."

Gray looked at the traffic around them and turned left, accelerating up a residential street. "Maybe we can shave a few minutes off the time." He reached into his jacket pocket and pulled out his cell phone, handing it to Jake, then quickly downshifting while scanning the intersection ahead of them. "Call it in to the PD. And tell them to alert UW campus security that we have a hostage situation at Liberty Hall."

Dodd waved Chloe and Winifred ahead of him into the tower. The room was octagonal, and each wall had wide glass windows, giving it the appearance of a lighthouse tower. The ceiling had a round opening, and high above, the automated bell hung, silent. A deep window ledge created a waist-high shelf that circled the room.

Chloe's gaze swept the space as she searched for an advantage, but there was nothing. No furniture, no drapes or blinds on the windows.

Only one object sat in solitary splendor on the window ledge directly across from them.

Gran's birthday clock. How did it get here? Puzzled, she looked at Dodd and found him watching her, a small smile on his thin lips.

"Ah, you recognize the clock, Chloe?"

"Yes, it was a birthday gift for my grandmother. How did it get here?"

"I brought it, of course. I took it from the house before I intercepted the limo driver and appropriated his car to collect Mrs. Abbott from the cruise ship this morning." He nodded approvingly. "Most accommodating of you to make plans that fit so perfectly with mine. Sit down on the floor, Mrs. Abbott." He waited until Winifred complied, then turned to Chloe. "Turn around and cross your wrists behind your back."

Chloe reluctantly obeyed, conscious of his firm, unwavering grip on the handgun.

He slipped a plastic tie around one of her wrists and threaded a second through the loop before he yanked the first one tight. Then he circled the second around her other wrist. Chloe winced at the pinching and bit back a cry of pain when he pulled it snug.

"Sit on the floor next to your grandmother."

Chloe did, and he swiftly looped and tightened nooses around her ankles, binding the ties together with a third length of plastic. Then he did he same thing to Winifred.

George Dodd stood and smiled down at them. "I suppose it's only fair that you understand what's going to happen to you." He glanced at his watch before walking to the rosewood clock. He turned the clock so they could see the back and opened the small door to expose the intricate workings. A whitish-gray substance now filled the entire space and a small object with wires leading from it was attached to the flashlight battery installed for the alarm.

A sense of dread overwhelmed Chloe. "What is that?"

"Dynamite. More specifically, dynamite from Jake Morrissey's company. It needed to be Jake's dynamite that destroyed you, Chloe, just as it was his dynamite that killed my son. You see the importance of the continuity and connection, don't you? Revenge isn't complete without all the parameters clearly defined."

Oh, God. He's completely crazy. Jake, are you listening? Hurry!

He checked his watch again. "I must leave you. It's time. You have precisely ten minutes. When the hands on the clock reach twelve, the battery will send electricity through the alarm to the detonator cap and set off the dynamite." He smiled benevolently. "Don't worry. You won't feel a thing. Only Morrissey will feel—he'll suffer when you're gone. I'm sorry to have to use you, but this was the only way to punish him." He looked out the window. "The Bell Tower at McGyver Hall has a perfect view so I can watch Jake Morrissey as his world explodes." He turned and walked to the door. "Goodbye, ladies."

And he left, quietly closing the door. The sound of his footsteps as he moved quickly down the stairs faded away.

"Gran, reach into my pocket." Chloe rolled to her knees and shifted closer to Winifred.

Winifred didn't question her. Instead, using both hands, she pulled the cell phone out of the square pocket of Chloe's full skirt and held it steady while Chloe bent over.

"Jake! Jake, are you there?"

"Chloe, thank God! Are you all right?"

"Yes. But Dodd put dynamite in Gran's clock and set it to go off in ten minutes."

"I heard." Jake's curse carried clearly over the phone. "Can you get out of the room to safety?"

"Our hands and feet are bound together. I don't think we'd make it down the stairs and away from the building in time."

"Tell me about the clock."

Chloe studied it. "Antique, glass face, musical figures on top. And it was modernized with a battery-operated alarm at some point."

"He's using the battery for ignition." Jake's mind raced. "You said it has a glass face?"

"Yes."

"Can you reach the hands on the clock?"

"I don't know. Gran, we need to get closer to the clock."

"Closer to the dynamite?" Winifred's eyebrows winged upward.

"If we don't find a way to disarm it, it's not going to matter how close we are. The whole tower will be gone and us with it."

Winifred nodded, clutching the phone in her bound hands, and rolled across the short expanse of bare wood floor after Chloe. Panting, both women struggled to their knees, their heads and shoulders even with the low window ledge where the clock sat.

"Gran, see if you can open the glass face."

Winifred lifted her hands, set the phone carefully on the ledge and slipped the little brass hook free to swing open the round glass face.

"Done," she murmured, her brow dotted with nervous perspiration. She picked up the phone and held it to Chloe's ear.

"We have the glass open, Jake, and we can reach the hands."

"This sounds too simple to work, Chloe, but it's the only chance. I want you to tell Winifred to slowly move the minute hand back thirty minutes."

"That's it? Are you sure it'll work?"

"I'm betting your life on it. And, Chloe, before you tell Winifred... I just want you to know, I love you."

Tears gathered in her eyes. "I love you, too, Jake."

"Tell Winifred to move the hands *slowly*." His voice was rough with emotion.

"Gran, Jake wants you to move the minute hand backward—thirty minutes. Do it slowly."

Winifred barely hesitated, drew a deep breath and, without a tremor in her fingers, lifted her bound hands and carefully, slowly, reversed the minute hand.

Both women held their breaths, waiting for an explosion. But the clock merely ticked steadily on.

"Chloe? Chloe!"

"I'm here, Jake. Gran did it—and the dynamite didn't go off."

"Good. Now, get the hell out of there, as fast as you can. We're in the parking lot. I'll be there in a few minutes."

"Right." Chloe looked at her grandmother. "Jake says to get out if we can."

Winifred nodded, dropped the phone and clambered to her feet beside Chloe. Hampered by the hobbles on their ankles, they could only take tiny steps. They managed to reach the door, fumble it open and step onto the landing before they heard the sound of a car below. Doors slammed, feet pounded on the stairs.

Jake reached Chloe first, swinging her off her feet and slinging her over his shoulder. Gray picked up Winifred and followed close on Jake's heels as he ran back down the stairs and out of the building. Sirens screamed;

police cars and fire trucks drove across the lawn to join the campus police and surround the building.

Jake lowered Chloe to the grass and knelt beside her to run his hands over her face, down her arms, testing to be sure she was whole. Ignoring the many onlookers, he retrieved his knife and cut her bonds.

"I'm fine, Jake, honestly." With difficulty, Chloe sat up. "Did the police catch Dodd?"

He lifted his head, looking swiftly at the surrounding chaos. "I doubt it."

"He might still be here. He said he was going to watch the explosion from the tower at McGyver Hall."

Jake's eyes flared, and his face grew hard.

"Go, I'm fine." She pushed at his arm, reading his unwillingness to leave her. "Gran's here—and so is half the campus and most of the police and fire departments."

"I'll be back." Jake pressed a quick, fierce kiss to her mouth and stood. Gray joined him and they ran toward McGyver Hall.

Moments later, Chloe and Winifred—whose ties had been released by a paramedic—were in the back seat of a police car. An officer had provided them with paper cups of hot coffee from a machine. They sat in semi-isolation, each cradling a cup while the organized chaos of a crime scene unfolded outside.

"Honey, I told you I wouldn't mind a little excitement in my life, but this wasn't exactly what I meant," Winifred said, her eyes twinkling.

"Sorry, Gran." Chloe studied her grandmother's crumpled linen pantsuit and silk blouse. Her white curls were disheveled, but her eyes gleamed with energy. "Gran, I need some advice."

"About what?"

"I think I'm in love with Jake."

"And?" Winifred waited, clearly expecting more.

"I know he's not active military anymore, but he's a soldier at heart and he looks at life from a warrior's viewpoint. And his job is dangerous."

"And that's a problem for you?" Winifred asked gently.

"I'm not sure. I've always chosen a quiet life." Chloe waved a hand at the campus around them. "I picked an academic career filled with books and study. How will Jake and I manage to blend our lives?"

"My Richard was a warrior."

Chloe felt her eyes widen. "Granddad? He was a sweetie."

"Yes, he was," Winifred agreed. "But he was also a warrior. I was a soldier's bride, as you know, and he went away to war when we'd been married for just two months. I thought we knew each other so well—after all, we grew up together. But war changes a man, or maybe it's fairer to say that war strips a man down to his very core. Richard was steel, solid steel. The bravest man I've ever known. But with me and the rest of his family, he was a teddy bear." Winifred's voice wavered and she paused, sipping her coffee. "We had a wonderful marriage, Chloe. More than fifty years, and though he's been gone for six years, I miss him every day."

"Oh, Gran." Chloe hugged her, moved beyond words at the wisdom and love apparent in her words and expression.

The door of the squad car opened and Chloe looked over her shoulder. Jake stood there, a frown growing as he searched her features. "What's wrong?" he asked.

"Nothing." She glanced at her grandmother.

"Did you arrest that awful man?" Winifred asked, leaning forward to look past Chloe at Jake.

Jake nodded. "A UW janitor saw Dodd toss his gun into the bushes outside Liberty Hall and followed him to McGyver Tower. When Dodd went into the tower room, the janitor locked him in and called the campus police to report Dodd for littering."

Chloe laughed out loud. "That must've been Fred."

"Yes. How did you know?"

"Fred tends to view any littering at Liberty Hall as a personal affront."

Jake lifted an eyebrow in query, but Chloe just smiled at him without explaining further. He turned back to her grandmother. "The Seattle PD have Dodd in custody. He confessed to assaulting the limo driver and forcing him to strip off his uniform before making him climb in the trunk. I'm guessing Dodd used the gun butt or a tire iron to knock the man out so he couldn't make any noise and alert passersby. All of which happened before Dodd picked you up at the cruise dock, Winifred."

"The poor driver!" Winifred exclaimed. "Was he badly injured?"

Jake shook his head. "He's been taken to Harborview Hospital, but the paramedics checked him out after the police removed him from the limo trunk. They seem convinced he wasn't hurt beyond a few bruises."

"Thank goodness." Winifred heaved a sigh of relief and made a shooing gesture with her free hand, the other occupied with balancing her cup. "Scoot, Chloe. I'll be fine here, drinking my coffee and contemplating my nice, quiet life."

Chloe slid across the seat and into Jake's arms. "I'm so glad you showed up at the tower when you did," she whispered. "To put it mildly…"

"Me, too." He nudged the car door shut and drew her away from the crowd to the far side of an empty ambulance. Then he wrapped her in his arms and kissed her breathless. Chloe kissed him back with all the emotion generated by the chaotic, terror-filled day.

He raised his head and stared at her, breathing harshly. "Marry me."

Stunned, she couldn't get her vocal cords to work.

"That's right, marriage. I realize we've only known each other a couple weeks, but we've been through more in these past days than most couples go through in a lifetime."

"Okay."

"Okay?" He sounded as stunned as she'd felt earlier.

"Yes."

He looked at her warily. "You're not shell-shocked from stress? You're not going to claim battlefield memory loss later on?"

Chloe laughed. "No. But I'm warning you, my grandmother wants great-grandchildren. And soon."

"I think we can manage that." He smiled lazily, his eyes hot. Then he bent his head and took her mouth with his once more.

Professor Weds Warrior, she thought blissfully. And then she stopped thinking and gave in to emotion.

From: Winifred@Codebreakers.org
To: Clara@AppleButterLadies.com
Sent: May 25th
Subject: Good morning—

Dear Clara,

So much has happened since we said good-bye and I left you at the Seattle docks yesterday. I hardly know where to start! I was kidnapped by the horrible man who's been following Chloe. He trapped her with me in the Liberty Hall tower with a dynamite bomb he'd set to explode. I swear, Clara, I thought

I was going to have a heart attack from sheer fright before Chloe spoke with Jake on her cell phone and he told us how to defuse the bomb. I had enough excitement yesterday to last the rest of my life—from now on if I ever think my life is getting dull, I'll watch a good British mystery on television!

All is well this morning, however. The villain is locked up in the King County Jail in downtown Seattle, I'm drinking tea while writing my daily e-mails, and Chloe and Jake will soon be planning a wedding. I can't wait to see her walk down the aisle. Now if I could only find suitable husbands for my other two granddaughters, I'd be completely content....

Have a wonderful day, Clara—we simply must get together soon. I miss seeing your smiling face.

All my love,

Winifred

THE APPLE ORCHARD
Katherine Stone

Dear Reader,

What a pleasure it's been working with Debbie and Lois on *Soldiers' Brides*! We've enjoyed sharing our grandmothers and granddaughters with one another, and creating a novel in which *their* lives intertwine. We've cared about them all, and rooted for them all.

Now it's Clara and Elizabeth's turn. So...welcome to *The Apple Orchard*. To those of you who've read *The Other Twin* and *Another Man's Son*, the charming town of Sarah's Orchard will be a familiar one. To those of you who are new to my stories, I hope you'll find the fictional locale, and its characters, a pleasant place to visit. I'll probably return to Sarah's Orchard in the future. I love the setting and can envision a wedding, with all the trimmings and intrigues, at the Orchard Inn.

I hope you enjoy *The Apple Orchard* and, if the spirit moves you, the other books. Please drop by my website – www.katherinestone.com – any time. I'd love to hear from you, too. My mailing address is Katherine Stone, PO Box 758, Mukilteo, WA 98275, USA.

Thanks for spending time with Clara, Elizabeth and Nick.

With all best wishes,

Katherine Stone

To those who serve, and those who love them

Prologue

Sarah's Orchard, Oregon
December 18
Twenty-seven years ago

His mom's boyfriend, Dennis, was going to be really mad. So would Marianne, his mom. Dennis would take Nick's being late out on her, too.

How many times, Dennis would shout, had he made it clear that if Nick wasn't home from school by three-thirty, the house would be locked, the burglar alarm set, and Nick would have to wait outside until his mom and Dennis returned from work at 1:00 a.m.?

It wasn't an idle threat. Since September, when Marianne and Nick had moved to Sarah's Orchard to live with Dennis, Nick had spent five nights outside. Dennis didn't care that Nick had an excuse for his tardiness. In each instance, the entire second-grade class—Nick's class—at Orchard Elementary had been dismissed late. It wasn't because of bad behavior, Nick had tried to explain. All five times there'd been something to celebrate.

Today's celebration, a Christmas party, was worth whatever punishment Dennis chose to inflict. It didn't matter how cold Nick would be by the time Dennis and Marianne returned. Nick's teacher had played the piano, and all the second-graders had gathered round to sing carols. The students took turns singing verses. No one laughed when words were forgotten or the tune was off key.

Nick wasn't sure his classmates even detected the discordant notes. He did. He couldn't help it. According to his teacher, he had perfect pitch. He hadn't known it before enrolling at Orchard Elementary. In fact, seven-year-old Nicholas Lawton hadn't even realized he could sing.

But he could, and he loved it.

He'd sing carols tonight, he decided as he ran toward the house—two miles away—where Dennis was probably shouting already. He'd sing as he froze on the porch. His carols would be sung quietly and in the shadows. The neighbors mustn't know he was alone every evening, Dennis had warned, whether he was guarding Dennis's house from the outside or within.

That was Nick's job, to make certain no one tried to break in while Dennis and Marianne were at the tavern where cocktail waitress Marianne served the drinks that bartender Dennis poured. Dennis made drugs in the basement of the dilapidated house on Center Street. Nick had never seen the lab. The door was always locked.

If not for his illegal enterprise, Dennis wouldn't have cared when Nick got home from school. It wasn't Nick's comfort—food, shelter, warmth—that made him furious when Nick was so late Dennis had to leave before he arrived. Dennis wanted Nick inside, awake and watchful, ready to call the tavern should anyone approach.

Nick had made a number of such calls. Dennis had never thanked him, but he'd come home right away. He'd yelled at the uninvited visitors, and on two occasions, he'd waved his gun around until they left. Even when he'd stopped yelling long enough to sell drugs to the intruders, he'd warned them that any future transactions would take place only at the bar.

Dennis could've given Nick the code for the burglar alarm. That way, Nick could let himself in on the afternoons he was late, reset the alarm once inside and be close to the phone if he needed it. Nick wasn't tall enough to reach the alarm panel. But if Dennis put a chair beneath it…

Nick made the mistake of suggesting to Dennis that he give him the code. Dennis laughed in a mean way, laughing at Nick for being so stupid as to imagine he'd trust him to begin with, much less trust that once he had the code, he wouldn't simply leave the house and spend the evening elsewhere instead of "earning his keep."

Nick was doing his best to make it home before Dennis locked him out. He was running as fast as he could. He didn't even slow his pace as he neared the apple orchard for which the town had been named.

Nick knew the town's history. All Orchard Elementary second-graders did. Their teacher believed it was important for them to know, and told the story in a fairytale way. Nick loved this story; he'd memorized its every detail.

Many years ago, the tale began, Dr. James Keeling and his wife, Sarah, moved from the big city, Portland, to what was then the farming community of Riverville.

The Keelings had an apple tree in Portland. Sarah

treasured the tree and its apples. The tree was too large to be transplanted, but the cuttings Sarah took flourished on the small piece of Riverville farmland the town's new doctor had purchased.

Apples hadn't been grown in Riverville until Sarah planted her orchard. But they became *the* crop of Riverville, which was renamed Sarah's Orchard in honor of the doctor's wife. Sarah's husband left a legacy, too. The Keeling Clinic. Renowned for its exceptional staff and unsurpassed expertise in any number of medical specialties, the clinic was a referral center for patients from coast to coast.

Sarah's acre of apples had been a family orchard, not a working one, and that was how it stayed.

All the town's orchards were beautiful when the apples were ripening and the leaves were green. But Nick thought the orchard that had been Sarah's remained beautiful even after the fruit was plucked and the branches were bare.

He didn't know what made the trees beckon to him on these wintry afternoons. He knew only that they did. Time permitting, he always paused to catch his breath against the orchard's three-railed fence. And on the afternoons when he dashed out of the classroom the moment the dismissal bell sounded, there was time, once his breath returned, to sing a song or two.

Nick wished he could sing carols, even one carol, to the apple trees on this December day. Or, having made sure that Dennis and his mom had already left the house on Center Street, he could go back to the orchard and spend the evening here. It wouldn't feel as cold—here. Somehow the barren trees would warm him.

But on the nights Nick was forced to keep vigil from the porch, Dennis would get tavern customers, drunken ones, to drop by. They were supposed to confirm that

Nick was there—and that, as they approached, he demand to know who they were and what they wanted.

Nick ran past the orchard, stumbling—but not falling—as he took his eyes from the path ahead to the trees he wanted to see. In the distance he saw the farmhouse.

When the Keelings lived there, it had been painted white and teal—which, his teacher explained, was a blend of green and blue. The new owners kept the original color scheme until the end of World War Two. With the help of the entire town, the young bride painted it daffodil-yellow with butter-cream trim. She wanted it to look like a beacon, to guide her soldier husband home.

The soldier must have liked the beacon. The farmhouse was still yellow and cream, glowing to Nick even on cloudy afternoons.

Today, the house also glowed from within. All the lights were on. The eaves were adorned for Christmas, as were the apple trees that lined the drive. Those closest to the house twinkled white. Along the drive itself the trees were wrapped in lights the color of ripe apples.

For the past three weeks, Nick had noticed the strands coiled around the trunks and limbs. Until today, the Christmas lights hadn't been illuminated when he ran by. It wasn't twilight even now. But the trees were shining. The family was celebrating, too. It was a large gathering, Nick saw. The partygoers had overflowed to the porch, and the grounds.

They seemed to be searching. And shouting. Their shouts weren't angry, like Dennis's—or his mom's previous boyfriends'.

These shouts sounded worried.

The road dipped, leaving the farmhouse and its noises behind. The orchard entrance lay ahead, at the bottom of the long, steep drive. The entrance was twin-

kling, an archway of red and white, and just inside, at
the base of a lighted tree, was a sobbing child.

She wasn't very old. Two or so. And she was *really*
sobbing. The kind of hiccupping wails that only grew
silent when it became necessary for her to breathe.

Nick had witnessed such sobbing before. Marianne's
boyfriend before Dennis had a two-year-old daughter
who cried like this. Nick hadn't been allowed to comfort her. She needed to learn not to cry, her father had
said.

No one was forbidding Nick to comfort this sobbing
girl. Without hesitation he ran to her.

"Don't cry!" he implored.

She looked at him and immediately wailed.

She didn't seem injured, although her holly-green
tights had dirt stains at the knees. Nor did she seem cold;
in her heavy Christmas sweater, she was probably
warmer than Nick.

Maybe she was scared.

Maybe a carol would help.

"Jingle Bells" wasn't Nick's favorite. "A Midnight
Clear" was.

But "Jingle Bells" might cheer her up, *if* she could
hear his singing above her cries.

She could, and when she did, she stared at him. It was
a bold stare and, at first, an indignant one—as if she'd
been enjoying a perfectly good cry and how dare he
make it end?

Then she smiled, *beamed.* Her stare had been one of
surprise, he decided, not indignation. Surprise that what
had felt like hopelessness could be vanquished by a song.

"You belong up there, don't you?" he asked, glancing at the drive. "You're the reason everyone's search-

ing. They probably figure there's no way you could've made it this far."

She didn't say anything, but the smile disappeared and new tears threatened.

"Don't start crying again, okay? I'd better carry you." Assuming he could lift her.

She was a healthy toddler. He was small for his age. *Very* small, as Dennis—and others—never failed to point out.

She was heavy. Nick staggered a little under her weight. It helped when she curled her arms around his neck and hung on.

Nick began singing, and she joined in.

"'Jingle bells,'" she crooned. "'All the way.'"

Her jumbled lyrics were nothing compared to the tune she couldn't carry.

But she had a happy voice, and the tears were gone. She'd obviously concluded that it wasn't so bad, in fact *fun,* to be carried up the hill. She pointed to the twinkling branches overhead and giggled as she sang.

When they reached the crest of the hill and were spotted by a searcher who shouted the wonderful news, she was immediately surrounded by the kind of love Nick wouldn't have believed existed if he hadn't seen it with his own eyes.

Whisked from his arms, the girl was held jointly by her weeping parents while the large circle of people who loved her wept, laughed and marveled that she'd wandered so far, so fast—especially since, or so they'd thought, they were all keeping an eye on her.

In moments, the toddler and her entourage were moving as one toward the farmhouse. Nick was halfway down the drive when he heard the male voice behind him.

"Wait, son! Please."

No one had ever called him *son*. His own dad "split" the day his mom told him she was pregnant. Whenever Marianne's boyfriends bothered to call him anything, they invariably came up with a cruel reminder of how small he was.

There'd also never been anyone who'd wanted to talk to him as much as the man who was jogging to catch him.

The man wasn't alone. A woman jogged beside him.

The driveway was so steep that the man and woman towered over Nick more than they would have if they'd all been standing on level ground.

The couple crouched down, and it didn't feel mean or insulting. They just wanted to look him straight in the eyes.

Their eyes, Nick noticed, glistened with tears.

"Who are you?" the man asked.

Nick hesitated. He could see this man showing up at Dennis's house and being shouted at by Dennis. Hating the image, he replied with a shrug.

"Well, I'm Charles MacKenzie, and this is my wife, Clara. We're Elizabeth's grandma and grandpa, and we can't tell you how grateful we are that you saved her. If she'd gone across the road…" The voice faltered.

"She was sitting down," Nick said. "She wouldn't have crossed the road. I don't think she was running away. Was she?"

"Heavens, no!" Clara replied. "She was just fascinated by the lights on the trees. The minute I turned them on, she started pointing to them. She loves bright colors. I'll bet she loved your bright blue eyes."

Nick didn't have bright blue eyes. At least, the last time he'd looked, they were gray. But if this nice lady wanted to think his eyes were bright blue, that was okay with him. He wished they were. For *her*.

"We didn't imagine Elizabeth would go outside," Charles murmured. "Or that she could *get* outside with all of us watching her. But she did, and you saved her. You must live nearby?"

Nick shrugged again. "I better go."

"Why don't you let us drive you home? It's getting dark."

"I'm okay."

"Could you join us for dinner? We could call your parents and invite them, too. We'd like to tell them what you did."

"*No.* I mean, they're—" Not home. Nick was certain it was true, that Dennis and his mom had already left for work. If he told these kind people he'd be alone for the evening, they'd really want him to stay for dinner, and when Dennis sent one of his customers to check on him and he wasn't there… "I have to go now."

"All right," Charles said. "We don't want to keep you. But here's something for you to remember. If you ever need anything—anything at all—you come to us. Just walk up this driveway, knock on the door and say 'I'm the boy who rescued Elizabeth.'"

"You don't even need to say that much," Clara said. "We'll see your blue eyes and know who you are. But if it seems that *our* eyes are failing us, if for some reason you think we might've forgotten, even though we never will, you can say 'I'm Elizabeth's hero.'" Clara didn't ask if that was okay with Nick. Instead, she added, "I really wish you'd let me send you home with some Christmas cookies."

"You should take her up on that, son. She's a terrific cook. Do you like apple butter?"

"I've never tasted it."

"Then it's time you did. My Clara makes the best apple butter in the world. Could we get you to take a jar or two?"

He was so tempted, not by the offer of food, but by the kindness that came with it. "No. Thank you. I have to go." *Now.* If he didn't, he might not ever leave.

"All right. Thank you, Elizabeth's hero. And please remember what we told you. We're here if you need us."

How could he ever forget? Nick wondered as he continued his journey home.

He ran, even though he knew his destination would be a locked house and a frigid porch. The sooner he put distance between himself and what he wanted so much—but would never have—the better.

He must have run faster than he'd ever run before. In no time he rounded the corner where Dennis's house would come into view.

Dennis's pickup was in the drive and a rental truck, like the U-Haul Dennis had rented to move Nick and Marianne from Medford to Sarah's Orchard, was parked out front.

Dennis, his mom and two of Dennis's friends were loading the vehicles. It wasn't just his mom's furniture that was being loaded, but Dennis's, as well. And there were things Nick had never seen. Equipment from the basement, he supposed.

No one shouted at him for being late. His mom simply told him they were leaving the second the trucks were loaded—about five minutes from now. Any belongings he hadn't put on the van by then would be left behind.

Would *he* have been left behind if he'd accepted Mrs. MacKenzie's offer of apple butter and cookies?

The question would haunt Nick for years to come.

How different his life might've been if he'd returned to the daffodil-yellow farmhouse in the middle of that very night.

I'm Elizabeth's...hero, he would've said through chattering teeth. Remember me? I've been waiting on a run-down porch on Center Street for my mom and her boyfriend to get home from work. It's been hours since they should've returned, and when I looked through the windows I didn't see any furniture inside. I'm pretty cold. And sort of hungry. Could I...could I come in?

But Nicholas Lawton did leave Sarah's Orchard that December night.

It would be twenty-four years before he made his way back. Found his way home.

One

Elizabeth Charlotte Winslow was smiling. She'd just picked up her wedding invitations and was delighted with the result. She'd designed them herself. And although her concept hadn't been a huge departure—a different font, a more interesting format—from what Atherton heiresses had mailed to their wedding guests for as long as anyone could recall, her mother, Abigail MacKenzie Winslow, had been wary.

It would be fine, Elizabeth had insisted. The gilt edging hadn't been forsaken, and the parchment itself was more expensive than paper had any right to be.

It *was* fine, as her mother would acknowledge when she saw the invitations…in forty minutes or so. Elizabeth wanted to make a brief stop before heading south to Atherton and her parents' Lilac Lane home.

She was in the second week of the nine she'd spend

living with her parents until her September wedding to Matthew Blaine. It was also the second week of her first carefree summer since she'd graduated from Atherton High.

She'd taken courses that summer. Advanced-placement courses that had helped her get her undergraduate degree from Stanford—and be admitted to Stanford Law—in three years, not four. She'd also taken classes each undergraduate summer and clerked during law school vacations and had spent the summer after graduation studying for the California bar.

Then it was off to L.A., where, as a prosecutor, she'd tried cases, and won cases, year round. There hadn't been any carefree summers in eleven years. No carefree autumns, winters or springs, either.

Two weeks ago, the jury had returned its guilty verdict on her swan-song case in L.A. She'd flown home the next day, and despite the occasional feeling that she was playing hooky, she was adapting well to her newfound freedom.

In fact, she was enjoying it so much, she hadn't yet made the offer to her new boss, the San Francisco D.A., that she'd intended to make. Even though her official start date was October 1, she'd tell him she was available to do preliminary work on the cases she'd be handling. So far the delights of a lazy summer had overcome that urge.

There were people—her mother, Matthew's mother and the wedding coordinator—who were unhappy with Elizabeth's notion of a carefree summer leading up to the Winslow-Blaine nuptials. There were myriad decisions to make, all of which they regarded as critical. Elizabeth's plan had been to be peripherally—but cheerfully—involved. Whatever the mothers wanted. She hadn't imagined there'd be issues, like the invitations, on which she'd felt strongly enough to voice a preference.

There were other choices she would've made differently. Fewer bridal showers. A less grand dress. And, as it became clear that her wedding—and the festivities leading up to it—was the event of the season, a nice middle-of-the-night elopement to Lake Tahoe sounded more and more appealing. But Elizabeth was picking her battles.

And Matthew, smartly, was remaining out of the fray. It wouldn't be a carefree summer for him. As an investment banker, her fiancé had several major deals in the works. He hoped to bring them all to lucrative conclusions before the wedding. It would require long hours and frequent travel, but he believed it could be done.

He'd been in New York for the past three days. He'd be coming home late tonight—too late, he'd said, for her to meet him at the airport, or at his Pacific Heights home, which would become theirs in September.

Matthew's house was Elizabeth's brief stop before driving to Atherton. Matthew wouldn't be seeing her tonight, but he'd be able to see their invitations. If he wanted to. Matthew wasn't any more desperate to see the engraved proof of their impending wedding than Elizabeth would've been if she hadn't insisted on the changes.

As Elizabeth made the short drive from Shreve & Company on Union Square, she confronted the real reason for her detour to Matthew's empty house before returning home. Once her mother acknowledged that the invitations were at least as elegant as the traditional ones, the logical next step would be for Elizabeth to begin addressing them.

There'd been a minor skirmish on that point. The mothers had wanted to hire a calligrapher. Elizabeth didn't do calligraphy, but her handwriting was legible. Presentable. Even if it wasn't, so what? This was *her* wedding. She wanted to address the invitations herself. She was a little surprised, she told the dismayed faces, that all brides didn't feel the same way.

The idea of spending the afternoon addressing invitations should have been a happy one. It would've been, had the recipient of the first invitation she was going to address been excited about receiving it—about the wedding itself.

But unless she'd magically changed her opinion of her granddaughter's groom-to-be, Clara MacKenzie wouldn't be excited at all. Elizabeth's detour to Matthew's was, therefore, a stalling tactic.

Since Monday night, Elizabeth had studiously avoided thinking about the phone conversation with her grandmother.

She needed to replay it, and there was no time like the present.

She'd made the call to Sarah's Orchard, a thank-you for the lovely July Fourth weekend she and Matthew had just spent at the farmhouse, and for the wonderful party Gram had thrown in their honor at the Orchard Inn.

The thank-you had been heartfelt. So was Elizabeth's hope that she'd hear Gram's enthusiastic approval of the man she was going to marry.

It hadn't been a far-fetched hope. She'd expected Gram to be as pleased with the match as everyone else.

But...

"Are you sure he's the one?" Clara had asked.

"Yes, I am. But you aren't. Why not?" When Gram hadn't been forthcoming with answer, Elizabeth had provided possible concerns herself. "Is it because he's ten years older than I am?"

"I didn't even realize he was."

"Or because he's thinking about going into politics?"

"More than thinking," Gram had replied. "It sounds like his run for the Senate is a sure thing."

"And that's bad?"

"Not at all. And with his beautiful, brilliant wife at his side, he's certain to win."

"That's *not* why he's marrying me." Elizabeth's statement had been emphatic, and so stern it had blocked the question that begged to be asked. *You think it is?* She'd sensed the question, of course. Rolled right over it. "Ours may not be the love you and Granddad had. What love is? But we're extremely compatible. I've done some dating, you know. I have my own previous relationships to compare this one to. That's what I *have* to compare it to, Gram. My relationships, not yours and Granddad's."

"And it's good?"

"Very good."

"You love him?"

"Of course I do! And Matthew loves me."

"Do you sing for him?"

Elizabeth couldn't carry a tune. She knew it. Anyone who'd ever heard her knew it. It had been years—decades—since she'd inflicted her tonelessness on the world. Not since the carefree summers she'd spent in Sarah's Orchard as a girl. "You *know* I can't sing."

"You always sang for Granddad and me."

"Yes, but…" *You're my grandparents. You love me unconditionally.* "Matthew doesn't need to hear me sing."

Before the phone call had ended, Gram had made an effort to soften her position. But it had been damning with faint praise. She didn't *dislike* Matthew. She didn't believe him to be a serial killer in disguise. She just didn't think he was the man for her only granddaughter. And she'd said, so quietly Elizabeth almost hadn't heard it, that Charles wouldn't think so, either.

Maybe that was what Gram's reaction to Matthew was really about. Granddad. The man Gram had loved for sixty-five years had died last November. It wasn't in Gram's nature to give up on life, and she hadn't. And she had the support of her family, her town and, perhaps most importantly, of Winifred and Helen. Both had known and loved Clara—and Charles—for more than sixty of those sixty-five years.

It had been their men, their soldiers, who'd brought them together. Sam had needed witnesses for his wedding, and friends for his friendless bride. They'd become close friends, all six of them. Over time, Helen and Winifred had lost their beloved husbands. Now Gram had lost hers. Elizabeth had no doubt that Gram's friends were reaching out to her as Gram and Granddad had reached out to them when Sam and Richard had died.

But Gram had to miss Granddad, deeply and desperately, every day.

That was how Elizabeth felt about losing Granddad, too.

Elizabeth wished Gram could be happy about her wedding, wished it'd given her something hopeful to look forward to.

It worried Elizabeth more than she'd been willing to admit—until this very moment—that it hadn't.

This very moment coincided with her arrival at Matthew's.

The silver Accord parked in his driveway was unexpected. And familiar. Its vanity plate confirmed its owner to be Matthew's executive assistant, Janine—the same Janine who'd been Matthew's date at the New Year's Eve gala at the Carlton Club where Matthew and Elizabeth had met.

Elizabeth had been home for the holidays, accompanying her parents to the social events of the season. Matthew had called her the following day, and by the time Elizabeth returned to L.A., she and Matthew were making plans for a future.

It was during a weekend visit in March that Elizabeth had seen Janine's Accord. She'd arrived at Matthew's just as Janine, who'd dropped off some financial statements Matthew needed to review, was leaving. She'd also learned from her mother that there'd been a "dreadful" few months when Matthew's parents had lived in "perpetual fear" that Matthew might marry Janine. Like Elizabeth, Matthew was an only child—and sole heir to a substantial fortune.

Matthew had told Elizabeth that rumors of his possible engagement to Janine were greatly exaggerated. She'd been a lover. That was all. He'd said it dismissively, as if the assistant who drove the Accord wasn't "wife material." When Elizabeth called him on what sounded like elitism, he'd apologized right away.

Elizabeth hadn't known Janine would be traveling with Matthew to New York. They must have rendezvoused early Tuesday at his home, where his Jaguar was parked in the garage, and shared a limo to SFO.

Must have, she reiterated silently as she parked the car.

So why hadn't she grabbed an invitation before heading toward the mail slot in his door? And why was she veering away from that door toward the master-bedroom side of Matthew's house?

Matthew never pulled the bedroom blinds. The neighbors' windows faced the other way, and it would take a slender voyeur indeed to traverse the narrow path. And a tall one to peer inside.

Elizabeth *was* slender, and tall. In the seconds before she witnessed the scene within, she knew what she'd see. And, in those seconds, the prosecutor known for her ability to distill seemingly random details into a coherent story distilled what she was about to witness into a single word.

Lies.

Elizabeth had never cast herself in such a drama. It would have been an idle exercise—and the attorney who hadn't spent a carefree summer since age eighteen was rarely idle. Besides, she'd met enough criminals and their victims to know that imagined reactions to hypothetical situations didn't necessarily forecast what would happen when the situation was real.

At the moment, the reality was excruciating. A glimpse through the window was all she needed.

And her reaction to the betrayal?

She felt detached.

And purposeful.

She returned to her car, opened the trunk and extracted one of the just-minted invitations—already of historical interest.

She toyed with writing "canceled" across the gold engraving. Or, and this was more appealing, drawing a circle with a slash through it.

That had a certain eloquence, succinct yet clear.

Less, however, was more.

After emptying an envelope of its invitation, she dropped her engagement ring inside and sealed the flap.

Very haiku, she thought as she slipped the envelope through the slot in the door.

Then, numbly but decisively, she began the seven-and-a half-hour drive to her grandmother's home.

Two

Sarah's Orchard
Friday, July 7, 8:00 p.m.

Nick paused at the foot of the steep driveway he knew so well. It was a reverent pause; it was also a chance to assert mind over matter.

His legs hurt, an acute pain on top of the smoldering discomfort that was always there. He'd been pushing hard the past three weeks, determined to complete the Tolliver Farm remodel today—so he could get going on the summer's project for Clara in the morning.

His legs weren't happy. But he was. And the Tollivers were.

He'd almost driven the mile from his home to Clara's. A concession to the throbbing in his legs. But the walk was good for his soul. Especially this final climb.

He'd made it countless times since his return to Sarah's Orchard. As he made the ascent now, he recalled the evening, three Aprils earlier, when he'd first knocked on the MacKenzies' teal-colored door.

He'd been in Sarah's Orchard for six weeks by then, his decision to come back an easy one to make. Sarah's Orchard was the only place he'd ever lived where he'd choose to live again.

There wasn't anything wrong with the other towns he'd lived in with his mother and Dennis, and Marianne's next boyfriend, and the next and the next—until, when he was seventeen, they'd gone their separate ways. Marianne had been ready to move. Again. He'd wanted to finish school. He'd never searched for her. Nor, he supposed, had she looked for him.

The towns had been pleasant. The memories weren't.

Nick hoped to live a quiet life for the rest of his life, and a useful one. As a soldier, he'd volunteered for impossible missions—and proved them possible, after all.

The military had been a good place for Nick until a spray of bullets fractured his legs and shattered his pelvis. He would've continued to serve if he could. But his recovery, though surprising to the doctors, was incomplete. His strength wasn't what it had been, nor was he as agile as he needed to be.

The military didn't compel Lieutenant Commander Nicholas Lawton to leave. Quite the contrary. Any number of high-level noncombat positions were his for the taking.

But Nick couldn't send soldiers into battle unless he was with them, leading them in—and leading them out.

He knew that emotional guidance was especially important for those unaccustomed to battle. No matter how well trained they were, how prepared they believed themselves to be, the first death, the first killing, was a shock.

No preparation was adequate for the sights and sounds of friends dying. Or enemies dying—young men who, in another world, might have been friends. Men who, like them, dreamed of playing with their children, caring for their elderly parents, making love to their brides.

Emotions were kept at bay during the fighting itself. Adrenaline and training saw the soldiers through. But until the aftermath, no soldier knew how he'd respond to what he'd experienced. Some were able to articulate their feelings. Nick listened to what they needed to say.

Others, like Nick himself had been, held everything inside. Nick was there for them, too, listening to their silence and speaking words that might have been of comfort had someone spoken them to him.

Nick had left the military, honorably and with fanfare he hadn't wanted. What lay ahead, after months of rehab, was a mission as challenging as any he'd ever known…and in which he was likely to fail.

Finding contentment, finding peace, might very well be impossible. Even in the only town he'd ever wanted to live in.

He'd chalked it up to morbid curiosity when he'd driven by the house on Center Street. He remembered it as dilapidated and menacing—where the danger to a seven-year-old boy was far greater than freezing to death on a winter night. The real peril had been to his heart and soul.

The house, with its For Rent sign, had remained an eyesore, a blemish in a neighborhood of charming homes. But it looked sad, not menacing, in need of care. The current owners, who lived in Medford, were waiting for the Sarah's Orchard housing market to appreciate enough that even their run-down property would sell. Their new tenant was welcome to make improvements, if he liked, at his own expense, assuming the structure wasn't devalued as a result.

It wasn't, and Nick's neighbors were thrilled. By the time he began knocking on doors—for that was how introductions were made in Sarah's Orchard—they'd spread the word that the new handyman in town was handy indeed.

Nick's reconciliation with his Center Street memories helped his quest for peace. As did seeing the orchards again, one orchard in particular.

But it wasn't enough. He needed to see the MacKenzies again. The kind eyes. He wouldn't introduce himself as "the boy who'd saved Elizabeth," of course. Much less as "Elizabeth's hero."

"Hero" had been as foreign to him on that long-ago December night as "son" had been. He'd clung to "son," treasured it, but even at age seven he'd believed "hero" was wrong. He'd only done what anyone would've done had they spotted the sobbing little girl.

He'd been called a hero many times in the intervening years. It continued to sound wrong. In combat as in life, he only did what he believed anyone would do.

Nick had intended to tell Charles and Clara the same thing he'd told the other townspeople who'd opened their doors to him. He was willing and able to do a range of repairs.

The orchard was in blossom on the April evening the soldier with splintered bones climbed the steep drive the small boy had ascended, carrying a giggling toddler, so many Decembers past.

In blossom, and magical. Those trees, he felt, wanted him to sing to them, the way he sang "Amazing Grace," when that was what the wounded needed to hear. Or

"Battle Hymn of the Republic." Or "God Bless America." Or any song that would make an injured soldier smile.

It was Clara who'd opened the door to his knock. Nick had been only a sentence into his introduction when she'd tilted her head and widened her eyes.

"You're him, aren't you?"

"Him?"

"Our boy. Elizabeth's hero. Don't deny it. I *know* you are. Charles! Guess who's here? At last."

Nick hadn't denied it. Nor, by the time Charles appeared, had he confirmed it. He'd been speechless in those moments, stunned that Clara had known.

The man he'd become bore no resemblance to the scrawny boy he'd been. True, Clara had promised she'd never forget his bright blue eyes.

But he didn't *have* bright blue eyes, not as a boy— and most certainly not as a man. Oh, there was a tincture of blue in the gray, a patch of sky amid the clouds. But in all his years, only Clara MacKenzie had remarked on it.

What she'd seen had been an illusion, the play of red Christmas lights on the hint of blue. Or maybe the entire illusion had been in the sparkling eyes of the beholder.

Others had made comments about Nick's eyes. Other women. Bedroom eyes, some concluded. Only wilder. As if a bed was too tame for his tastes. And that was before he went to war.

No, Nick didn't have bright blue eyes. Never had. And the hair that had been blondish when Clara had last seen him had turned brown when he reached his teens.

But Clara had known who he was.

Because of his expression, she'd eventually informed him. It was identical, she said, to the hopeful way he'd looked when she and Charles had promised to be there for him—always. Hopeful yet skeptical, she'd added. Hope against hope.

Charles and Clara MacKenzie had kept their promise, welcoming him into their lives when he'd needed them most. Charles and Clara had needed Nick, too. Both of them. And, in the seven months since Charles's death, and to the extent she'd permit it, he'd shared with Clara her enormous loss.

Beginning tomorrow, he'd be with Clara all summer.

He'd find a way to help her, and the lovely eyes that had once seen colors and emotions no one else could see.

Three

"Oh, Clara," he said when she opened the door and he saw her tears.

"You miss him, too."

"I do," Nick said. "All day, every day. Charles was the finest man I've ever known."

Clara nodded and wiped her eyes. "Are you dropping by for dinner?"

"Just dropping by." Nick smiled. "But I wouldn't turn down food."

"Then come on in."

They'd both known she'd ask, and that he'd accept the offer. He'd shown up often—at suppertime—since Charles's death. And at dawn, when her curtains signaled she'd awakened for the day. And midmorning for coffee, and in the afternoon for tea.

Both knew he was checking up on her, and why he never called in advance. She'd tell him what she told everyone else who worried about her. *You don't need to come over. I'm fine!*

She'd made such assertions to Nick in the beginning. *You can't possibly be fine,* he'd tell her when he appeared despite her protestations. He'd arrive within fifteen minutes of his phone call, and she always seemed relieved when he did. *And even if you're fine, Clara, I'm not.*

Nick didn't care about the food she inevitably served him. He could cook his own meals. But if he permitted Clara to feed him, she'd end up nibbling on something, too.

It was past her usual suppertime. But Nick had the feeling she might have forgotten to eat. His impression was confirmed when they reached the kitchen.

On the table where her dinner might have been, four round boxes sat instead. Glossy boxes, he noted, each in a different shade of yellow.

"Hatboxes?" Nick prompted.

"They contain the letters Charles wrote me during the war. I haven't read them since his return. I didn't need to. I had him. And," Clara said, "I knew every one by heart."

"I'll bet you still do."

"I don't know. Getting them down from the attic is as far as I've gotten."

"The attic? Clara—"

"I'm perfectly ambulatory, Nick! And the railings a certain *dear* friend of ours added to all our walls and staircases make climbing up and down a breeze." Clara smiled at the dear friend who, following Charles's stroke, had made it easy for him to spend the remaining year of his life with the woman he loved in the farmhouse he'd always known. "Elizabeth painted these boxes for me."

"Oh?" Nick asked, moving closer.

The varying shades of yellow were background. On each lid was an apple tree. One for every season. The style was primitive and bold, painted by a girl who couldn't draw any better than she could sing.

The boxes weren't works of art. But they were works of love. And passion, Nick thought. An exuberant affection for the trees, be they barren for winter, blossom-laden during spring, bountiful with summer fruit or brilliant with the leaves of autumn.

Elizabeth's wintertime tree wasn't entirely barren. Oblong splashes of red dangled from its outermost reaches. Christmas lights—like the ones that had illuminated a sobbing little girl.

"When did she paint these?"

"The first year she spent the entire summer here. She was eight, and we had *such* fun. On rainy days, we poked around in the attic, trying on old clothes, looking at old photographs, playing with the mah-jongg set Charles inherited from his father. Charles's letters didn't pique her interest. But she could tell how important they were to me. She wondered if they needed brighter homes than the white hatboxes I'd stored them in. They definitely did, I told her, and asked if she'd be willing to decorate them for me."

"Did you suggest what she should draw? The seasons of the orchard?"

"I made no suggestions whatsoever. But, being Elizabeth, she shared her every thought. The boxes had to be yellow, she said, because I'd painted the house yellow to welcome Charles home from the war."

"She didn't go with the same yellow."

"No. She felt it would be all right—if I agreed—to pick four brighter shades. You remember her affinity for the bright and shiny."

"I do," Nick said softly. "And the apple trees? Why did she choose to paint them?"

"Because she loves them. She's always viewed them as the living things they are—as friends." Clara touched an apple blossom on Elizabeth's springtime tree. "When she was finished, Charles lacquered each box inside and out, sealing the cardboard and, or so we hoped, preserving her vivid paintings. But they've faded, haven't they?"

Not at all, Nick thought. He felt quite sure they were as bright as the day eight-year-old Elizabeth had dabbed her final drop of paint. *But Clara couldn't see it.* It was the worry he would find a way to address. Beginning tomorrow.

Tonight, he broached the worry that was foremost on Clara's mind. "Have you heard from Elizabeth?"

"Not since Monday night. I don't expect to hear from her, Nick. Not on that topic. She's not mad at me because of what I said about Matthew. Sad, maybe. Disappointed. But not mad." She sighed. "If anyone owes anyone a follow-up phone call, it's me who should call her."

"But you haven't."

"It wouldn't be fair unless I was calling to tell her I'd decided my instincts were wrong and he was perfect for her after all."

"You haven't decided that."

"Not even close. The more I think about it, the more convinced I become. It's better just to let some time pass."

"Is Elizabeth still coming for a visit at the end of the month?"

"We didn't discuss it Monday night, but I'm sure she will. She's not going to hold my concerns about Matthew against me. And she *is* going to marry him. I wasn't trying to talk her out of it. I probably shouldn't have said anything."

"That's not your style, Clara, not when the happiness of your family's involved. Especially Elizabeth."

"But I've made her unhappy. I wish you'd come to the party at the Orchard Inn."

"I was behind on the remodel for Pete and Celia."

"Ha!"

"Ha?"

"You were afraid I'd have a glass of champagne or two, and start reminiscing about Elizabeth's Christmastime adventure and say this is the boy who saved her. *This* is Elizabeth's hero."

Clara had made the pronouncement with fondness twenty-seven years ago. There was more fondness now.

"I was behind on the remodel," Nick repeated, smiling. "I'm not *afraid* of your introducing me as that boy. I just don't want you to."

"I know, Nick. And I won't. I do wish you'd been at the party, though."

"I don't know Elizabeth, Clara. There's no way I would've been able to tell if she and Matthew were right for each other."

"You'd have been able to tell. You'd have been able to see…" Clara sighed again.

"See what?"

"That Matthew's not in love with my granddaughter. There," she continued without a pause. "I've said what I could never say to Elizabeth. But it's what I believe, Nick. And it scares me for her."

Nick hadn't had a chance to reflect upon, much less dispute, Clara's assertion that he'd be able to see—or even sense—the presence or absence of love. But he heard himself say something astonishing. "It scares me for her, too."

Four

In what should have been the final hour of Elizabeth's seven-and-a-half-hour journey to Sarah's Orchard, the drive became treacherous. The two-lane road from Medford was somewhat perilous in broad daylight when the pavement was dry. But in darkness, when rain fell…

Eight hours and forty-five minutes after she'd pulled away from the curb in San Francisco, Elizabeth reached the crest of a driveway down which—or so she'd been told—she'd scampered on a long-ago winter night.

It was almost ten. Would Gram be awake?

The glowing house lights told her yes.

The lights were blurry. The rain was drenching. The downpour was not, however, the only reason for the watery blur.

Since her glimpse into Matthew's bedroom, Elizabeth had kept her emotions as tightly sequestered as a deliberating jury in a high-profile trial. But as she neared the safe haven of her grandmother's home, those emotions escaped in a flood of tears.

* * *

"Now who could that be?" Clara wondered when the doorbell rang.

"No one you want to see," Nick replied. "Not at this hour."

Nick had personally installed the farmhouse's burglar alarm. It was state-of-the-art—every window, all the doors, panic buttons at various locations throughout the home. He had an uneasy feeling that Clara hadn't turned it on since Charles's death.

Now, at 10:00 p.m., she had no qualms about opening the door to whoever happened by on what had become a soggy night.

"You've come over this late."

"Not without a warning call."

"This is Sarah's Orchard, Nick." She stood up from the kitchen table and gave Nick, who was washing dishes, a gentle pat. "I'll scream if it's anyone sinister."

Nick wiped his soapy hands and followed. He stopped short of the door and off to the side, invisible to the visitor, but a step away from intervening if Clara needed him.

"Elizabeth!"

"Hi, Gram."

"Come in, darling girl." The hand that had patted Nick's arm went to her granddaughter's cheek. "Tears."

"And rain." Elizabeth lifted the rain-spattered box she'd taken from the trunk before dashing to the covered porch. "Lots of rain. Not that it matters if these get soaked."

"What are they?" Clara asked as Elizabeth walked inside.

"My wedding invitations. I thought we could build a fire with them."

"The design didn't work out as well as you'd hoped?"

"The design's fine. It's the wedding that's not so good."

"Oh, Elizabeth."

"How did you know, Gram? About Matthew?"

"What happened?"

"He was supposed to be in New York, on the business trip he told you about last weekend. I went to his house, to leave one of the invitations for him. He wasn't in New York. And he wasn't alone. He was with the woman he'd been involved with before he and I got together."

"Is he still alive?" Nick stepped into her line of sight as he spoke.

"Oh!" *You.* Whoever you are.

She'd seen him twice, briefly—but memorably. The first time had been eighteen months ago, in the neurology ward at the Keeling Clinic, the day Granddad was admitted with his stroke. He'd been standing at the periphery of the crowded waiting room of friends who'd remained at the medical center until Clara's family arrived. He'd disappeared shortly thereafter. But in the few moments before he'd vanished, and even though her focus had been on rushing to Gram's side, she'd been acutely aware of him.

It felt as if he, too, was at Clara's side. Despite how far away he stood. At Gram's side, protecting her—and Granddad. Guarding them with his life.

The second time she'd seen him had been seven months ago, in late November, at Granddad's funeral. He'd stood a distance away then, as well.

Now he was here. Whoever he was. And he was asking if Matthew Blaine had survived his faithlessness.

"I'm Nicholas Lawton."

This—*he*—was Nicholas Lawton? Elizabeth knew of him, of course. Three years ago, he'd been the talk, and worry, of the MacKenzie clan. Granddad had been wanting to remodel Gram's kitchen. Her "small" business, The Apple Butter Ladies, was becoming a force to be reckoned with.

Clara and her friend and business partner, Eve, needed more space not only for the batches of apple butter the marketplace was beginning to demand, but for the support staff that processed orders, packaged the jars, unloaded the crates of apples delivered from nearby orchards, and shipped off the cartons of apple butter.

Granddad knew what the new kitchen needed to be. His years as owner and manager of MacKenzie's Market had made him a wizard at designing flow patterns conducive to happy shoppers. And workers. His sketches for Clara's new kitchen were based on sitting in the midst of the Apple Butter Ladies' operation during its busiest time of year—from harvest through the holidays. He'd observed the near-collisions, the conversations that took place over shoulders, not face-to-face, and other obstacles to what should have been as enjoyable and productive as a quilting bee.

The changes were major. Walls would have to be moved. The bids he'd gotten had been pricier than he'd imagined. But the cost hadn't been the primary sticking point. The contractors didn't "get" his vision. They'd suggested modifications Charles had known wouldn't work. The idea of spending hard-earned money for the privilege of arguing over the placement of every cupboard and countertop wasn't something Charles was eager to do.

He would, though, if he had to. For Clara.

He was on the verge of accepting a bid when, out of the blue, a man named Nicholas Lawton arrived in town. A "handyman," Charles reported to his family. Who, he assured his concerned children—and grandchildren—was fully capable of handling the entire renovation. "Nick can do anything," Clara cheerfully added…which alarmed the family all the more. Who was this stranger who'd bewitched Gram and Granddad so completely?

Two of Elizabeth's six cousins, all of whom were male, made an immediate surprise visit to the farmhouse. No one was going to take advantage of their grandparents.

But they'd liked Nick. Proclaimed him to be a "great guy." The assessment was affirmed within months by two additional cousins and, over time, by the entire family. Not that everyone met Nick. But they saw Gram's kitchen and, after Granddad's stroke, the railings Nick installed.

They heard, too, the affection for Nick in their grandparents' voices. Gram's fondness was easy and familiar. Her emotions were always effortlessly conveyed. With the exception of his family, however, Granddad had been reserved. But there was emotion in Charles's voice when he talked about Nick. It was different from what one heard for his sons and grandsons. But no less important, or impassioned.

Like the rest of her family, Elizabeth spoke highly of Nicholas Lawton, and was grateful for Nicholas Lawton, although—as it happened—every time she was in town, he was involved with projects elsewhere and unable to drop by.

She'd be meeting him this summer, Gram had said. At the farmhouse. Assuming, of course, that Nick hadn't finished the painting he planned to do before Elizabeth's visit in late July.

Elizabeth knew very little about painting houses. But she felt certain she and Nick would meet. Ten years ago, when then-mayor Clara MacKenzie decided the "may-orly" thing to do in honor of Sarah's Orchard's centennial celebration would be to return James and Sarah Keeling's farmhouse to its original teal and white, the painters Granddad hired were at it for three months.

There'd been a team of painters then, not a solitary one. And their task, to cover cream with teal, had to be far easier than what Nick would face when he did the reverse, restoring Charles and Clara's farmhouse to the colors it had been ever since it had served as a beacon to welcome a soldier home.

"You're going to paint the house."

"I am."

"Inside and out," Clara said.

"Inside, too?"

"Why not?" Nick asked.

"It needs to be spiffed up, Nick says, all except the kitchen. We've been discussing color schemes," Clara murmured, "Nick has all sorts of options and he wants me to decide. He says he's showing up at dawn tomorrow with a zillion paint chips. I can't make such decisions. Now that you're here, Elizabeth, I won't have to."

"You don't want me choosing colors!"

"Of course I do. But—and here's what I was going to do—just agree with whatever Nick thinks will look best. He's the artist."

"Hardly," Nick said. "I look forward to your input, Elizabeth." He untied the daisy-print apron he wore. "Now, I think I'll leave you ladies alone."

"Why don't you take my car?" Clara asked. "It's pouring."

Nick didn't glance outside. "I'm fine." He looked at Elizabeth. "What time's good for you tomorrow?"

"Anytime. Including dawn. Wasn't that what you and Gram had planned?"

"Only," Clara said, "because Nick knows I'm an early riser when I don't have my granddaughter to chat with through the night. We should be up by noon, though, wouldn't you say?"

"I'd say so," Elizabeth replied. "I'd also say I've never slept past eight in my life, Gram, and neither have you. So if you'd like to come by earlier, Nick…"

"Noon's good," he said. "I'll see you then."

The downpour was a suitable companion for Nick's thoughts.

As he left the farmhouse, he headed away from Center Street, not toward it. He needed to walk for a while. Run for a while.

And think—for a while.

Clara and Charles hadn't forgotten the boy who'd rescued their granddaughter. And Elizabeth's vanishing act in pursuit of brightly lit apple trees was a cautionary tale remembered by every MacKenzie old enough to recall the terror of that evening.

All MacKenzies knew that a nameless youngster had carried their girl to safety. But Charles and Clara alone had been waiting for his return. They'd seemed to know he *would* return, and even when, since the kitchen Charles had designed for Clara was ready for Nick to build.

Nick had always known that the rescued girl would have no memory of her Yuletide misadventure. Much less of him.

Nick wouldn't have recognized Elizabeth, either, if he hadn't seen photographs of her in her grandparents' home. Despite that, the Elizabeth who rushed into the

Keeling Clinic on the evening of Charles's stroke had been a surprise.

The camera had captured her elegant bones and wholesome allure. But it had failed to capture *her*. She didn't have a freeze-frame sort of face. Or a freeze-frame sort of life. She was beauty in motion, as vibrant as the bright colors she chased. As bold as the emotions it wouldn't occur to her to hide.

Until that evening at the clinic, Nick figured it was just a matter of time before he and Elizabeth were introduced. The well-bred heiress would offer a gracious hello, while the granddaughter-turned-prosecutor searched for proof that he meant no harm to the grandparents she loved.

He'd pass inspection, and that would be that. From her standpoint, anyway.

Nick had known, even before seeing her, that the protectiveness he felt toward Charles and Clara would extend to their only granddaughter.

It did, but with a twist.

Elizabeth needed his protection, all right. Protection from him.

The attraction he'd felt for her was immediate. And powerful.

But as powerful as the physical desire was, it paled in comparison to a longing that was entirely new. He wanted to be with her. Simply be. For better, for worse. In sickness and in health. Forsaking all others.

Forever.

Nick dealt with his longing in a way that was best for Elizabeth, most protective of her. He kept his distance, avoiding any and all opportunity for the two of them to even meet. And, on a sunny day in early May, Clara told him Elizabeth was engaged.

He ached at the revelation. And, at the same time, he

felt relieved. Elizabeth had found the kind of man she should marry.

And now…

Now.

Nick could run all night in the storm. Until his every shattered bone screamed for mercy.

But Nicholas Lawton couldn't outrun, could never outrun, his feelings for Elizabeth.

They were part of who he was.

The best part.

Five

Gram insisted that her rain-soaked granddaughter change into slumber-party attire before they convened in the kitchen for hot chocolate and a chat.

"I will if you will," Elizabeth had said.

They'd gone to their separate bedrooms, the one where Clara and Charles had slept for more than sixty years—and where Charles had died in his sleep—and the guest room down the hall that had always been Elizabeth's.

Her farm clothes were there, the wardrobe from the final teenage summer she'd spent at Sarah's Orchard. The wardrobe had been baggy even then. She'd liked wearing loose clothing over her plumpish frame.

The plumpness had gone the way of carefree summers. The jeans and T-shirts would be baggier now.

When Gram, in robe and slippers, emerged from her bedroom, Elizabeth, similarly dressed, emerged from hers.

"He wasn't what I expected," Elizabeth said as they walked down the stairs.

Gram's hand slid along the satin-smooth railing Nick had made. "You only dated him for four months before getting engaged."

"I meant Nick."

"Oh?"

"Not that my expectations mean very much. Witness Matthew."

"Matthew's history."

"That's definitive."

"Well, isn't he?"

Elizabeth's mind's eye viewed again the image she'd glimpsed through his bedroom window. "Yes. He is."

"Good. Let's talk about Nick. In what way wasn't he what you expected?"

"I don't know. I guess I thought he wouldn't be so…"

"Handsome?"

"Gram."

"Gorgeous?"

"Gram."

"What then?"

"Solemn." *Intense.*

"Nick is solemn. He reminds me of Granddad in that way. In many ways, come to think of it."

Granddad? Solemn? And like Nick in many ways?

Elizabeth might have pursued the inquiry. They'd reached the kitchen, where, on one of the many countertops Granddad knew the Apple Butter Ladies needed and which Nick had built, sat the hatboxes she'd painted twenty-one years ago.

"Granddad's letters," she murmured.

"Yes. Please feel free to read them."

To discover, Elizabeth mused, *what true love really is.* "I couldn't."

"I *want* you to. In fact, I'm hoping all our children and grandchildren will. They're a little mushy, I suppose, but there's nothing too private for you to read."

"Then I'll read them, Gram. We all will. If that's what you want."

"It's the reason I brought them down from the attic. I'd like to make copies, a complete set for each of you—and Nick, of course."

Nick, of course? "That would be wonderful," Elizabeth said. "We could even have them bound into books."

"We could?"

"Absolutely."

Clara touched a glossy box. "That would be nice. There's a bit of organizing to do. The letters are in chronological order, but I carried some of them with me all the time. I'm not sure I tucked them into their correct bundles when I received word that Charles was on his way home."

"That sounds easy," Elizabeth said. So easy she wouldn't have mentioned it if not for Gram's frown. "Gram?"

"Would you be willing to put them in order for me?"

"I'd be delighted to. But wouldn't you like to do that yourself? And read them again while you're at it?"

"I'm not ready to read them yet. So if you wouldn't mind…"

"As I said, I'd be delighted. Gram? Is there something else?"

"I'm afraid they may not photocopy very well. The paper was thin to begin with, and he wrote on both sides."

"That won't be a problem."

"It won't?"

"Nope. You'd be amazed at the smudged, machine-washed, written-on-both-sides bits of paper I've been able to present to juries in all their legible glory, thanks to the magic of computers. That's what we should do,

Gram. Scan the letters directly into your computer. We can tinker with contrast, resolution and so on at the scanning stage, and make additional improvements once we've scanned them in."

"I'm glad you're saying 'we.' When it comes to computers, my forte is e-mail."

"You're still frowning. What's wrong?"

"I was thinking it's been a while since I e-mailed Winifred."

"Like before meeting Matthew last weekend?" Elizabeth guessed.

"A while before that," Gram admitted.

"You were busy planning the reception for us at the Orchard Inn. It was a wonderful party, Gram, my unfortunate choice of fiancé notwithstanding. If you'd liked Matthew, you would've e-mailed Winifred right away. But you didn't like him, and not wanting to worry her, you held off. And, of course, you were concerned about my feelings, too. The good news is you have a doozy of an e-mail to send now. With my permission."

"I won't get too carried away."

"The truth is the truth, Gram. There are men who'd never lie to their fiancées, or spend clandestine afternoons with other women. Men like Granddad," Elizabeth said. *And Nick?* "Then there are the Matthew Blaines of the world. He wasn't in love with me. You were able to see it, even though I couldn't."

"I saw something else, Elizabeth. You weren't in love with Matthew, either."

"You're just saying that to make me feel better." Elizabeth smiled. "It *would* make me feel better—if it was true."

"It's true, darling girl. Mark my— Nick," she predicted as the phone began to ring.

"Nick? Why?"

"He'll want to make sure there's nothing we need." Clara lifted the receiver. "We're fine! Hello? Well, yes, as a matter of fact, she is here." *Your mother,* she mouthed. "Safe and sound, thank goodness, and having dodged an unfortunate matrimonial bullet. No, Abby, she's not going to marry him."

Clara winked at her granddaughter. Abigail Mac-Kenzie-Winslow didn't like being called Abby. Her mother knew it, and reserved it for times such as these, when sternness was required.

"The engagement ring Matthew found in his foyer *was* a major clue. He's bewildered? I'd suggest he put on his thinking cap. He's a smart fellow. He ought to be able to figure this out." Clara was silent for a moment. "She's resting. I'll have her call you tomorrow. She won't be changing her mind. And, as her mother, you shouldn't *want* her to." Another silence. "I don't know when she'll be returning to San Francisco. I'm hoping she'll stay here for a while. She'd be a tremendous help with a project I'm working on. Give my best to Thomas, will you?"

Clara replaced the receiver and smiled at her granddaughter.

"Thank you, Gram."

"That's not the end of it," Clara said. "We both know your mother better than that."

"She really wanted this marriage."

"Too bad! If Matthew's last name wasn't Blaine, and she wasn't in a tizzy about how her society friends are going to react, her focus would be where it belongs—on you. Despite that, she *is* concerned about you."

"I know."

"How a daughter of mine could be such a snob, I'll never know." Gram paused. Sighed. "That's not entirely accurate. The truth is, she comes by it honestly."

"She does? From where? Dad's not a snob. And she certainly didn't get it from you or Granddad."

"That's the problem. I'm afraid she did. Who knew snobbery could be carried in the genes? Old money isn't even supposed to be snobbish. Your father being a case in point. But, as I know well, it's the exception that proves the rule. One of San Francisco's oldest and wealthiest families—mine—is such an exception."

"Your family, Gram?"

"The San Francisco Carltons. Even when I was a girl, the Carlton fortune was generations old. But talk about snobs. My mother especially."

"Your mother?"

"My father was almost as pretentious. He was a Bronxville Smith. But we lived in San Francisco, not New York, and she was the Carlton of the two."

"So…you're a Carlton."

"I *was* a Carlton. Granddad knew, and his parents. To everyone else, I was simply Clara Anne Smith, who couldn't wait to become Clara Anne MacKenzie. It wasn't a secret as much as an irrelevance."

"Mom doesn't know."

"And never needs to. Like your relationship with Matthew, my pedigree is ancient history."

"But how did you and Granddad meet? I always thought he'd never left Sarah's Orchard before he went to war—and that the two of you met and fell in love before that."

"We met here, in September 1941. I'd just celebrated my sixteenth birthday and in two months he'd turned eighteen."

"And a month after that," Elizabeth said, "Pearl Harbor was attacked."

"We were in love by then. Long before that day of infamy, we knew we'd spend our lives together."

"What were you doing in Sarah's Orchard?"

"What all San Francisco heiresses did in those days, attending finishing school. Because of the war in Europe, stateside boarding schools were popular, and new ones kept cropping up. Rogue River School for Girls was in its second year when I arrived that September."

"I've never heard of Rogue River School for Girls."

"But you know the building well. After the war, it became the Orchard Inn."

"Which is a short walk to MacKenzie's Market."

"Where Granddad helped his parents on weekends and after school."

"And where a Rogue River schoolgirl happened by?"

"A classmate and I loved the apples we were served at lunch. One day, we decided to buy some for snacks. One day became every day. Granddad always had an apple waiting for me, shined to a mirror finish on his shirtsleeve. His parents were amused by how smitten he was. Girls had been stopping by the store for apples—or whatever else was in season—for a while. But he'd never taken an interest in any of them the way he was interested in me. And, of course, he was my one and only love."

"And you were his."

"We knew it. His family knew it."

"And your family?"

"I'd planned to tell them that Christmas. Charles and I talked about his coming to San Francisco for New Year's to ask my parents' permission for us to marry that spring. But everything changed, the world changed on

December 7. I went to Portland with him. That's where he enlisted. And where we spoke our wedding vows—privately, just to each other." She closed her eyes for a moment. "We thought he'd be sent to the Pacific. But Congress had declared war on Germany and Italy, too, by then, and that's where he went."

"How long was he gone?"

"Three years, eight months, six days. He came home a month after VE Day."

"You missed him desperately."

"Every second of every day. I was lucky to have his parents, and this town. They welcomed me and my babies, your twin uncles."

"And *your* family?"

Clara shook her head. "They didn't want any part of a daughter who'd gotten pregnant out of wedlock with a country boy whose dream was to carry on the tradition of his family's store. My parents threatened to disown me, to cut me off from the wealth and social status that were my birthright, unless I went into hiding until after I'd had my babies and given them away."

"They were serious?"

"Oh, yes. And so was I. I didn't threaten to disown them. I just did it."

"That must've been difficult."

"I won't pretend it wasn't. Not the decision—that was easy. But it hurt me deeply that they hadn't even wanted to meet the man I loved, hadn't given him a chance."

"Mom's not that much of a snob. But," Elizabeth said, "I wonder if Matthew is."

Six

April 13, 1942
Midnight
Clara, my love,
I'm remembering the first night you sneaked out of the dormitory to be with me. I was so worried you'd fall as you climbed down the tree. You laughed at my worry. I can hear that fearless laughter even now.

You scampered down the oak, long skirts and all, as if you'd been climbing trees all your life. We walked to the river. Do you remember? And lay beside each other on the grass. We listened to the sounds of the autumn night. The owl talking to the moon. The river lapping at our feet.

I listened to you breathe. When you breathed out, my Clara, I breathed in. I wanted to draw deep within me the air still warm from being deep within you. I wondered if you were doing the same.

It was the only way we could touch on that September night. We'd known each other just one week. We *lay as close as we could without touching, didn't we?*

I wanted to touch you, Clara. You discovered, later, how much. But I'm glad we didn't touch on that night. I can lie here, so many miles away—a world away, my darling—and pretend you're beside me now, and that the night air that's giving me life, giving me hope, is doing so because it was breathed first by you.

I love you, Clara. More than life, and long beyond death.

I'm lying beside you, my love.

Always,

Charles

"Oh, Granddad," Elizabeth whispered as she placed the letter beside the others she'd read. *"Granddad."*

After a moment, and through the blur of dampness in her eyes, she glanced at the stovetop clock.

Eleven forty-five. Time to get ready for Nick. *Mentally* ready, she amended, for the switching of cerebral gears from Granddad's letters, Granddad's love, to choosing colors schemes for the house—with Nick.

Mental preparedness was required there, as well. She felt wary about seeing Nick. Quite wary. But quite eager, too.

It was an unsettling paradox, and a crazy one. *Crazy* being the operative word.

A little head-clearing fresh air was in order, and it was hers for the taking. Last night's rainstorm was now a memory. The world it left behind sparkled fresh and clean.

She walked the length of the driveway. At its farthest reach, she sat on a patch of grass beneath an apple tree. Eyes closed, she lifted her face skyward. The air was warm, as if from the lungs of a loved one lying close by. She inhaled deeply and was rewarded with a gift from an orchard of friends, the delicate scent of apples ripening beneath the summer sun.

Elizabeth Charlotte Winslow didn't have a freeze-frame kind of beauty; Nick had already decided that.

But the face that smiled at the sun was as motionless as a painting, and more beautiful than any he'd ever seen.

She was sitting beneath the very tree where he'd found her, sobbing, as a girl, and he was approaching from behind her, as he had on that December afternoon.

He would've been happy to watch her forever. But she had no idea she was being observed, and he had no right not to tell her.

"Elizabeth."

Her eyes flew open and she scrambled to her feet.

"Nick."

"On the lookout for Matthew?"

"No. I…" *On the lookout for you.* "Gram said you'd be coming from Center Street."

"I came early. There's a fence rail that needs replacing. I wanted to check for others before making a run to the lumber store."

"You take such good care of her."

"I'm honored that she lets me." Nick gestured toward the hill up which he'd once carried a singing, clinging little girl. "Shall we?"

"Sure." They ascended in silence, except for the swishing sound of her jeans legs brushing against each other. Finally she said, "Matthew won't be coming to Sarah's Orchard."

"So he's dead, after all."

"What? No!"

"No?" Then why isn't he moving heaven and earth to win you back? "What *did* you do?"

"When I saw…what I saw, I put my engagement ring in a wedding-invitation envelope, slid it through the mail slot in his door and drove away."

"That's nice. Classy." His smile was solemn. But it was a smile. "Very haiku."

She stopped. The denim stopped.

"What's wrong?" he asked.

"Nothing. I thought it was very haiku, too. Are you a poet?"

"I'm a handyman, Elizabeth." Nick resumed walking. "So you think your haiku message will keep Matthew away?"

"No. But I'm hoping the conversation we had when he called last night will. I believe I made it clear that any further discussions would be a waste of his time—and mine."

"You meant it."

"Absolutely."

"I'll bet he wasn't happy."

"He was…surprised. He tried to convince me that what he'd done had 'just happened,' as if he'd had no more control over it than if he'd been struck by lightning. And, of course, he said it meant nothing to him. *Janine* meant nothing."

"You obviously weren't convinced."

"I told him I thought he was in love with Janine and should have the courage to marry her, no matter how his parents felt about it. That wasn't what he wanted to hear. He was still trying to persuade me to forgive him. I said I already had, but that the marriage was off."

"Why?"

"*Why?*"

"I'm not questioning your decision. I'm just wondering if you expanded on your reasons."

"I did point out that lies don't 'just happen.' And that he'd lied to me *in advance* about where he'd be yesterday afternoon."

"A premeditated lie."

"Yes."

"Betrayal in the first degree."

"I wish I'd said that. Are you an attorney, Nick?"

"Elizabeth," he said, "I'm a handyman."

"Who can do anything, according to Gram."

"I can do a few things."

"Have you always been a handyman?"

Not always, Nick thought. Not until a December afternoon. Before then, he'd been a boy no one wanted, or valued.

He hadn't believed—until then—in a better world than the one he'd always known. But there *was* a better world, he'd discovered. And, just maybe, it was a world in which he could belong. He'd vowed to try.

"From the time I was seven, when I've seen something that needed fixing, I've done my best to fix it."

"Do you think I should've tried to fix my relationship with Matthew?"

"Not in a million years. Not even if you loved him." This time it was Nick who stopped. He waited until she met his dark gray eyes. "Did you?"

"Love the man I was going to marry? And whom I *would* have married if I hadn't caught him in flagrante with Janine?"

"Yes," Nick said. "That man."

"No." It began as a whisper, as if it were a confession almost too shameful to reveal. Once exposed to the summer sun—or perhaps to the gray eyes that glittered with sparks of blue—the *no* took on a life of its own. A happy life, relieved…and giggling. Bubbling. "No. No! I didn't love him."

Seven

"Where's Clara?" Nick asked when they entered the kitchen.

"She's at Eve's."

"Ah."

"Lemonade?" she offered.

"Sure. Thank you." Tossing the folder he'd brought with him onto the kitchen table, Nick walked to the counter where Charles's letters lay, taken from their glossy boxes. "Are you reading these?"

"Yes. Gram wants all of us to read them. *All of us* is her family…and you." It surprised him, Elizabeth thought. And moved him. He swallowed and looked away. "After making copies, I'm going to have each set professionally bound."

"That's nice." Nick touched the stack that had been removed from their envelopes. "Are these the ones you've read so far?"

Elizabeth nodded as she gave him a glass of lemonade. "I put the envelopes in order first. That didn't take as long as Gram figured it might. Then I started reading. The letters begin the day Granddad said goodbye to her in Portland. He introduces each fellow soldier he meets like an author introduces the characters in his story—who each of them is, where he comes from, who he loves, who and what he left behind. It's a diverse group, but they're united in their commitment to what they've chosen to do. Granddad doesn't portray their journey as a grand adventure. And yet, as they're crossing the country—and then the ocean—it feels that way. There's a sense of excitement, of eagerness for what lies ahead."

"Do you think they know what lies ahead?"

Elizabeth shook her head. "How could they? They're only eighteen. And, like Granddad, they've enlisted because of Pearl Harbor. The country they love has been attacked. They want to defend it. They believe what they're doing is right and good. And because it *is* right and good, they also believe they'll return triumphant and whole. But they can't, can they? Not all of them."

"No," Nick said. "Not all of them. In the letters you've read, have they gone into battle yet?"

"Yes. Just. And they all survived. Granddad says it that succinctly, that *flatly,* without any description of what actually happened." Elizabeth handed him the letter Charles wrote at midnight on April 13, 1942. "A few hours later, he wrote this."

Nick's expression as he read revealed nothing. When he finished and looked at her, his eyes were the color of stone. "What do you think?"

"About the letter? That it's beautiful. He loves Gram so much."

"Yes, he does." Nick hesitated briefly. "I'm sensing you have other thoughts."

"I get the feeling something horrible happened. He needs to tell her what it was."

"He won't. Ever."

"What?"

"He'll tell her succinctly, flatly, when one of his band of brothers dies. But he'll never describe how his friends die, or the way it feels to aim a rifle at another human being and pull the trigger and watch him fall, or how frightened he is, or angry, or if there comes a time when he wishes he could take a bullet instead of firing one."

"He *has* to tell her those things."

"Does he? Why?"

"She's the woman he loves! The woman who loves *him*. He can't hide such important emotions from her. It would be wrong."

"Wrong?"

"Yes." It was so clear to her. How could it not be to him? But it obviously wasn't. A new darkness shadowed his eyes. It looked like sadness, she thought. *Loneliness.* He didn't agree with what she was saying. And yet, it seemed, he wasn't going to argue the point. Maybe, if she quit arguing, he'd explain. "Why would he hide what he was feeling?"

"Because he loves her. He wants to protect her, Elizabeth. Her—and them. The love they share."

"You're saying he did something in combat that would make her love him less—or stop loving him at all? Because if so, I don't believe it. Granddad would never, *ever,* have committed the kind of atrocity that… Never."

"You're right," Nick said. "He wouldn't have. He'd have died first. You know that. I know that. And he trusts that your grandmother will know it, too. War can't change a man like Charles MacKenzie, Elizabeth. Not even war can do that."

Elizabeth heard in Nick's voice the same emotion

she'd heard in Granddad's when he spoke of Nick. She couldn't define it. But it was solemn. Important. And very deep. Gram had said the two were alike. And close, Elizabeth realized. Bonded in some special—reverent—way. Maybe Granddad had told Nick about the letters, what he'd shared and hadn't shared with Clara...and why. Or maybe Nick was only guessing.

Either way, Nick seemed to know.

"You're not going to find any premeditated betrayal here."

Nick gestured toward the letters as he spoke. *Here* referred, of course, to what Charles had written to his love. And yet, for a crazy unsettling moment, it felt as if *here*—where there was no betrayal—was anyplace she happened to be. With Nick.

"No betrayal," she murmured. "But you said Granddad wants to protect Gram. And them."

"He needs to believe that the world he knew before he went to war still exists. That's the world he's fighting for, where a girl climbs down a tree to meet the boy she loves, and you don't have to strain to hear an owl above the sounds of mortar and the cries of wounded men. That's why he's fighting, Elizabeth, to protect that innocence, that ideal."

"So when he writes about Gram being beside him, he's not bringing her to war with him."

"No," Nick said softly, "he's going home."

Home felt like *here.* Crazy. Except, in his blue-gray eyes, the sadness—and the loneliness—were gone.

What filled the void was so unsettling, in a giddy, glorious way, that she turned from him...and started babbling.

"Maybe we should look at your color schemes. Not

that I'm going to make any suggestions. In fact, don't *let* me. I'd never have come up with the choices you made for Gram's kitchen, and they're *wonderful*…"

"She's going to love these." Elizabeth's assertion, made thirty minutes later, was a grateful one. "The colors you've chosen are so cheerful. Just walking from room to room will make her smile."

"I hope so," Nick said. "Assuming she can see them."

"She's having trouble with her vision?" Elizabeth frowned. "She didn't say anything about it."

"I'm not so sure she would, even if she knew."

He was right, of course. Gram wasn't one to complain. "She doesn't know?"

"She's aware that her vision isn't what it used to be. But if it's what I think it is—cataracts—the impairment has come on so gradually she's adapted to the changes without realizing how significant they are."

"But you think they're significant."

"Very, and probably have been for a while. But because she has adapted, it's only been three weeks since I first began to wonder."

"What made you wonder?"

"Because of what happened when she looked at the sky on a crystal-clear night. She grabbed my arm and pointed to the moon. She was alarmed by what she saw, didn't know what it was. I thought she was confused. But as I was deciding how to suggest that to her, she began to describe what she was seeing. An immense sphere of light, she said, bright and glaring. A UFO, she thought, and was stunned I wasn't remarking on it, too. When I told her all I saw was the moon, she tilted her head, changing the angle of the incoming light and, with a laugh, chalked it up to her eyes playing tricks on her."

"But it wasn't."

"No. I did a little reading online and began to notice other things. Her reaction to oncoming headlights, for instance. She squints at them and, sometimes, she even recoils."

"I didn't think she drove at night."

"She doesn't, and hasn't for a while. But she's been a passenger in my truck. I've made a point of being a passenger in her car, too, during the day. She's okay if the ambient light is good and it's a familiar route. She's a careful driver. Cautious."

"But if her overall vision is significantly impaired… What else have you noticed?"

"She doesn't read the way she used to. Not for pleasure."

"Or," Elizabeth said, "maintain what was once a daily e-mail correspondence with Winifred."

"And that's after increasing the magnification of her reading glasses to the strongest she can buy at the market. She listens to the radio, and listens to, but doesn't watch, TV."

"You said she might not see the colors you've chosen."

"I'm not sure she sees color at all anymore. When she showed me the hatboxes you painted, she was dismayed that they'd faded despite the lacquer finish."

"They haven't faded."

"I didn't think so."

Elizabeth searched her memory for what else she'd observed since her arrival. "She uses the railing to go up and down stairs. And she was very eager to turn the letter-scanning project over to me. And equally eager not to be here when you showed me the color schemes. And last night, while we were sitting at the kitchen table, she got up a couple of times to flip a light switch."

"Only to discover the light was already on."

"All the lights were on. The kitchen was bright."

"Her world may be very dark."

"A visual darkness," Elizabeth said thoughtfully, "that makes sense to her, feels appropriate to her, given the emotional darkness of losing Granddad. Not being able to see must make that loss, and the prospect of her life after Granddad, seem even more hopeless. But it was *her* idea, she said, to have you paint the house."

"The outside."

"The gold that guided Granddad home after the war. She wants him to see the glow from wherever he is—even though she can't." Elizabeth saw a glow then. Or believed she did. A glitter of wanting, of longing, in his solemn gray eyes. In a flicker it was gone. Its impact left her momentarily confused. She forced the moment, and the confusion away. "Gram needs to see an ophthalmologist."

"She has an appointment for eleven on Wednesday morning. I made it once I figured out what was going on. I called Charles's neurologist at the Clinic and asked who he'd recommend. Next Wednesday was the earliest opening, but the timing was good. I didn't want to talk to her about her vision until after you and Matthew had come and gone, and I knew that beginning today I'd be here all the time. My plan was to show her the color schemes I'd chosen…"

"And to gently, patiently, point out to her what she couldn't see."

"Something like that. She knows her vision is failing. She just doesn't know there's a chance it can be improved. I'm expecting resistance to the idea of seeing an ophthalmologist."

"Eye surgery *is* daunting, even for an intrepid climber

of trees. She's been in such wonderful health all her life. As far as I know, she's never had surgery of any kind."

"Daunting," Nick agreed. "And not without risk—assuming my diagnosis is even correct."

Elizabeth was certain it was, that his research had been thorough, his conclusions sound. And if she asked him whether he happened to be an ophthalmologist, she could predict his stern reply.

No, Elizabeth, I'm a handyman.

"They're just *old*," Gram said when Nick and Elizabeth raised the issue of her eyesight. "*I'm* just old."

"You're not old, Gram, and once your vision's restored to what it can be, you'll be as active as ever. Not being able to see has gotten in your way. You would've gone on the cruise to Victoria with Helen and Winifred, you *know* you would have, if you hadn't felt uncomfortable about making the trip from Sarah's Orchard to Seattle. The thought of trying to read signs in airports, and finding your way in unfamiliar places in what felt like darkness…don't you think that influenced your decision not to go?"

"I don't know, Elizabeth. Since Granddad died, everything's been difficult."

"Of course it has, Clara," Nick said. "The loss is immense. But that's all the more reason to fix what can be fixed."

"The two of you spent the afternoon rehearsing your pitch, didn't you? I feel like I'm in the middle of one of those interventions."

Elizabeth smiled. "Maybe we rehearsed a little, Gram. Is it working? If not, we have reams of information downloaded from the Internet that we're prepared to read aloud to you."

"You're dear things, both of you. And I'm very grateful for your concern. But—"

"You could at least have an ophthalmologist do an exam. Cataracts or not, having your eyes checked is a good idea."

"I'm not going to have an exam unless I'd be willing to have surgery if something was found. I'm all right the way I am. I'm getting along fine. I see the two of you *quite* well. And you're both gorgeous."

"Just think how much more gorgeous we'd be, Gram, not to mention how *colorful*."

"Nice try, Elizabeth. But it's really my decision, isn't it?"

"Entirely your decision," Nick said. "Just promise us that you'll consider it."

"I promise. Now, can we please talk about something else?"

An hour later, Nick announced he was going home to get a good night's rest before the painting project that would commence the following day.

Elizabeth walked him to the porch.

"What do you think?"

"That she's her granddaughter's grandmother."

"Argumentative?"

Nick smiled. "Determined. And smart. Like you, she's able to listen and argue at the same time. She heard every word we said, and she's going to give it some serious thought. Ultimately, though, it's her decision."

"You're the man who likes to fix things."

"That's right. But we can't make her do this."

"And pushing her is likely to backfire." Elizabeth sighed. "You're probably thinking we shouldn't mention it again?"

"Not unless she brings it up."

"And we don't tell her about the appointment you made."

"No," he said. "We don't. Not yet."

She admired the reasonableness of his approach. When she shook her head, it was with resignation, not protest. But her movement was forceful enough to dislodge a strand of auburn hair from where it belonged, behind her ear, into her eyes.

As she reached up to tuck it away, another hand moved to touch it—touch her—too.

Her hand was quicker. Impatient. She watched his hand, as if in slow motion, drop away.

By the time she looked up, it was too late to tell what expression had accompanied his gesture.

It was just as well, she told herself after they'd said good-night. Gram's eyes were seeing too little, and hers were seeing too much.

Nick was a sensual man. He undoubtedly touched women, casually, all the time. And he was polite. Chivalrous. He'd brush a lock of hair from a woman's eyes as reflexively as he'd open a door for her.

She might have misinterpreted his expression as longing. And completely misunderstood his touch....

Eight

The sanding of teal-colored paint, to create a pastel canvas for the cream that would cover it, was hard work, hot work, even in the morning.

Elizabeth appeared, at 9:00 a.m., with a glass of lemonade.

"Thanks," Nick said.

"You're welcome. Gram probably has a cooler somewhere. We could fill it with ice and a few pitchers of lemonade, and you could—"

"I prefer this." *You.* Nick raised the glass in a silent toast and met her eyes over its frosted rim. "If you don't mind."

"I don't mind."

"Good. What have you and Clara been doing since breakfast?"

"I've been scanning. She's been puttering."

"And?"

"The scanning's going to work. It'll take time, but I have time, and the result will be worth it. That's the good news."

"Clara hasn't mentioned her eyesight."

"No."

"Are you surprised?"

"Not really. But I've been watching her. And you're right. The impairment's significant. And that's from the perspective of someone on the outside looking in. I keep thinking what it must be like for her, peering through prisms that both block her view and scatter light."

"She's thinking about it, too."

Elizabeth nodded, and frowned. "I lay awake last night worrying. What if she decides not to do anything? She could get in an accident, Nick. Even in broad daylight on a familiar route. The idea of her being hurt is terrifying enough. And if she injured someone else… She'd never forgive herself."

"We're not going to let that happen, Elizabeth. No matter what she decides." There was nothing idle in Nick's reassurance. It was a quiet promise. A solemn vow. "Agreed?"

"Agreed."

After a moment, he smiled. "I could use another one of these in forty-five minutes or so."

"You'll have it," Elizabeth said as she took the empty glass. "More lemonade coming up."

"Not just lemonade," he said. "Lemonade and conversation." Lemonade, he thought, and you.

By midafternoon, forty-five minutes or so had become forty-five minutes *on the dot* from when the last lemonade-and-conversation rendezvous ended.

And, for both of them, forty-five minutes had never felt so long.

By late afternoon, when the sun blazed its hottest, they'd moved to the shade of a nearby apple tree.

And talked.

And talked.

She wanted to know all about him. He said there was really nothing of interest to tell.

She responded in kind about herself. He proved her wrong, greeting her replies to his questions—question after question—as if he'd spent his life waiting to hear them.

She told him, because he wanted to know, about her girlhood summers in Sarah's Orchard.

"My happiest memories are here," she said as she gazed at the orchard. "I wonder if I've ever realized that before."

"What made you happy?"

"Everything. Being with Gram and Granddad, of course. And spending time with the trees."

"With them?"

"Until I was big enough to be *in* them. I remember Gram's horror the first time she saw me scrambling up. Little did I know that I'd inherited my tree-climbing ability from her."

"You didn't fall?"

"Never! Nor," she added, "did any of these trees ever so much as creak in protest. I was a sturdy girl. Heavy."

"Healthy," Nick countered.

Elizabeth smiled. "Very. But the trees held my weight as if I was just another bird dropping by." She shook her head. "Poor trees. My weight was the least of what I subjected them to. I'd climb up, as high as I could go, and sing to the orchard at the top of my lungs."

"That doesn't sound so bad," said the man whose life had been joyless until, as a boy, he'd discovered the same joy. "Singing to the trees."

"It wasn't bad for me. I loved it. Love to sing. Unfortunately, I can't begin to carry a tune."

"I'm sure the trees didn't care. You said they never creaked in protest."

"They're pretty gracious. Like my grandparents. I serenaded them endlessly, too. The price of unconditional love, I suppose."

"A price they were delighted to pay."

"Yes," she murmured. "They'd even suggest that I sing, if I hadn't for a while."

"Happy memories."

"So happy. So lucky. What about you, Nick?"

"Go right ahead," he said. "Sing for me."

"That *wasn't* what I was asking." I wasn't asking, she thought, for *your* unconditional love. But the serious eyes that met her startled ones seemed willing to offer it. Another mirage, she told herself. And a lingering one… "I— What I meant was, are *you* a singer? Do *you* love to sing?"

The questions were logical. Their answers, she'd have imagined, straightforward.

But Nick frowned.

"I can sing," he said at last. "And there was a time, when I was a boy, that I loved singing. Since then, I've only sung when people needed me to."

"Needed you to? Because you sing so well and your voice is so comforting?"

"Something like that."

"You don't love it anymore?"

"I haven't sung for a while. Perhaps if I sang with someone who loved to sing, it would come back to me."

"Assuming that someone could carry a tune."

"It wouldn't matter a bit."

"I can't just break into song." Not now. Not yet.

Nick smiled. Neither could he. Not now. Not yet. "Maybe later."

"Maybe."

"You probably like Christmas songs."

"I do."

"Do you have a favorite?"

"I've never thought about it. But I suppose, if I had to choose, I'd say 'Jingle Bells.' What about you?"

"If I had to choose," he answered softly, "I'd say 'Jingle Bells,' too."

During the three days until the Tuesday afternoon when Nick would have to cancel Gram's Wednesday-morning eye appointment, he and Elizabeth ate breakfast with her, and lunch and dinner.

And, at forty-five-minute intervals in between the home-cooked country meals, Nick and Elizabeth talked.

And, in between that, Elizabeth scanned the letters she'd already read, and read several more. She wasn't searching for proof that Nick was right in saying Charles would withhold from Clara the horrors of war. But she found it. Even when war claimed the life of a friend.

May 18, 1942
My dearest love,
Danny died in battle three days ago. We brought him back to camp with us, and he's on his way home to Cedar Rapids.

I need your help, my darling. As you know, Danny's family opposed his decision to enlist, and there was anger on both sides when he boarded the train.

Danny never regretted his decision. He wouldn't regret it even now. But he regretted the pain he caused his parents, and that he hadn't made things right with them before he left. He'd been planning to write, to apologize for hurting them and to plead—again—with them to understand. Of all of us, Danny had the clearest vision of the importance of what we're doing, and must continue to do.

He was a hero, Clara. In life and in death.

He was also a loving son.

I couldn't save Danny. But I have to try to save his parents from suffering more than the immense anguish they'll feel at his death. The enclosed letter is to them. I've written about Danny's life since they last saw him, the good things, the memories that will make them smile. The jokes he told. The poker face he didn't have. The way he spoke of them. They need to know his anger was gone. And that he believed, long before he died, that theirs was, too.

Will you see that my letter gets to Danny's parents? I don't have their address. The army will, of course, but it will reach them more quickly if I send it to you. His mother teaches school in Cedar Rapids. Her name is Rose. And his father, Daniel, is a dairy farmer. Danny's last name, as I'm sure you remember, is Small.

I love you, Clara. Please know that without the slightest doubt. And never doubt, either, your support of my decision to go to war.

It was the right decision, my love. I'm where I need to be, doing what I need to do. For our children, and our children's children.

I'm going to see our babies, Clara. And their babies. I will return, my Clara, to you. It's more than a hope, or a wish, or a dream. It's a belief, deep inside. I don't know why we're meant to be the lucky ones, only that we are.

I'm already the luckiest man on earth, because of you.
I love you,
Charles

Elizabeth and Nick didn't touch during those sunny days. Just as Charles and Clara hadn't touched at the beginning of their love. But the air they breathed was warmed by the sun, and by each other.

Elizabeth was breathing some of that air, holding on to it, when, just hours before Nick was going to call the clinic, Gram spoke the words she and Nick had been hoping to hear.

"Maybe I should see someone about my eyes."

"Okay," Elizabeth said with impressive calm.

"There might not be anything that can be done."

"But it's worth finding out."

"I guess so. I suppose the next step would be to make an appointment. One of the perks of living in a town with a state-of-the-art medical center is that there's likely to be a good ophthalmologist close by."

"There are several. All terrific. But Nick's arranged for you to see the one he felt you'd like the best. You have an appointment with her at eleven tomorrow."

"He's a lovely young man, isn't he?"

"Yes," Elizabeth whispered. "He is."

Nine

Clara's cataracts were "ripe," the doctor said. That was good. From a surgical perspective, they were ready to be removed. And, Dr. Diana Hathaway added, Clara was very likely to benefit from the surgery.

The standard of care, to which the Harvard-trained ophthalmologist resolutely adhered, was to operate on one eye at a time. Assuming the outcome was positive and complications hadn't occurred, surgery on the other would be deferred to a later date.

Typically, she liked to do the surgery three weeks following the initial evaluation. That gave the patient an opportunity to prepare, and to have the physical and lab exams that were prudent before anesthesia.

Dr. Hathaway had an opening in three weeks. She'd hold it for Clara, unless… It turned out there was a last-minute cancellation, a patient with the flu. The surgery had been scheduled for tomorrow afternoon. The internist, whom Clara hadn't seen for far too long, since before Charles's stroke, could examine her today, and labs could be done immediately.

"Let's do it," Clara said.

* * *

"I really like your drawings of the orchard."

Elizabeth looked from her clenched fists to the calm face from which the improbable words had come.

She and Nick were in the surgical waiting area. They weren't alone, but whoever had arranged the furnishings had done so as if each group of chairs was a private island. Their two chairs were angled so that they faced each other and no one else.

"You do not. But," she said, "as a ploy to distract me from worrying about Gram, it was pretty good."

"It might have been a ploy, but it was also the truth. I've been thinking they'd make nice labels for the apple butter jars. The company needs a logo. What better than seasons of the orchard, as drawn by Clara's granddaughter?"

"They were drawn by an eight-year-old."

"Who was passionate about the apple trees. I really like the drawings, Elizabeth. The winter one, especially."

He seemed on the verge of saying something else. Whether he'd thought better of it, or simply sensed the approach of Diana Hathaway, Elizabeth would never know.

Dr. Hathaway wore scrubs, a white coat, surgical booties and a smile.

"She's in recovery. The surgery went fine."

"No problems?"

"None. She should be awake within the hour, and, once she's steady on her feet, she'll be ready to go home. As I mentioned yesterday, her eye needs to remain covered until I see her tomorrow afternoon, and to the extent it's possible, keeping both eyes closed is best. It will be possible, I think. It'll be dark by the time you get her home, and since she may not have slept terribly well last night, she should be able to sleep."

"I think we all will," Nick said.

He didn't touch the dark circles beneath Elizabeth's eyes. But the worry in his voice was a gentle caress.

Elizabeth tucked Gram into bed while Nick waited downstairs.

"Comfy?"

"Very comfy," Gram said.

"And sleepy?"

"Getting there. You do not, however, need to stay with me till I drift off."

"Maybe I want to."

Gram smiled, and because Elizabeth had been so adamant about it, resisted opening—and winking with—the unpatched eye. "What shall we talk about?"

"Whatever you like, Gram."

"Well," Clara said. "I've been thinking that if my vision does improve, maybe it is time for me to read Granddad's letters. I know you could—and would—read them to me. But seeing his handwriting would be nice."

"You'll be able to see it. They're wonderful letters, Gram. He loved you so much."

"As I loved him."

"I haven't read all the letters yet, but Nick says he doesn't believe Granddad would ever tell you what he saw in battle."

"Nick's right."

"Did that bother you?"

"That he wasn't sharing everything? I suppose it did at first. But I realized he needed *not* to tell me."

"He never talked about what he saw?"

"Never," Gram said.

"What?" Elizabeth asked softly when Gram's frowning expression told her there was more.

"I've wondered if he talked to Nick. If they talked to each other. There were times, especially after Charles's stroke, when they'd go to the orchard and stand side by side gazing at the trees. I'd think they weren't speaking, but maybe they were, in the way men do. One word, when we might have used a thousand. And, on occasion, a solemn nod. They wouldn't have needed many words, of course. Wouldn't have *needed* to explain. They'd both seen the unspeakable."

"Both?"

Gram's unpatched eye opened, concerned.

"Both, Gram?"

"Nick hasn't had a chance to tell you yet."

Oh yes, he has. Whatever it was Nick hadn't told her, it wasn't because he hadn't had the opportunity to do so. Choice, not chance, determined what he'd shared. A choice Nicholas Lawton had every right to make.

"Tell me what?"

"He spent some time in the military."

Enough time, Gram had already revealed, to see the unspeakable. "Close your eye," Elizabeth ordered.

"Not until you stop looking so upset."

Elizabeth flashed a smile. "How's that?"

"Unconvincing."

"I'm fine! So Nick hasn't mentioned his military service to me. Why should he?"

"My vision may have been problematic, but my hearing hasn't. Nick cares about you, Elizabeth. And you care about him. Please remember, darling girl, that our men, our soldiers, need to be able *not* to tell us about their battles. And because we love them, and trust them, we can give them that gift."

Gram closed her eye then, and moments later drifted off to sleep.

"'Night, dearest Gram," Elizabeth whispered as she withdrew. "I love you."

She stood at the top of the staircase, gathering her emotions. So Nick had omitted that key bit of data about his life. So what? He was under no obligation to tell her anything—much less everything.

This was far from a betrayal. Elizabeth knew betrayal—Matthew's—and had weathered it admirably.

The only trouble was she hadn't been in love with Matthew....

Nick was outside, in the orchard, standing in the precise spot—perhaps—where he and Granddad had shared in silence as much as in words the secrets of men who went to war.

He smiled as she approached. "How is she?"

"Sleeping."

Nick's smile went away. "How are you?"

"How long were you in the military?"

"Twelve and a half years. Elizabeth—"

"You told me you'd always been a handyman."

"I told you," he said quietly, "that from the time I was seven, whenever I saw something that needed to be fixed, I wanted to fix it. That's the reason I became a soldier. I believed I could help make the world a better place. I knew, at least, that I had to try." He met her eyes. "I didn't lie to you. And when I told you about the things Charles might have seen in battle, the fear and rage he might have felt, I was talking about myself. I was telling you, Elizabeth, more than I've ever told anyone...more than I ever believed I would."

"Is there anything else you want to tell me?"

"About my military service? No. There isn't. And I understand what that means. You didn't know the man

I was before I went to war. You can't know, as Clara knew about her Charles, that I'd have died before committing—"

"I do know that, Nick!" On faith, she thought. On love. "I *do*."

"There is something else I want to tell you."

Elizabeth shivered, but not from fear about what he'd reveal. She trusted this man. Believed in this man. "Okay."

"I love you."

"Nick…"

He shivered, too. Not from fear. Her shining eyes gave him her reply.

Elizabeth saw his joy. His desire.

Then he was touching her, holding her head as he gazed at her, wanting her.

"Nick?"

"I love you."

As his mouth found hers, her hands curved over his wrists. She tasted his desire, felt his strength. He had the power to crush her…or to protect her with everything he had.

The kiss ended with a sigh, and a promise. There'd be more, so much more.

His lips caressed her fingertips as he spoke. "I've been wondering what kept me alive, kept me believing the fight was right and good. I'd always thought it was the memory of these trees, this orchard, a farmhouse glowing gold."

"You moved here three years ago."

"I returned here then."

"Oh."

"But there was more to the memory, one I'd give my life to protect—a place where a lovely little girl was free to chase the twinkling Christmas lights on the apple trees she loved…and where, even when she sat sobbing at the end of the driveway, she was safe from harm."

"Because," she whispered, "her hero happened by."

"A lonely boy happened by."

"And she stopped crying."

"He sang to her. And," he said, "she sang to him."

"Off key."

"In her key. A happy key. One he'd love to hear again and again."

"If you'll sing with me."

"Always."

The fingertips he'd been kissing moved to his eyes.

Gram had said the boy who'd rescued her granddaughter had the most brilliant blue eyes. And she was right. Elizabeth saw in his eyes what Gram had seen, the color Nick's eyes became when the loneliness was sent away.

Elizabeth didn't know, although it was true, that tonight's blue was far brighter. For on this night, and all the coming nights and days, his eyes would be filled with love.

Epilogue

To: Winifred@Codebreakers.org
From: Clara@AppleButterLadies.com
Date: July 18
Subject: Happiness! Seeing clearly! Love!

Dearest Winifred and Helen (for whom I'm popping a colorful copy of this colorful e-mail in today's post),

Please accept my apologies for being so remiss in not responding to you before now. As both of you knew, losing Charles has been difficult. I'll always miss him, as you miss your beloved Sam and Richard. I feel he's closer to me now than in those impossible months after he died. He was never very far away, I realize. I just wasn't able to find him. I'm letting the memories of our love come back to me now, and smiling when they do, and he's right there with them.

I have fabulous—and interesting—news.

The fabulous, first. Elizabeth and Nick (yes, Nick!)

are in love. Matthew was wrong for her, and, fortunately, she discovered it in time. But Nick is so right for her and loves her as she should be loved, and she loves him—as he should be loved—right back.

They're planning to live in Sarah's Orchard. She'll be the Apple Butter Ladies' "in house" counsel to begin with, and if the legal spirit moves her, she'll branch out from there. Her first corporate responsibility will be to register the official Apple Butter Ladies' logo (the .JPEG is attached, and, Helen, you have an eight-by-twelve-inch glossy). She drew the pictures when she was eight, and we've scanned them into the computer (I'm becoming quite good at scanning) and made the four-quadrant design. The winter apple tree, with its red Christmas lights, will—I think—also become the invitation to Nick and Elizabeth's Christmastime wedding. (You'll each be receiving one.)

I'm so thrilled for both of them. And I know, *know*, that Charles is, too. As for my social-butterfly daughter, we'll discover what she's really made of (ancient blue-blood genes or motherly love) when she and Thomas visit next weekend. Call me an optimist, but I'm betting on her daughter's happiness trumping every snobbish impulse she might have.

My interesting news is that I've recently had cataract surgery. (Cataract-surgery advocate that I've become, I plan to have both eyes done). I'm more than an advocate. I feel like sharing what feels like a miracle to everyone I know (or don't know!). That's why I'm attaching (and including) a few articles on the topic. If any of the signs or symptoms seem familiar to you, please, please, please make an appointment with an ophthalmologist. Or, even better, come on down and see mine, Dr. Diana Hathaway, the loveliest and most competent surgeon you'll ever meet. If the prospect of making the trip to Sarah's Orchard is off-putting, too much of an ordeal, that may be a symptom in itself. Elizabeth, Nick and I would be delighted to provide door-to-door service—anytime!

You can see how giddy I am about this. But it's such a gift to see colors again. Without my even realizing it, the world had become a dull, dull gray. And I can read again. And play cards. And smile at the night sky. And send belated messages to my two dearest friends.

I'll write often, now that once again I can. Our friendship means so much to me and has meant so much for so long, I can hardly bear to think it might have faded (as colors did) because of tiny deposits in my eyes—aaaaaah! Never.

Take care, dear ones. All my love,

Clara

0507/010/MB087 V2

Queens of Romance

Were these sisters destined to be wives?

To Have a Husband

Harriet found enigmatic stranger Quinn McBride incredibly
attractive, but she wasn't sure she could believe or trust him.
Could she really be falling for the enemy?

To Become a Bride

Right from the beginning Danie crossed swords with Jonas
Noble, but the secretive, handsome male was still unwittingly
tempting her to imagine herself as his blushing bride!

To Make a Marriage

Her unborn baby had been conceived in a moment of
irresistible passionate madness. But how much longer could
she keep her secret? How was Adam Munroe going to react
to impending fatherhood?

Available 20th April 2007

Collect all 4 superb books in the collection!

M&B

0507/009/MB088 V2

Three utterly romantic, red-hot stories of heroines who travel back in time to meet the one!

What if you had the night of your life...

60 Years Ago?

80 Years Ago?

200 Years Ago?

"The idea of finding your soulmate in the past is romantic and all three contributing authors have done an excellent job providing a little bit of magic in this anthology."
—*Romantic Times*

Available 20th April 2007

FORTUNE TELLING

TELLING

SCOTT CUNNINGHAM

The Crossing Press • Freedom, CA

For information on bulk purchases or group discounts for this and other Crossing Press titles, please contact our Special Sales Manager at 800-777-1048.

Visit our Web site on the Internet: www.crossingpress.com

Library of Congress Cataloging-in-Publication Data

Cunningham, Scott, 1956-
  [Art of Divination]
  Pocket guide to fortune telling / Scott Cunningham.
        p. cm. -- (The Crossing Press pocket series)
    Originally published: The art of divination. Freedom, CA: Crossing Press, c1993.
    ISBN 0-89594-875-3 (pbk.)
    1. Divination I. Title II. Series.
  [BF1751.C86   1997]
  133.3--dc21
                                                      97-26024
                                                          CIP

Contents

1

Introduction

BEGINNINGS

The practice of foretelling the future through the use of tools predates history. Perhaps the earliest forms consisted of gazing into lakes, watching the smoke rising from cooking and heating fires and observing the shapes of clouds. In pre-literate times, all such phenomena were invested with spiritual energies, and it seems logical that it was to these that our ancestors turned for glimpses of tomorrow. In the great cultures of the past, divination was usually linked with religion. The deities, it was believed, were willing to provide hints of the future if they were given the opportunity to do so. This was provided to them by the presentation and use of specific tools, which the deities manipulated to provide specific responses. The earliest diviners thought that divination revealed the will of the deities. The future, they thought, was unchangeable.

After many centuries, however, it became obvious that this concept could easily be challenged. Why did some events revealed in predictions never occur? Some cultures answered such questions by altering their definition of divination. Rather than revealing a fated future, divination provided glimpses of *possible* future events. The future could be altered by human action. Thus, divination provided a window into potential tomorrows—not of fate. Negative messages came to be considered useful warnings, not inescapable messages.

Divination attempts to discover the past, present or future, while magic is an active process by which the future is thought to be changed. Though magic and divination can be used together, they're in no way related.

HOW IT WORKS

It's believed that our actions and thoughts produce non-physical "waves" of energy that extend into the future and, thus, shape it to a certain extent. They produce a map of tomorrow based on our current speed and direction, but we can change course at any time.

Divinatory techniques examine these energy waves (which may not be consciously known to the diviner) and, by taking them as well as other forces into account, paint a picture of the future—if things continue on the present course for some time.

The tools reveal the unknown information in a wide variety of ways. Some of these (the use of the pendulum and sand divination) seem to rely on the subconscious mind.

Other techniques are completely free of our conscious or subconscious control, relying on other forces to manipulate the objects and to produce the prediction. In these forms, which are usually the most reliable, we simply present the tools and allow them to do the work.

THE MAJOR TYPES OF FORTUNETELLING

By studying the hundreds of techniques used in cultures throughout history, scholars have divided divination into two basic forms: *operational* and *natural*. Operational divination consists of the manipulation of tools (smoke, oil in water, eggs, dice, pieces of paper, knives, stones and so on) to determine the future. Such tools are used in specific ways for this express purpose. These represent later developments of divinatory technique.

Natural divination consists of the observation of occurrences in the natural world. A specific time and place is set aside for the express purpose of asking that omens derived from natural physical phenomena present themselves to reveal the future. The casual observation of omens that may unexpectedly occur at any time isn't true divination. Omens must be preceded by a request for information in order to be classified as divination. These are known as "provoked omens." Such omens are created by the world around us. The behavior of animals, observation of the stars, clouds, and wind, the sudden appearance of meteors and lightning are some popular forms.

THE RESPONSE

Messages received during fortunetelling are known as responses. They usually take one of three forms. The nature of the technique determines the message's form.

The first produces so-called "binary" responses. The techniques that create binary responses are the easiest to perform and often produce the clearest answers. Questions are asked that can be answered with a yes or no; hence the term binary. Occasionally, a third option, "maybe," "perhaps," or "no answer," is also included.

The second response consists of the creation of symbols or images. These forms are termed "symbolic." The divinatory tools (particularly crystal spheres, clouds, fire, smoke and oil dropped into water) produce symbols that are interpreted in conjunction with the diviner's question. Forms that produce such responses aren't limited to answering specific questions; they can be used to determine the general future. The symbols thus produced are interpreted to provide information such as "it will be a prosperous year" or "expect losses" and so on.

Symbolic responses rely both on the diviner's powers of observation as well as on her or his ability to unlock the symbols' inner meanings. Generally speaking, only symbols familiar to the diviner will appear, and this enhances the probability of a successful interpretation.

The value of techniques that produce binary responses is obvious: no such interpretation is necessary. Both of these forms, however, can produce satisfactory results if used with the proper attitude.

The third type of divination produces what we may term "selective" responses. A number of likely future events are written on pieces of paper, leaves, stones or on other tools. These are then manipulated (placed in a windy spot or chosen at random) to provide the most likely prediction.

DIVINATION ISN'T PSYCHIC AWARENESS

Anyone, psychic or not, can successfully practice divination. It can certainly be argued that our psychic minds may be at work during some techniques; that they examine waves of future energy and then relate them (through symbolic responses) to our conscious mind. However, no such awareness can be at work during techniques that produce binary or selective responses. Yet all three systems can produce insightful answers.

Some diviners still believe that higher beings manipulate the tools or, alternately, place symbols within the tools for us to see. Such a belief isn't necessary, for even nonreligious persons can satisfactorily perform divination.

WHY THE PAST IS IMPORTANT

Some question the need to examine the past to discover the future. We assume that we know everything about our pasts because we've lived them.

Why, then, do so many divinatory techniques focus on both the past and the future? Most Tarot spreads (see Chapter 17) include a placement for a card that symbolizes the past as well as one that represents the future. Magic mirrors and other tools are utilized to illuminate the past, especially to see the circumstances surrounding a crime that has been committed at an earlier time.

The fact remains that divination has always been used for this purpose. The explanation is simple: every day, we're building our futures. Every decision that we make affects tomorrow. When we're faced with a difficult situation, we may ask ourselves, "Why?" The answer often lies in the past.

Though most of us can remember our pasts, we may not be able to make the conscious connection between past and present. We're incapable of seeing that we reap the fruits of our actions. If, yesterday, a man decided to sit on train tracks for twenty-four hours, and is then run over by the train, he's feeling the effects of his past decision.

If we make unwise choices we'll suffer because of them. Deciding not to take an important medication last week may result in a severe relapse this week. If we allow another person to steer us away from our goals and dreams, we may find ourselves living an unfulfilling experience bereft of happiness. The fact remains that many of us are simply unable to link past actions to the present state of our lives.

The past also affects the future, for the streams of energy not only follow us, they race on into the future, continuing to mold our lives. Becoming aware of these past streams can not only answer questions concerning our present lives, they can also provide hints of the future.

Divination remains a mysterious art. Perhaps this is part of its appeal. Scientific inquiry and education have largely stripped our lives of mystery. Though the purpose of divination is the clarification of the future, the manner in which this is achieved is highly romantic and evocative. This may explain why divination has never lost its popularity during the 5,000 years of its practice.

2

The Fine Art of Fortunetelling

Virtually anyone can successfully practice divination. With practice and a sincere acceptance of the underlying theories, we can gain information concerning the past or future and analyze our present situation.

A few techniques require years of study, but most of those presented in this book can be performed easily, and most of the tools are readily available at little or no cost.

THE APPROPRIATE ATTITUDE

First, your attitude toward the practice is of the utmost importance. If you perform divination to entertain others, chances are that incorrect messages or nothing at all will come through. Why should an oracle accurately respond when the diviner possesses no genuine interest in its messages?

Doubt, in the earliest stages of your work, is perfectly understandable. You lack the experience that will eventually convince you of divination's genuine ability to assist you with your life. Once you've grown comfortable with the proceedings and have gained true insights into the future through your practice, release this doubt and replace it with the firm knowledge that divination is a remarkably effective art. If you're a spiritual or religious person you might view divination as a process that reveals messages sent by a higher being. This can help to erase all doubts concerning its viability.

SELECTION OF A SUITABLE FORM

This book contains detailed instructions for performing over 100 different types of divination. With so many available options, it may be difficult to decide which to use. Ideally, one type will immediately draw your attention, and this may well prove to be the most effective method. Always listen to your intuition. If you enjoy plants, botanomancy may be right; if you play cards, cartomancy.

By way of example, I've always been attracted to water in all forms—rivers, lakes, oceans, fountains and even sprinklers whirling on the lawn of my childhood home. When I first began practicing divination I used water as my tool. If no one system immediately attracts you, work with a number of techniques until you find the one best suited to you. This should produce the most accurate responses. In matters of great importance you may wish to ask the same question using two or three different methods and then compare the answers.

THE QUESTION

Most forms of divination produce responses in one of three ways: "binary" (a yes/no response), "symbolic" (the creation of images or symbols), and "selective" (the technique chooses a specific prediction). All of these can be used to answer questions. Divination isn't always performed to answer specific questions. Indeed, readings may be used to provide general insight into the future. Still, most of us need responses to specific queries regarding the future.

Clear questions will produce clear answers. Use common sense. Asking something like "Will I go to Cleveland or Portland next spring?" cannot be answered in a binary system. The question actually contains three queries: "Will I go to Cleveland?" "Will I go to Portland?" "Will I go there in the spring?" When using a system that's limited to yes or no answers each possible future event or choice must be separately questioned.

On the next page is a typical series of questions used, in this case, to discover the whereabouts of a lost set of keys. The responses were gained through the movement of the pendulum.

Q. "Are my missing keys in the house?"
    R. Yes.
Q. "Are my missing keys in the bedroom?"
    R. No. (If a positive response is here received, the following question would be skipped.)
Q. "Are my missing keys in the living room?"
    R. Yes.
Q. "Are my missing keys in the trash can?"
    R. No.
Q. "Are my missing keys in the couch?"
    R. No.
Q. "Are my missing keys behind the couch?"
    R. Yes.

Such a series of questions is often necessary to cover all possible options. Repeating the technique several times to obtain the needed information may seem to be a great deal of work but actually requires little time.

Such questions may be written, stated aloud or thought. Different systems use different methods. Unless introductions specifically state otherwise, use what feels best.

REPETITION OF DIVINATION TO ANSWER THE SAME QUESTION

In some cases, the response may be unclear, or you may be unsure of the oracle's response. When this happens it's best to repeat the divination three times. This repetition provides a more comprehensible response and may lessen the possibility of misinterpretation on your part.

PREPARATION FOR DIVINATION

Though many forms of divination were designed in ancient times to be used at a moment's notice, some required ritual preparation: prayer, offerings, the burning of incense and aromatic woods, bathing, donning special garments and so on. None of this preparatory work is necessary today but may be used prior to divination if desired.

The rationale for preparation is clear. The work calms the diviner, allowing her or him to concentrate on the question to be asked. Ritual is a process, usually of conscious origin, that accomplishes a specific need. In divination, this need consists of preparing the diviner for the coming act.

If you feel the need for some kind of pre-divinitory rite, one of the most effective is accessible. Sit quietly for a few moments. Breathe deeply. Don't strain your lungs; simply allow a slightly longer period of time for each inhalation and exhalation. Think your question. Then move on to the actual technique itself.

Most diviners agree that, if circumstances allow, it's best not to eat a large meal immediately prior to divination. This is thought to desensitize the diviner and to make certain forms such as gazing more difficult to perform successfully. Still, divination should be used when needed.

No special costume is needed: no mystical headgear, no sacred jewelry, no star-covered robe. Some techniques were traditionally practiced naked (such as divination through mirrors), but nudity is unnecessary.

APPROPRIATE TIMES FOR DIVINATION

If you've used a method of divination that produces images or symbols, interpret them immediately after they're received. You must rely on your intuition.

Though symbols can be astonishingly clear, others need close scrutiny. Try to think in symbolic ways. Open yourself to the answer. Keep your question in mind. If you still encounter problems, repeat the divination.

A LACK OF RESPONSE

Some forms of fortunetelling include an option of "no answer is possible at this time." When this occurs, don't despair. A lack of response isn't always an indication of failure. It may simply mean that too many energies are at work for an accurate prediction. Try the technique again at a later time. Receiving no response is far better than receiving an inaccurate answer. If desired, use divination to determine why no response can be produced.

WHEN DIVINATION "FAILS"

As stated in the beginning of this book, every decision, thought and action may dramatically alter the course of our lives. The waves of energy that we radiate, and those of others who are in our lives, can change the future. Thus, sometimes a reading may produce a response that isn't true.

Many forms of divination produce warnings. If a reading indicates that you'll be involved in a car accident on a specific day, and you don't get into a car that day to avoid such an accident, you've changed the future—and, thus, have voided the prediction. This isn't a sign of failure of the chosen technique but rather a sign of our ability to change our own futures.

While some forms of divination are certainly open to error in interpretation (not only of the foreseen events but also of their time frames), those with which the practitioner is most comfortable should produce reliable responses.

Reasons for experiences to the contrary include: the technique isn't the most successful for the diviner; the technique isn't the best for the specific situation; or the technique wasn't repeated at least twice to provide further, clarified information. Vague questions may also be the culprit. Switch systems if necessary. Always ensure that your question is properly formulated.

READING FOR OTHERS

Once you have discovered divination and have reaped the many benefits that can be gained from its usage, it's only natural to want to assist your friends with the same techniques—particularly those who are experiencing problems and who have come to you for some type of assistance.

I don't recommend that you do so until you've gained proficiency in at least one system. By proficiency I mean that you've successfully performed the divination on several occasions and have worked sufficiently with symbolic thought. Nothing is more disconcerting that watching the diviner surreptitiously consulting a book to find the meaning of a response. The only exception to this is the I Ching.

You may want to use these techniques to discover your friends' futures without their knowledge. It's an invasion of privacy. In this age of wire taps, computer files, even machines that display the number from which a telephone call is originating, the future may well be one of the few private areas that we have left. It simply isn't ethical to perform divination concerning other persons without receiving their prior, explicit consent.

If you do gain proficiency, and others ask you to perform divination in their name, keep these things in mind:

- You are not a professional diviner. Be prepared for the occasional mistake.
- Realize that you're placing yourself in a position of power over another human being. Never joke or jest during the divination itself. Maintain the appropriate attitude. Think carefully before you speak. Some persons will believe everything that you say and feel the need for frequent sessions. When reading for such persons, limit sessions to once a week or month so that they don't become dependent on your advice. You have a responsibility to those who come to you.

- Never charge for such work unless you set yourself up as a "reader." This is certainly not recommended (and may cause problems with local officials).

- Search for positive signs or responses. If you see accidents ahead, don't say "You'll break your leg on Tuesday." Instead, advise the friend to be extremely careful on that particular day. It is, however, fine to mention "possible health problems."

- Realize that symbolic forms of divination may be more difficult to interpret when performed for others. Simply describe the response to your friend and let her or him solve the puzzle.

- Inform your friend that the future isn't carved in stone. Explain that a negative future can be avoided by making changes today. Dismiss all ideas of fate and divine will and put their minds at ease.

THE DANGERS OF READING FOR YOURSELF

The conscious mind and the subconscious mind can cause us deliberately or unknowingly to misinterpret a response. This illustrates the importance of clearing your mind of anything but the question directly prior to divinitory rituals. Don't think of your desired answer. Avoid seeing negative signs as positive. Don't allow your desires to alter your interpretation of the response.

Never allow yourself to become totally dependent on divination. We can certainly make decisions based on other sources of information. Divination is simply an additional source—it needn't (and shouldn't) be our only one.

3

Symbolic Thought

Our culture possesses many symbols. A heart is widely known as a modern symbol of love, as is a ring placed on a finger. Colors have great symbolic value: red, for example, means "stop" or "pay attention." Some containers of poisonous substances still bear a skull and crossbones.

We're taught that symbolism has its place, but that spoken and written language is the ultimate form of communication. Consequently, our ability to interpret symbols has waned. We even think in language.

Symbolism can certainly be expressed in language, both spoken and written, but symbolic thought consists of the recognition of non-alphabetic symbols and their interpretation. As has been previously mentioned, this is of vital importance in all symbolic forms of divination.

Once you've seen symbols in the fire, in clouds, in a crystal sphere, even in a cup from which you've drunk tea, it's usually necessary to interpret them. This is impossible without thinking in a symbolic way.

Sometimes in-depth thought isn't necessary in interpreting divinity responses. If you've asked whether you should continue on your present course, and you see an eight-sided figure attached to a straight stick, the meaning could well be "stop"; that is, change your life and alter your course. However, the formulation of even this simple interpretation requires the ability to view symbols in relation to the question asked and to find the common link.

LOOK FOR SYMBOLS

This may seem obvious, but many of us aren't used to this practice. If all you see in the clouds are clouds, you're not involved in symbolic thought. Don't see the symbols as consisting merely of their outer forms. Avoid being dazzled by their physical structures. Expand your consciousness.

INTERPRET ACCORDING TO YOUR SYMBOLISM

Trust your instincts. If, for example, you see a dog while cloud gazing, allow its inner meaning to come to you. If you think of dogs as loyal and faithful friends you may view this appearance as a positive sign. If, however, dogs have always terrified you, you may well have a different interpretation.

Most books of fortunetelling include long lists of symbols and their "correct" interpretations. This type of information is usually of little use, for it isn't linked with a personal symbolic system. Such information can be safely ignored.

How do you discover the meanings of symbols? The divinitory tools that you choose usually produce symbols that will speak to you. Think about them for a while after they appear. Interpret them in conjunction with the question. Give yourself permission to think in a symbolic manner.

IF DIFFICULTY ARISES

Occasionally, the symbols produced may not seem to have any specific meaning. If you asked about your future love life, and all that you saw during divination was a frog, you may wonder if the technique has failed you.

It may be necessary to pursue symbolic thought at a greater depth. What do frogs do? They live near the water. They hop around. This symbolism may mean that you won't settle down with a specific person for some time.

Additionally, no system of divination will produce accurate responses every single time. Too many factors are constantly at work. This uncertainty of the future may be revealed by the appearance of nonsensible symbols. If you find that you simply can't make a connection between the symbol and your question, you have two options. Either perform a second divination to clarify the response or wait and repeat it at a later time.

AN EXERCISE TO DEVELOP SYMBOLIC THOUGHT

This exercise takes only a few moments for concentration. No matter where you are study the things around you. Your eyes may fall on a coffee pot. Use symbolic thought—what does coffee symbolize? Wakefulness? Morning? A friend who visits every day for a cup? Or, you might see a pencil. Communication? Problems with communication in a relationship? Creativity? You're not performing divination here; you're honing your ability to think in a symbolic manner. Performed several times a day, this exercise will prepare your mind for symbolic thought when the need arises during divination.

If you have difficulty in recognizing symbols, you can practice one form of symbolic divination on a regular basis. Allow no more than ten to fifteen minutes for each session. As you retrain your consciousness you'll eventually become aware of the symbols.

Fortunately, not all forms of divination produce symbolic responses. The binary (yes/no) and selective systems are usually quite straightforward. If you have difficulty with symbolic thought, and if you have specific questions concerning the future, you may wish to rely on these techniques for the time being.

4

The Nature of Time

In some systems of Asian philosophy, time is seen as an illusion. It's useful for ordering our lives. Time is viewed as a convenient tool whereby we can organize our existences, but it doesn't truly exist.

Even when viewed at the most simplest level, our perception of time may be somewhat confusing. When you began to read this chapter, it was the present. That moment is now in the past. You're currently experiencing a new present, and the future is but a moment away.

Thinking about time in a different way is important to the diviner, who can't assume that time moves inevitably from A to B to C. Only in viewing time from a less physically based viewpoint can we be successful in looking into the past, present and future.

The most common explanation of time is that it consists of a one-way path or stream. Birth puts us into a ship on this stream. We sit facing the past, able to see the past and look to either side to gain knowledge of the present but unable to look behind us to see the future. We continue our voyage until we leave this plane of existence. This theory doesn't support the practice of divination. It implies that we can never know the future, for it simply hasn't happened yet.

In a related theory time is seen as a river. We float down this river, directing our voyage to the future. Though the strong current impels us to move forward, we can through effort move backwards and revisit where we've been, or jump ahead for short periods to see what lies around the river's bend. This allows us the flexibility of perceiving the future, but it still sees time as a linear phenomenon, not particularly suited to divination.

Yet a third concept of time is that of a book. We can start reading at the beginning and continue on through the end, but it's perfectly possible to look ahead and read how the story ends; that is, to look into the future. This theory is based upon the assumption that the future is already written, and that we can read these words. Though this concept supports the practice of divination, it's dependent on the concepts of fate and destiny; thus, divination doesn't support it.

In a fourth concept time is a spiral that has always existed. Our lives lead to the center, but the path is preset. We can jump from one part of the spiral to another to see what has been or what will be and then return to the present to live out our lives. This, too, is based on predestination, on fate, and so doesn't fit our definition of divination.

Some believe, however, that time is far more complex than any of these theories. It consists, not of linear (straight) motion or of a spiral, but of motion in all directions; of zigzags and curves and circles and spirals. It's this activity that's responsible for the creation of what we perceive to be the past, present, and future. Time itself is seen as a dimension that intersects with our physical world; that measures it but doesn't in any way control it. It also brings order into our lives; to paraphrase Einstein, time is what prevents everything from happening at once.

In this view, the past, present and future don't exist and yet simultaneously do exist. It is, again, our perception of events as occurring yesterday, today or tomorrow that provides a structure on which to build our lives.

Think of yourself as standing in the middle of a large plain. Hundreds of paths stretch out from your position, each representing the past or a potential future. The position that you occupy is the present. You can look down the roads that you traveled to arrive at this time and, by examining them, can determine which of the future paths you'll likely take. This is the process of divination—of finding the most plausible path. However, you can alter the future by taking an alternate path.

It's impossible to discuss divination without resorting to the use of such terms as *past*, *present* and *future*. Our perception of time is a valuable ally in our lives, allowing us to view our experiences as linear, even though we know that this isn't so. We stand in the center of all those paths, walking toward that center and traveling away from it…simultaneously.

In summary: Time is an illusion. Today is built on yesterday; tomorrow on today. Divination offers a means of reaching beyond the constraints of time; of seeing the past, present and future. The present is in the past; the future is already here.

5

Determinations

I use Tarot cards here not as symbols of the future, but only to point out the most appropriate method of divination to answer a specific question. This is a new method of handling an old tool.

Never use a deck that others have owned. Remove the Minor Arcana (the Wands, Swords, Cups and Pentacles) and set it aside. Place the twenty-two remaining cards face down on a flat surface. Mix the cards with your hands. Ask for guidance in the selection of the best divinitory technique. Choose one card at random. Turn it over and read, from the below list, the most appropriate method. (Some decks use alternate names for the Major Arcana.)

The Fool: None should be immediately used.

The Magician: Crystallomancy

The High Priestess: Moon gazing (either directly or at the moon's reflection on the surface of water)

The Empress: Plants and Herbs

The Emperor: Knives

The Hierophant: Stones

The Lovers: Roses and apples

The Chariot: The hearing of chance words in public

Strength: Fire, candles, incense and smoke

Hermit: Omens seen on journeys; bibliomancy

Wheel of Fortune: Pendulum

Justice: Birds

Hanged Man: Dactylomancy
Death: None should be immediately used.
Temperance: Wine
Devil: None should be immediately used.
Tower: Casting of lots
Star: Stars, meteorology, provocation of sky omens
Moon: Water
Sun: Candles
Judgment: Fire
The World: Any form

DETERMINING THE TIME FRAME OF A RESPONSE

Because much of divination is designed to reveal the future, it's often necessary to place these events in a time frame. Will the omen take place next week? Next month? Next year? You could, of course, consult many other forms of divination to determine the time, but the methods below are easy and may be used if desired.

For Immediate Events

To determine the possible hour of an event, collect fourteen smooth, flat stones of the same size. Paint each stone with a number from one to twelve. Allow to dry, turn the twelve stones over, and repeat the same number on the back. Paint the thirteenth stone black. Allow it to dry and paint the other side black also. Leave the fourteenth stone plain.

When all fourteen stones have been prepared and are fully dry, place them in a cloth bag. State your question: "At what hour will such and such occur?" Reach into the bag without peering within and remove a stone. If it's one of the numbered ones, this represents the hour. Choose again and again until you obtain the black or plain stone. If the plain stone is found first, the hour will be in the a.m. If the black, in the p.m. If either the plain or the black stone is retrieved before the numbered stone, the question can't be answered at this moment.

Within a Week

Paint the names of the days of the week on seven stones. Add two blank stones, mix them in a cloth bag, ask when, and retrieve one as usual. If you select a blank stone, no answer is possible. Otherwise, the stone will reveal the day.

Within the Next Few Months

Obtain four stones of the same approximate size. One should be white, one green, one red and one brown. Mix these up in a small bag or bowl and, with your eyes closed, select a stone at random. Remove the stone and determine the time frame:

White: In one month
Green: Two months
Red: Three months
Brown: Four months

Within a Year

Utilize the same four stones. Ask for information concerning the time of the prediction's manifestation.

White: Winter
Green: Spring

Red: Summer

Brown: Autumn

These methods can provide us with opportunity to take action either to alter negative future events, or to prepare us for positive occurrences. Failure of the event to occur at the predicted time doesn't always indicate a failure of this technique. See this as a demonstration that the future is always in motion.

In any case, countercheck and confirm all of these divinations until you're certain that they're as correct as possible. If you receive conflicting or confusing answers, try another system or wait for another time.

6

Changing Your Future

One of the most common misunderstandings concerning divination is the belief that it reveals our destiny. This is incorrect, for the future as seen in divinitory responses can be changed. Even within most religious doctrines, humans are regarded as possessing free will. We certainly have the power to alter the future.

It would be wonderful if every divination produced positive responses. This rarely happens. We make mistakes; allow others to guide us down dark roads; rely on our emotions when we should think, or use our brains when we need to feel. Overcoming these challenges is a part of our daily existence. Our futures aren't pre-set flight plans. We create them with every choice in action that we make.

Karma

How does karma affect the future? Karma is often described as a phenomenon that has a direct influence on our lives. Past actions (especially negative ones) will be returned to us through a mystical process that's little understood. If we make mistakes, we'll receive lessons that instruct us to avoid such behavior.

Some say that the effects of karma are inescapable. Moreover, there are those who state that even our actions in previous lives can return to haunt us in our present existences.

Many persons see karma as a type of universal teacher. According to this view, at least part of our future is predetermined by our own actions. Some persons use divination to reveal these karmic debts. Once they're aware of the problem, they take action. These persons do their homework so that the coming test will be of minimal pain. Though they may be unable to escape the effects of karma, they are able to work with the process.

Karmic lessons may be viewed as the phenomena of the return of energy waves that we radiated at previous moments of our lives. Thus, like our futures, we create our karma on a daily basis. Though we might not be able to fully escape being faced with these lessons, we can certainly alter our current behavior to avoid future painful situations by acting positively and living a positive life.

THE STUMBLING BLOCK OF FEAR

Fear is one of the most harmful and imprisoning of all human feelings. It can literally destroy a person's life, whether the fears are grounded in fact or not. In divination, fear often arises from ominous messages concerning the future.

Fears that are created in this manner are dangerous, for they may actually assist the warning to manifest. Subconsciously or consciously, we give life to the prediction through fear.

We need to release such fears in order to divest them of their power. Failure to do so will negatively reprogram our energy waves. A lack of positive action is the worst possible avenue in such situations.

If you suffer from fear of the future, you may wish to write a short affirmation. It may run something like the following: "Fear of the future has no role in my life. I have the power to change my future".

Such a simple statement, repeated several times a day, may be a boon to releasing fear. Once this has been accomplished it's time for positive thought and positive action.

ACTION AND THOUGHT TO PREVENT NEGATIVE FUTURE EVENTS

One word of advice: warnings concerned with important matters received during divination should always be double- or triple-checked to ensure that no error in technique or interpretation has created the response.

1. Retrain your mind. Focus on a positive future. True, other types of problems may occur, but *never* think about the negative response. Block it out of existence; don't consider it as an inescapable part of your future.

2. Use further divinations to determine the most effective method of creating the change. Techniques that produce yes or no answers are favored here, for there's no room for erroneous interpretations.

3. Work at correcting one problem at a time. If you're faced with many warnings, choose the most negative. Once you've successfully achieved the necessary changes (determined through divination), take a rest. Begin to work on lesser problems at a later date.

4. Act in accordance with your need. If, for example, you've foreseen that a planned move will cause you heartache, illness or financial loss, take steps now to change your plans if you wish to avoid this future.

Or, you may see trouble concerning a relationship. If so, reexamine your feelings toward the person. Increase communication. Lay it all out on the line. Some relationships need hard work to be emotionally fulfilling for both parties. Don't allow the warning to be manifested.

If sickness is foretold, change the patterns of your life. Get regular, non-intensive exercise. Eat low-fat, low-sodium, whole and healthier foods. Attain a positive outlook on life. Because stress has been clinically proven to cause illness, reduce stress by all available methods. Break life-draining habits.

After releasing fear, use affirmations on a daily basis to celebrate the coming positive change as well as to strengthen your conscious and subconscious resolve. These need be no more than one or two sentences.

Many of us are stubborn. We don't like to change our plans. Such feelings must be released if we wish to be successful at altering our futures.

5. Take responsibility for your life as it is now. Realize that no higher being has predetermined its course. Steer toward calmer waters. Also assume responsibility for the way you've allowed others to adversely affect your life. Forgive yourself for your mistakes, release guilt, and get on with the process of creating your future.

THE NATURE OF SUCH TECHNIQUES

Some argue that these methods rely solely on the powers of our subconscious minds. This is only half the picture.

While it is true that positive thinking and affirmations can indeed change our lives, the energy waves from present actions can cause much greater changes. Many events can't be affected by positive thinking.

This theory has severe flaws. Saying an affirmation every morning and evening won't stop an earthquake or prevent a storm that will cause widespread flooding. However, we can avoid being caught in such disasters by taking steps to ensure that we won't be in these areas. We can move out of the area to avoid the harmful situation. Thus, positive thinking must always be combined with positive action to affect lasting change.

The energies of those whom we know can greatly affect our futures. We all know someone who, upon meeting a new acquaintance or lover, completely changes her or his life in accordance with the desires of the new companion. Such changes may be positive or negative and, indeed, may well be the stimulus for a received warning.

Positive thinking can't directly affect the energy waves of others with whom our futures have become entangled. If divination reveals that these waves are negative, it may be necessary to make a difficult choice between continuing the friendship or going off on our own, thus removing their energy waves from ours.

Don't surrender yourself to fear. Recheck all warnings to be sure of their veracity. Use positive thinking and positive action in accordance with your needs. End damaging or dangerous relationships. Gain the confidence that you are, truly, the captain of your soul and the creator of your future. See the concepts of destiny and fate as products of fatalistic humans who take no responsibility for the state of their lives.

ACTION TO ALTER POSITIVE FUTURE EVENTS

It may become apparent that some future events revealed by divination aren't in alignment with our wishes and desires. A divination may foretell an impending pregnancy. These messages can be seen as warnings if we don't desire the predicted change.

Such revealed future events can also be altered. Some positive actions necessary to change the future are obvious: if a woman doesn't wish to become pregnant she can avoid sex during her fertile times or she could use a more reliable form of birth control. In either case, she will have used positive action to change her future. Other positive omens can be altered in similar ways.

Fortunetelling Using Water

Water is traditionally considered to be a feminine element. Its moist coolness generally symbolizes growth and purification; love and psychic awareness; healing and peace. Due to these and other qualities, it should come as no surprise that water has been and continues to be a popular tool in many forms of divination.

WATER GAZING

The simplest technique is known as gazing or scrying, in which water is used to create symbols of the future. To perform this ancient rite, pour water into a blue ceramic bowl. Ask your question. Sit with your back to the light in a darkened room and gaze into but not at the water. (Some persons add a few drops of blue food color or ink to the water to darken it; this is particularly useful when using a light-colored bowl).

As with a crystal ball, the water may cloud. Eventually you may begin to see symbols within its cool depths. Make note of any such symbols. When no further symbols are seen, begin the process of interpretation.

Some water gazers prefer to have the light of a candle reflected on the water's surface. Others take the bowl outside on a cloudless night and, capturing the moon's reflection, divine by its appearance on the water.

A method related to water gazing involves wine. Pour wine into a clear glass. Place a candle behind it and light it. Sitting in front of the glass, ask your question (if any), gaze into the illuminated wine and search for symbols to appear.

In scyphomancy the reader can discern the past, present and future. Three cups of three various materials are needed.

Old instructions state that the weather must have been calm for three days prior to the divination, and that the diviner be dressed in white. Fill a silver cup with wine, a copper cup with oil, and a glass bowl with water. Scry in the silver cup to view in the past, in the copper cup to see the present and the glass bowl to discover the future.

You can place a gold ring into a glass of water. Set this glass before a mirror and gaze into the ring's reflection in the looking glass.

Natural bodies of water provide excellent gazing tools. A calm lake or a small pool which is continuously filled by a running stream is ideal. Sit before the lake or pool. Shut out all distractions and gaze into the water. If appropriate, ask a question. You will see what you need to know.

Finally, toss a lump of gold or silver into a well. The water will become clearer and, thus, more conducive to scrying.

Other methods of water gazing include watching the waves at a beach, gazing into the sea from a high point and scrying in the reflections of the sun sent up by water against a flat surface.

OTHER FORMS OF WATER DIVINATION

Floating

Take a specific object—a slice of bread, a leaf or some other light object—to a lake or spring. While asking a yes or no question, throw the object into the water. If it sinks, the answer is yes; if it continues to float, or sinks but rises and is washed up on the bank, no.

To determine the faithfulness of a lover, toss a scarf onto the surface of a pond or lake. If the scarf floats to the north, she or he has been faithful. If to the south, there is doubt in this regard.

Place a small flower in the bottom of a large bowl. Asking your question, pour the water into the bowl. If the flower floats after a few moments, the answer is yes. If it remains at the bottom of the bowl, the answer is no. If it rises but then sinks, no answer is possible at this time.

A similar divination requires nothing more than three pieces of paper, a large bowl and water. Write yes on one piece of paper, no on the second, and leave the third blank. Place them into the bowl. Ask your question and pour water into the bowl. The first that rises to the surface of the water answers your question. If this is the blank paper, it indicates that no answer can be produced at this time.

To discover the state of the weather at sea, throw a piece of bread into a well. If it floats, all will be calm. However, if it sinks, foul weather is predicted.

Wells and Ponds

To find the answer to any binary question, toss a stone into a well. The number of bubbles that arise reveals the response: an odd number signifies no, while an even number of bubbles is a yes.

Go to an operational well alone at dusk or dawn. Gaze into the water. If you see a symbol, remember it. After it has disappeared, toss a rock into the well. If you can hear an echo of the rock's splash, the message is true.

Go to a shallow, artificial pool at night. The water in the pool must be still. A nearby light should shine nearby on the water. Wait until it begins to rain. A gentle rain, one with widely interspersed drops, is absolutely necessary. Sit or stand beside the fountain and ask a question. If the light is bright enough, it will illuminate the rain drops falling onto the water. Each drop will send a single ring radiating outward as it hits. Watch the size of these rings. If most are small and last less than a second, the answer is yes. If most are large and last for a longer time, no.

Listening to Water

Lie down beside a stream running over rocks. Listen to the murmuring of the water. A picture may form in your mind in response to your question.

Goldfish

Place a fish bowl containing goldfish on a table. Position a bright light so that it shines through the bowl onto the wall above and behind it (block the light so that its beam is narrow; a flashlight may prove effective). As the light shines through the bowl, the fishes' movements will create shadows on the wall that may reveal the future.

Steam

Find a mirror hung on a wall with a low table placed before it. Fill a large pot with water and heat it to boiling. Remove the pot and place it on a hot pad before the mirror. As the steam rises, it will cloud the mirror. You may gaze in the misty mirror, or wait for the steam to condense and drip down its silvered face. The drips may form themselves into a letter or letters, which can then be interpreted.

Fortunetelling Using Fire

FIRE GAZING

Sit before a roaring fire. Ask your question. Gaze into the flames while the fire burns down. Within the flames, or in the sparkling, glowing coals below them, images of the future may appear. Interpret them with symbolic thought. It's best to limit gazing time to about five minutes.

FIRE READING

- If, after stirring the fire, it burns brightly, a loved one far from home is safe and happy.
- Pale flames foretell the approach of bad weather.
- If the fire suddenly blazes up in a raging inferno, a stranger will soon arrive.
- Blue flames indicate the approach of a storm.
- Showers of sparks from a fire indicate that news of some importance will reach you shortly.
- When the fire seems to be buzzing (as opposed to crackling), storms are at hand.
- Sparks flying from the fire indicate a coming altercation in the household.
- If a fire refuses to light, hard work will be required in the future.
- If the fire lights quickly, visitors are to be expected.
- A very bright fire is a sign of rain.
- A sputtering fire betokens snow.

•When the fire talks, trouble is ahead.

You may see other signs; interpret them accordingly.

HEAT AND STRAWS

Heat a skillet with a flat bottom. Carefully turn it over and place it on a heat-proof surface. Scatter several straws (the type the cows eat is fine) on the skillet's heated bottom. Watch the straws gyrate and dance as they begin to burn and smoke, and discover the future from their actions.

BURNINGS

Write a question concerning the future on a small piece of paper. Place it face down on a flat, heat-proof surface. Light one corner of the paper with a match. If the entire paper burns, the answer is yes. If only part of the paper is destroyed, the answer is no.

Toss laurel branches or leaves into a fire. To find the answer to a yes or no question, say the following directly to the fire:

Fire, fire, blessed fire,
Unto fortune I aspire.
Now I hope that I may see
The future that will come to me.

Then state your question while tossing five bay leaves on the fire (or on its coals). If they crackle and splutter while burning, the answer is yes. If they burn silently, the answer is no.

Alternately, throw a flammable object into the fire while asking a question. If it doesn't burn or if it burns more slowly than usual, the signs are favorable, or the answer is yes. If it does burn, unfavorable or no.

Light a match and hold it straight up. If the head curves toward the left while burning, the answer is no. If to the right, yes.

SNAPDRAGON

Place a pile of raisins on a heat-proof dish. Pour rum or some other flammable liqueur over the raisins. Carefully light the alcohol with a match.

Hold a metal cup in one hand and, with the other, snatch ("snap") flaming raisins from the pile, one at a time, and throw them into the cup. The number of raisins that you collect before the fire dies out determines your future.

For numbers between one and nine, consult the following list. For larger numbers, find the sum and keep reducing it until it becomes a single digit. (For example, if you successfully snapped thirty-eight raisins, add three and eight. This produces the number eleven. Add one and one (the number eleven) and you'll come up with two).

Following is a list of numbers and their divinitory meanings relevant to this particular technique:

1. Don't rely on others.
2. Love and relationships will be of importance.
3. A positive future is ahead.
4. Change is in the air.
5. Trouble ahead.
6. Maintain balance.
7. Peace and happiness will be yours.
8. Justice will be done.

9. Look to your dreams for advice and answers.

Or, simply count the number of snapped raisins. An even number is yes, odd no.

CANDLES

Choose a room not usually subject to winds or drafts. Night is preferred, and it's best to lower the lights. Use white candles except where otherwise indicated.

Light a candle in its holder. Search for signs from the flame itself and its wick. If the candle refuses to light, a storm is probably on the way. If the flame seems dim, it may be best to hold off on plans for the time being. An extremely bright flame is a sign of good fortune, but if it quickly grows smaller, the luck will be temporary.

If the flame waves about, some other form of bad weather may be coming, or a great change in circumstances is foretold. A spark visible in the wick indicates the imminent arrival of good news. If the flame turns in a circle or seems to form a spiral, danger is forecast. Finally, a halo around the flame indicates an approaching storm.

Another method of reading candles involves watching the way wax drips down the candle's sides. Though white candles can be used for this purpose, you may wish to choose one whose color matches the nature of your question, as listed below:

White: All questions
Purple: Position, authority
Blue: Sickness, health and recovery
Green: Family, children, births, money, jobs

Yellow: Relocation for work, moving in general, passing tests, communication (upcoming meetings, letters, phone calls), theories

Orange: Physical actions and activity of all kinds

Red: Love, relationships

Pink: Friendships

Place the candle in a holder. Ask a yes or no question while lighting its wick. If wax drips only on the left side, the answer is no. If on the right, yes. If equally on both sides, no response is possible. If no wax drips down, ask again later.

An exceedingly easy way to obtain an answer to a question: obtain two small candles, such as those placed on birthday cakes. Choose their colors according to the above list. Place these candles in their holders and stick them into a block of clay, a piece of foam or a potato, cut in half, laid cut side down.

With two matches, simultaneously light the candles. Settle before them while asking your question. The first to burn out reveals the answer: the left one, no. The right one, yes.

Alternately, light a candle, ask a question, and observe the flame's motion. If the flame or the wick bends toward you, the answer is yes. If it bends away from you, no.

A technique geared to predicting the future happiness or otherwise for those living in the same house can also be used.

Place two candles in holders on the mantle above the fireplace or on the kitchen table. Light their wicks and watch the flames' movements. If the candles burn well with bright, long flames, good fortune for the household is predicted. If the flames are short, dim, spluttery or if they send up clouds of smoke, troubles will have to be faced. If, on the other hand, they seem to burn in a normal manner, so too will life continue on its present course for those who live in the house.

To determine the character of the coming year, wait until Halloween or New Year's Eve. On that night, light a candle and go outside. Walk around your house clockwise and return inside. If you can accomplish this without the flame being extinguished, the coming year will be most fortunate.

A rather unusual form of candle divination involves the remarkable properties of fresh lemon juice. Obtain a clean, non-ball point pen or felt-tip pen (the type once in common use in which the writing tip was dipped into a bottle of ink). A sharpened, short stick may be substituted.

Squeeze the juice from one lemon into a small bowl. Lay three, five or seven pieces of paper on a flat surface. Dipping the pen into the lemon juice, "write" a possible future on each piece of paper with the juice; the juice here acts as the ink. Since lemon juice is invisible and difficult to write with, reduce these futures to just a few words. Allow them to thoroughly dry.

Light a candle. Place the slips of paper into a bowl. Mix them thoroughly with your left hand, then choose one at random. Hold the chosen paper close enough to the flame to heat it but not to burn it. The heat will reveal the future written on the paper as the lemon juice darkens. This will determine the possible future.

SMOKE

Light a candle. Pass a plain white card through the flame three times while asking a question. (Do this quickly to avoid setting the card on fire.) Interpret the resulting carbon deposits left on the underside of the card with symbolic thought.

Build a fire outside in a safe place while asking a yes/no question. Watch the smoke. If it rises straight and lightly into the air, a positive answer has been received. If, however, it hangs heavily around the fire, the reverse is true.

A second method involves the burning of specific objects and observing the smoke that rises from them. Asking your question, throw a handful of poppy seeds onto the burning coals of a dying fire. The responses are read in the same manner described in the above paragraph.

Alternately, throw a handful of cedar shavings (available in almost all pet supply stores and many supermarkets) onto the coals while asking your question and read the omens according to the first method described above.

An easier technique requires nothing more exotic than burning an incense stick. Though any type can be used, sandalwood seems to produce the best results. Hold the incense stick between your hands and ask your question. Light it, set it in its holder, and gaze into the smoke. A message may be revealed to you by the smoke's appearance or actions.

And finally, watch the smoke rising from extinguished candles. If it moves to the right, the answer is yes. If to the left, no.

ASHES

Collect ashes. Outside, in a place where the wind usually blows at some time, scatter the ashes to a good depth in a rectangular shape on the ground. While asking your question regarding the future, use a finger to write the word yes in the ashes to the right and no to the left. Leave them undisturbed overnight.

In the morning, study the ashes. If both words are clearly legible, no answer is possible at this time. If one has been obliterated, the remaining word reveals the answer to your question. If both words are gone, again, no answer has been given.

Alternately, write in the ashes two or three words that encapsulate your question, such as "Move next month." The next morning you'll probably find that some of the letters have been destroyed. Piece together the remaining letters to reveal the future.

9

Fortunetelling Using Wind, Clouds and Birds

WIND

Go to a place where few trees or buildings block the wind. Wait until the air grows calm. Ask a yes or no question and watch the winds.

If they blow to the north, the answer is favorable. To the east, unfavorable. To the south, unfavorable. To the west, favorable. (You may need to bring along a compass.) If no wind rises within nine minutes, no response is immediately possible.

In an unlikely event that a whirlwind (sometimes known as a "dust devil") suddenly appears, it is an unfavorable omen.

In another method write five possible future (or five choices that you're currently facing) on five round pieces of paper. Take these outside to a windy place. Draw a circle on the ground and lay the papers within it. The wind will eventually rise and blow the papers from the circle.

The last paper to remain within the circle reveals the best possible choice (or the most likely future event). If all are simultaneously removed by the wind, no response is possible at this time. If no wind rises, again, there is no answer.

The wind has also been used in a number of other ingenious ways. Sit beside a lake or a swimming pool. Ask a question and watch the water's surface. If the wind picks up and produces ripples on the water's surface, the answer is yes. If not, no.

CLOUDS

On a day when clouds race across the sky, or when thunderheads build up to an impressive size, sit or stand with your back to the sun and look up toward the sky. Think of your question and gaze into the clouds. Study their shapes, blinking normally. Soon they may form a symbol, or you may become aware of a symbol that was already present. Examine this image and determine what connection it has with your questions.

BIRDS

Go to a place with many trees with a source of water and food for the birds. Stand or sit and ask your question. Turn your face toward the sky and watch for birds.

If birds suddenly fly across the sky from the left to the right, the answer is favorable. If from the right to the left, unfavorable. If no birds appear, ask again later.

If birds fly directly toward you, the answer is yes; if away from you, no.

Some birds are thought to be fortunate, others unfortunate. To see a fortunate bird on the left greatly diminishes its positive aspects; an unfortunate bird on the right will bring a small degree of bad luck. However, fortunate birds on the right and unfortunate birds on the left are clear signs and need little interpretation.

The number of birds pursuing the same path or perching on the same object during your observation also determines the answer: an even number is positive; an odd number is negative. Four birds flying from the left to the right is considered to be the most auspicious sign. Three birds flying from the left to the right is unfavorable. Thus, their number may also be taken into consideration. If an odd number of birds flies in the positive direction, ascertain their message as best as you can.

The cries of birds, when heard during divination, can also be of divinitory use. One or two calls are positive; three, negative. A greater number of cries indicates that the birds aren't immediately available for answers.

The height at which birds fly plays its role in this form of divination. Birds of good omen flying high foretell extremely good luck; lower, a lessened positive event. Similarly, unfortunate birds flying at high altitudes are extremely ill-omened; at lowered elevations, less so.

When you begin to work with the birds of your area (and they needn't be the predatory type, though hawks and eagles are ideal) you may find that a particular species seems to give the best results. If so, it's safe to ignore omens from other types of birds and rely on this species for messages.

Another type of bird divination relies on the appearance of specific types of birds during a session. The following list has been largely gathered from European and American sources, but could easily be expanded a hundredfold. (Note: fortunate birds indicate positive responses to question; unfortunate birds, negative responses.)

Blackbird: A *fortunate* omen whenever seen, especially two blackbirds sitting together.

Bluebird: A *fortunate* symbol of happiness.

Crow: Usually thought of as an *unfortunate* omen, though the number of its cries is considered to be of greater significance. One is favorable, two unfavorable, three favorable.

Dove: Highly *fortunate*. Predicts peace, love and happiness.

Duck: *Fortunate*. Your relationship will be stable.

Eagle: Often considered to be *unfortunate*, though eagles can also be viewed as symbols of power and strength. Sighting one may indicate that you'll rise above current problems and emerge successfully.

Gull: *Fortunate*. You may soon travel. If the trip involves business, it will be financially successful. If a vacation, you'll enjoy yourself.

Heron: *Unfortunate*. Hard times ahead.

Hummingbird: The appearance of these delightful birds is quite *fortunate*, for they betoken love, marriage or pregnancy.

Lark: Another *fortunate* bird representation of love, the lark can also predict future health or illness. If a sick person watches a lark sitting on a branch she or he can determine the likelihood of recovery. If the lark turns its head from the ill person the sickness will continue for some time. If, however, it stares directly at the diviner, recovery will soon occur.

Magpie: Both *fortunate* and *unfortunate*. Usually thought to be an omen of disaster, the number of these birds is indicative of a wide range of predictions. One, misfortune. Two, happiness (and possibly marriage). Three, a delightful trip. Four signifies the arrival of good news, while five indicates that friends will visit. Any number higher than five is considered to be unfavorable.

Oriole: *Fortunate*. Happiness and peace are in the future.

Owl: Usually considered to be *unfortunate*, for in most countries owls are seen as omens of death or disaster.

Quail: A peaceful household is predicted by the appearance of a quail. A *fortunate* bird. If arguments are raging, they'll soon end.

Raven: Despite its sleek black appearance, the raven can be a positive omen, depending on the number seen. One raven betokens sadness; two, happiness; three, marriage; four, birth. Ravens are considered by some cultures to be the most prophetic of all birds. Both *fortunate* and *unfortunate*.

Robin: *Fortunate*. The appearance of a robin portends a harmonious home life.

Sparrow: This homely little bird, when it appears during divination, ensures domestic tranquillity. Quite *fortunate*.

Stork: Fairly *fortunate*. The future will largely be positive; children may be involved.

Swallow: A *fortunate* sign, whether perching or flying to the right. Joy is in the future. Love and luck.

Wren: A *fortunate* sign concerning the future. Wrens are the luckiest of all birds.

Fortunetelling Using Plants and Herbs

A GENERAL PLANT DIVINATION

Fill five flower pots with the same kind of dirt. Plant in each pot a seed of the same type of flower, on the same day and at the same time. Ensure that they have the same exposure to sunlight and water. For best results, do this on the day of the full moon.

On a small piece of tape, write an expected or hoped-for future and apply this to the side of one pot. Continue until all five pots have been designated with five different futures.

The seed that first germinates determines the event that will most likely occur in the near future.

THE APPLE

Using a silver knife, peel an apple so that it comes off the fruit in one unbroken strip. (If the peel breaks while paring, try it again at a later time.)

Ask your question and throw the peel over your left shoulder. It will produce a shape on the floor behind you. If this shape is anything other than an O or U, the answer is yes.

Find an apple that still has its stem attached. Ask your question. Hold the apple in your left hand and, with your right, begin twisting the stem. With each twist, say yes or no. The word that you say when the stem twists off (or directly prior to this occurrence) signifies the answer to your question.

THE DAISY

Remove each petal from a daisy while saying "she/he loves me, she/he loves me not." The sentence stated as the last petal is removed reveals the truth. Any daisy-like flower can be used for this technique.

A second form of daisy divination isn't limited to matters of love. Ask a binary question. As you pluck each petal, say yes or no. As the last petal falls, the answer has been given.

THE DANDELION

Find a dandelion that has gone to seed. Ask whether some desired wish will come true. Blow hard against the seeds. If all the seeds fly off, your wish will be shortly granted. If a few seeds remain, a bit of time will be necessary for this to occur. If many seeds are left, your desire will not be granted.

An alternate method consists of thinking of your husband, wife or mate while blowing on a dandelion. If all the seeds immediately fly away, the relationship is stable. If not, problems may be in the offing.

A third method: blow away the winged seeds. If they immediately fall to the ground, the answer is no. If they float away on the wind, yes.

LEAVES

Find a large leaf. Write a question upon the leaf. Place it in a safe spot. If it quickly withers and dries, the prospects aren't rosy. However, if it remains fresh and dries slowly, the signs are favorable.

Alternately, sit beneath a large, leafy tree when the sun is shining, the sky is clear and a breeze freshens the air. Face west to discover your past, north the present and east the future. Ask your question. Watch the shadows created by the sun shining through the moving leaves. Look for symbols and interpret them in accordance with your query.

Leaves are used in other ways. To know if the coming year will be happy or sad, go to a tree in autumn as it's losing its leaves. Every leaf that you catch in mid-air as it falls portends a lucky week. An alternate version is to stand beneath an apple tree in spring and to catch the petals of the fragrant blossoms as they fall. Each petal is a sign of a month of good fortune.

ONION

Obtain three fresh round onions. Place them in a spot where they can remain undisturbed for some time. Name the left onion yes, the middle onion maybe, and the right onion no. The first to sprout determines the answer to your question. If the onion's sprout points toward you, the accuracy of the response is strengthened.

ROSE

Place a fresh rose petal in the palm of your left hand, then smartly snap your right hand against the petal. If this creates a loud sound, the signs are favorable or the answer is yes. If little sound, the reverse.

Obtain three fresh roses. Place these in three vases that aren't filled with water. Name the left rose yes, the middle rose no answer and the right rose no. The flower that remains fresh after the other two have withered reveals the outcome. (Check them several times a day to observe their progress.)

Fill a basin with rose water—or plain water. Pluck three leaves from a rose plant. Name each for a specific person that you wish to become involved with (but are having difficulty making up your mind). Place these on the surface of the rose water. The leaf that floats for the longest time on the water's surface indicates the favored choice.

PLANT OMENS

Aloe: To see this common plant in bloom (a rare occurrence) is an omen of fortune.

Daffodil: Though it's considered unlucky to see the first daffodil in spring, the observer will, somewhat curiously, earn "more gold than silver" in the coming year.

Fir: Seeing a fir tree in an unusual locale is a sign of future mischief and challenges.

Four-Leaf Clover: The nearly universal sign of good luck.

Hay: Seeing a load of fresh hay is a positive sign.

Holly: Good luck.

Laurel: Peace and goodwill.

Lilac: Finding a rare five-petalled lilac is an omen of great luck. This is highly unusual, but it does occur.

Lily: Celibacy.

Mistletoe: Mysteries.

Myrtle: Seen flowering, a sign of good fortune.

Nettle: Challenges ahead.

Poppy: An ill omen.

Rose: Seeing the flower is an omen of love.

Wisteria: In bloom, seen unexpectedly, this is an omen that your love is faithful, or that she or he is thinking about you at that moment.

11

Fortunetelling Using the Casting of Lots

CLEROMANCY

Place three dice of the same size either in a cup or between your hands. Shake and drop them onto a piece of velvet. Add the numbers that appear on the upper surfaces of the dice, then determine your fortune.

Three: Pleasant surprises in the very near future.
Four: Unpleasantness of some kind may occur.
Five: Plans or a wish will be granted.
Six: A loss of some kind is forecast.
Seven: Possible difficulties.
Eight: Expect criticism.
Nine: Marriage; unions.
Ten: Birth, either of a child or of a new project.
Eleven: A parting, which may be temporary.
Twelve: A message of importance will soon arrive.
Thirteen: Sorrow.
Fourteen: Friendship; help from a new friend.
Fifteen: Begin no new projects for a few days.
Sixteen: A pleasant journey.
Seventeen: A change in plans may be necessary.
Eighteen: Success, a wish will be obtained.

A similar version uses dominoes. Different futures are determined by the combination of numbers that appear on a domino selected at random from a pile.

STONES

Gather thirteen white and thirteen black stones. (If you can only find white or light-colored stones, paint thirteen of them black.) All should be of approximately the same size.

While asking your yes/no question, place the stones in a small cloth bag or a metal bowl. Shake the stones. Repeat, then state the question a second and third time. Reach into the bowl or bag and, with your eyes closed, grab a handful of stones. Remove them and place them on the surface of the table or the ground.

Count the number of each color of stones. If there are more white stones than black, the answer to your question is favorable. If more black stones have been collected, the answer is no. If you've retrieved an equal number of black and white stones, there is no answer at this time.

A modern form of stone divination apparently originated in Europe. Obtain thirteen stones of uniform size. Using white paint, mark each with one of the following words on one side only: Sun, Moon, Merc. (Mercury), Venus, Mars, Jup. (Jupiter), Sat. (Saturn), Home, Love, Money, News, Travel, Health.

The first seven are the planets, together with the sun and moon. The last six represent various aspects of life.

To use the stones, draw a circle one foot in diameter. Shake the stones in a bag and throw them over the circle. Only those stones that are within the circle face up are consulted.

Here's a list of the stones and their divinitory meanings:

Sun: Great activity; illumination.

Moon: Dreams, fantasies, changeability, the future in motion, healing, secrets.

Mercury: Thought is required.

Venus: Love, beauty, compassion.

Mars: Fights, danger, arguments, altercations, energy.

Jupiter: Money, employment, business.

Saturn: Old age, sustainment, possible health problems.

Home: Family relations, the structure itself.

Love: Relationships, marriage, companionship, separation or divorce (if near Mars or Saturn).

Money: Employment, raises, bills, business, security.

News: Messages of all kinds, letters, faxes.

Travel: Short trips, long trips, business trips, relocation of the home.

Health: Matters of healing and sickness.

Stones that are close to each other are read together. For example, if love appears beside news, you'll receive a message from or about a relationship. If near the Sun, all will become clear concerning your relationship in the future. Near the Moon, your love is mostly a fantasy. If near Mercury, reexamine your relationship. Close to Venus, you are greatly loved. If near Mars, be prepared for a confrontation with your love. Near Jupiter, you've been placing too much importance (love) on money. Near Saturn, the relationship may end soon. Alternately, it may last well into the future.

Other nearby stones can provide additional insight into the situation. If Jupiter appears beside money, look to the next closest stone to determine the nature of the response. If it's news, you may receive a message concerning money, a bill, or even a check.

This system of lot casting can create surprising results if the stones are read with thought and intelligence.

WOODEN LOTS

A third method is quite simple. Obtain two straight branches. Remove all the twigs, then peel off the bark on one side of each branch.

Holding the branches, ask your question and roll them on the ground. If, when they come to a complete stop, the two peeled sides are face up, the answer is yes. If the two unpeeled sides, no. If one of each appears, no reply is possible at this time.

A modern version of this art uses small, square pieces of wood, each of which is marked on one side with the letters of the alphabet (such as tiles that come with the popular game Scrabble). Place the tiles (there can be more than one for each letter) into a bowl or urn. Shake them while asking your question, or clear your mind.

Pour out the tiles onto a flat surface. Gather those that have landed face up and set aside those that are blank. With these letters, spell out words that may reveal your future. The first word that you thus spell (unless it's a common word such as and) will usually pertain to your question. Further words created from the tiles may clarify the response.

12

Fortunetelling Using Crystal Gazing

Ideally, a crystal sphere is at least 2 1/2 inches in diameter. It should be cut from quartz crystal, not glass or plastic. The reason usually given for this particular size is that the larger the crystal, the larger the symbols that will be created in it and, thus, the easier it will be to see and interpret them.

The best crystal sphere is perfectly round and clear. Usually, however, most crystal balls of this size contain what are known as veils. Fortunately these in no way hinder the practice of crystallomancy.

As has become common knowledge, quartz crystal is a product of nature possessing a unique set of energies. One of these is its ability to act as a focal point for the seer. The center of the ball seems to draw in the diviner and thus clears the mind of extraneous thoughts.

The purpose of crystal gazing is to produce images within the crystal itself, not in the mind. Some argue that these images actually appear within the gazer's mind, but most practitioners disagree. While the crystal may, indeed, stimulate psychic awareness, the ball itself creates the images. The awakened psychic awareness is of use simply to assist in the interpretation of the responses received.

This is why crystal gazing requires a seer of a sensitive and receptive nature. Though you needn't be psychic, it helps. Still, most anyone with the willingness to trust the sphere and to be open to its messages will eventually succeed in garnering a symbolic response. Continued practice will only enhance the effectiveness of this technique.

Now to specifics. Crystallomancy is best performed at night, ideally on the full moon or during its waxing. Lower the lights but leave at least one candle or light burning; the room shouldn't be completely dark. Sit with your back to the light source.

The room should be absolutely silent. No crackling fires, music, fans, or conversation overheard from another room. Sounds will jeopardize the possibility of seeing anything at all, for they'll distract your mind from the process.

Lay a small piece of black velvet in your left hand. Place the crystal on the black velvet, then cradle it between both your hands. (Alternately, cover a table with black velvet and place the sphere on its stand on the velvet.) Breathe deeply for a few moments to relax your body and mind.

Ask your question. Questions asked of the crystal can concern the past, present or future. (In fact, during the 1300s crystallomancy was widely used in Europe to discover thieves and to recover stolen property.)

Gaze *into* the sphere, not at its outer surface or at any reflections from the room that may be visible. Let yourself go. Blink when necessary—there's no reason to strain your eyes. Also, don't concentrate. This is precisely the opposite state in which you should be. Open your awareness.

The first sign that something is happening will be a clouding of the crystal. It may seem to be filled with a milky white substance that swirls around within the sphere. Relax and keep gazing. The milkiness may change from white to other colors but not all seers have experienced this phenomenon. Eventually it will turn black.

Images will then appear within the sphere. Though words are never seen (unless they happen to be written on a piece of paper that's related to your question), the symbols created within the crystal will usually relate to your question. Remember what you see—this is vital for later interpretation. Don't attempt to unlock the message while actually gazing; focus on the symbols themselves.

Eventually, the images will dissolve into the mist, and the mist itself will seem to disappear, as if a curtain had been drawn across the ball. This always marks the end of the gazing session.

Wrap the crystal sphere in the velvet. Place it safely away and immediately interpret the symbols. This can be surprisingly simple if you think in a symbolic manner. For example, if you asked about the future of a loving relationship, and you saw a heart, the message is quite clear. if you experience any difficulty in interpretation, write down the symbols seen, in the order in which they were received, and study them at a later time.

Not all crystal responses rely on symbolism. If you've asked to discover the whereabouts of a lost object, you may well see within the crystal the place in which it resides—a drawer, behind the couch, and so on. If several options have been presented to you in some sphere of your life, and you asked which of these is the best to take, that option may be clearly expressed.

In the beginning of this work, many find it difficult to move past the point at which the ball appears to cloud over. This may last for weeks. When this happens, wrap the sphere in velvet after an appropriate time and wait at least a day before making the attempt again. Keep practicing on a regular basis. Images will eventually come to you.

13

In Matters of Love

In an earlier chapter, we discussed the inadvisability of performing divination to examine the lives of others. However, some of the techniques described here and elsewhere in this book seem to break this rule. The reason? When you are in a relationship, you give up some control over your life to your partner, and vice versa. Assuming that you act in trust and love, you're truly not snooping, and you can use these techniques without fear of breaking a divinitory rule.

These rites can be used if your partner is unresponsive. They are also useful if you haven't yet decided on a mate. This chapter describes only a few of these time-honored rites. I've deliberately omitted those designed to discover the occupation of a young woman's future husband as well as many others that simply don't speak to modern times.

DREAMS

The most popular means of producing dreams of love is the practice of placing certain objects beneath the pillow. Plants most frequently used for such divinations include the four-leaf clover, plantain, yarrow, poplar, mugwort, daisy and bay. Inquiries regarding the diviner's future love life are stated while falling asleep; the answers are revealed in the dreams that take place that night.

On Midsummer night, collect the flowers or small branches from nine different plants (they needn't be those listed above). Place these beneath your pillow and sleep on it. You'll dream of your future love.

Valentine's Day is considered to be a most efficacious time for divining a future love. On this night, to see in a dream the face of one who will marry you, obtain two bay leaves. Sprinkle them with rose water and lay them (crossed over each other) under your pillow. As you lie down, say

Good Valentine
Be kind to me,
In dreams let me
My true love see.

A dream will reveal the face of your future spouse.

A related practice makes use not of plants but a mirror. On the first day of May in which the moon is visible, hide a small mirror on your person and go out to stare silently at the moon. Repeat this for nine consecutive nights. On the last night, place the mirror beneath your pillow to dream of a beloved.

The moon figures into many love dream oracles. On the night when the new moon is first visible, say

New moon, new moon, I hail thee!
By all the virtue in thy body,
Grant this night that I may see
He who my true love is to be.

She or he will appear in a dream that night.

On seven consecutive nights, count seven stars. Go to sleep. On the seventh night, you'll see the man or woman that you'll marry.

Or, stare at the brightest star that you can find. Wink three times and go to bed. A dream will be produced.

Here is a lemon divination: remove the peel from two lemons. Place these in a small piece of cheesecloth and slip this packet inside your night clothes. If you dream of your desired one presenting you with two lemons, he or she surely loves you.

Pluck nine leaves from a smooth (that is, non-prickly) holly bush. Tie these up in a scarf with nine knots. Place this beneath your pillow and sleep. You will dream of your future partner that night.

And finally, cut an apple in half on the night of the full moon. Eat one half before midnight and the other half just after the clock strikes twelve. Sleep and you'll dream of your love.

PAPER

Some love divinations don't depend on dreams to produce the response, but on sleep. Write the names of three possible future spouses on three pieces of paper. Fold each twice and place these under your pillow. Immediately remove one slip of paper before sleeping (do not read it). On waking the next morning, remove yet another slip. The remaining paper reveals the best choice.

THE APPLE

Cut an apple in half. Count the number of seeds that you find. If this number is even, marriage is in the offing. If an odd number, not. If one of the seeds has been accidentally cut in half, the road of romance will be somewhat rocky.

Similarly, to discover whether someone truly loves you, throw two apple seeds into a fire while saying:

If you love me, pop and fly;
If you hate me, lie and die.

If, while burning, the apple seeds make a sharp crackling sound, the person does have affection toward you. If no sound is made, not.

An old practice involves discovering the initial of one's future spouse. Stand before a mirror. Stick an apple seed to your forehead. Immediately begin saying the alphabet. The letter at which the seed falls off reveals that person's initial. If you get through the entire alphabet and the seed hasn't dropped, no response is possible at this time.

A related practice involves naming two seeds for two specific possible spouses and sticking them to your forehead. That which remains the longest indicates that the person named for that seed is indeed in love with you.

There are many more apple rites, but we'll end with just one more. This divination uses both the fruit and a mirror and was often performed on Halloween—considered an efficacious time for love divination of all types. After dusk, place a candle before a mirror. Stand before the mirror so that you can look into your reflection. Eat an apple and brush your hair. In time, your future lover will appear to be reflected in the mirror, peering eerily over your shoulder.

BASIL LEAF DIVINATION

Obtain two fresh basil leaves. Name one for yourself and one for your intended. Place them on a fire. If they lie still and don't burn, or burn slowly and/or silently, love is strong. If, however, they burn quickly, snapping and popping, a fight between the two of you may soon occur.

STRAW

Find a piece of dried straw (hay). Pinch it at one end while saying "loves me." Pinch next to it and say "loves me not." Continue until you've pinched the entire straw. The last statement is the true one.

MISTLETOE

This is another plant that has long been associated with both love and magic. Save mistletoe after it has been taken down once Yule is past. When in next December it's time to hang up another bunch, burn the now dried mistletoe in a fire. If it burns with a steady flame, your future mate will be steady and true. If it crackles and splutters, she or he will be of a bad temperament. Alternately, place fresh or dried mistletoe under your pillow to dream of a future love.

THE LADYBUG

Capture a ladybug as it rests on a leaf. Ask it to reveal the location of your true love. The direction in which it flies off reveals this information. Or, if the ladybug seems content to sit on your finger or hand for a few moments, count the spots that speckle its wings. If the number is even, you are certainly loved. If odd, not.

THE BULB OF LOVE

Finally, we'll end with a rite that utilizes a flower bulb. Any type of flower may be used. This is best done in the spring. Plant the bulb in a pot filled with the appropriate soil. Water it and care for it as usual. If it seems to sprout more quickly than normal, the signs are favorable. Keep watching it. If it blooms, the one that you love certainly loves you. If not, love hazards may be ahead.

14

Fortunetelling Using Mirrors

TYPES OF MAGIC MIRRORS

The first European mirrors seem to have been made of highly polished metal—brass or silver were particularly favored. Before divinitory use, they were moistened with oil or water to improve their reflective properties. Such mirrors were used for grooming purposes as well as for divination. Even so, these mirrors produced poorly defined reflections. Other cultures used stone mirrors. These were the only two forms of artificial mirrors available (as opposed to natural mirrors, such as lakes).

However, even after glass mirrors were available, a number of specialized metal mirrors were utilized in divination. These were related to the planets and had to be made at auspicious astrological moments. Each was used on a specific day and was consulted concerning specific subjects.

The Sun mirror was made of gold. It was used on Sundays for information concerning those in power.

The Moon mirror was made of silver. It was consulted on Mondays to determine if wishes would come true and for dream interpretation.

The Mercury mirror consisted of a globe of glass filled with mercury (the liquid metal). It was used on Wednesdays to discover the answers to inquiries regarding money.

The Venus mirror was made of copper. On Fridays, it could be used to answer love questions.

The Mars mirror was made of iron. It was consulted on Tuesdays for advice concerning arguments and lawsuits.

The Saturn mirror was composed of lead. Used on Saturdays, it revealed lost articles and uncovered secrets.

Other forms of mirrors were also made and used. One common type consisted of glass globes that were filled with various substances and placed, cork downward, on a table. One of these was filled with pure water. A sort of artificial crystal ball, it was used as a gazing object. Recent books recommend creating similar globes, though most advise that the water be dyed blue or black.

An alternate form of these mirror globes was known as the narcotic mirror. This consisted of water in which powdered narcotic herbs such as belladonna, poppy, hemp and henbane were mixed. This water, it should be noted, wasn't imbibed.

A modern mirror is a concave piece of glass painted on the convex side with black paint. This allows the unpainted glass to provide a reflective surface. The mirror is held in black velvet and acts as a gazing tool.

Perhaps the simplest of all divinitory mirrors consists of a plain piece of black paper inserted in a frame. No glass is used. A square frame is useful for obtaining knowledge of the physical world, while a round frame is most suited for information related to metaphysics and the spiritual world.

USES OF DIVINITORY MIRRORS

Take a glass mirror to a lake, pond or stream. Ask a question that can be answered with yes or no. Dip the mirror completely into the water three times, retrieving it each time. As you bring it up the last time, look into its mirrored surface. If your reflection is clear, the answer is yes. If it's distorted, the reverse. (This can also be performed by dipping a small mirror into a large bowl or bucket of water, or even in the bathtub before bathing.)

To inquire after the state of a loved one or family member, place a mirror so that it only reflects the ceiling. Light the room with white candles. Sit before the mirror. Gaze into it and ask "How is (name)?" An image of the person in question will eventually appear. If she or he seems to be smiling, all is well. If frowning, all is not well. If no expression is visible, or the face doesn't appear, there is no answer.

A curious ritual for divining the future is used on New Year's Eve. Go to an empty building. Sit on the floor. Place one mirror behind you and one in front of you. Each should be laid flat on the floor. Light a candle and pass it between yourself and the mirror before you. At the stroke of midnight, gaze into the candle's flame as it's reflected on the mirror.

To know if an unexpected event will actually occur, use a grease pencil to write the question on a small mirror. Wrap this in several layers of cloth, place it beneath your pillow, and sleep on it. If you dream of the hoped-for event, it will occur. If not, it probably won't.

Finally, take a mirror to a window on a day and at a time when the sun shines into the house. Hold the mirror so that it reflects the sun's light onto the ceiling. Watch the moving patterns that this creates and see symbols of the future.

15

Fortunetelling Using the Stars, Moon and Lightning

STAR DIVINATIONS

Go outside on a clear night. Ask a question. If the stars seem to glow brighter, or if you see a shooting star, the answer is yes. If nothing seems to occur after fifteen minutes, or if clouds blot out the stars, the response is no.

Before going to bed, walk outside, look up at the sky and say the following: "Stars, stars, show me the future." It will appear in a dream that night.

Wishing on a star is a popular practice. Outside, look at one particular star for several minutes. State your hoped-for future. Close your eyes for three seconds. If, upon opening your eyes, they immediately fix on the same star, your future is as you wished. If you can't find it at once, your future will be different.

THE MOON

When the moon first appears in the sky as a crescent, go outside and point a dull-bladed knife (preferably silver) at the moon. Say the following words:

New moon, true morrow, be true now to me
That I ere the morrow my true love may see.

Place the knife beneath your pillow. Speak to no one as you prepare for bed. Remember your dreams.

The position of the moon on the evening that you first spot it is considered to be of importance. When you first see the moon after her change (the new moon) directly before you or on your right side, the month will be of the utmost good fortune. If, however, you happen to see the moon over your left shoulder, or if you have to turn your head behind you to see it, the month will be decidedly less lucky.

To produce a dream of future events hold a piece of silver up to the moon at the time of its full phase. Ask your question, return home and place the silver beneath your pillow. If the query is to come true in the near future you'll dream of it that night.

On the night of the new moon's reappearance after her period of retiring, say the following directly to her:

New moon, true moon,
Star in the stream,
Pray tell me my fortune
In my dream.

At one time, the day of the moon (not the day of the week) upon which a person was born indicated that person's future life and character. Each of the twenty-eight days of the lunar calendar also betokened specific influences. This was a crude form of astrology that anyone could practice. Here, in a highly abbreviated form, is one common European version of this ancient form of divination:

Day One (the new moon): A person who is born on this day will have a long life and be happy.

Day Two: Finances may be a problem.

Day Three: An inauspicious day on which to be born.

Day Four: Political success is assured.

Day Five: No omens concerning birth. However, it is very fortunate for women to conceive on this day.

Day Six: The child born will become a skilled hunter.

No omens for days Seven through Nine.

Tenth Day: A person born on this day will widely travel but will never achieve lasting tranquillity.

No omens for days Eleven through Twenty.

Twenty-First Day: A child born on this day may become a thief.

No omens for days Twenty-two through Twenty-eight.

LIGHTNING

Go outside on a night that will probably bring a storm. Stand facing in any direction and wait for the first flash. If it appears to the left, it's a sign of trouble and heartaches. If, however, it appears on the right, this portends a happy, prosperous future. If it's directly overhead, a mixture of both. If you've asked a specific question it's answered in the same manner: to the left, no; to the right, yes. If it appears directly overhead, no answer is possible.

Go outside after the first bolt. Ask a binary question. At the second flash, begin counting one thousand and one, one thousand and two, and so on. Stop counting as the thunder rumbles across the sky. If the number that you've reached is even, the answer is yes; if odd, no.

16

Other Forms of Fortunetelling

CLOTH

Collect several small pieces of cloth (or paper), preferably of the same type of material. One each of the following colors is required: yellow, red, gray, blue, green, black, and orange.

Cut each into small squares of uniform size, perhaps two inches square. Place them in a box. For a general divination, mix them up, reach into the box and draw one out at random. The color chosen determines the future.

Yellow: Jealousy
Red: Love, fortune, success
Gray: Inaction, delay
Blue: Health, peace, happiness
Green: Money
Black: Sadness, trouble
Orange: Misfortune

EGGS

Fill a clear, tall glass with water. Using a pin, prick a hole in the egg's smaller end. Hold the egg over the water until the white begins to drip from it into the glass. Ask a question, if any. Watch the egg whites create shapes as they hang and float in the water. Through the use of symbolic thought, determine the future.

Hard-boil seven eggs. Allow them to cool in the water. Then, using combinations of food colorings, dye each egg one of these colors: red, orange, yellow, green, blue, and purple. Leave the seventh egg white.

Once the dyes have dried, place the eggs in a bowl. Ask your question. Close your eyes and select one egg at random from the bowl. Read the future according to the following interpretations.

Red: Things are moving; beware.

Orange: Great change is ahead, positive or negative.

Yellow: Thought is necessary; not emotions.

Green: A creative period is ahead.

Blue: Love and relationships are forecast.

Purple: Higher forces are at work.

White: No response is possible at this time.

In another version, use three eggs. Dye one dark blue, one orange, and leave the third white. Place them in a bowl and, with your eyes closed, mix them around with your hands. Ask a yes/no question. Choose an egg.

Dark blue: No.

Orange: Yes.

White: No answer is possible at this time.

KNIVES

Place a knife on a table. State your question and vigorously spin the knife by its middle. The direction to which its blade points indicates from where the misfortunes are emanating.

This method can also be used to find an object that has been lost in the house. For this purpose, the tip will point to its hiding place.

Create a circle of small pieces of paper on which you've written each of the letters of the alphabet, from A to Z. Place the knife in the exact center of the circle, its sharp tip pointing away from you. Ask a question and spin the knife by giving it a twist. The letter to which the knife's sharp tip points determines the response. If the first letter indicated by the knife is *y*, you need not continue; the question has been answered (yes). If an *n*, no. If neither of these two letters turns up, continue asking the same question and spin the knife a total of thirteen times (keep track of the letters in the correct order between spins). These may spell out words that reveal the future. You may have to jumble around the letters a bit to receive a clear understanding of the message.

NEEDLES AND PINS

Place twenty-five needles on a plate. Pour water over the plate until the needles float. If any of the needles cross, the future looks ill. If, however, none cross, all will be fine.

Fill a white bowl eight inches in diameter with water. After a prayer, float two pins on the water about two inches apart. If the needles maintain this distance or move farther apart, an ill person may recover. If the left needle drifts toward the right needle, a poor prognosis has been made; she or he may not be healed.

Collect water from a flowing stream. Pour this into a vessel. Ask a yes or no question. Place a needle on the middle finger of your right hand. Slowly dip your hand into the water until the needle floats on its surface. Watch the needle. If it floats for a long time, the future is positive or the answer is yes. If it sinks, the omen is negative or the answer is no.

Attach a pin to a thread. Hold this over a pregnant woman's wrist or her stomach. If the suspended pin swings in a clockwise direction, it will be a boy. If counterclockwise, a girl will shortly arrive.

OIL

You'll need a bowl of water and a jar of oil. Put the bowl on a table and sit before it. Ask for a general reading of the future and slowly pour a bit of the oil into the water. The oil will rise.

- •If the oil divides into two sections, an argument may be in the offing. Or, a negative answer.
- •If the oil forms a ring and remains unbroken, a business journey will be profitable, or the sick will recover. A positive response.
- •If smaller droplets of oil emerge from a large one, it may indicate pregnancy. This is also a favorable sign for the sick, for it predicts recovery.
- •If oil spreads thinly and covers the entire surface of the water, troubles are ahead.
- •Many small, unconnected globules of oil indicate the coming of money.
- •A crescent or a star shape is extremely fortunate.

Sit at a table before the bowl of water. A candle should be the only source of illumination. Ask your question. Pour oil into the water until it forms a circle on its surface. Gaze into the flickering reflection of the candle's flame on the oil and determine the future.

Fill a bowl with water. Add a quantity of oil as well as a great deal of ground black pepper. Place a few fingers into the bowl and swirl it around in all directions, so that some of the pepper adheres to the sides of the bowl above the surface of the water. Ask your question while performing this. Stop, remove your fingers and interpret the symbols created by the pepper blots in the manner of tea leaf readers.

PAPER

Write questions on five small pieces of paper. Roll them up into tight cylinders. Place these in a metal strainer and hold it in the steam rising from a pot on the stove. The first of these to unroll has been affirmatively answered; the other questions, no.

Cut two squares of the same size from the same piece of white paper. Using a black marking pen or ink, color one piece of paper black. Go to an upstairs window and, asking your question, throw the squares at the same time out of the window. Carefully observe which square first lands on the ground to determine the answer. If it's black, the answer is yes; if white, no.

Alternately, you can cut a five-pointed star from a piece of paper. On each leg, write one of the following: yes, no, maybe, probably. Leave the fifth leg blank. Write lightly with a pencil, not a pen; you shouldn't be able to read the answers when the paper is turned blank side down.

Ask your question. Place the star under your pillow face down. Each evening for four nights, fold over one leg of the star without turning it over to see which answer has been eliminated. On the fifth night look to see which corner hasn't been folded. This will answer your question.

PENDULUMS

Virtually any small object that can be tied to a string can be used as the required weight. Pierced stones, buttons, coins and rings are some popular choices. Attach the object to a natural-fiber string of about six to eight inches in length.

To use the pendulum, sit at a table. Rest the elbow of your writing hand on the table and hold the end of the string between your thumb and forefinger. Ask a question that can be answered affirmatively or negatively. Hold your arm and the string perfectly still and wait.

The pendulum will begin to swing. There are differing methods of interpreting these movements. Say your name. Record the way the pendulum swings. That is your "yes" answer. When asking a question, if the pendulum swings the way it did when you spoke your name, the answer is yes. If otherwise, the answer is no.

If the pendulum swings in a circle either clockwise or counterclockwise, the answer is yes; if in a back and forth motion, no. If it refuses to move, no answer can be produced.

A third method of interpreting the pendulum's movements involves only circular motion. A clockwise circle is yes; a counterclockwise motion, no.

Some believe that the subconscious mind is responsible for the pendulum's movements. This certainly seems to be true. Thus, its ability to foretell our futures is limited. It can't predict major events (which may be caused by a number of outside factors). Still, as a tool of contacting the subconscious mind, the pendulum has proven effective more often than not.

RINGS

Attach a thread to a ring (gold wedding rings are preferred, but any can be used). Suspend this in an empty glass. Ask your question. If the ring knocks only once, the answer is yes. If twice, no.

Alternately, observe the direction in which the ring hits the glass. If it knocks against the left, the omen is bad. If the right, good. Against the far side of the glass, bad. Against the near side, good.

SAND

Pour dry sand into a square or rectangular tray to the depth of three inches. Place this on a table before you.

Hold a pencil loosely in your hand and place its point on the center of the sand. Close your eyes and state your question. Breathe deeply and relax.

You'll have a strong urge to move the pencil. Let it move of its own accord across and through the sand. Continue this until the pencil stops moving, or in about three minutes, whichever comes first. A longer period of writing may create a jumble of confusing messages incapable of interpretation.

Remove the pencil and look down at the symbols on the sand. Sometimes, legible words will be created by the pencil's movement. There may also be a *y* for yes, an *n* for no, or a *p* for perhaps. More usually, symbols will appear. Some of those most commonly seen in sand divination include:

Large circle: Misfortune
Small circle: News, especially pertaining to work
Triangle: Success
Square: Obstacles
A long line: A journey
A short line: A visitor
Heart: Love, relationships, friendships
Broken or uneven heart: Partings
Flower: Beginnings
An x: Love

Pour fine sand into a sieve. Shake this over a flat, light-colored surface while asking your question. Gaze into the patterns created by the sand as it falls onto the surface. Use symbolic thought to decode their messages.

17

Fortunetelling Using the Tarot

As the popularity of the Tarot continues, writers and artists have continually altered the designs found on the cards and, thus, have changed their divinitory meanings.

Most experts recommend the Rider-Waite deck when first beginning to use the cards. Students who are offended by the Christian symbolism and sexist undertones of this deck can choose from a variety of others.

THE DECK ITSELF

The Tarot consists of seventy-eight cards, which are divided into two decks: the twenty-two Major Arcana cards and the fifty-six Minor Arcana. The Minor Arcana closely corresponds to our modern playing cards; the Major Arcana is unique in decks.

Unlike modern playing cards, which are double-headed and, thus, are identical whether upside down or right side up, the images on the Tarot have only one side which is up. "Reversed" interpretations are thus an important part of most Tarot readings. In general, upright cards are interpreted in positive ways; reversed cards in negative ways.

THE MINOR ARCANA

The Minor Arcana, often considered to be of lesser divinitory importance than the Major Arcana, consists of four suits of fourteen cards each: Ace through Ten, Knight, Page, Queen and King. In general, these suits are concerned with the following matters:

Pentacles: The Earth, the material world, money and business.

Wands: Fire, feelings, intellect, beginnings, direction, creation.

Cups: Water, intuition, emotions, love, love-making, happiness.

Swords: Strife, strength, difficulties, challenges, energy, mystery.

These suits correspond to our playing cards in the following manner: Pentacles: Diamonds, Wands: Clubs, Cups: Hearts, Swords: Spades.

In most pre-twentieth-century decks, the Minor Arcana aren't as richly illustrated as the Major Arcana. This has changed, however; many modern decks are fully illustrated.

THE MAJOR ARCANA

The Major Arcana consists of twenty-two cards (numbered 0 through 21, which often confuses those first using the cards). The cards are sometimes seen as archetypes. Each card can trigger your subconscious, setting off associations. These symbols cover the whole range of human experience, life and death, good and evil, love and hate, success and failure, truth and falsehood.

Pentacles

Wands

Cups

Swords

The name, number and symbolism of each card in the Major Arcana follow. The possible divinitory meanings are based on a survey of the literature as well as personal experience. There will be differences in many decks, so you may discover different meanings for some cards as you work with them.

0: The Fool Upright: The subconscious mind. *Reversed:* Negligence. Refusal to open one's eyes to see what lies ahead. Foolishness. Carelessness.

1: The Magician Upright: Strength of will. Skill. Subtlety. Diplomacy. Mastery of natural forces. *Reversed:* Use of powers for evil ends. Illusion. Insecurity.

2: The High Priestess Upright: Knowledge. Secrets. Wisdom. Intuition. Balance. Foresight. The future. Spiritual enlightenment. The female mysteries. Mystery traditions. Initiation. Natural forces. *Reversed:*

Ignorance. Superficiality. Surface knowledge. Wisdom used for unwise purposes.

3: The Empress Upright: The Earth Mother. Motherhood. Emotions. Fertility (of all kinds). Sensuality. *Reversed:* Domestic strife. Poverty. Fear. Anxiety. Indecision, but also possibly truth, light and rejoicing.

4: The Emperor Upright: Competence. Worldly influence. Intelligence overcoming emotion. Realization of all goals. Protection. Authority. *Reversed:* Immaturity. Weakness of character. Uncontrolled emotions. Loss of wealth. Lack of authority.

THE EMPEROR.

5: The Hierophant Upright: A religious vocation. Teaching. Fatherhood. Mercy. Compassion. Ritual. Authority. A High Priest. *Reversed:* Misuse of spiritual authority. Control of others. Generosity to a fault. Unconventionality.

THE HIEROPHANT

6: The Lovers Upright: Love. Union. Beauty. Attraction. Reconciliation. Harmony. *Reversed:* Infidelity. Unfulfilling relationships. Obsession with love object. Foolish plans.

7: The Chariot Upright: Control of inner energies. Mastery of the elements. Obstacles that have been faced. Confrontations. Effort. Victory. Conquest. *Reversed:* Failure to succeed. Defeat. Plans falling apart. Failure to face responsibility. Bad news will arrive. War and conflicts. Vengeance.

STRENGTH.

8: Strength Upright: Fortitude. Energy. Hidden forces. Heroism. Physical and spiritual power. Vitality. Success. *Reversed:* Tyranny. Weakness. Discord. The abuse of power. Obstinacy and stubbornness. Disgrace. Danger.

THE HERMIT.

9: The Hermit Upright: The inner search for truth and wisdom. Circumspection. Thriftiness. Meditation. Withdrawal. Silence. The need for caution. Secrets will be revealed. *Reversed:* Delays due to unreasonable caution. Fear. Loneliness. Fanaticism concerning a spiritual path. Disguise.

WHEEL of FORTUNE.

10: The Wheel of Fortune Upright: Unexpected events. Cyclicity. Evolution. Fortune. Unforeseen change. Probability. Chaos. *Reversed:* Increase (some say poverty, fear, loneliness).

THE HANGED MAN.

11: Justice Upright: Absolute justice. Judgment. Impartiality. Virtue. Success in legal matters: lawsuits, wills, contracts. Balance. Karma. *Reversed:* Unfair condemnation. Bigotry. Excessive severity. Bias. Intolerance. False accusations.

12: The Hanged Man Upright: Initiation. Wisdom. The power of prophecy. Sacrifice necessary to obtain a goal. Divination. Transformation.

Prophecy. Rebirth. Devotion. *Reversed:* Unwillingness to make necessary sacrifices. Selfishness. Punishment. Loss. Enforced sacrifice. Defeat. Hypocrisy.

DEATH.

13: Death Upright: Destruction, change and renewal. A major positive change in circumstances. Reincarnation (and, thus, events in past lives that affect this one). The death of old ideas and cherished beliefs. *Reversed:* Stagnation, negative change. A major unfortunate change in circumstances. Ruin. Endings. (Note: this card virtually never refers to physical death.)

14: Temperance Upright: Self-control. Moderation. Friendship. Fusion. Patience. Frugality. Working harmoniously with others. Mixation. Combination. *Reversed:* Extravagance, perplexity, over-indulgence, discord, inability to work with others.

THE DEVIL.

15: The Devil Upright: Unnecessary bondage to others, to ideas and concepts, or to material objects. Suffering. Violence. Delusion. Fear. *Reversed:* The throwing off of all forms of bondage. The overcoming of fear and delusion. The finding of the path to enlightenment. The conquering of one's base desires and beliefs. A controlled subconscious mind. (This card is an example of how a reversed interpretation may be positive, while an upright may be negative.)

16: The Tower Upright: Transformation of existing forms to make room for the new. Destruction. Violence. Overthrow. Loss. Reversal of fortune. Ambition. Tyranny. *Reversed:* The same but to a lesser degree.

THE STAR.

17: The Star Upright: Hope. Trust. Optimism. Insight. Opportunity. Bright promises. A favorable future. *Reversed:* Restriction. Self-doubt. Pessimism. Dis-appointment. Dreaminess. Unfulfilled hopes. Broken promises. Expectations dashed.

18: The Moon Upright: Promise. Fulfillment. Women in general. Dreams. Twilight. Deception. Hidden enemies. Dissatisfaction. Lying, Trickery. Scandal. Revealed secrets. Mistakes. *Reversed:* The same to a lesser degree.

THE SUN .

19: The Sun Upright: Fruitfulness. Sacred truth. Pleasure. Riches. Gain. Glory. Success in employment. Achievement. Recovery from sickness. Joy. Success. Happiness. *Reversed:* Vanity. Shamelessness. Arrogance; the upright meanings in a minor degree.

20: Judgment Upright: Rejuvenation. Rehabilitation. Recovery from addiction. Improvement in all things. *Reversed:* Difficulty in coming to a decision. Maintaining old habits. Lack of positive change. Delay. The desire not to face facts.

21: The World Upright: Success. Completion. Joy. Perfection. Attainment of all things. Triumph. Travel. *Reversed:* Fear of change. Fear of success. Lack of vision. Inability to accept the positive.

THE WORLD.

USING THE TAROT

When consulting the Tarot, pick your question and hold it firmly in your mind while shuffling the cards. Shuffle in such a way as to have approximately half the cards appear upside-down. The suggested way of doing this is to cut the deck in half. Then turn one half of the deck upside-down and put it on top of the other half. Shuffle the cards thoroughly. Repeat this procedure up to three times. Shuffle the cards in this way each time you use them.

Significator: After shuffling, choose a Significator. This is the card that represents you, or if you are doing a reading for someone else, the person on whose behalf you are acting. Choose a Page for boys under twenty-one and the same for girls, too, unless they are married. Then choose a Queen for any woman over twenty-one. Select a Knight for a young man, a King for a married, mature man.

Different authors give different interpretations of the ages and colorings that are represented by the cards. Do not attach too much importance to the card chosen. It can be appropriate to select it according to temperament or even occupation. Following are some general guidelines:

- King, Queen, Knight and Page of Pentacles—Very fair; blond to light brown hair; blue, gray or green eyes.
- King, Queen, Knight and Page of Swords—Very dark person; brown to black hair; brown or black eyes.
- King, Queen, Knight and Page of Cups—Medium coloring; sandy to medium brown hair; usually blue, gray or green eyes.
- King, Queen, Knight and Page of Wands—Medium dark coloring; light to dark brown hair; brown eyes.

You can choose to remove the Significator from the deck before shuffling. It can be placed on the table, serving as a focus, around which the cards of the reading are placed.

One method of consulting the Tarot is very easy. Concentrate on your question as you shuffle the cards. Shuffle at least nine times. Lay the pack on the table and cut it. Shuffle once more.

Select the top card. Turn it over carefully so that you do not accidentally invert it. Study the card's symbolism. Then interpret the card in relation to your question. That's the whole of it.

Another simple method looks at the past, present and future. Shuffle the deck and cut it into three piles. Now turn the piles face up. This will give you three of your cards. From the bottom of each pile, take the bottom card and place it face up, just above the pile from which you have taken it. The two cards on the left are the past. The two cards on the right are the future or a likely outcome. The two middle cards are important; they represent what is going on now, what your present attitudes are. You can draw additional cards from the piles, reading them in relation to your question and the previous cards.

Although these methods give only limited information, they are adequate for simple questions. By experimenting with these simple spreads, you will learn how to combine the meanings of cards into a coherent whole. Then you can go on to more complicated layouts.

While this process is easily explained, it can be difficult to practice successfully. The Tarot is a complex tool with many layers of symbolism. It must be studied carefully to produce the best results. Develop your own way of seeing and interpreting its symbols; this will assist you in using other forms of divination as well.

1. Find the most appealing Tarot deck. Many metaphysical shops have opened decks so that you can examine the cards contained within them. Choose the one that calls to you.

2. Set aside a certain period of time each day to study one Tarot card. Doing this with all of the cards will require seventy-eight days. Don't look up the card's meaning in books; study the card itself. Become aware of its symbolism. Try to fit it into your daily life. It's a good idea to write down your observations for each card. Then, as you become familiar with each card, notice how cards relate to one another. Keep a journal of your observations.

3. Read books on the subject, but realize that different books contain different interpretations. Compare the information contained within books to your own interpretations of the cards. Notice the similarities and differences and decide which are most appropriate. Your interpretations may well be the best for you.

4. Then, and only then, begin using the Tarot for divination. Attempting to do this before gaining knowledge of the deck is likely to end in failure, for you must become familiar with the tool before using it. Read only for yourself at first. Later, when you've gained proficiency, you can read for friends.

5. Keep studying and practicing. Respect the Tarot. Divining with the Tarot is a responsibility. It must always be remembered that a negative interpretation may throw a person off balance. Never state that a thing will happen; say only that it appears probable in the course of events. The cards are a means of placing the past in a more meaningful perspective, understanding the present, and revealing the alternatives for the future. The future is in each person's hands, and everything is subject to change.

18

Fortunetelling Using Palmistry

Palmistry is a complex art. Far from the quick perusal of a hand, it requires an in-depth knowledge of human nature and of the dozens and dozens of lines and symbols that may appear on the palm. This art is so complicated that many students soon abandon their studies. However, some major points of palmistry can be included here. The interested student should consult any of a number of books currently available for further information.

I should perhaps make it clear that most palmists make no claims that psychic powers are at work during a reading. They believe that everything that needs to be revealed is right there on the palm. Though great familiarity with these signs is required, psychic awareness is not.

In brief, palmistry consists of two parts: the study of the shape of the hand, fingers, joints, nails and thumb, and of the markings and lines on the palm and wrists.

Both hands are read. An old saying, "the left hand is what we're born with; the right hand is what we make" perfectly sums up the difference between the two. The right hand is compared to the left hand to judge how we've lived our lives; the right hand reveals the present and future.

The overall shape of the hand reveals the person's temperament. It is usually studied first by palmists.

1. Intellectual   2. Practical

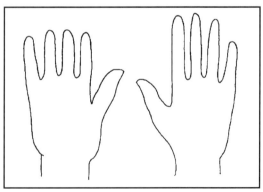

1. Intuitive   2. Sensitive

- The intellectual hand (sometimes called the earth hand) has a square palm and fingers approximately the same length. Persons possessing this hand are usually practical in worldly affairs and in love.
- The practical hand (sometimes called the air hand) has a short square palm with longer fingers. Persons possessing this hand are mercurial in nature, quick to respond to any situation.
- The intuitive hand (sometimes called the fire hand) has a long oblong palm with shorter fingers. Persons possessing this hand are often easy-going extroverts.
- The sensitive hand (sometimes called the water hand) has a long, thin palm with long, thin fingers. People possessing this hand are often artists.

After the shape of the hand, the lines in the palm are studied. These are the principal lines in the palm.

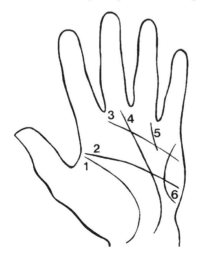

The Life Line (1) (one of the most important lines in the hand) curves around the base of the thumb. If the sweep into the palm is great, the person's constitution and energy are strong. Branches in the line indicate a change in manner of living or occupation.

The Head Line (2) indicates intelligence. If your head line starts above the life line, the person will have confidence and an independent attitude, with a desire to forge ahead.

The Heart Line (3) represents emotional and physical qualities. This line should be read together with the head line to show the balance of the head/heart alliance. If the line originates under the pad of the index finger, the person will be capable of great affection. If it originates between the pad of the index finger and the pad of the second finger, the person's emotions will be checked by practical matters. If it originates under the pad of the second finger, a very sexual nature is indicated.

The Destiny or Fate Line (4) indicates the changes in a person's life, changes made by the person or brought about by external forces.

The Sun Line (5) indicates artistic trends and chance of success.

The Intuition Line (6) shows a person's insights.

These are the barest glimpses into the mysteries of palmistry. The available information is massive, requiring a remarkable memory and intensive study and practice.

19

Fortunetelling Using the I Ching

The I Ching, or the Chinese Book of Changes, consists of a group of sixty-four special symbols, known as hexagrams, together with their divinitory meanings, as well as commentaries and other ancillary information.

CREATING THE HEXAGRAM

There are two methods of using the I Ching for divination. In the first older method, fifty yarrow stalks are thrown and counted in a complex fashion; or three coins of the same weight and material are thrown as dice and counted. Today most people use the coin method because it is much simpler and faster. Pennies or quarters can be used.

The three coins are tossed onto a flat surface. Heads are given the numerical value of three; tails the value of two. After tossing the coins, their values are added to determine the type of line to be drawn. When using three coins, there are only four possible combinations. These are two heads, one tail (6 + 2 = 8); one head, two tails (3 + 4 = 7); three heads (3 + 3 + 3 = 9), and three tails (2 + 2 + 2 = 6).

The number 6 for a throw indicates a broken line; 7 a solid line; 8 a broken line, and 9 a solid line. The coins are tossed six times, and the hexagram is built up from the bottom line, the way a house is built from the bottom up. The bottom three lines are called the bottom trigram. The top three lines are called the top trigram.

```
9=  ——————
8=  — — —
7=  ——————
6=  — — —
```

READING THE I CHING

The symbolism and divinitory meaning of the hexagram is read in relation to the diviner's question. Many persons find that the I Ching is most useful in clarifying a present situation, or in determining whether she or he is living in harmony with personal objectives.

A times, the hexagram's meaning will be quite clear, though couched in symbolism. At other times, thought and reflection may be necessary to understand its message. The I Ching isn't an instant form of divination; it relies on the diviner to comprehend its meaning.

In the back of the I Ching (see a book on the I Ching or page 106) is a chart which indicates the Chinese name for the top trigram and the bottom trigram. Simply read the top trigram first and go down the chart until you see the Chinese name for the bottom trigram. This will indicate the number of the hexagram and the name of the hexagram to consult for your future. For example, if the entire hexagram reads as follows:

(top trigram)

(bottom trigram)

we find that the top trigram = the Chinese name "Chên" and the bottom trigram = "Tui." The place where the bottom and top trigram meet on the chart is number 54. There are two readings of this hexagram in the I Ching, an older one at the beginning of the book, a newer one at the end of the book. We turn to hexagram 54.

We can read commentary from that point on. If you wish corroboration of the way you feel, you will find it in the I Ching. As for your future, the I Ching suggests alternatives. Nothing, no future course is set in stone. Free will is a base on which the I Ching operates.

Upper / Lower	Ch'ien ☰	Chên ☳	K'an ☵	Kên ☶	K'un ☷	Sun ☴	Li ☲	Tui ☱
Ch'ien ☰	1	34	5	26	11	9	14	42
Chên ☳	25	51	3	27	24	43	21	17
K'an ☵	6	40	29	4	7	59	64	47
Kên ☶	33	62	39	52	15	53	56	31
K'un ☷	12	16	8	23	2	20	35	45
Sun ☴	44	32	48	18	46	58	50	28
Li ☲	13	55	63	22	36	37	30	49
Tui ☱	10	54	60	41	19	61	38	58

Key for Identifying the Hexagrams

20

The Future Is Now

In this age, when self-help books reach the top of the sales charts, it's apparent that we as humans are no longer content to live our lives without direction. We search for the perfect techniques to improve ourselves. We read books, attend seminars and spend a period of time each day in pursuit of our quest. These measures are quite effective for some individuals. Others, however, realize that something is missing: they have a goal, and a map to reach that goal, but they're uncertain of the best route to take. They may lapse into despair and do nothing to improve their lives.

As we have seen, divination provides us with that vital information. It presents us with a view of the direction in which we're heading. By analyzing this information and applying it to our present lives, we can detour around unpleasant destinations and improve the quality of our lives.

This and the knowledge that we can recreate our future lives before they occur are the greatest lessons that divination has to offer. Divination can also assist us in planning events, ease the process of making difficult choices, provide advice and bring order into our lives.

As a tool designed to access otherwise unknowable information, divination can play a vital role in conforming our lives to our expectations, dreams and desires. It can assist us in learning the lessons that we haven't yet mastered, thus smoothing the path that we tread into the future.

Accepting responsibility for the state of our lives isn't an easy task. "How could this have happened?" we may ask in moments of crisis. Once we've accepted that we have created our present and future by past choices in action, we begin to lose the feeling of powerlessness over our lives. This spurs us toward living well today so that tomorrow won't present further avoidable challenges.

Divination can be seen as a friend who possesses a great wisdom and knowledge. However, the information that we receive from its practice must be put to use if it's to be of any value.

This chapter's title presents a message of vital importance. We usually consider the future as being a hazy possibility completely unconnected to the present. This is erroneous thinking. The past, the present and the future simultaneously exist in this moment, in this nanosecond. They don't consist of three separate compartments; they're one. Once we are aware of this fact we can utilize it to our advantage.

Tomorrow is but a heartbeat away. The illusion that we know as time may be useful, but only if we recognize its flexibility. We can stretch time and move within it.

The use of divination, then, can be far more than the simple satisfaction of our natural curiosity. It can provide invaluable information. Using the responses that we receive, we can build our lives into more positive, fulfilling experiences.

The future is now.

Pocket Guides from The Crossing Press

Pocket Guide to Acupressure Points for Women
By Cathryn Bauer
$6.95 • Paper • ISBN 0-89594-879-6

Pocket Guide to Astrology
By Alan Oken
$6.95 • Paper • ISBN 0-89594-820-6

Pocket Guide to Ayurvedic Healing
By Candis Cantin Packard
$6.95 • Paper • ISBN 0-89594-764-1

Pocket Guide to Bach Flower Essences
By Rachelle Hasnas
$6.95 • Paper • ISBN 0-89594-865-6

Pocket Guide to Good Food
By Margaret M. Wittenberg
$6.95 • Paper • ISBN 0-89594-747-1

Pocket Herbal Reference Guide
By Debra St. Claire
$6.95 • Paper • ISBN 0-89594-568-1

Pocket Macrobiotics
By Carl Ferre
$6.95 • Paper • ISBN 0-89594-848-6

Pocket Guide to Meditation
By Alan Pritz
$6.95 • Paper • ISBN 0-89594-886-9

Pocket Guides from The Crossing Press

Pocket Guide to Naturopathic Medicine
By Judith Boice
$6.95 • Paper • ISBN 0-89594-821-4

Pocket Guide to Numerology
By Alan Oken
$6.95 • Paper • ISBN 0-89594-826-5

Pocket Guide to Shamanism
By Tom Cowan
$6.95 • Paper • ISBN 0-89594-845-1

Pocket to Self Hypnosis
By Adam Burke
$6.95 • Paper • ISBN 0-89594-824-9

Pocket Guide to the Tarot
By Alan Oken
$6.95 • Paper • 0-89594-822-2

Pocket Guide to The 12-Steps
By Kathleen S.
$6.95 • Paper • ISBN 0-89594-864-8

Pocket Guide to Visualization
By Helen Graham
$6.95 • Paper • ISBN 0-89594-885-0

BOOKS BY THE CROSSING PRESS